T<

by Beate Boeker
www.happybooks.de

ISBN-13: 978-1492273448
ISBN-10: 1492273449

Praise for Delayed Death

"Delayed Death seems to prove the cliché that no good deed goes unpunished. Carlina was only trying to help when she decided to delay the news of her grandfather's death for a day. Her generous impulse results in a series of misadventures for the close-knit, unpredictable Mantoni family and a laugh-out-loud funny read for the rest of us. This cozy mystery is set in Florence and told with good-natured charm and an eye for detail that makes you feel you're in that beautiful city. Once I started reading it, the dust bunnies under the bed had to wait. I couldn't put it down."
Sandra Cody

"What a fun, fun, FUN start to this series. I hadn't heard about this series before I was approached to review, and I'm so glad I discovered it. Right from the beginning I was laughing along with Carlina and her outrageous family, as she tries to keep them in line, solve the mystery and keep her lingerie store in business."
Bella Mcguire

"Beate Boeker's voice is light and conversational, as if sitting down and talking with a friend. She paints the scenes so well you can feel the timbre of the city and taste and smell the delicious food offerings of Florence. With a sprinkling of Italian-speak thrown in, I swear I was bi-lingual by the time I finished. This is cozy mystery writing at its finest."
Jayne Ormerod

Chapter 1

"I've never seen such a sexy bride." Carlina stepped back and looked at her cousin Emma with a smile. "The gang will faint."

Emma twirled on her pearly high heels and checked her rear view in the mirror that went from the ceiling to the floor. Seventeen spotlights illuminated the white painted bedroom and showed the bride in full splendor. "That's the least I expect." She wriggled her shapely bottom in the skintight dress. "The sexiest bride of Florence." Her smile was triumph made flesh.

Carlina took the veil and held it up. It felt soft like a cobweb, and a faint trace of Emma's perfume wafted up to her. Probably Emma had already tried it on several times, admiring herself in the mirror. "Your new mother-in-law might have a stroke, though." She smiled at her cousin with affection.

"Why?" Emma slipped underneath the veil and adjusted the position with her fingertips. "Just because it's sexy?"

Carlina glanced at Emma's legs and swallowed her answer. The late September sunlight poured into the bedroom and shimmered on Emma's exquisite nylons. Her legs looked a mile longer today because the wedding dress was short enough to make everybody wonder why it had cost more than a month's salary.

Emma didn't notice her cousin's hesitation. "Can I go like this?"

Carlina nodded. "You're perfect." The family had been blessed with many good-looking women, and Emma had inherited the long legs and peachy skin, but on top of that, she had an energy about her that made her even more attractive. A faint feeling of melancholy grabbed Carlina. Emma was getting married. Things would be different now. *Why should they be different?* A voice inside her mocked her thoughts. *Emma will continue to live two floors below you, Lucio has lived here for months, and she will always remain your little cousin. Don't become maudlin, just because it's a wedding.*

Emma took a deep breath. "I'm glad I sent mother and the rest of the gang away. They would have driven me crazy."

Carlina nodded. "I couldn't agree with you more." She glanced sideways at her beautiful cousin. "But they were a bit huffed. I was surprised they obeyed, particularly Benedetta. I expected her to insist. After all, you're her eldest daughter, the first one to get married, and . . ."

"It's because I'm the bride today." Emma opened her arms and threw back her head. "Today, I'm the star."

Carlina suppressed a smile. "You're always the star, and I do hope your big day will be perfect."

"Of course it will!" Emma laughed. "Think of all the hours of preparation! I've thought of every detail. Nothing will go wrong."

A shiver ran through Carlina. *I hope the gods don't listen.* "Don't you think the house feels strange with the whole gang gone? It's never been so quiet."

Before Emma could reply, a ringing tone came from Carlina's black evening bag lying on top of the white dresser.

"Oh, no, not again!" Emma bent forward with one fluid movement and grabbed Carlina's arm. "Don't answer that. I think your shop assistant should for once manage without you. She has already called twice. Why does all of Florence want to buy underwear on my wedding day?"

Carlina gave her a reassuring smile. "It's the first time I've left Elena all alone at the store, and I said she could call whenever she has a question." She shook off her cousin's hand and clicked open the tiny clasp of her handbag. "We have plenty of time, so don't worry." With a flick of her wrist, she pulled out her phone and checked the caller ID. "Oh, no." She closed her eyes as if that would make it go away. "It's *mamma*."

"Don't answer it!" Emma's voice rose. "I know she will spoil my wedding!"

"Nonsense." Carlina shook her head and laid a calming hand on Emma's arm. *Emma is more nervous than she wants to admit.* "I bet she only forgot something." She pressed the green button. "Ciao, *mamma*."

She listened to the quaking voice on the other end. Her face twisted.

Emma frowned. "What's up? Why do you look so strange?"

Carlina made a soothing motion with her hand. Then she said, "All right. Don't worry. We're almost on our way. Ciao."

She pressed the red button, threw back her head, and exploded into laughter.

Emma circled around her, too impatient to stand still. Her high heels left tiny imprints in the creamy carpet. "I didn't understand a word. What does she want? Why are you laughing?"

Carlina gasped for breath. "I was right. She forgot something."

"What?" Emma placed her hands on her hips. Her red mouth pulled down at the corners.

Carlina took a deep breath and said with relish, "She forgot grandpa."

Emma's mouth dropped open. "She forgot grandpa? How can she do that?"

Carlina shook her head. "I have no clue. It seems he didn't want to join her for the hairdresser and the manicure this morning, wasn't even dressed yet, so *mamma* decided she would leave without him but forgot to tell me." She started to laugh again. "That's so like *mamma*."

Emma flattened out an imaginary crease on her skirt. "She's not normal, that one."

"No one in our family is normal." Carlina gave her a cheerful smile.

"I don't know why you look so happy about it." Emma twitched her veil to the side and glared at her.

"No?" Carlina's smile deepened. She opened her mouth, but before she could say something, Emma interrupted her.

"No, don't tell me. I don't want to know." She looked at the mirror once again. "When did you say Uncle Ugo would come?"

Carlina checked her wristwatch. "In twenty minutes."

Emma sighed. "I wish he could drive to our door."

Carlina grinned. "If you hadn't insisted on the biggest limo to be rented in the whole of Italy, he could have done just that. As it is, you will have to walk the few steps to Via Ghibellina. He said he would wait in the car."

"I still think he could have tried."

"So do I." Carlina made sure her voice sounded ironic. "It must be great fun to squeeze a limo through a historical street that was created long before cars were invented. But who would have paid for the scratched paint on both sides of the limo? You?"

Emma pursed her lips. "You're not supposed to be nasty to me on the day of my wedding. Now let's go." She turned on her high heels and sashayed to the white door. "I just hope grandpa has dressed in the meantime."

"You forgot to pack your makeup into your handbag." Carlina held up the slim rectangle in glittering gold. "Why don't you do that, and I'll go downstairs and get grandpa ready."

Emma pulled her finely plucked eyebrows together. "I hope grandpa will hurry. What if he takes one of his sudden ideas into his head and--"

"Don't worry; all will be fine. I promise." Carlina pushed Emma in the direction of the bathroom, a modern wonder in black with spotlights hidden in the floor. "Pack your stuff. I'll take care of grandpa." She slung her evening bag over her shoulder and left Emma's apartment to go downstairs. As always, she put one hand on the polished wooden railing because she loved to feel the smooth surface and enjoyed the way it led her in soft curves from the top of the house to the ground floor, passing all the family apartments. Today, she also used her other hand to gather her long evening dress and hold it up. The staircase smelled of beeswax. *Benedetta must have polished it yesterday.* Carlina took a deep breath.

The bells of Santa Croce chimed the full hour. Carlina stopped for an instant on the landing and listened. How often had she heard the bells chime; how much their sound was part of her life. She loved this house, her home. For as long as she could remember, it had been special to her, first as a child, when she had come with her family during the long summer vacations, and later, when they had moved to Florence after the death of her father. A pang went through her. *I wish he could celebrate with us today.* After all these years, the pain had lessened, but from time to time, the sharp feeling of loss jumped at her without warning.

She pushed the thought away and forced herself to descend the worn wooden stairs a bit slower than usual so she wouldn't trip in her high heels. The rustling of her dark-red dress made her feel festive. *I've never seen Emma so nervous, but maybe that's normal if you're getting married. I hope she'll be happy with Lucio. He's so . . . fierce sometimes.* Carlina frowned. *But then, Emma isn't a mellow dove either. She'll be fine.*

She arrived on the ground floor, turned to the left, and knocked on the green wooden door. When she didn't hear a sound, she knocked again, louder this time. Without waiting for a reply, she took out her key, turned it in the lock, and pushed the door open. The apartment was stiflingly warm and smelled of grandfather's peppermint drops. As she went through, she called out, "Grandpa! It's me, Carlina. Are you ready for Emma's wedding?"

He wasn't in the sitting room.

Carlina frowned. "Now what?" *I'm not in the mood to play hide and seek with a nervous cousin and a disgruntled grandfather.*

She opened the door to the kitchen and froze.

Emma's heels clicked behind her on the crooked stones that made up the floor in the old house. "Carlina, is he ready? We have to go."

Carlina stared at her grandfather, slumped in his chair, with his chin sunk against his still chest. His eyes were wide open. "He . . . he's not ready." Her voice spoke all by itself. It sounded devoid of all feeling.

Emma came up. "He has to hurry. I'm not willing to be late for my own wedding, just because--" She stopped mid-sentence, grabbed the door frame, and screamed.

Carlina twisted around and grabbed her arms. "Shh. It's all right. Don't scream." Her whole body quivered from shock.

Emma pointed a pearly painted fingernail at their grandfather. Her hand shook. "He's dead!" Her shriek reverberated through the old kitchen.

Carlina gulped. "Yes. He's dead." Her eyes filled with tears. "I'm so sorry." A feeling of sorrow and helplessness swamped her.

"Sorry?" Emma narrowed her eyes. "He has destroyed my wedding!"

"But Emma," Carlina laid her hand, suddenly cold, on Emma's arm. "It's not his fault."

"Not his fault!" Emma stuck her hands on her hips and stared at her grandfather with clenched jaws. "I'm not so sure. He always got me into trouble, always."

Carlina stared at her. "That's not fair. Of course he was a bit unusual sometimes, but . . ."

"Unusual?" Emma rounded on Carlina with such a vicious hiss she took a step back. "Don't you remember the time our dear grandfather was supposed to collect me from hospital and didn't show up? He said he had to worship the sun that day because it had come out for the first time in weeks. That was the sun-worshiping period. I stood in front of the hospital for two endless hours, thinking my family had forgotten me. Don't you remember that?"

Carlina bit her lips. "I do. But please, calm down now. We have to--"

Emma interrupted her, "And the day we were supposed to leave on vacation, all together, and he made us jump out of the train at the last minute because he felt a bad vibe on the train? That was the vibe-feeling period. Don't you remember that?"

Carlina searched her cousin's face with worry. Her cousin's violent reaction perturbed her.

"Do you remember the bad vibe period?" Emma's voice became louder with each word.

A small smile escaped Carlina at the memory. "I do. It was the period I liked most." A tear rolled down her cheek. "I'm going to miss him so much."

Emma threw her a look full of contempt. "And now he dies, minutes before I get married. It's unbelievable! He was fine this morning, fit enough to tell me my wedding dress is way too short."

Carlina caught her breath. "Do you mean . . ." she had to swallow before she could continue, ". . . something's not right with his death?"

Emma made an impatient move with her hand. "No, of course I don't mean that. He's seventy-nine, for heaven's sake. People his age die all the time. I just wish he hadn't chosen this exact moment!" She stamped her foot.

"He couldn't help it." Carlina wiped away the tear. She opened her handbag and pulled out her phone with a shaking hand. "I have to call *mamma*."

"No!" Emma pounced on her and took the phone away.

"But Emma!" Carlina stared at her, nonplussed.

Her cousin pressed her lips into one determined line. "He won't destroy my wedding." She emphasized each word. "I don't accept it."

"But . . . what do you want to do?" Carlina lifted her hands. "We don't have a choice. I mean, he--"

"We'll leave him as he is."

Carlina's mouth dropped open. "What?"

"It doesn't make a difference if he dies today or tomorrow." Emma lifted her chin underneath the veil.

Carlina blinked. "You make it sound as if it was a matter of choosing."

"But it is." Emma bent forward and took Carlina by the arms. Her dark eyes glittered. "Today, his death is inconvenient. Very inconvenient. Tomorrow, he can die as much as he wants. Tomorrow, I'm on my honeymoon, far away in Africa, where he can't bother me."

Carlina didn't know if she should be scandalized or laugh. "But . . ."

"Please, Carlina." Emma opened her eyes wide. "For him, it doesn't matter one bit. For me, it makes all the difference in the world."

Carlina felt herself soften. In a way, Emma was right.

Emma narrowed her eyes and pressed her point. "Besides, think of Uncle Teo. You know the doctor told him only last week to avoid any stressful situations because of his weak heart. He almost forbade him to join the wedding today, and that's nothing compared to the sudden death of his twin!"

Carlina hesitated. "But surely . . ."

"If we tell him now that grandpa died, Uncle Teo might immediately drop dead, too."

"Oh, God. Do you really think so?"

"Yes." Emma pressed her lips together. "After all, they're identical twins. Better let Uncle Teo enjoy the party and all the excitement of the wedding, then get a good night's rest, and tomorrow, you can break it to him gently."

Carlina bit her lip in indecision. "You make it sound so sensible. But everybody expects grandpa." She shook her head. "They'll ask us why he didn't come. They'll worry!"

"Nobody will worry." Emma took Carlina's phone from her cousin's hand, placed it on the kitchen table, and watched her grandfather out of narrowed eyes. "We'll say the bad vibe period has come back, and Nico decided it would be unlucky to join the party. Nobody will think twice about it."

Carlina felt as if she had strayed into an out-of-body experience, disconnected from reality. She shook her head, but the feeling didn't go away. "That won't work. Everybody knows the bad-vibe-period stopped a year ago. Right now, he has the dangerous past period. Had, I mean." She hugged herself.

Emma shrugged her perfect shoulder beneath the filmy material of her wedding dress. It shimmered in the soft sunlight coming from the window. "So grandpa changed his mind."

"He never changed his mind. He never went back to old

periods. I knew him." A lump formed in Carlina's throat.

"Now he did. Never too old for surprises, aren't you, Grandpa?" She nudged Nico's shoulder with an impatient expression on her face and recoiled when he toppled to the side.

Carlina jumped forward and steadied him. She had never touched a dead body before. It felt heavy and warm. Warm?

She swallowed. "Emma?" Her voice sounded unsteady. "I . . . I think he must have died a minute ago."

Emma stared at her. "Why?"

"Because he's still warm."

Emma recoiled. "*Madonna*."

Something smelled strange. A cloying feeling grabbed Carlina by the throat. "I can't make him sit up again."

"Then place his head on the table." Emma took back one step. "My dress--"

Something inside Carlina cracked. "I don't give a damn about your dress." She glared at her cousin. "If you want to continue with your wedding, help me to put him into a decent position. Now."

Emma came closer with obvious reluctance. Just as she stood in front of the kitchen window, a man walked past on the street. He whistled when he saw her. Emma turned her back on him with a hiss and stared at her cousin out of eyes wide with fear. "I can't turn around," she breathed. "Is he still there?"

"Who?"

"The guy on the street!"

Carlina froze. She shifted her grandfather's weight as best as she could and craned her neck to look around Emma's slim form. "No."

Emma swallowed. "We can't leave grandpa here where everybody can see him."

Carlina closed her eyes. Her grandfather's weight hurt her arms, and the sickening smell made her gag. "Whatever you want, but come here and help me!"

Emma turned around and closed the white curtain. "Maybe we should put grandpa to bed," she said. "Then nobody will find him too early."

"Fine." Carlina clenched her teeth. "Now take his feet."

"But I . . ."

"Emma." Carlina knew Emma would recognize the underlying threat in her voice and obey her elder cousin, just as she had done all those years ago when they were teenagers. She didn't use that tone often, but it still worked.

Emma sighed and grabbed Nico's feet. "My dress will tear. It wasn't made for a workout."

Carlina didn't reply. Nico had been a small man, and he looked smaller than ever without his personality to fill the space around him, but he was so heavy, she started to pant.

"He weighs a ton." Emma gasped.

"Don't drop him." Carlina tottered forward on her high heels and kicked open the old door to the bedroom.

They both heaved a sigh of relief when they placed him onto his bed. The mattress sagged in the middle.

"We have to take off his shirt and pants." Carlina felt sick.

"What? Why?"

Carlina held onto the brass bed-frame to stop herself from shaking. "How likely is it that he goes to bed, dressed in his best suit for your wedding?"

Emma glanced at her and pulled her slim eyebrows together. "Your face is green."

Carlina pressed her hand to her mouth. "Ugh." She ran to the bathroom.

When she came back several minutes later, she had to place one hand on the wall to assure herself that something firm existed.

"I've done it." Emma tucked a corner of the cotton bedspread behind Nico's shoulder and straightened. "We can go now." She looked cool and composed, as if she undressed the dead every day.

"Where did you put his trousers?"

Emma made a vague move with her hand. "They're over there."

Carlina willed herself to leave the support of the wall and crossed the room. "We have to hang them up. Grandpa was pedantic. He would never have thrown his best trousers across a chair like this."

Emma sighed. "Maybe he felt ill already."

"No way."

"Oh, all right." Emma picked up the trousers and folded them along the crease, then smoothed them over the back of the wooden chair in the corner.

"I've forgotten my shawl." Emma left the room without closing the door. "I'll just run upstairs to get it. And I'll open the curtain in the kitchen so nobody will wonder. Don't forget your phone. It's still on the table. Please hurry." Her last words were drowned out by the clattering of her high heels on the floor.

Carlina folded Nico's white shirt and placed it next to the trousers. She glanced one last time around the room, taking care not to look at the shrunken figure beneath the bedspread, then she closed the bedroom door behind her. For an instant, she leaned against the door, her hot brow pressed against the smooth wood. *This is the biggest mistake of your life.*

"Carlina? Are you coming?"

Carlina straightened. "Sì, sì."

II

"Where's father?" Carlina's mother sidled along the pew closer to her daughter. Her long blue skirt twisted around her legs, and she pulled it free with an impatient tug.

"Ssshhh." Carlina placed a finger on her lips and pointed at the altar where Emma and Lucio stood in front of the priest.

Fabbiola stood on tiptoe and brought her mouth to her daughter's ear. "Why were you so late?" Her perfume smelled of lily-of-the-valley.

"I'll tell you later." Carlina stared straight ahead, her back stiff. *Stop pestering me. Please.*

"Where's your grandfather?" Fabbiola poked her in the ribs.

Sweat formed on Carlina's brow. She lowered her voice so only Fabbiola could hear her. "He didn't want to come."

"Why not?" Fabbiola's voice rose.

Aunt Maria, seated in the pew in front of them, turned her head and frowned. The three gigantic feathers adorning her hat wiped across Carlina's face and tickled her on the nose.

Carlina sneezed.

"Be quiet," Fabbiola whispered. "You're disturbing the service."

The priest turned to the congregation. "Dear sisters and brothers in the Lord, let us now sing hymn 232, the Golden Gates of Paradise."

Amid the rustling of book pages, Fabbiola poked her daughter again. "You're hiding something, Carlina. Out with it."

Carlina took the folded program and waved it in front of her face. "It's hot in here." Thank God her dress was cut low on the front and back.

"Caroline."

Oh, God. Now she was Caroline instead of Carlina. Two more minutes and she would be Caroline Arabella. Desperate, she bent to her mother's ear. "He said he felt bad vibes." The organ started to play the first notes.

"Bad vibes?" Fabbiola's blue hat wobbled. "But he had gotten over the bad vibes!"

"Shh." Carlina placed a finger over her mouth. "You're disturbing the service." She took a deep breath and warbled together with the congregation. "Yes, the golden gates of paradise, of paradise, of . . ."

"Caroline Arabella!"

Carlina broke off in mid-paradise. "It came back."

"What came back?" Fabbiola had painted her fingernails bright red to celebrate the occasion. They looked like fat drops of blood.

Carlina averted her gaze. *I'm not going to be sick again.* "The bad vibe period is back."

"Oh, *Madonna*."

"Yes, the golden gates of paradise, of paradise, of paradise . . ." Carlina sang as loud as she could. Maybe her mother would get the message and stop talking.

"Did he say this bad-vibe-thing in front of Emma?" Fabbiola's whisper penetrated the music.

Carlina closed her eyes for a brief moment. "Yes."

Fabbiola's brown eyes grew round. "I bet she threw a fit."

That much at least is true. Carlina nodded and trilled a last high note. Too bad the song was so short.

They all sat down, and for a minute, only the shuffling of feet, the rustle of clothes, and a cough from Uncle Teo filled the church.

The priest opened his bible.

"Did father feel all right?" Fabbiola directed a look of reproach at the priest who dared to interrupt her with the beginning of his sermon.

"Never better." The words came out of her mouth before she could stop them. Carlina blushed. *This is not the right moment for black humor, Carlina.*

"But--"

Aunt Maria turned around again. Her black eyes swept over them with a mixture of reproach and curiosity. A wave of garlic aroma wafted into Carlina's direction.

Carlina glared at her mother. "Not now, *mamma*. I'll tell you later."

Fabbiola sighed, then shrugged. She looked at the priest for an instant.

Carlina watched her from the corner of her eye with misgiving. She knew what was going to happen. It never took Fabbiola more than one minute to decide the priest wasn't interesting enough to keep her awake. Today, it took even less.

Fabbiola grabbed her trusted cushion which was already waiting on the pew, slid lower, and placed it behind her head.

Carlina suppressed a sigh. *If she wasn't so short, she couldn't sleep in church. On the other hand, if she was taller, she might decide to stretch out on the pew in the middle of the service. Now that would be a sight.* The thought brought a smile to her lips. *At least she doesn't snore.*

She turned her gaze back to the priest. The huge altar, the life-size golden cross, and the flickering candles in five massive chandeliers made the man of God look small and unimpressive in spite of his white robes. *But he has a soothing voice. A bit like Grandpa's.* Carlina swallowed. *I'm going to miss him. It was never boring with him around.* She bit her lip. She was not going to cry. If she did, several family members would think she was crying because she wasn't married yet. She had better rustle up some clever answers to the inevitable questions that would come later.

The priest droned on and on. He never seemed to change his text. Carlina felt as if she could soon hold the ceremony herself. How many Mantoni marriages had he conducted this year? Carlina counted back in her mind. Five? Six? The last one had been Angela and Marco's, three months ago. They had been the most beautiful couple she had seen so far. Not as sexy as Emma but classy and graceful. *Marco has enough sex appeal for two, no matter if he's in a tux or a pair of jeans.* Carlina could see his dark head two pews further down. *He'll become a successful doctor, even if he's new to Florence. The women will come to him in droves.*

When the service was over, Carlina hid behind a column at the side. She didn't want to talk to anyone.

At long last, the church had emptied, and only the priest remained. His steps echoed on the stone slabs as he went past her. Carlina forced herself to follow him. Her heart felt heavy. The portals of the Catholic church stood wide open, and the

September sun danced in dusty beams across the ancient wooden pews. A peal of laughter greeted Carlina as she arrived at the steps. She closed her eyes against the bright light and took a deep breath. The air smelled pure and clean, a welcome change to the heavy scent of incense in the church.

"Please gather on the steps." Uncle Ugo waved his big camera and spread out his arms, shooing stray family members like sheep back into position. "Now smile!"

Carlina stayed where she was, everything but her head hidden behind her fat Aunt Maria. Obedient, she smiled past the waving feathers on Aunt Maria's hat, but her gaze swept beyond the crowd.

To her left, the lilac hills of Tuscany stretched in soft waves. From her position, she had an enticing view over Florence and its ancient center, down in the valley. The Duomo's vast dome gleamed in the sunlight, a rich gold, with the Campanile tower, spearing the sky with its slim elegance, by its side. The reddish color of the terracotta-tiled roofs all around them made the town look warm and inviting. Carlina's heart swelled with happiness. She loved Florence, its beauty, its busyness. She had fallen in love with it during her summer vacations as a child, but even when she had come to live permanently in Florence - a scared and sad thirteen-year-old - the magic had never abated. *Maybe it's different if you're born here, then you don't see it as a gift.* She looked at the faces next to her. Did anybody spare a glance for the town, sitting like a sleeping beauty at their feet? She caught her brother's eyes. Enzo had been six when they had moved from Seattle. Maybe he was more of an Italian than she was.

Her brother waved. "Carlina!"

She waved back but stayed where she was because their mother stood next to him. She had to keep an eye on her mother to make sure she kept her distance all day long. Fabbiola knew how to drag a secret out of her daughter.

To Carlina's right, beyond the church grounds, five cypresses stood in a row like slim sentinels. A soft haze lingered in the air and softened their dark green. Summer was over, even if it was still warm enough to go in shirtsleeves. Behind them, the cemetery stretched down the sloping hill. It brought her back to ground with a thud. Grandpa was dead. She would return next week for the funeral service. Carlina stifled a sigh.

Aunt Maria's feathers wiped across Carlina's face as she

turned. "It'll be your turn soon, Carlina." Her small eyes blinked at her.

Carlina, nodded, clenched her teeth and forced a smile. She backed up one step to avoid the feathers a third time.

Alberta, her mother's eldest sister, appeared out of nowhere and glanced at Carlina from beneath her hideous green hat.

Damn. She must have overheard Aunt Maria's remark.

Aunt Maria turned away with a quick reflex that made Carlina bite down a smile. Then she steeled herself. Her aunt Alberta was famous for her vicious tongue.

"You should stop chasing them all away, Carlina." Alberta pushed her hat higher so she could see better. "You scare men. Nobody wants an independent woman. I understand why Giulio broke off the engagement."

I broke off the engagement. He didn't. Carlina wanted to sweep that stupid hat off Alberta's head. *Besides, that was five years ago, so we can talk of a more recent scandal now.*

Alberta chose not to notice Carlina's stormy silence. "You should try to be a bit more understanding. You're not getting younger, you know. At thirty-five, you're on the verge of becoming a confirmed spinster." Her false smile stretched the wrinkled skin above her lips.

"Thirty-two," Carlina said through clenched teeth.

Alberta waved. "'Whatever. My Angela now, she found a wonderful husband." She gave a sentimental sigh. "But then, she's a beauty."

And she knows it. Carlina looked beyond her aunt. *I want to take out my Vespa and go for a ride. The vine leaves will be red by now, and the earth smells so rich this time of the year.*

Her aunt scrutinized her. "You don't look much like the other girls in the family." She sniffed. "Must be the father."

Enough was enough. "I don't have a tongue like a steel knife either, which seems to be another family characteristic." Carlina pretended a smile and hoped it would come out serene.

Carlina could tell by Aunt Maria's heaving shoulders that she chuckled.

Alberta turned red. "I'm going to talk to your mother about your manners." She moved her hat once again. It now looked like a crooked egg. "Where's father?" Her voice carried over the crowd. "I haven't seen him at all. Your mother said I should ask you."

Several people looked around.

Carlina squared her shoulders. "He decided to stay at home."

"What?" Alberta frowned so hard, her face looked like a wrinkled walnut. "He's becoming very odd."

He always was odd. And a dear.

"Why on earth didn't he want to come?"

"The bad vibe period has come back. He said it would be safer to stay at home." The more often she said it, the more it sounded like the truth.

"But he had left that period!" Alberta pressed her lips together. "These past months, he only talked about the bad past catching up with us."

"Really?" Carlina pretended she had never heard about Nico's latest tic. "What event from your past did he mention?"

Alberta pulled herself up to her full height. "Nothing that concerns you."

Bravo, Grandpa. I hope you rattled her, even if you invented it all. Carlina nodded a cool dismissal and pretended to see someone on the far side of the crowd. "I have to go. See you later, Alberta."

The rest of the day, she dodged her mother and changed the subject whenever someone asked her about Nico. Every time she caught Emma's gaze, she wondered how her cousin could act as if no cloud had ever appeared on her horizon. Emma seemed serene and happy, poised and in control of herself. *But Emma is a very focused woman. Her feelings are never all over the place.* Carlina didn't dare to sigh, though she felt like it, but she'd had enough commiserating glances for one day.

At a quarter to nine, she dropped into her chair at the festive dinner table with a feeling of relief. The worst was over. Dinner, some dancing, and she could go home. Tomorrow . . . no, she wouldn't think of tomorrow. She would--

"Oh, hello," a dark voice said above her.

Carlina looked up in surprise. "Hello."

Angela appeared and took her husband by the arm. "This is Caroline, Marco. She's my cousin."

"We've met." Carlina smiled at Marco and got up to place the obligatory family kisses on his cheeks. He smelled good, of cedar wood and something else she couldn't place.

"I'm sorry." A smile crept into the corner of his mouth. "It's a bit hard to remember all the names, though I do remember your face." He held her chair and waited until she was seated, then helped his wife and sat down. "There seem to be so many cousins around."

"There are." Carlina liked him. "My mother has six brothers and sisters who are all married with several kids. It's hard to cross Florence without tripping over a family member of the Mantoni clan."

He chuckled. "I noticed."

"We call them the gang." Carlina wrapped both hands around the elaborate arrangement of orchids in front of her and pushed it to the side to get more room.

Marco lifted his eyebrows. "Sounds dangerous."

"It is." *And if you knew I've just shifted my dead grandfather, you would believe me.*

Angela bent forward, her dark hair falling over her shoulder. "Now don't you scare him, Caroline. We are a normal family."

"That depends on your definition of normal." *She's the only one who never calls me Carlina.*

"Nonsense." Angela fingered the linen napkin with nervous fingers. "There's nothing wrong with any--"

"Carlina!" The booming voice behind Carlina caused the crystal glasses to rattle.

Marco gave a start of surprise.

"Uncle Teo!" Carlina jumped up and kissed her great uncle. "How are you?" She searched his face for any signs of fatigue or exhaustion.

"Never better, never better, my girl." Uncle Teo's few white hairs stood up in tufts, in stark contrast to his impeccable dark suit and white shirt, but his eyes were bright, and his cheeks had a rosy glow that showed how much he enjoyed himself.

He reminded Carlina so much of Nico, it felt as if someone had punched her straight in the stomach.

"What do I hear from Fabbiola?" Uncle Teo grinned at her with delight. "Nico is ill?"

Marco gasped. "For a moment I thought it was Nico himself." He said under his breath to Angela.

Carlina caught the words. *Ha, ha. Our normal family is already getting to him.* She added a hug to the kiss. Uncle Teo felt fragile and small in her arms. Sadness swamped her.

Angela bent closer to her husband. "No, this is Teo. He's better dressed than Nico. That's the only way you can tell them apart."

Carlina straightened her back with an effort. "The bad-vibe-period has come back," she said. Her voice didn't sound quite firm. "So he decided not to come."

Uncle Teo cackled with laughter. "That bad, eh?"

Carlina's mouth went dry. "What do you mean?"

"I bet he felt weak and decided not to stay up all night." He paraded two steps in front of her with a swagger. "Well, we can't all become younger every day." A wink at Carlina. "I'm not finished yet, no matter what that old doctor tells me!" He looked across the room at his wife. Aunt Maria lifted one large arm and waved at him. "Maria says I have to return to our table. See you later." He wriggled his white eyebrows at her. "Don't forget I want to dance with you. I want to dance with all my beautiful nieces." He grinned at Angela. "I'm not too old for that. Bad vibe. Ha. I bet Nico is nowhere near as fit as I am."

Carlina swallowed. *How true.*

Uncle Teo waved at them again and strutted off.

Phew. Carlina felt as if all her muscles had turned into water.

Marco shook his head. "Why is he happy that his twin brother is sick?"

Angela sighed and pushed her hand through her long hair.

Carlina said, "Because they are in eternal competition. From the day they were born, they wanted to outdo each other. Some say they had seven kids each because every time one of them got a new baby, the other went straight home and told his wife he wanted one more."

"Caroline! You make them sound so disagreeable." Angela pulled her slim eyebrows together.

Marco chuckled into his glass.

"But not at all." Carlina played with the white sugarcoated almond on her plate. *Now the competition is over, but Uncle Teo doesn't know it yet.*

"Why did they stop at seven kids?" Marco put a hand onto his wife's arm but kept looking at Carlina.

"Because my grandmother died after the birth of her seventh child." She turned the almond in a circle, lost in thought. "My grandpa raised all his kids on his own; though to be fair, Aunt Maria and Uncle Teo helped a lot."

Marco whistled. "Wow."

Angela withdrew her hand. "You know I hate that."

"What?"

"That whistling. It's so vulgar."

Mamma mia. Carlina suppressed the urge to roll her eyes. *She's so prissy, I wonder if she isn't a changeling.* She smiled to herself.

"What's so funny?" Marco's dark eyes probed her face.

"Oh, my family. They're a source of never ending amusement to me." *When combined with my thoughts, that is.*

Chapter 2

"Carlina!"

Someone pulled the bed cover away. Carlina held onto it with as much strength as her sleep-drugged arms would allow, but her fingers slid off the soft cotton, and a cold draft of air wafted around her legs. Carlina shuddered.

"Carlina! Get up!" Fabbiola sobbed. "Father died."

Carlina shot up, the shock coursing like hot lightning through her body. "Oh, God, I overslept." Her voice sounded drunken with sleep.

"What?" Fabbiola's eyes were red-rimmed. "What did you say?"

"Nothing." Carlina jumped out of bed and ran to the door of her apartment.

"Carlina! Stop!"

Carlina swiveled around. *Wake up, stupid. You need all your wits now.* "I . . . I can't believe it, *mamma*. I need to go downstairs and see it for myself." She rubbed her eyes.

"You can't go downstairs in this . . . this lacy nothing." Fabbiola pointed with a shaky finger at Carlina's nightdress.

"Oh. Right." Carlina hurried to her small bathroom and grabbed her white silk bathrobe with the red belt. She bent over the sink, turned on the faucet, and splashed cold water into her face. Things became clearer. She toweled off her face and turned to her mother who stood on the threshold to the bathroom.

Fabbiola's henna-red hair hung in strands, and last night's mascara smudged her eyes with huge black shadows. She was wearing her yellow silk dressing gown - a gift from Carlina - inside out.

Carlina felt a wave of tenderness rise inside her. "Who found him?"

Fabbiola wrung her hands. "Teo did. He said he wanted to chat with his brother about the wedding."

"Oh, God." Carlina turned cold. "Is he all right? What about his heart?"

"He's fine." Fabbiola said. "He says his heart doesn't bother him at all."

Carlina sighed. *Probably he wanted to gloat about having been awake all night and having eaten all kinds of indigestible things without side effects. Damn. I wanted to spare him the shock.* "And then?"

"He found him dead and came upstairs to wake me."

Oh, no. Carlina went to her mother and hugged her. "I'm so sorry, *mamma*. He was a wonderful man."

Fabbiola returned the hug with a sob. "It was so unexpected. Yesterday, he was just the same as always, and today . . ." She shuddered and wept without restraint.

Carlina held her tight. She waited until her mother calmed down, then said with a gentle voice. "Have you called the doctor?"

Fabbiola wiped her eyes. "I tried to. But I only got an answering machine. He's ill. It said I should call the hospital." She sniffed. "Just when you need Enrico, he's ill. That's so typical."

"But *mamma*, he was always here when one of us was ill. He can't help it if it he's not able to work right now. Did you call another doctor?" Carlina looked around for her cell phone.

Fabbiola drew herself up to her full size. "Of course not! What an idea. As if I would call someone I've never seen in my life." She eyed her daughter who was searching through her handbag with a determined face. "Don't you dare call a stranger either. I don't want an unknown man in my house."

"*Mamma*." Carlina fished out her cell phone and held it up. "We have to call someone. Without a death certificate, you can't move him. We need a doctor to get a death certificate."

"Oh, *Madonna*, I don't want to discuss this!" Fabbiola hugged herself. "My father is dead, and we're fighting about trivialities."

"It's not a triviality, *mamma*." Carlina tried to keep her voice calm. It helped her to cope with the grief by focusing on something to do. Anything. "It's the law. We don't have a choice." She looked at her phone and frowned. "Maybe --"

"Wait!" Fabbiola stretched out her hands. "I have an idea! We'll call Marco."

Carlina's hand sank to her side. "Marco? Why should Marco be able to help us?"

Fabbiola gave an impatient hiss. "Not Marco the mason. I mean Angela's Marco. Your new cousin! He's a doctor, isn't he?"

"Well, yes, I guess, but doesn't it seem a bit unfair? He has just finished medical school and--" Carlina shivered and pulled the bathrobe tighter around her.

"Nonsense." Fabbiola held out her hand with an imperious gesture. "Give me your phone. I will call him. He is family. That counts."

II

By the time Marco arrived at Via delle Pinzochere 10, the bells of Santa Croce had chimed eleven o'clock. Carlina listened to the familiar sound with a feeling of relief. In five minutes, Emma's plane would leave from Pisa airport, and nothing could stop her vacation in Africa. The wedding had been a success, the honeymoon would be fine, and when Emma returned, the worst would be over. *I just have to be strong for another day or two. As long as I remember my story and stick to it, nobody will start to ask awkward questions.*

Half the family had gathered in Nico's small kitchen. Those who didn't fit stood around in the entry. Carlina shook her head. She still didn't understand how news traveled faster than light within the Mantoni gang.

Aunt Maria leaned against the gas stove and breathed heavily, expelling clouds reeking of garlic with each breath as a small dragon would expel fire. Carlina frowned. Where was Uncle Teo? Was he still with his dead brother? In the other corner of the kitchen, as far away from Aunt Maria as possible, she saw Angela, who had crossed her arms in front of her chest and tapped a well-shod foot on the worn linoleum. *I bet she isn't happy that her husband was hauled in to sign the death certificate.*

Next to her, Carlina's cousins Ernesto and Annalisa stood with wide open eyes, their red hair flaming in the late morning sun coming through the window. At the ages of seventeen and nineteen, they were more impressed by death than the older folks. Their mother Benedetta had an arm around Annalisa's shoulders and sniffed into a handkerchief, but she had found the time to put on her bright red lipstick as always. Behind her, Carlina discovered her sister Gabriella with her husband

Bernando, both with red-rimmed eyes. Gabriella's brown curls looked tangled, as if she had last brushed them a week ago. *Where have they come from? They live thirty kilometers away.* Thank God they hadn't brought little Lilly. She would mourn her great-grandfather enough without seeing him dead.

Fabbiola reigned over the crowd by standing at the center and distributing paper handkerchiefs. Carlina sidled into the kitchen and avoided eye contact. She knew she would start to cry the minute she saw sympathy in someone's face.

A commotion at the kitchen door made her turn around. It was Marco. His handsome face looked pale. He hunched his shoulders as if he expected a blow and addressed Carlina. "Do you have a pen?"

Carlina nodded and opened the rickety drawer where Nico had kept all the odds and ends needed in a kitchen. She passed him a cheap ballpoint pen and watched him take a folded paper from his jacket pocket. The room fell silent. The only sound left was Aunt Maria's heavy breathing and the rustling of the paper beneath Marco's hands. It sounded eerie.

Carlina shuddered. It felt unnatural, the way they all watched Marco with immobile faces.

Marco filled two lines with an illegible scrawl. Then he checked the time on his wristwatch and noted that too, but just as he lifted the pen one last time to sign the death certificate, Uncle Teo shot through the door, stopped right in front of Marco, grabbed his arms, and shook him.

"Uncle Teo!" Carlina started forward. "Calm down."

"Something is wrong!" Uncle Teo's gnarled hands looked like claws on Marco's jacket. "I feel it! I know it!"

Carlina grabbed the edge of the table to steady herself. "What?"

"I tell you!" Uncle Teo let go of the young doctor and looked around the room, his eyes wild. "Something is wrong!"

Carlina took a chair and pushed it in Uncle Teo's direction. "Sit down, Uncle Teo." *And hush up. Now!*

Uncle Teo jumped away from the chair as if it was contaminated. "I don't want to sit. I tell you - me, Teodoro Alfredo Mantoni," he pointed with his right thumb at his breast, "I know. Something is wrong." His usually impeccable shirt looked crumpled and made him seem older.

His wife frowned and bent forward. "Why, Teo? How do you know?"

"I guess he inherited the bad vibe period," Angela muttered under her breath.

Uncle Teo glanced at her with acute dislike. "Nico is still wearing socks."

Carlina's thought she had misunderstood. "What?"

Her great-uncle nodded so hard, his white hair flopped forward. "Yes. He never wore socks in bed. Never! I know him. I'm his twin. I know."

Carlina felt as if the universe was turning around her in ever quickening circles. She placed a hand onto Uncle Teo's arm, not sure if it was a gesture to steady herself or to restrain him - or both. "I guess he changed his habits. We all do from time to time."

"No!" Uncle Teo shook his head. "An old man doesn't change his habits."

"Maybe he felt cold when he went to bed." *He sure started to be cold.*

The family watched the conversation in fascination, their heads turning as if they were watching a tennis match. Benedetta clapped a hand in front of her mouth, her eyes wide. The bright red lipstick peeking from between her fingers looked out of place in her white face.

"Nonsense." Uncle Teo hissed air between his teeth. "Nico didn't feel cold. It was hot yesterday. Too hot for late September."

I have to stop this. I have to divert him. Carlina pretended to give a nonchalant shrug. "I guess he must have felt ill already. That's why he didn't take off his socks."

"No." Uncle Teo shook his head. "He always took off his socks first."

Why, oh, why have I insisted on undressing Grandpa? How stupid of me! Desperate, Carlina turned to Marco. "I'm sure everything looked normal, don't you think so, Marco?" She fixed him with a compelling stare. *Say yes, Marco. Come on!*

Marco returned her look with a vacant expression as if he hadn't heard her.

"I think you should believe Teo." Aunt Maria moved her considerable bulk forward until she stood right next to Uncle Teo. "He knows what he's saying."

"I'm sure there's a perfectly normal reason why Grandpa is still wearing socks." Carlina clenched her teeth and smiled at Marco in what she hoped was an encouraging smile. "I suggest you sign the death certificate, and then we move on."

Marco nodded and lifted his pen, but before he could start to write, Fabbiola stuck her hands on her hips and said to Uncle Teo, "Are you telling us father was murdered?"

Silence. Even Aunt Maria stopped breathing. All eyes stared at Marco.

"Of course not!" Carlina felt hot and cold at the same time. She faked a laugh. "What an absurd thought!"

Marco placed the pen with care on top of the death certificate and straightened. He looked at Fabbiola, his face set like a mask. "I think you should consider what you are saying. If it was indeed murder, it would cause quite a scandal."

Wrong answer, wrong! Carlina winced. If only he knew the family better. Promising a scandal was a surefire way to get them interested. She could already see Ernesto and Annalisa perking up. Aunt Maria took one of her garlic snacks from the voluminous pocket of her skirt and cracked it between her large teeth by way of celebrating the occasion.

"Murder!" Fabbiola stared at Marco, her eyes wide, but Carlina could see the glittering that showed she was already checking the possibilities in her mind. "You're not serious."

"Of course not!" Carlina made one last attempt to save the situation. "So Grandpa died with his socks on. What's the big deal? He must have felt bad and forgotten them."

"No." Uncle Teo shook his head. "He wouldn't have done that."

Damn you, Uncle Teo. This is not the time to become stubborn. Carlina looked around the room in the faint hope of finding someone to support her, but they were all hugely entertained by the thought of having a family murder. Her sister Gabriella lifted her eyebrows so high, they disappeared beneath her tumbling curls, and her husband Bernando looked as if he had just been promised an exciting night out.

"Marco." Angela pushed Fabbiola to the side and stopped next to her husband. "I suggest you call some other doctor. It's a bit much to expect you to shoulder the responsibility when you've only just started work." She glanced at Fabbiola, her eyes cold.

Marco looked at his wife, his expression hard to fathom. He picked up the pen and held it cocked at an angle as if he wanted to sign the death certificate but didn't want to contradict his wife.

Carlina studied his immobile face, her thoughts running ahead in a panic. Was he relieved that Angela tried to shield him or did he resent it? Theirs had been a whirlwind romance. Was he having second thoughts? Maybe her beauty had swept him away, and now he was starting to get to know the lady underneath the veneer. *Quick, Carlina, quick. You have to find a solution to make him sign the paper.* What could she do to overcome Angela's influence and make him sign up now?

Fabbiola shook her head and pouted like a five-year-old. "I didn't push Marco to do anything at all. I just asked him."

Carlina gulped. Of course. Her mother never commanded anything, she asked. Like royalty . . . and it was just as hard to say no as if a real queen had asked the favor. Her throat constricted. She had to make Marco sign the Paper. "Marco, I think --"

Uncle Teo crashed a fist onto the table.

Everybody jumped.

"Enough!" His voice sounded higher than normal. "We won't discuss this anymore. Nobody is going to sign the death certificate, and nobody is going to treat this as a natural death. I will call the police."

Several family members gasped with delight.

Carlina gasped in dismay. "No!" She placed her hand on Uncle Teo's arm. "I'm sure there's a perfectly normal explanation." She tried to convey with her eyes that she knew the explanation and would share it with him as soon as they had gotten rid of the rest of the gang, but Uncle Teo shook her off. "Nobody is going to stop me." His voice rose, and two cords stood out on his neck like knotted ropes. "Nico was my twin." His cheeks turned puce. "I know something is wrong!"

Carlina stared at him. *If I try to stop him now, he's going to have a heart attack, and I will be responsible.* She bit her lips. *Damn.* "All right, Uncle Teo." She made sure her voice sounded soothing. *I'll talk to him as soon as I can get him all alone.* She smiled and opened her mouth to suggest that Teo take a rest, when her mother beat her to it.

Fabbiola straightened her shoulders, looked around the room, and delivered the verdict like a fanfare. "Let's call the police." She went to the phone in the corner of the kitchen and punched in the emergency number 113.

Carlina's mouth dropped open. Her mind went blank.

Before she could make up her mind what to do, Uncle Teo jumped forward and snatched the phone out of Fabbiola's hands. "He was my twin! I call the police!" His face turned from puce to lilac, and his eyes bulged.

Carlina balled her fists and took a steadying breath. *I can't stop him now . . . he would suffer a heart attack. Damn, damn, damn.*

Uncle Teo pressed the phone against his ear and listened without moving.

The whole family waited with bated breath.

Maybe the line is busy. Carlina bit her lips in agony.

"Pronto?" Uncle Teo knew the important role of a family entertainer. He spoke with relish and enough emphasis to shame a poet declaiming his favorite work. "I have to report a murder." He switched the phone on loudspeaker.

Oh, no. Carlina suppressed a groan. *Please. This is not a theater show. This is real.*

"Can you give me your name, please?" The policewoman wasn't aware she was supposed to take an active part in the theater; she even seemed bored.

Gabriella shook her head in disgust at this meager performance until all her curls wobbled.

"I'm Teodoro Alfredo Mantoni." When the operator didn't react, Uncle Teo repeated, "Mantoni. You know the Mantoni name, don't you?"

All Mantonis waited with bated breath for the reply, but the operator proved to be a disappointing partner. "Right." she said. "Where are you now?"

A sigh went up. The Mantonis had counted on a better show.

Uncle Teo frowned. "I'm at home, of course."

"Where is home? Could you please give me your address?"

"Of course." Uncle Teo sounded affronted now. "It's Via delle Pinzochere 10, in the historic center of Florence, next to Santa Croce."

"Noted. Now please tell me where you found the body."

Uncle Teo frowned. This wasn't going according to plan. "In his bed."

"Who is the victim?"

Carlina winced. Nico wasn't a victim. He had died a normal death, and his grandchild had moved him around a bit. That was all.

"It's my twin, Nicolò Alfredo Mantoni," Uncle Teo said. "You surely have heard about the twins Teodoro and Nicolò Mantoni, haven't you?"

The operator was well trained; she ignored questions that

only lead to trouble. "How do you know the death wasn't natural?"

Uncle Teo took a deep breath. Now this was the climax of the drama. "He was wearing socks."

Carlina started to shake with suppressed laughter.

"Excuse me, *signor*? Did you say he was wearing socks?" A sense of humor had not been part of the operator's job description.

"Yes."

"And you believe these socks were lethal?" Not a trace of amusement crept into the operator's voice.

"I never said that!" Uncle Teo's eyebrows bristled at the dumbness of the question. "But it was unusual."

For an instant, no sound came over the phone.

"Hello?" Uncle Teo shook the receiver as if that would improve the connection. "Are you still there?"

"Yes." The operator sounded patient now. Too patient. "How old was the victim?"

"Seventy-nine," Uncle Teo said with dignity. "Seventy-nine and four months and three days, to be exact, and fifteen minutes older than I am."

"Excuse me?"

"He was my twin." Uncle Teo repeated as if that explained everything.

"Are you telling me the victim was seventy-nine years old; he died with his socks on while he was in bed, and that's why you believe he was killed?"

"Exactly." Uncle Teo didn't catch the note of incredulity in the operator's voice. "Now we're understanding each other."

A chuckle escaped Carlina. She smothered it with a fake cough. Limp with relief, she sank against the table. *Thank God Uncle Teo made such a hash of it. The police will never come.*

The operator said, "I'll send an officer around within the next thirty minutes."

Chapter 3

Dust danced in the Sunday morning sunlight that came through the window next to the reception desk at the Florence police station. Gloria finished the call, shook her head and dialed three numbers in quick succession. After four years on the police force, she knew the internal numbers by heart.

Stefano answered after the first ring. "Tell me!"

"Ever heard of the Mantoni family?"

Stefano didn't reply.

Gloria inspected her fingernails as she waited. She knew Stefano well enough to picture him, his thick hair brushed back, his eyebrows pulled together in thought. A pity he wasn't interested in her.

"No."

Gloria smothered a smile. Never one to waste a word, Stefano sounded rude, but she knew him better. "I just got a call from an excited seventy-nine year old. Full name Teodoro Alfredo Mantoni." Gloria spoke slowly, as she knew Stefano would write it down. "He introduced himself as if he belongs to the royal family."

"Go on. I'll run a background check on him while you speak."

Gloria heard the clicking of Stefano's keyboard. "He said his twin was murdered because they found him dead in bed with his socks on."

Stefano laughed.

"My thoughts exactly. However, this guy claims it was unusual."

"Fat chance."

Gloria hesitated. "As it's quiet today, and as he seemed so excited, I said I would send someone over. Paolo is ill, so I wondered if you . . .?"

Stefano groaned. "I have a pile of work on my desk. What about Sergio?"

"Sergio is working on the Bellini case."

"All right." Stefano sighed. "Where do I have to go?"

"Via delle Pinzochere 10. Do you know it?"

"I do." Stefano said without hesitation. "It's a tiny street in the historical part of town, right next to Santa Croce."

"Nice area." Gloria looked out of the dusty window. "At least you'll get some fresh air in the sun."

"Hmm." Stefano didn't sound convinced.

Gloria heard a keyboard clicking. "What are you doing?"

"I just got the background check," Stefano said. "It shows a few speeding fines. Nothing else. But it seems to be a huge family."

"If you're lucky, it'll be over in ten minutes." Gloria made her voice upbeat. "Who do you want with you?"

"Roberto. Maybe for once, he'll be able to say it was a natural death without an autopsy." Stefano sounded resigned.

"Roberto has some days off and is out of town. He won't be back before Tuesday."

"Great. What am I supposed to do? Look at the guy's socks and give a verdict as if I am God Almighty?" He broke off. "Sorry, Gloria. I guess I'll just listen to what they have to say. I hope it won't take the whole day."

"Who's coming with you?"

"I'll ask Piedro, but you don't need to call him. I'll tell him myself."

"Fine. Good luck." Gloria disconnected the line with a sigh. She wished she had the courage to ask him for an evening out, but every time she mentioned something in that direction, Stefano became icy. A shame, really.

II

"I have to come up with a strategy. What is my best course of action?" Carlina held her face to the hot water coming from the shower. She owed the best ideas in her life to her shower, so when Uncle Teo had finished his conversation with the police, she had bolted for her bathroom as a fox bolts for his hole. Besides, she couldn't welcome the police dressed in a silk bathrobe.

But today, the shower didn't help. Her brain felt blocked as if all the intelligent fibers were frozen by fear. "First, I have to relax." Carlina concentrated on the steady stream of water, on the patter of warm drops on her shoulders, on the soothing steam swirling around her, and waited for relaxation to kick in.

It didn't. Her nerves were as taut as a thong two sizes too small. It hurt.

She switched off the water and leaned forward to pull a soft towel from the rail. As she toweled herself off, she wondered what was going on downstairs. If she knew her family well, Benedetta would refresh her lipstick and start to cook a gigantic meal to feed everyone. Not a hope that anybody would return home while the prospect of sharing a murder investigation kept them entertained.

Damn Emma. *I shouldn't have listened to her*. Now her cousin was far away in Africa, out of reach of the police, while she was sitting in the soup. Damn Uncle Teo, too. Did he have to make a scene? Did he have to call the police?

Carlina pulled her favorite bra and slip out of the drawer and put them on. For once, the imitation leopard fur on the straps and cups failed to give her pleasure. She picked a blue cotton blouse and a pair of jeans at random and dressed without noticing what she was doing. Just before she left her apartment, her glance fell on her cell phone. She stopped dead. An idea flashed through her mind. *I could call the police and explain it was all a mistake.*

Carlina grabbed her phone and started to punch in the number, then hesitated. What could she say? "I'm sorry, but please forget about that call you got some minutes ago? My grandfather died a natural death, but the timing didn't fit, so I stuffed him into his bed to hide him, only, I forgot to take off his socks?" How did that sound?

Her heart sank. *I can't tell them on the phone.* She pressed her lips together. *It'll be easier to tell them in person.* She would ask the police for a confidential talk, and then she would tell them the truth. It would be the most embarrassing thing ever, but she didn't have a choice.

As she descended the worn wooden staircase from the top floor, she realized she was walking twice as slowly as usual, her fingers caressing the smooth wooden railing out of habit. She didn't want to arrive. She didn't want to face the police. She didn't want to explain how stupid she had been.

In front of her grandfather's green door, she pulled back her shoulders, shook her hair, and took a deep breath. But before she could touch the handle, someone flung it open from inside. A flash of red hair, then her cousin Ernesto called over his shoulder as if he was seven and not seventeen, "Here she is!"

Carlina's stomach curled up. "Are you waiting for me?"

"Yes!" Ernesto grabbed her arm and led her to the kitchen like a prize he had won at the local carnival. "The *commissario* is here. He has looked at every detail, and we've already explained everything, but now he wants to see you."

What? He was supposed to come in thirty minutes, not in five! Carlina stopped. "I think I forgot something," she said. "Let me just run upstairs, and I'll . . ."

The kitchen was still full of people, but it now looked more like a party. Benedetta was busy handing around little slices of bread with tomato cubes, and already, voices were raised in heated discussions.

"Carlina!" Fabbiola rushed toward her. She had found the time to dress and brush her hair, but she carried her trusted cushion under one arm.

Carlina looked at it with dismay. If her mother started to carry the cushion around inside the house, it was worse than she'd expected. For some reason, her mother felt safer with cushion than without and took it with her whenever she left the house, but as a rule, she didn't carry it around if she stayed inside.

Fabbiola gave her a lopsided hug. "Why do you look so afraid?" she asked with a stage whisper. "He's nice, the *commissario*. I've already explained everything to him."

Everything? Oh, no. "That's all right, *mamma*." Carlina's voice sounded as uncertain as she felt.

A man appeared in the kitchen door, tall enough to tower over her. "Are you Caroline Arabella Ashley?"

Carlina nodded. Her throat felt tight. He had his back to the light, so she couldn't make out his features, but he seemed lean and athletic. He was wearing a crisp white shirt and black trousers, formal enough to scare her.

"My name is Stefano Garini. I'm the *commissario* at the homicide department."

Carlina winced. The homicide department. It was all so wrong.

Her mother grabbed her arm and gave her a reassuring smile.

"Would you please step into the sitting room?" He led the way, then opened the door and stood to the side.

Carlina cleared her throat. "Sure."

"I won't leave you." Fabbiola declared in a voice that brooked no opposition.

"That's not necessary, *mamma*." Carlina's voice sounded flat.

Commissario Garini inclined his head. "If you wish to have your mother with you, it's not a problem."

Carlina looked at him. His thick hair was dark-brown, brushed back from his brow. He was tanned, as if he had been in the sun all summer long.

"See?" Fabbiola shook Carlina's arm. "I told you he's nice."

"*Mamma*, I can talk to him on my own. I'm not a teenager anymore."

"I know, my dear." Fabbiola smiled at her daughter. "But what kind of a mother would leave her daughter all alone with the police?"

It sounded as if the police was equal to a wild beast, bent on devouring Carlina until not a hair was left.

The *commissario* didn't bat an eyelid. "This is *signor* Cervi." He made a motion with his hand toward the corner of the room. A young man with an impassive face nodded at them. He was seated on a low stool.

Grandpa used this stool to put up his feet. He'll never do it again. The loss hit Carlina like a wave.

The *commissario* glanced at her. "Are you all right, *signorina* Ashley?"

Carlina pulled herself together. The *commissario* had sharp eyes. She had to keep her wits about her. "Yes."

Commissario Garini nodded. "*Signor* Cervi will take notes about our conversation. Do you agree to this?"

"Of course!" Fabbiola sat on the sofa. "Don't we, Carlina?"

Carlina nodded. "Yes." She felt like a puppet on strings, moving without her own will.

Signor Cervi took out a notebook and a pen.

"Come here, my dear." Fabbiola patted the place next to her.

Carlina dropped onto the sofa and looked at the *commissario* who took a seat in the battered armchair to her left. His face was lean and thin, and his nose reminded her of a hawk. No, the resemblance with a hawk came from the eyes. They were light and hard and gave her the impression he could spot a detail at a distance of several kilometers. He didn't look like someone who would understand a silly mistake or two.

"I understand from your family that you were the last person to see Nicolò Mantoni alive."

"Together with her cousin, Emma, that is." Fabbiola pushed the cushion behind her back and leaned into it as if she wanted to talk for an hour.

Commissario Garini nodded. "Quite, *signora* Mantoni-Ashley. However, I would appreciate if you could let your daughter tell me in her own words." He focused on Carlina and waited for her to begin.

Carlina met his eyes. They were cool and expectant, and for an instant, she thought she saw an ironic twinge in the faint lifting of an eyebrow. Her heart plummeted. How could she tell this unemotional man she had moved her dead grandfather around?

Fabbiola took her hand and pressed it so hard, Carlina thought her bones would crack. "Tell him about father's phases, dear."

Carlina frowned. Why was her mother so protective all at once? "My grandfather . . ." her voice cracked. *Damn.* Carlina could feel herself blushing. The *commissario* would think she was an emotional wreck. She cleared her throat and recommenced, "My grandfather was a bit . . . eccentric."

Fabbiola lifted both hands, still holding onto Carlina's hand. "He wasn't eccentric; he was crazy. But lovely crazy, if you know what I mean."

Commissario Garini gave her a look as if "lovely crazy" didn't exist in his dictionary.

Carlina tried to free her hand, but Fabbiola held onto it.

"My mother means he had different phases, but they didn't do any harm," she said.

Commissario Garini frowned. "What phases?"

"Well, he had a phase when he joined the Sun Worship Church. Have you heard of them?"

He shook his head.

"They adore the Sun and sink into meditation whenever it comes out."

She had been right about that ironic eyebrow. It twitched higher. She could tell Garini wasn't a man to waste sympathy on anybody's foibles. *Oh, God.* "He also had a health food period, when we were only allowed to eat homemade bread. During that period, he drank vinegar for breakfast."

"Vinegar and honey," Fabbiola corrected. "It's supposed to be good for you."

"I see." It sounded as if the *commissario* was wondering why Nico hadn't been locked up years ago.

"Another period was the bad vibe period," Carlina said.

"That's when he felt bad vibes that prevented him from doing some things."

"How convenient." *Commissario* Garini's voice was dry.

"It had nothing to do with convenience!" Fabbiola fired up. "It was a real feeling, and it made him sick to do things that went against his conviction." She patted the cushion behind her back for support.

The *commissario* inclined his head. "I understand."

He thinks we're a bunch of lunatics. "These last weeks, he had the bad past period." Carlina tried to convey with her voice that she was in full control of all her intellectual capacities, even if the same couldn't be said of all her family members.

The *commissario* lifted his eyebrows. "What does this mean?"

Fabbiola made a throw-away gesture with her hand. "Oh, it was nothing. He told us we had bad things in our past that would catch up with us. We laughed so hard about some of the things he invented." Without warning, she started to cry. "I'm going to miss him."

Carlina put her arm around her mother, her own eyes filling with tears.

"*Signorina* Ashley, I don't wish to make your life difficult at such a sad time, but could you please corroborate the statements I heard earlier?"

"Of course." Carlina bit her lips. Had she just agreed to confirm everything? *Oh, no.* Her mother pulled the cushion from behind her back and sobbed into it.

The *commissario* watched her without twitching a muscle.

He won't understand. He won't believe me. He's a police computer with a body wrapped around it. He has no idea how a human being feels.

Fabbiola's sobs made Carlina wince. *I can't embarrass her so much. She'll never forgive me if I present them all as liars now.*

"*Signorina* Ashley? Would you please answer?"

Carlina met his cool gaze for a fleeting instant. He seemed dark and menacing, though she couldn't tell where the impression came from. *I never want to see him mad.* She opened her mouth and heard herself say. "My grandfather didn't want to come to the wedding. He said it would be unlucky. We had the impression the bad vibe period had returned, and we couldn't change his mind, so we left." The words rushed out of her mouth. There. She had said it. She had crossed the point of no return. *Oh, Madonna.*

The *commissario's* light eyes seemed to penetrate into her brain. "You're quite sure he was fine and well when you saw him?"

Her heart started to race. *What does he know?*

"Of course she's sure." Fabbiola said. "Do you think my daughter would lie to the police?"

The *commissario* didn't take his gaze off Carlina. "*Signorina* Ashley?"

Carlina cleared her throat. "Yes." Her voice sounded higher than normal.

"Then how do you explain the socks?"

Carlina shrugged. *Did that look nonchalant enough?* "He probably felt too bad to take them off."

"Did he seem different compared to his usual self?"

Very. Carlina bit her lips. "No."

"Thank you." The *commissario* got up. "I have all the information we need. Due to the circumstances, we will arrange an autopsy, but it will take some days. You will hear from us. In the meantime, I would like to seal the apartment."

Fabbiola gasped. "What?"

He looked at her. "It's standard procedure. We're treating this case as a murder investigation until we have further evidence. I understand your father lived on his own?"

"Yes." Fabbiola clutched her cushion tight.

"Then it won't create too much of an inconvenience." He held the door open for her to leave the sitting room. "Please ask the family to leave the apartment."

Carlina shook her head, but the feeling of having strayed into a surrealistic movie remained.

As soon as the *commissario* was out of earshot, Carlina rounded on her mother with a hiss. "Why did you behave as if I'm a five-year-old?"

Fabbiola pouted. "I don't think you should be alone with a policeman."

It sounded as if policemen were a dangerous species. "Why?" Carlina put her hands on her hips. "What did you think would happen?"

Fabbiola hitched her cushion higher and gave her a dark look. "He kept asking who had last seen father alive. He said it was important to speak to you. It sounded . . . " her voice trailed out, then she shrugged. "It sounded sinister."

"Oh, *mamma*." Carlina gave her a quick hug. "Thank you, but it wasn't necessary at all." *In fact, you rendered me the worst possible service.*

When the *commissario* and his assistant had left, she extricated herself from the family and ran upstairs to her apartment on the top floor. It was a relief to be alone, to stop acting, and to be just herself. She felt hollow and exhausted and dropped onto her bed with the leopard print cover. *I have lied to the police.* She felt like a criminal.

Carlina placed her hands behind her head and looked at the slanted ceiling painted in a soft lilac. Now what? Call the *commissario* and tell him it was all lies?

She shuddered.

No way. He would look at her with those cold eyes and would decide it was time to lock her up.

Carlina shook her head. "Now relax, my girl," she said to herself. "Forget the policeman made of stone and think about it without emotions." She forced herself to think through her options. Even if the interview didn't go the way she had planned, nothing worse could happen. They would make that stupid autopsy; they would realize it had been a natural death, and that was it. She could relax now.

She bit her lips. Just one problem remained. What if the autopsy revealed that Grandpa had died earlier than Carlina had claimed? She had no idea how long he had been dead when they had found him. Not very long, but what did that mean in hours or minutes? Hadn't she seen on TV that it was almost impossible to pin down a death to an exact moment? Surely they wouldn't be able to do that. If they did the autopsy in a few days, it would be even more difficult. Hadn't she read this somewhere?

Carlina got up and decided to put all thoughts about her grandfather's death behind her. But in spite of all her reasoning, she felt jumpy all day long. When she couldn't stand it anymore, she grabbed her keys, took her trusted Vespa, and roared around the hills of Florence. For once, it didn't help. The *commissario's* lean face and hard eyes were imprinted on her mind like an image of Nemesis. *Cool down, silly.* Carlina stopped her Vespa on top of a hill, took off her helmet with the leopard print, and breathed the soft evening air. It smelled of rosemary from a nearby hedge. *You're exaggerating him. The image you remember is distorted by emotion. Nobody can look as fierce as that.* Carlina sat without moving and looked around the scenery she loved. Already dusk settled below a mauve sky. The evening light spun a golden haze over the dark outline of the trees on the hilltops around her, and on the fields, fog gathered like foamy water. In the valleys, windows sprung to light, warm islands of comfort. Carlina took a deep breath. *Don't worry. You'll never see him again.*

III

"So what do you make of the Mantoni family?" Stefano led the way to his office and pushed open the gray door. It squeaked as always, and Stefano thought for the hundredth time that he should remember to bring oil for the hinges.

Piedro shrugged. "From what they said, the victim must have been bananas."

Stefano nodded. "To me it seemed as if the whole family was odd." He smiled at his subordinate. "Sit down, Piedro." He waited until Piedro had taken a seat in front of his old desk, then stretched himself out in his own chair. "Anything else?"

Piedro took out his notes and studied them before he looked up. "Nothing. I don't think there was anything suspicious at all. Of course some were nervous, and some were excited, but that's pretty normal, isn't it?"

"Yes." Stefano looked at Piedro and decided to help him along. "Who was nervous, and who was excited?"

"Let me see." Piedro leafed through his notes. "The twin, Teodoro, he was excited. Loved the whole thing. Am not sure about the daughter of the victim. Name of Fabbiola Mantoni-Ashley. Funny name, that one."

"She said she had been married to an American. Didn't you note that?"

"No."

Stefano frowned. *I have to read his notes later and add the things he forgot.* "You should add it. How did her behavior strike you?"

"Well." Piedro looked at his notes as if he hoped for inspiration. His gelled-up hair stood up in spikes. "First, she was excited, but later, she seemed worried about her daughter."

"Yes. Do you think that was unusual?"

Piedro shrugged. "Not really. I just wondered why she got all worked up. She didn't look as if she needed to be protected. The daughter, I mean. What was her name? Carlina."

"No. Caroline Ashley."

Piedro frowned. "Everybody called her Carlina."

"A nickname." For an instant, Stefano saw Carlina's pale face again. The freckles had made her look younger than she was. Her eyes reminded him of a cat, slanted and intelligent.

Piedro shrugged off the name. "She acted real nervous."

"Yes, I noticed that too."

Piedro grinned. "Maybe she never talked to an investigating officer before."

"Who knows what she has to hide." Stefano sighed. "So many lie to us for many different reasons." He frowned. "Didn't her mother tell us she owns a retail store?"

"Yes." Piedro leafed through his notebook. "They sure talked a lot, all of them, if you don't count this Carlina." He turned another page. "Here it is. It's a store for luxury underwear called Temptation." He grinned. "Think something is wrong with that store?" He checked his notes once again. "It's on Via dei Tornabuoni. Expensive area."

"Yes." Stefano frowned. "It might bear looking into. We should keep our eyes open." He pushed his hand through his hair. "One other thing, though. Did you notice anything unusual about the body?"

Piedro looked as intelligent as a pair of boxer shorts. "Unusual?"

"That's what I said." *Be patient, Stefano. He's still young.*

"No. He was dead."

Spot on, Piedro. "Yes. I know he was dead. But did you see the marks on his backside?"

"No."

Stefano felt like he was explaining things to a kangaroo. "They come from the blood. It pools when the circulation stops, and they indicate the position of the body when he died." He shook his head, puzzling over it. "The marks on this victim were faint, but they seemed unusual to me, as if he had died in a sitting position." He shrugged. "Then again, the mattress was sagging like a hammock. I guess that's why."

Piedro's eyes glazed over. "I'll type the report, then," he said.

I wonder if he heard a word I said. Garini suppressed a sigh. "Yes. Please leave it on my desk when you're done."

Piedro nodded and made a move to get up.

Stefano stopped him by lifting his hand. "Wait a moment."

"Yes?" Piedro looked wary.

"Why did you decide to become a policeman?" Garini bent forward.

His subordinate blinked. "My father said it was a good job."

No doubt. "And you? What did you think?"

Piedro looked around the room as if the answer was written on the walls. "I dunno."

Stefano remembered the first day he himself had started work. Naive? Yes. Full of lofty ideas? Oh my. He smiled a little at himself. But also with a strong desire to protect, to help, to keep injustice at bay. With the years, he had become more of a cynic. He had discovered beautiful faces with black holes where their souls should have been; had been shocked more than once by the depth of human wickedness; had started to mistrust the surface of things, the smiling faces, the easy answers. His probing had become harsher, his search for truth more ruthless. But underneath, he still knew why he was doing his job. He fought for stability, for justice. It was easy to forget that when faced with paperwork, with politics, with stupidity, but whenever he solved a case, it gave him a satisfaction nothing could equal. Did Piedro feel any of this? Did he sense a mission?

Piedro got up. "I'll do the report, then."

He doesn't even ask how we will proceed. Stefano forced himself to explain the next steps in spite of the bored expression on his assistant's face. "We won't get the autopsy before Tuesday. Roberto's assistant is already checking the most important points, but we need to wait for Roberto's return before we get the official file. I do wonder about those marks . . ." He shook his head. "Still, I think it doesn't matter. This case will be over before it begins, Piedro. An old man dies in his bed, and his over-excited family tries to make a story out of it." He sighed. "We only have one result: I have to stay an hour longer tonight to deal with the paperwork."

Chapter 4

"Stefano!" A man waved at Stefano from the other side of the street.

Stefano looked up from the hot pizza in front of him and lifted his hand. "Ciao, Roberto." *Please don't come over.* He inhaled the scent of the aromatic salami and watched the pathologist with a wary eye. *Of course he arrives the minute my pizza is served.*

Roberto crossed the narrow street with a jaunty step. He passed the terracotta pots filled with boxwood that separated the restaurant from the sidewalk and came closer with a grin on his round face.

The red-and-white checkered tablecloth fluttered in a sudden gust of wind.

"Roberto." Stefano nodded at him and lifted his fork. "Sorry if I start, but my pizza will get cold."

Roberto pulled up an iron chair with a flat red cushion, dropped onto it and stretched his legs in front of him. "No problem." He waved at the waiter. "Bring me some of that red wine I had the last time."

Stefano suppressed a sigh. He had counted on a quiet meal, and now he had to share it with the most voluble of his colleagues. *If only he doesn't start to talk about work.*

"Why are you eating so late?" Roberto pointed at the pizza. "Or should I say early? Is this lunch or dinner?"

"Lunch. I wanted to finish a case first." Stefano cut a good-sized bit out of his pizza wedge. "Had a good weekend?"

Roberto shrugged. "It was all right. We went to see my wife's family, up in Milano."

"Hmm." Stefano munched the first piece of pizza. It tasted crisp and spicy, just the way he wanted it. He liked this pizzeria, hidden from the steady stream of tourists, with simple, wholesome food.

"You can be lucky you're not married." Roberto rolled his

eyes. "I can stand my mother-in-law for two hours, but any minute longer is torture."

"You shouldn't go if you don't like it." Stefano took the next piece of pizza. *Delicious.* He glanced at a sparrow that fluttered from the boxwood to the pavement. It looked like a tiny ball of feathers on the gray stone slabs.

"You don't know my wife!" Roberto threw his hands into the air. "Silvia would pulverize me if I ever suggested such a thing."

Stefano felt an old feeling of boredom creep up. *Why do people complain all the time about things they can change?* "So get a divorce."

The sparrow cocked its brown head and looked at Stefano out of unblinking, black eyes, as if it wanted to say "Want to share, mate?"

Stefano threw him a crumb.

Roberto burst into laughter. "That's so typical for you, Stefano!"

Stefano lifted his eyebrows. "What? A divorce? I've never been married."

"No, no." Roberto shook his head. "You're so rude. You have quite a reputation for blistering one-liners, you know that, don't you?"

Stefano blinked. "I do?"

The waiter arrived with the wine and filled Roberto's glass from a slim glass carafe. Three more sparrows landed on the pavement.

"Grazie." Roberto nodded at the waiter and picked up his glass. "No wine for you?"

"No, thanks." Stefano lifted his glass filled with water. "Salute." *I thought I'd kept most of my scathing comments to myself.*

Roberto looked at him, a grin spreading over his round face. "Maybe it's good you're not married. I can't imagine you making compromises."

"God, Roberto, you're hitting hard today." Stefano put down his fork. "I may not be the world's best choice for small talk, but I've never seen myself in such a bad light."

Roberto crossed his ankles and looked with satisfaction at his polished shoes before he glanced at Stefano's abandoned fork. "Sorry, I didn't want to destroy your appetite."

Stefano lifted his eyebrows. "You could have fooled me."

The pathologist grinned. "Hey, I haven't even started to talk about work."

"Thanks." Stefano's voice sounded dry. He picked up his fork and continued to eat.

"In fact, I wanted to tell you about that old man you sent on Sunday."

Stefano lifted both hands. "Sorry for that. For once, I obeyed my nobler instincts and humored a crazy family. You can see where it got me."

"It wasn't a natural death."

The fork fell with a clatter onto Stefano's plate. "What?" His voice thundered through the small street.

The sparrows flew up in a flurry.

The waiter came running. "Is everything all right, *signori*?"

Stefano forced a smile. "Yes, thanks." He turned back to Roberto. "You're kidding me."

"Not at all." Roberto chuckled into his fist. "That got you, didn't it?"

"It sure did." Stefano's voice sounded grim. "I wondered about the marks on his body, but I thought they were due to the sagging mattress. What was it?"

"Morphine. Enough to kill a horse." Roberto moved his shoes a bit, so the light would move on the shiny surface. "The kind you get on prescription when you're in pain. He took it with a drink."

"Damn."

Roberto cocked his head. "Is there a problem?"

Stefano frowned. "I was sure it was a natural death, so I didn't dig as deep as I usually do."

Roberto shrugged. "You can still ask all the questions you want." He emptied his wine glass and refilled it from the glass carafe. "You sure you don't want a glass?"

"Yes, thanks." Stefano frowned at his last piece of pizza. "Anything else?"

Roberto moved his head from side to side. "Two things."

Stefano clenched his teeth. "Tell me!"

"You just mentioned the spots on his body. I would say the victim died sitting, but you found him in bed, is that right?"

"Yes."

"Hmm. If you had asked me, I would have said it was impossible."

"Even with a mattress like a hammock?"

Roberto frowned. "Yes. We found some marks on his legs

too, and they would not have been there if he had died stretched out. Very faint, though. No wonder you missed them."

"I see." Stefano wanted to hit something hard. "What else?"

"The time of death seems to be . . . off-key. From your report, I know he was supposed to have died sometime between one thirty in the afternoon and the next morning at ten forty-five, is that right?"

Stefano nodded. "That's what the witnesses said."

"My assistant took him in and checked him through." Roberto emptied his glass and put it back onto the table with a satisfied sigh. "Of course, he's not very experienced yet, and when I came back from Milano, it was much too late to tell, but he said several signs hinted at an earlier death."

"Earlier?" The image of a nervous woman with cat eyes rose in Stefano's mind. "How much earlier?" *She lied to me.*

Roberto shrugged. "Difficult to say. It was a hot day, and I don't know about the room temperature, so I can only give you some very loose information. Don't look at me like that; I didn't see him when he came in, so I can't be certain of the time."

Stefano waived at the waiter. *"Il conto, per favore!"*

"Hey, you haven't finished your pizza!" Roberto pulled up his feet and bent forward. "No need to run off in a panic. The guy has been dead for days. Some minutes more or less won't make a difference."

Stefano pulled out his wallet. "I've lost my appetite."

Roberto watched him. "No wonder people are afraid of you, Stefano. In a black mood, you look more dangerous than any killer I've ever seen."

"You've only seen dead ones."

"Thank God." Roberto shuddered. "But you . . . who do you want to kill?"

"Me." Stefano slapped two bills on the table. "For having been so stupid. And -- " he broke off.

"And?" Roberto's eyes were alight with curiosity.

"A woman called Carlina." *I felt sorry for her.*

Stefano hurried back to the police station. He had two options now. Either the old man had killed himself or he had been eliminated. *If only I had taken the whole thing seriously right from the start.* He skipped over a pile of dog poo, pulled out his cell phone and called his assistant. "Piedro?" Stefano pressed the phone against his ear. *What's that noise?*

"Sì!" Piedro's voice almost drowned in a clanging sound.

"Where are you?" Stefano tried not to sound as impatient as he felt.

"I'm still at the garage. They say they'll have my motorbike repaired within the next hour."

"They've said so twice already."

"I know." Piedro managed to sound harassed. "But when they had checked the brake fluid, they realized it can't have been the source of --"

"Don't explain." Stefano interrupted him. "If your bike can't be repaired within the next hour, take the train back to Florence."

"But that takes more than an hour!"

"A little less. The train connection isn't that bad. After all, you're only in Pisa, not at the end of the world."

"But how do I collect my bike?"

"By the very same train. On your next day off." Garini made sure his voice sounded sweet.

Piedro sighed. "All right."

"Hurry. We have a new case, and I need you here."

"A new case?"

"Yes. Remember the grandfather who died with his socks on?"

"Yeah. The one with the mad family."

"Exactly. He was poisoned."

"Cool."

Garini sighed and rang off. *If only Piedro wasn't the son of my boss.*

As he hurried back to the station, his mind clicked off the things he had to do. Get a search warrant. Kick himself for having been taken in. Get a tape recorder from the station and start with another round of interrogations, first tackling that woman called Carlina. He shook his head at his own stupidity. *It's not like you to be taken in by a pair of cat eyes and some freckles, Stefano.* If only Roberto had for once given him a tighter frame of time. Vague as it was, it didn't help at all. The whole Mantoni family had been milling around the house all morning, bringing flowers, helping each other get ready for the wedding, collecting stuff. He had already established that during the first round of interviews. *Damn.* He had to scare someone into talking. It was his only chance.

Chapter 5

Carlina hummed to herself as she undressed the mannequin in her store. Thank God she had switched to the new models. They weighed less than the former style of mannequins, were a lot easier to handle and looked sexier too. She slung the old bra and slip over her shoulder, then bent down to pull the new collection from the box at her feet. The bra came up first, and she held it against her mannequin to check the effect. Hmm. Creamy white with lace. Gorgeous, but on the mannequin it looked kind of weak. Carlina stopped humming and frowned. Maybe she needed to buy a darker mannequin. After all, white was still the best-sold color, and if she could never show it on her pale mannequin, it hurt sales. She dropped the creamy bra and fished out another in chocolate brown with white lace.

Better. Much better. Carlina started to hum again. Lovely for autumn. She would hang up a poster of a dark-skinned woman with the creamy bra behind the mannequin, then she could show both. The new nylons in soft brown with golden swirls would fit so well. She could--

"*Buona sera, signorina* Ashley."

Carlina jumped and dropped the bra. She swiveled around and stared at the tall man in front of her. "*Commissario* Garini." As she met his eyes, she knew her memory hadn't faulted her. He looked as intimidating as ever. No, he looked worse. The blue jeans and black leather jacket seemed too warm for this late September day, but that wasn't the problem. His eyes scared her, those hawk-like eyes, too light and cold. She felt like a mouse and wanted to run for cover. "What can I do for you?"

The *commissario* looked around. "Is anybody else in the shop?"

Carlina's heart started to beat faster. "No. My assistant has already left."

"Can you close up?"

Her hand started to tremble. "I'd rather not."

He checked his heavy wristwatch with an impatient gesture. "When will you close?"

"At seven."

"I can't wait that long. I need to talk to you."

God, he was rude. Carlina pressed her lips together. "One moment, please." *I won't leave my mannequin naked in the window, even if you have to wait.* She turned back to the mannequin, laid it on the floor with an expert flick of her wrist, slipped on the new thong, fixed the bra, and put it back into the window. The nylons would have to wait. His presence made her too nervous to handle the fragile material.

Then she stepped out of the window and went past him to the entrance of her store.

Quick as a flash, he was behind her, a hand on her arm. "Where are you going?"

She jumped with fear. "I just want to put up a sign that the store is closed." She narrowed her eyes. "Unless you prefer to interrupt our conversation whenever a customer comes in."

His hand dropped from her arm. "Go ahead."

With stiff legs, Carlina went to the door. *This is not going well. Oh, my God. I should have told him the truth. They have found out that grandpa died earlier. Damn, damn, damn.*

She took the sign from its hiding place, hung it on the inside of the glass door and closed the door with the key. Then she turned around and faced him. "Come to the back," she said. *No need to be polite with this humanized police computer.*

He didn't take his eyes off her, not even for one second. "Why?"

"Because I don't want the whole world to see that I'm having a long conversation with a *commissario* from the homicide department."

Those hateful eyebrows twitched. "Is it going to be a long conversation?"

Carlina clenched her teeth. "Yes." She brushed past him and went to the back of the store. He was right on her heels, so close she felt stifled. "Do you have to walk so close behind me?" It sounded like a hiss.

"Yes." His voice was free of emotions. "Otherwise, you can pull a gun on me."

"I'm not wearing a gun!"

"I know. But you might have one in a drawer somewhere."

How did he know she wasn't wearing a gun? Had those light eyes scanned her from top to toe? Carlina felt hot, then cold. "I don't own a gun."

"Officially, you don't," he agreed.

Oh, God. "How come you're on your own?" She drew the curtain to the side and stepped into her tiny storage room. "I thought policemen only come in sets. Are you sure I'm not too dangerous to handle all on your own?" She heard her own words and stopped, appalled. What on earth was she saying?

His gaze became arctic. "I don't underestimate you, if that's what you fear. However," he leaned against the door frame and crossed his arms in front of his chest, "you shouldn't underestimate me either."

I sure don't. On the contrary. Carlina took two small folding footstools off a hook on the wall, unfolded them and placed them on the floor. Her storage room was small to begin with, and her clever storage system diminished it even further. She was proud of the tiny cubicles that covered every free space on the walls from the ceiling to the floor, plus the second layer of storage racks that could be moved to the side on rails. She pushed the racks to the end to enlarge the room close to the curtain. Now the door to the small bathroom in the back was blocked, but that didn't matter. "Sit down."

He lifted his eyebrows.

The way he stood there seemed insolent, as if he was relaxed and at his ease, but she wasn't fooled. He had a coiled energy about him that reminded her of a panther. If she made a wrong move, he would pounce on her quicker than she could blink.

"I prefer to remain standing," he said.

"Suit yourself." *Damn. Now I have to look up at him if I want to rest my feet.* Carlina sat on her footstool, leaned her back against the shelves and, to make up for her inferior position, put her feet onto the stool he had rejected as if she was the most relaxed tourist Florence had ever seen. If she rested her head against the shelf, she could even look at him without getting a crick in the neck.

Was he grinning? She stared at him.

He returned her gaze unblinking.

I must have imagined that twitch around his mouth.

He reached into the pocket of his black leather jacket.

Carlina jumped.

"Nervous, are you?"

She didn't reply.

He pulled out a small box in black and pressed a button. A red light came on. "I want to record our conversation. Do you agree?"

What choice do I have? "Yes." The tiny room felt overcrowded with him at the door.

"Your name is Caroline Arabella Ashley, living at Via delle Pinzochere, 10 in Florence. Do you confirm this?"

"Yes." Carlina bit her lips. God, this was hard. She felt like a total idiot. How could she ever have lied to that unforgiving, inhuman man?

"*Signorin*a Ashley, do you wish to add anything to your statement of last Sunday?"

I don't want to play cat and mouse with him. He's better at this than I am. Carlina pulled herself up. "I do."

He waited without twitching a muscle.

"I lied about . . . about the time when I saw my grandfather last. He was dead when Emma and I went downstairs to pick him up for the wedding." *God, he doesn't make it easy. I was so stupid.*

"How did you get access to his apartment?"

Carlina stared at him. "With my key, of course."

"You have a key to your grandfather's apartment?"

"Yes and no." Carlina crossed her legs at the ankles to look more relaxed, but she had the uneasy feeling he wasn't fooled. "Our keys are universal fits. I can enter any apartment in the house with my key."

His mouth went slack. "What? You have access to all apartments with one key?"

"Yes." Carlina nodded.

"Good grief. How many apartments are in that house?"

"On the ground floor, we have two - my grandfather on the right." She swallowed. *Not anymore. No, better not think about it.* "Uncle Teo lives with Aunt Maria on the left. They are --," she broke off and started again. "They were identical twins. They painted their doors bright red and bright green, the colors of Italy."

She could tell he wasn't interested in the colors of Italy and suppressed a sigh. "On the first floor, we have Emma with her fiancé, I mean husband, Lucio, and on the right, her mother Benedetta with my cousins Ernesto and Annalisa. Benedetta is my mother's youngest sister."

He looked a bit dazed.

"Benedetta is the one with the bright lipstick." No, he wasn't interested in the lipstick either. "Ernesto and Annalisa both have red hair. It's funny because their older sister Emma is a lot darker and . . ." Her voice petered out when she saw the expression in his light eyes.

"And the second floor?"

"On the second floor, my mother lives on the right hand side. The apartment on the left is rented to the neighboring house, and they have made a hole into their wall instead and closed the door to our staircase."

Now he looked as if he wanted to congratulate the neighbors for their decision. "I understand you have one brother and one sister."

"Yes."

"Why don't they live with you in the house?"

Carlina shrugged. "Enzo works in Pisa and doesn't want to commute each day, though grandpa told him a hundred times he should live at home." She smiled a little at the thought of her irrepressible brother. "My sister Gabriella is married to Bernando, and they live next to Bernando's mother, thirty kilometers away. The apartment would be too small for them anyway because of Lilly. She's my niece, and she has just turned seven. But they visit us often, and Lilly likes to stay with me because--" She stopped herself. The *commissario* wasn't interested in hearing how well she got along with her niece. It wasn't her style to rattle along like a woman without a brain. God, he made her nervous.

"And you? Where do you live?" he asked.

"I live above my mother, underneath the roof."

"Where did you find your grandfather?"

Carlina throat tightened. The preliminaries were over. Now came the hard part. "Grandpa was sitting at the kitchen table." Her voice cracked.

"Go on."

She felt as if he was pushing her bit by bit forward, until she would drop off a cliff. "My cousin . . . Emma threw a fit."

His eyebrows twitched. "Why?"

"Emma was the bride! His death destroyed her wedding."

Commissario Garini looked as if he had no clue what she was talking about.

Do you have no imagination at all? "Can you picture the

bride coming up to church and saying that her grandfather just died?" Carlina closed her eyes. It was easier to speak without looking at the man made of steel next to her. "Everybody bursting into tears, the wedding canceled, no dancing, no party, the flowers wilting, the ceremony postponed, the honeymoon annulled . . ." She shook her head so hard, she felt the edge of the shelf beneath her hair.

"I like the wilting flowers," he said. "Nice touch."

Her eyes flew open. *I hate you.*

He returned her gaze without emotion. "Go on."

Another step closer to the edge. "In the end, we said it would make no difference to my grandfather if we pretended he had died later, but for Emma, it made all the difference in the world."

"Interesting." His voice was dry as dust.

Damn that man. He wanted to provoke her, and he managed all too well. "We had another reason, too."

"Well?"

"The doctor told Uncle Teo to avoid stress because of his heart. He almost forbade him to join the wedding party. Emma and I were afraid that Uncle Teo would have a heart attack if we told him in the middle of the wedding."

He lifted a skeptical eyebrow but didn't comment. "What happened then?"

Carlina took a deep breath, but for once, the smell of dust and boxes and brand-new products, the smell of her own universe, failed to soothe her. Where had all the oxygen gone? "Everybody could see my grandfather through the kitchen window, so we decided to put him into bed."

"Fully dressed?" His eyebrow twitched.

"Emma undressed him, but she forgot the socks."

"What were you doing in the meantime?" He sounded as if he thought she had used the interim to dance a solitary waltz in the kitchen.

Carlina clenched her teeth. "I was sick in the bathroom."

"So you did feel some emotions. Congratulations." His voice was vitriolic enough to make a hole in the floor if it dripped.

Don't reply, Carlina. Ignore him.

"Let me get one point clear," Garini said. "If I understood correctly, you were both fully dressed for the wedding in long evening gowns."

"Mine was long." Carlina looked at her hands. "Emma's was short."

"Both with high heels, I assume?" His light eyes seemed to pierce her.

"Yes." Carlina glared at him. "Want to know our hairdos as well? If you wish, I can send you a picture."

"That would be helpful," he said. "Wasn't it difficult to carry a dead man in that outfit?"

"It was."

"Anything unusual strike you?"

Carlina wanted to hit his immobile face. "I don't do this kind of thing every day, if that's what you mean!"

"I meant with the body."

Carlina crossed her arms in front of her chest. "I've never seen a body before. Ever. I wouldn't know if anything was unusual, even if it came up and bit me in the face." Her hand flew to her mouth. "Ugh. Didn't want to say that."

He laughed.

Her gaze flew to his face. He knew how to laugh? The laughter transformed his lean face, made his eyes sparkle. He looked like a different man. Carlina bit back an answering grin.

He looked at her, his head placed to one side, as if he was considering something. "Would you describe how you carried the body?"

Carlina's face twisted.

"Please."

Her mouth dropped. He could be polite? She took a deep breath. "Grandpa was sitting at the kitchen table. His eyes were open. Emma nudged him, and he fell to the side. I - I managed to catch him before he fell. He was heavy - and warm."

"Warm?" His sharp voice interrupted her.

"Yes." Carlina swallowed. "I said to Emma he must have died a short time ago."

"But you were sure he was dead?"

Carlina's mouth dropped open. "Oh, *Madonna*, yes, of course. If you had seen him . . . there was no doubt."

"Was it cold in the apartment?"

"No. It was stifling. I remember thinking so when I came through the door. It smelled of peppermint." Her throat hurt at the memory. "Grandpa used to eat peppermint drops all the time." *Don't cry, Carlina.*

"What happened then?"

"I couldn't make him sit up again." Her throat tightened. "Emma said I should place his head on the table, but it felt so . . .

irreverent." *Damn.* She shouldn't have used that word. Nothing in her behavior had led him to believe that she gave a damn about reverence for the dead. She cringed and waited for a scathing comment from Garini. When nothing came, she looked up at him.

His light eyes searched her face. "Go on." It didn't sound quite as commanding as before.

"I made Emma take his feet. We carried him to his bed. It felt . . . indecent, and there was that smell."

His eyebrows pulled together. "What smell?"

"I . . I don't know. I've never smelled it before. Sort of sweet, but in a cloying way."

"And then?"

"And then I was sick." She felt sick now.

"What did his face look like?"

Carlina's mouth was dry. "I tried not to look. I wanted to remember him the way he had been."

"So you didn't see anything? Not a glimpse?"

Carlina swallowed. "It was . . . bluish."

He gave a sharp, short nod. "Did Emma say it had been difficult to undress him?"

"No." Carlina shook her head. "She was real quick. But then, she was in a hurry."

"I see." The ironic note was back in his voice.

Carlina pulled herself together. "I thought it wouldn't make a difference. I only wanted to help Emma." She sounded pleading now. "I also planned to get up early the next morning, to find him. Then nobody else would have suffered the same shock."

"But you didn't?"

"No." Carlina could feel herself blushing. "I overslept." *He'll think I'm a total loser.* "Uncle Teo found him."

"His twin."

"Yes." Carlina sighed. "I was so glad that he didn't have a heart attack right there and then. However, later, just as Marco wanted to sign the death certificate, he . . ."

Garini held up one hand. "Hold on. Your mother told me Marco was called because your family doctor was ill."

"That's right."

"What's the name of your family doctor?" Garini was back to his true form. He shot his questions like bullets at her.

"Enrico Catalini."

"Is Marco the official stand-in for *signor* Catalini?"

"I don't know." Carlina frowned. "But my mother wanted to have Marco because he's a family member. He married my cousin Angela some months ago."

Garini's light eyes narrowed in thought.

Carlina was glad she had chosen to sit. The shelf in her back gave her a bit of much needed stability to face those x-ray eyes of his.

"What happened next?"

"Uncle Teo exploded into the kitchen and made a big scene because Grandpa still had his socks on." She sighed. "I didn't know he always took off his socks first when he undressed. I never even thought about his socks."

The *commissario* didn't comment.

Carlina threw him a glance. No sympathy there. "Next thing I knew, Uncle Teo called the police." Something scratched her ear. Carlina reached up and blushed. Damn. She still had the bra and slip from the mannequin over her shoulder. What a sight she was! She pulled them off with a quick move and stuffed them behind her back. Hopefully he wouldn't start laughing.

His light eyes never wavered. "Why didn't you stop your Uncle Teo?"

Carlina bristled. "How could I? Wrestle the phone from his hands?"

"For example." His voice was mild. "I'd have thought you're a woman with enough resources." For some reason, it didn't sound like a compliment.

"Uncle Teo turned beet red." Carlina didn't look at Garini. She didn't want to see the disbelief in his eyes. "I was afraid he would have a heart attack if I stopped him. Besides, all the family was listening in."

"Fine." His voice sounded hard. "And can you explain why you didn't tell me the truth when I came?"

She looked at her hands. They had clenched themselves into a tight knot. "I wanted to, but you came early. When I came downstairs, the gang, I mean my family, had told you everything."

"Everything but the truth."

"Well." Carlina felt short of breath, as if something was strangling her. "I wanted to speak to you alone." She lifted her gaze and frowned at him. "You remember that, don't you?"

He lifted his eyebrows. "You didn't try very hard."

Carlina closed her eyes for an instant. "I didn't want to shake my mother. She was so upset."

"Was she?"

How she hated his snarky questions. "Yes, she was!" She balled her fists. "I don't know if you saw her cushion?"

"I did."

"Well, she usually carries that cushion around with her when she's on the road, but in the house, she doesn't take it. When she came up to me and had that cushion in her arms, I knew she was shaken to the core."

He blinked. "Are you telling me your mother never leaves the house without a cushion?"

Oh, God. She shouldn't have mentioned it. "Yes." She hoped her voice conveyed dignity. "It's a little idiosyncrasy."

"Did she take it to the wedding?" He sounded intrigued.

"Yes."

"And did she use it?"

"I don't know why you need to know that! It doesn't have anything to do with my grandfather." Carlina pressed her lips together.

His mouth twitched. "Humor me."

"Oh, all right." Carlina sighed. "She used it to sleep in Church."

"I take it the service wasn't fascinating?"

Carlina suppressed a giggle. "It was the sixth family wedding this year."

"In that case, I understand completely."

Carlina smiled. "Later, *mamma* used the cushion to sleep on the table."

"She slept on the table?" Now he sounded scandalized.

"Just with her head." Carlina hastened to add. "It doesn't matter; everybody is used to it. In fact, I think it's very considerate of her."

He blinked. "In what way?"

"Well, we always share a taxi back, and when she's tired, she simply goes to sleep. Other mothers would start to nag until the party broke up."

"I see." His tone spoke volumes.

He thinks we're a bunch of idiots. Carlina stared at her hands and concentrated on relaxing them. Out of the corner of her eyes, she saw that he was still leaning against the door frame as if he belonged there, a relaxed panther.

From the street, she heard the faint noise of people walking by, talking, laughing. Inside, it was so quiet, her own breathing seemed too loud.

"To sum up, *signorina* Ashley. You moved your dead grandfather because you didn't want to upset your cousin Emma. You allowed your great uncle Teo to call the police with a crazy tale because you didn't want him to have a heart attack. You lied to the police because you didn't want to upset your mother Fabbiola. I'm impressed. You're quite the philanthropist."

Carlina's ears turned hot.

"Well? Don't you wish to comment?"

His icy words cut through her like a steel blade. "No. I may not have told you the truth the first time, but this time, I have."

"Are you going to stick to this version?" His friendly voice sounded false.

"Yes." She pulled up her feet. "I take it the interview is over. Please go now. I can't keep my store closed for hours on end."

"Just a minute, *signorina* Ashley. I have one more thing to tell you."

"Well?" Carlina bent forward on her footstool, ready to get up. *Go. Just go away.*

"Your grandfather was poisoned with an overdose of morphine."

A rushing sound like a giant waterfall deafened her ears. The floor came up to meet her, then everything turned black.

Chapter 6

When she regained consciousness, her nose was pressed against black leather. It smelled good, with an added hint of fresh air and soap. Two strong hands pulled her back into an upright position and leaned her against the shelf, only this time, she sat on the floor.

His lean face bent over her. He looked grim.

With detached interest, Carlina discovered a small scar next to his mouth. She concentrated on breathing. It was a full-time job.

"Weak moment over?"

She winced and managed to find her voice. "Repeat your last sentence." *Maybe I misunderstood him.*

"Your grandfather was poisoned with an overdose of morphine." He said it without emotion, as if he was the computer she had suspected all along.

So I've heard him right. Carlina closed her eyes.

"You going to faint again?"

She shook her head. "No. You can take your hands off me."

He snatched his hold away.

She almost toppled forward and had to place both hands flat on the floor to stabilize herself. "What happens now?"

He looked at her. "Now, I'm going to find out who killed him."

She didn't reply. Her head felt as if it had been filled with cotton wool, soft and sort of mushy.

"*Signorina* Ashley."

"What?"

"You still have to answer a few questions."

She bit her lips so hard they hurt. "Go ahead."

"Do you think it's possible that your grandfather killed himself?"

Carlina snatched up her head. "No. Absolutely not. Granddad enjoyed every moment of his life. He relished his phases and was constantly on the hunt for something new to do. He was mentally alert and very competitive. He once said that killing yourself was giving up too soon."

"He was competitive?"

"Oh, yes." She nodded. "You see, he was in eternal competition with his twin, my Uncle Teo. They constantly tried to outdo each other." Carlina took a deep breath. She still felt shaken. "When Uncle Teo was diagnosed with a weak heart a short time ago, granddad went to get a general check-up, too. On account of their being twins and having the same genes, you see."

"Yes."

Carlina's throat felt tight. "Granddad got an official certificate that he was as healthy as a horse. He showed it to everybody and said he would live to be a hundred." Tears pooled in her eyes as she remembered him strutting around the house, waving the certificate.

The *commissario* lifted his eyebrows. "And in spite of that, you had no hint of a suspicion when you found him dead?"

She felt stupid now. "No."

"Why not?"

"I don't know. As I said, suicide would have been totally out of character . . . and . . . and murder . . ."

"Yes, *signorina* Ashley?" It sounded as if he was ready to pounce on her any second now.

"Murder never crossed my mind."

He straightened. "Do you happen to have any plans to leave the country?"

A chill ran up her back. "No."

"Good. If you should change your mind, inform me."

Her throat hurt. "Yes."

He got up.

Carlina realized he had knelt next to her. She hurried to follow him, but the world still seemed a bit shaky. With a quick grab, she steadied herself on the shelf.

His gaze followed her hand. "If you should ever contemplate a change of career, try acting. You're quite convincing."

Fury exploded inside her. "And if you should ever contemplate a change of career, try garbage collector. Garbage doesn't have feelings."

His eyes narrowed. "Cat."

"Computer."

For the first time, his face registered surprise. "What?"

Carlina gave an arrogant shrug; at least she hoped it was arrogant. "Work it out."

She accompanied him to the door. As she unlocked the door and took off the sign, she was aware of his quiet presence behind her. He unsettled her more than she wanted to admit.

She stepped to the side to let him pass.

He stopped in front of her. "You are aware that I have to talk to your family, aren't you?"

Carlina's face went blank. "Oh, *Madonna*."

"I am going to your house right now," he said. *"Arrivederci."* He nodded at her and turned left, toward the Arno River. His black motorbike stood on the sidewalk in a strict no-parking zone.

Carlina watched him start the motor with a roar. Her thoughts jumped around in futile jerks like boxed-in fleas. *I have to stop him. I can't. I have to talk to my mother. Grandpa has been murdered. Oh, God. I'm a suspect. I have to talk to Uncle Teo. I have to be home before Garini.* The last thought arrived home like a gear kicking in. She flew into action.

II

Carlina raced home through several forbidden shortcuts, parked her Vespa at a rakish angle, and ran into the house. The unbroken seal on Nico's door made her feel sick. She raced upstairs. Her mother wasn't in her apartment, though all the windows stood open. Damn. Where could she be? Had Garini arrived already? She stopped in Fabbiola's kitchen and listened. The house was silent. No door slammed, no footstep could be heard, no wailing, no shouting.

But wait. Wasn't that a murmur of voices? Carlina rushed to the kitchen window and leaned out. She could hear Uncle Teo's voice. He was on the first floor, in Benedetta's kitchen. They had opened the door to the small balcony, otherwise Carlina would not have heard them.

Carlina turned on her heels and ran downstairs again.

"Benedetta?" Carlina pushed open the door to her aunt's apartment. "Is my mother here?"

It smelled of frying onions with a bit of *aceto di Modena* – balsamic vinegar - as spice. It was the only kind of vinegar her

aunt ever used. A homey smell, a smell that made her feel
welcome. Carlina pressed her hands together. With clenched
teeth, she went forward until she could look through the open
door into the kitchen.

Benedetta looked up from the dough she was kneading. She
had flour up to her elbows and a small mountain of dough on the
marble working slab in front of her. "Yes, she's here, Carlina."
Her red lipstick glowed through the gloomy room. The
neighboring house stood so close, little light came into
Benedetta's kitchen.

Carlina went through the door and stopped dead. Benedetta
had not mentioned the room was stuffed full with Mantoni
family members.

Next to Benedetta, her children Ernesto and Annalisa had
gathered at the kitchen table. Ernesto slouched in his chair, his
right thumb flying over his cell phone as he composed a text
message.

His sister Annalisa grated a piece of Parmesan cheese with
the easy moves that came from long habit. The pile of grated
cheese on the marble slab in front of her was already ten
centimeters high.

Without stopping composing his message, Ernesto leaned
over and picked up a bit of cheese with his left hand.

Annalisa slapped his arm.

Uncle Teo sat in front of a glazed terracotta bowl filled with
black olives. He looked unfamiliar, all dressed in black, but the
usual innocent expression on his face, as he chewed without a
sound, was well-known to Carlina.

Aunt Maria, also in black, peeled garlic gloves next to him
while humming to herself, and Fabbiola stood at the sink and
washed spinach. A yellow curtain moved with the breeze in front
of the open balcony door.

"You're early today, Carlina." Her mother turned around and
pointed with her chin at the fridge. "Could you get out the
Ricotta?"

Carlina obeyed without a word. *So I've beat Garini. I wonder
how many minutes I have until he shows up.* Sweat ran down
between her shoulder blades as she reached into the fridge and
took out the cool plastic containers filled with Ricotta cheese. *I
need more than two minutes to explain what happened.*

An idea flashed through her mind. "I'll be back in a second."
She placed the Ricotta cheese onto the table, swiveled around

and ran downstairs to the front door. As she reached the landing, she moved to the side and glided along the walls of the entry hall. Garini had better not see her shadow through the etched glass panes that filled the better part of the wooden front door.

Next to the door, she reached up. Thank God, the central box for the door bell cable was within her reach. She pulled the cable from the box with one swift move. There. Now Garini could ring until he turned blue. Nobody was home.

She ran back upstairs and stormed into the kitchen.

"Close the door, Carlina," Benedetta said. "The pasta shouldn't sit in a draft."

Carlina closed the door. She felt sick with fear. What would they say? She tried to swallow, but her mouth was too dry. "Listen, everybody. I have to tell you something."

Uncle Teo looked up. "Carlina, you're so pale."

Carlina bit her lips.

"Yes, I've thought so, too." Fabbiola nodded and stirred the spinach once more in the sink filled with cold water. "Hand me that dish cloth, will you Carlina?"

Carlina gave her mother the dish cloth.

"You're not coming down with an illness, are you?" Benedetta frowned. "I think you work too much." She lifted the pasta machine from the shelf and shifted it into the right position on the table, so she could flatten the dough into a thin sheet as soon as it had rested long enough.

"But she's early today," Fabbiola smiled at her daughter and spread out the dish cloth next to the sink.

"*Mamma*, I have to tell you something." Carlina started to feel desperate.

"Benedetta, I think you should close the balcony door." Fabbiola said. "The pasta will become too dry."

"Oh, no." Ernest looked up from his cell phone. "Please leave it open. It's already too stuffy in here."

"Then you should put the dough somewhere else to protect it." Fabbiola gave the pasta mountain an affectionate little pat.

"Place it into that bowl." Aunt Maria pushed a garlic clove into her mouth and conjured up a battered stainless steel bowl with the other hand.

Carlina lifted her voice. "Listen, I don't have much time, and I need to tell you something important."

Fabbiola frowned and placed a wet hand onto Carlina's brow. "Are you coming down with a fever, dear?"

"No." Carlina felt like screaming. "*Commissario* Garini stopped at Temptation today and --"

"He, he," Uncle Teo picked another black olive. "Wanted to buy underwear for his sweetheart, didn't he?"

Carlina closed her eyes. *Can you please let me finish my sentence?*

Annalisa looked up with such a quick move, her red hair swung back like a wing. "Does he have a sweetheart?"

"I don't think so." Fabbiola shook the wet spinach above the sink until the drops flew in all directions.

"Why not?" Benedetta placed the pasta dough with care into the stainless steel bowl. "I think he's a very attractive man, and in general, attractive men are not single."

"It doesn't matter if he's single or not," Carlina cut in.

"Now, why are you not interested?" Aunt Maria winked at her.

Uncle Teo chuckled. "So maybe he came to the store to chat with Carlina."

"Exactly." *I have to tell them in a rush. I can't prepare them.* Carlina took a deep breath. "He came to tell me that grandpa has been poisoned."

Everybody froze.

The rustle of the thin curtain remained the only sound in the room.

Ernesto's phone hit the kitchen floor with a crash.

"Damn!" Ernesto dived under the table.

Uncle Teo banged his balled fist onto the table. "I told you! I knew something was wrong!" He grinned in triumph.

With a splash, Fabbiola dropped the spinach into the sink as if she hadn't tried to shake it dry for several minutes and turned around. "Why did he tell *you*?" She emphasized the last word.

Benedetta closed her red mouth with a snap. "Why shouldn't he tell Carlina?"

Aunt Maria nodded. "Carlina is an attractive woman. He --"

"He came to tell me because I lied to him." Carlina clenched her teeth. This was the hardest part.

"You lied to him?" Annalisa's mouth dropped open. "I wouldn't try that too often. He's scary."

Ernesto emerged from beneath the table, but he didn't look at his phone. He stared at his cousin. "Wow."

"Why did you lie to the police? What about?" Fabbiola pressed her mouth into one thin line.

"I told him Grandpa was still alive before the wedding."

"But he was!" Fabbiola stuck her hands on her hips.

"No." Carlina shook her head. "He was dead. Emma and I placed him into bed." She nodded at Uncle Teo. "But we forgot to take off his socks." There. Now the worst was over. Maybe.

Ernesto's mouth dropped open. "You put Grandpa to bed after he was dead?" His eyebrows almost touched his red hair. "Wicked!"

"I don't believe for a minute that Emma would do anything like that!" Benedetta fired up in defense of her eldest daughter.

Carlina swallowed.

"Of course she would," Uncle Teo crossed his arms in front of his chest. "Emma probably had the idea."

"But why did you do it?" Aunt Maria held a forgotten garlic clove in her hand.

"Because we didn't want to destroy the wedding." *It sounds so silly now.*

Annalisa's mouth dropped open. "Are you crazy?"

"You lied to me!" Fabbiola stared at her daughter.

"And to me." Uncle Teo frowned at Carlina.

Carlina stood up straighter. "Yes, I did, but that doesn't matter."

"It doesn't matter?" Fabbiola's voice rose higher. "You say it doesn't matter that you lie to me, your only --"

"*Mamma*." Carlina took her mother's hands. "We have other problems now."

Fabbiola withdrew her hands. "I don't see what you mean! I say things have come to a pretty pass when --"

Carlina interrupted her with a rising feeling of desperation. "Listen to me!" Didn't they get it? Hadn't they heard what she'd said?

Aunt Maria contemplated the garlic clove. "Who killed Nico?"

Everybody whipped around and stared at her.

"Thank you, Aunt Maria." Carlina dropped into a chair. "That's the big question."

Silence.

The yellow curtains fluttered in the breeze as if the world was still in order.

Fabbiola took two small steps and bent over her daughter. "Father was murdered?"

Carlina nodded. "That's what Garini said."

Ernesto's eyes widened. "Did you kill him, Carlina?" His red hair stood up like a flame.

His mother turned on him with a hiss. "Of course not, stupid! How can you say such a thing of your cousin?"

Carlina shook her head. "Ernesto isn't stupid. The *commissario* thinks the same."

Benedetta covered her red mouth with her hand. "Oh, *Madonna*."

Fabbiola straightened and placed her hands on her hips. "I can't believe the *commissario* is so dumb. He looked like a clever man. How can he think my daughter is a criminal?"

Carlina bit back a smile. "Because said daughter behaved like an idiot."

"What did he say to you?" Fabbiola's tone turned belligerent.

"He took me apart, looked deep into my soul, and found nothing trustworthy there."

"Is that a poem?" Ernesto eyed his cousin with mistrust.

"No." Carlina sighed. "It's the truth."

"But . . . " Fabbiola shook her head until a henna-colored strand slid out of her bun. "We have to call Emma. Emma can tell the *commissario* that you said the truth."

"We can't call Emma." Carlina shrugged. "Her cell phone doesn't work in Africa. I tried at least seven times. Her mailbox is switched off, too."

Fabbiola gave an exasperated hiss. "Why did she have to go on a nature safari? I said all along that it was stupid! She will return with Malaria and intestinal worms and --"

Benedetta wrung her hands. "Emma has nothing to do with this." It sounded more like a prayer than a statement.

Uncle Teo got up. "Carlina." His voice sounded serious.

"Yes?"

"Tell us once again, from the beginning, how you found him."

Carlina cleared her throat. "I told Emma I would help get grandpa ready and went downstairs. We still had about twenty minutes before meeting Uncle Ugo with the limousine at the end of the street. Grandpa was already dressed for the wedding. He was sitting in the kitchen, his chin on his chest. At first, I thought he had fallen asleep. But then I saw his eyes . . . " Her voice trembled. "His eyes were open. At this instant, Emma came. When she saw Grandpa, she threw a fit."

"I can imagine." Ernesto grinned.

Benedetta gave him a sharp look. "That's enough, Ernesto. What then?"

"We wondered what to do. Just then, someone walked past the window. He looked in, but fortunately, Emma was blocking the view. That's when we realized everybody could see grandpa dead in his chair. So Emma suggested placing him into his bed."

"That was a sensible thing to do," Fabbiola said.

Carlina suppressed a nervous giggle. *Only mamma would say that.*

Uncle Teo frowned. "But . . . do you have any idea why Nico was killed?"

Carlina shook her head. "No. I mean, I never, ever thought anybody would hate him enough to kill him." For an instant, she heard Emma's heated voice again, saw her twisted face when they found Nico. *How well do I know my family? To what lengths will they go if under pressure?* She shuddered. *But Emma wouldn't have killed grandpa on the very day of her wedding.* She felt weak like overcooked spaghetti. "The *commissario* also asked a few other questions."

"What questions?" Aunt Maria frowned.

"He seemed to wonder if grandpa had reason to kill himself."

"No way." Ernesto shook his head. "That would have meant he would lose the competition with Uncle Teo. He kept saying that the one who dies first is the ultimate loser."

The rest of the family nodded. Nobody who knew Nico could for one minute accept the idea of suicide.

"Exactly." Carlina smiled at her younger cousin. "That's what I told the *commissario*."

Aunt Maria sighed. "In a way, it's a pity."

Fabbiola blinked. "What is a pity?"

Uncle Teo gave his wife a sharp glance. "I know what you mean. If Carlina had accepted the idea of suicide, he might stop looking for a murderer."

Carlina's head started to turn. "Are you kidding? I'm through with lying. He's not human, that man. He's a sort of police machine. If you want to lie to him, go right ahead, but I won't play along."

"But if father was killed, then we have to find the murderer!" Benedetta pulled the ends of her red mouth down.

"Even if it means that one of us will be convicted?" Aunt Maria munched a garlic clove as if her words hadn't frozen the rest of the family.

Annalisa rallied first. "I'm sure it was someone from the outside. None of us would do this kind of thing. How was he killed, exactly? I mean, what stuff was used, Carlina?"

"It was an overdose of morphine." The now familiar feeling of sickness rose inside Carlina.

"Morphine?" Aunt Maria lifted her head. "Who in the family uses morphine?"

Carlina shrugged. "As far as I know, nobody." *But that doesn't mean anything.*

Ernesto shook his phone and mumbled to himself.

"Is it broken?" Annalisa bent closer to her brother.

"I don't think so." Ernesto frowned. "But I don't get a connection. Maybe when I go outside . . ." He jumped up and went to the open window.

"How can you talk about cell phones when your cousin is accused of murder?" Benedetta frowned at her children.

"Carlina isn't accused of murder!" Fabbiola placed a protective arm around her daughter's shoulders.

Something cold ran up Carlina's spine. *Accused of murder.* Garini hadn't said it, but she had seen it in his eyes.

Ernesto gave her an apologetic smile, shrugged, and went onto the small balcony.

In two seconds he was back, his face white. "Carlina. The *commissario* is having coffee with *signorina* Electra. He's sitting at her open window."

Carlina's heart plummeted. *He overheard every word we said.* Her mind raced back. Had they said anything incriminating? Anything the *commissario* could use to build a case against her?

Ernesto swallowed. "He says you should come out to him."

Six stricken faces turned to Carlina.

"I'm coming." *Does my voice sound firm and confident?*

She stepped onto the balcony. Right in front of her, so close she could touch its stone wall if she stretched out an arm and bent forward, was the opposite house. *Signorina* Electra lived in the apartment right across from Benedetta, but she didn't have a balcony. Her living room window started to the left, where Benedetta's balcony stopped. *Signorina* Electra was a great fan of geraniums, and every spring, she crammed as many plants as she could into her window boxes. Sometimes, to Benedetta's irritation, she even used a part of Benedetta's balcony, though how she managed to reach this far at her age remained a much discussed mystery. The red and white blooms cascaded over the window sill, their bitter smell strong and pungent.

Garini sat in *signorina* Electra's living room at a spindle-legged table. He lifted a fragile teacup in silent salute, looking as out of place as a panther in a kindergarten.

I hope her herbal tea makes him sick.

"*Signorina* Ashley. I hope you're having a pleasant time off."

Carlina was aware of the family behind her, listening with bated breath to her every word. "Quite. Want to come over to interrogate us?"

He lifted his eyebrows. "What a charming invitation. I rang your bell, but when nobody answered, I figured I might just as well visit my old friend *signorina* Electra." He turned in his seat as the door of the living room behind him opened.

Signorina Electra glided into the room, her wide gown flowing behind her. Golden stars glittered on her garment as she lifted her teapot. "Here's the tea. It's a different type this time, chamomile-peppermint."

Garini's face became even more wooden than usual.

Carlina bent over the railing and said in a low voice, "Don't you love her teas, Garini?"

Signorina Electra came closer and peered out of short-sighted eyes at Carlina. "Is that you, Carlina? My, I haven't seen you for a long time. You're not as pretty as Emma. Are you married yet?" Her voice echoed through the slim gap between the houses.

"No." Carlina shouted back loud enough for all the street to hear. "Are you enjoying your visitor?"

The family behind Carlina gasped.

"But of course. We go back a long time, don't we, Stefano?" She winked at Garini.

Carlina clenched her teeth. "Well, when you've finished your chamomile-peppermint drink, don't hesitate to come over, Garini."

"I will." His light eyes held her gaze. "Make sure the bell works."

III

Carlina stood on a ladder and held the screwdriver as well as the cover of the bell in her left hand when Garini appeared behind the etched glass panes. She eyed his lean shadow for an instant. *Why does he always make me so nervous?* She descended the ladder with care and pulled the door open. "The bell isn't working yet, but you can come in."

"Thanks." He followed her in and watched as she climbed the ladder. "What happened?"

"Cable fell off." Carlina already regretted her rash action. She had more trouble than she wanted to admit to get the thing going again.

"Just like that?"

"Hmm." From the corner of her eye, she saw his eyebrow twitch. *Damn him.* He always seemed to know when she was lying.

"You can repair electrical problems by yourself?"

"Yep."

"Who taught you?"

"My father." She handed him the cover of the bell. "Would you hold this for a minute?"

He accepted it without comment. "Can you talk while you repair the bell?"

"I'm a woman." Carlina grinned down at him. "I can do plenty of things simultaneously. But I should warn you that this is no place to discuss confidential things."

"Why not?"

"Because every word you say down here carries through the staircase as if this was the famous opera-house La Scala. It can be heard on every floor."

He leaned against the door. "I don't have anything confidential to discuss."

She glanced at him. "Neither do I."

"Good."

Why does he always sound so ironic? Carlina pulled at the cable that seemed to have gotten too short. Her hands were dusty and the round window above the door didn't let in enough light.

"Tell me about your grandfather," he said.

"What do you want to know?" She sounded short and out of temper, which she was.

"Did he take medication?"

Carlina shook her head. "No. He was proud not to depend on anything at his age."

"I will have to check his bathroom later." It was a statement, not a question.

"Didn't you already do that?"

"This time, I'll look deeper."

I don't like the sound of that. Carlina clenched her teeth. "I see."

The *commissario* didn't take his gaze from her face. "You said your grandfather had phases?"

"Yes." *No more friendly talk from me, Mister.*

"The last phase was about the bad past, is that right?"

She glanced down. "Are you recording me again?"

He put his hand into his leather jacket and pulled out the recorder. "Thanks for reminding me. Do you agree that we record this conversation?"

"Of course, of course. Record every damn sneeze, if it makes you happy." For an instant, she was tempted to drop the screwdriver onto the small box.

"I will." He sounded unruffled. "Tell me about a typical episode from that bad past period."

Carlina shrugged. "It was always the same. Grandpa dropped a reference to our bad past like a bomb, usually in the middle of some family gathering or other. Sometimes, it was downright hilarious. Other times, people became embarrassed or even angry." The cable finally remained where it belonged. She gave a satisfied nod. "That's it." She held out her hand, still looking at the cable. "The cover, please."

He placed the bell cover into her hand. "What did he say to you?"

"To me?" Carlina glanced over her shoulder at him. "What do you mean?"

A ray of sunshine touched the round ornamental window above the door. It shone through the colored glass panes and painted yellow and red blobs of color onto the white wall at the side. Carlina smiled. *One day, I'll clean that window, then it'll be even more spectacular.*

The *commissario*'s voice pulled her back to earth. "Did your grandfather mention an episode from your bad past?"

"Oh, yes." Carlina placed the cover over the cable. "He said I had chased away a prince and would end my days as an old maid or married to --" she broke off just a second before the next words slipped out. . . . *a garbage man. That's what he said, but I won't tell you so, after the things I said at Temptation. Don't want you to get the wrong idea.*

"Or what?" he asked.

Of course Garini had caught her hesitation. "A butcher," she improvised.

"And had you?"

Carlina fixed the last screw that held the cover. "Had I what?"

"Chased away a prince?"

She dusted her hands and climbed down. "No."

"So the tale was completely invented?"

Carlina threw him a look and sighed. If she didn't tell him her story, someone else would. "No." She opened the front door. "I'm not running away, don't worry. I just have to check the bell."

He held the door for her as she went out.

Carlina pressed the lowest bell next to a row of shining brass plates engraved with their names. The bell in Nico's apartment rang so loud, it could be heard outside. Carlina smiled. "Good."

Then she straightened her shoulders. An uneasy feeling pooled in her stomach. She wasn't going to enjoy telling her story to this man made of steel. "We have two choices," she said. "Either we sit on the stairs or we go upstairs to my apartment."

"Can't we remain standing?"

"No." She shook her head.

"Why not?"

Was he laughing at her? She was sure his mouth had twitched. "Because I have to stand all day long at my store. That's why I choose to sit whenever I can."

"I noticed."

"Good."

"Your apartment, then," he said.

Now why did I give him a choice? She gave a sharp nod.

"But first, I'd like to check your grandfather's bathroom." He took a folded piece of paper from his leather jacket. "I need to show this to your Uncle Teo."

Carlina eyed the paper. "What is it?"

"It's the search warrant."

The word triggered a surge of fear inside Carlina. *He's going to arrest someone, someone from my family. They will be put away behind bars, away from life, away from the sun, away from happiness. For what? Twenty years? More?* Her head swam.

"*Signorina* Ashley?"

"What?" Her mouth felt dry.

"You're not going to faint again, are you?"

She clenched her teeth. "No." She could feel herself sway and sat on the first step so hard, she hurt her backside. "Uncle Teo is upstairs, in Benedetta's kitchen. You go and find him." With a deep breath, she closed her eyes and leaned against the banister.

"I'm here, Carlina." Uncle Teo's voice came from above. "What do you need?"

"I'd like you to see this search warrant." Garini held out the piece of paper.

Uncle Teo came down the stairs and took the paper. He unfolded it, fished his glasses from his breast pocket, placed them on the tip of his nose and read the paper. "The whole house?" He sounded surprised.

"Yes." Garini didn't elaborate.

"Are you planning to search other houses as well?"

Garini lifted his eyebrows. "Like whose?"

Uncle Teo lifted both hands. "The rest of the family. Gabriella, Bernando, and little Lilly's house. Alberta, Angela and Marco's villa."

"Not yet." Garini didn't twitch a muscle. "We'll start here."

"All right." Uncle Teo inclined his head. "I will inform the others."

He turned and narrowed his eyes at Carlina. "Are you all right, dear?"

Carlina got up. "Yes."

"One more thing, *commissario*." Uncle Teo focussed his rheumy eyes onto Garini. "When can we have the funeral?"

Garini frowned. "We'll need a few more days. I'll be in touch as soon as I know more."

"All right." Uncle Teo sighed and went upstairs again.

Carlina's heart went out to him. He looked so frail and alone, without the competition of his twin brother to push him to new heights every day.

The *commissario* waited until Benedetta's apartment door had opened and closed, then he nodded at Carlina. "Would you now open the door, please?"

"Yes." Carlina pushed her key into the lock of Nico's apartment door. The police seal broke as the door swung open. She stepped back with a motion for him to go through.

"Please come with me," he said.

"Why?"

His cool eyes assessed her. "I'd rather have you near me."

Great. Just great. "If you're trying to imply that I might tamper with the evidence while you're gone, you should remember I had plenty of time to do so already." The words rushed out before she could stop herself.

"Not inside this apartment, you didn't. Don't forget to close the door."

Carlina snapped her mouth shut and followed him without a word.

Uncle Nico hadn't been vain. Above the sink, on a rickety cupboard with mirrored doors, they found some cheap shaving lotion, toothpaste, shampoo, a toothbrush crooked with age, and a simple bar of soap. Garini pressed a button on his infernal recorder and spoke into it, listing each item. Then he closed the small doors. "The mere basics." He turned around and looked at her, his face inscrutable. "Did you ever give him anything?"

"Just an Aspirin, once or twice. He hated to take medicine."

"Do you have access to morphine?" He made it sound casual, as if he had asked for a tissue.

Carlina clenched her teeth. "No, I don't."

"Do you know if anybody else gave him something to take?"

Carlina hesitated. *If you don't tell him, someone else will.* "I know he once asked Aunt Maria for something against heartburn."

Garini sighed. "Then I need to check her bathroom and yours," he said. "But before we do that, I'd like another look around the apartment."

She nodded and followed him. He went into the bedroom first, his hands in his pockets, his eyes sharp and inquisitive, as if he was a tourist who was not allowed to touch anything but absorbed every atom of information.

He stopped in the middle of the bedroom and looked around. Carlina stood next to him and tried to see the room through his eyes. On the wall, a row of pictures showed all her uncles and aunts and her grandmother. The pictures were yellow at the edges. The wardrobe was slim, a cheap thing made of pressed wood. Behind the wardrobe, the ceiling had a smudge. Carlina suppressed a smile. It dated back to Annalisa's early teens, when she had fallen asleep in the small tub while the water was still running. She had managed to inundate the whole bathroom before Benedetta came to wake her up.

The chair in the corner was covered with green brocade, but it had scuffed armrests. The bed looked as if it came straight from 1950, but the bedspread was thick and bright green. Garini frowned. "Was your grandfather poor?"

"He wasn't rich." Carlina said. "But most of all, he wasn't interested in decorating."

"Who gave him the bedspread?"

Carlina caught her breath. "I did. Green was his favorite color." She swallowed. "I assume you deduced that he would never have bought it himself?" *God, how stilted I sound.*

A glimmer of a smile. "You assume correctly, *signorina* Ashley."

He went into the sitting room. "Your grandfather loved the arts." He looked at the reproduction of Botticelli's Birth of Venus above the sofa and the collection of glossy art books on the low table in front.

"Yes." Carlina smiled. "He always wanted to drag me into museums."

"I take it you don't like the arts?"

Carlina shrugged. "I don't like the darkness and dreariness of the medieval paintings. I much prefer the impressionists with their light and warmth." She lifted her chin, waiting for a condescending remark, but none came.

Garini wandered into the kitchen and looked around. Then he opened the fridge with the help of a handkerchief. For an instant, he looked at a bit of cheese, two eggs, and some butter. "Nothing much there."

"He usually had dinner upstairs."

"Does the whole family eat together every day?" He made it sound as if that was his personal nightmare.

Carlina shrugged. "Benedetta works as a secretary for the town council and she always finishes early. She loves to cook, and so we often eat in her kitchen."

"He doesn't have anything to drink in the fridge."

Carlina nodded at the window. "He drank one carafe of tap water each day. We all told him it wasn't enough, but he said he wasn't tall, so it would do." She smiled a bit at the memory. "He filled it each morning and drank it all through the day."

Garini went to the window. The carafe stood on the sideboard, a glass stopper on top. "Is that where he always kept it?"

"Yes."

Garini looked at the liquid. "Did anybody touch it on Sunday?"

She shrugged. "I don't know. There was so much coming and going."

The *commissario*'s eyes went from the window to the side board. "Did he sometimes leave the window open?"

"Yes." As the *commissario* didn't seem to approve of her

answer, she added, "But it wasn't dangerous; nobody can get in because of the iron bars."

"I know." Garini shook his head. "But you can easily reach through the bars and drop something into the carafe."

Carlina caught her breath. "Is that how it was done?"

"I don't know." Garini looked at her. "It seems a hazardous way to kill someone. After all, anybody might drink from that carafe."

Carlina shook her head. "No. It was Grandpa's alone. He said he had to know that he drank his minimum each day, and if anybody else wanted a drink, he gave them fresh water."

Garini's eyes narrowed. "Then somebody knew him well enough to use that knowledge."

Carlina felt as if something hard pressed against her chest. *Someone from my family. No. Please not.*

"Can you find a plastic bag and a towel inside this kitchen? I have to take the carafe to the police station."

"Yes." Her voice sounded flat.

When she had unearthed the plastic bag and the towel from a drawer, he wrapped the carafe with care and stowed it in an old wine box.

Then he opened another cupboard and lifted his eyebrows. "You said your grandfather ate peppermint drops?"

"Yes. All the time."

"That would explain the five packages I found in the cupboard."

Carlina grinned. "Yes."

"What happened to your grandfather's cat?"

"Grandpa didn't have a cat."

His eyes narrowed. "Are you sure?"

"Yes, of course."

He pointed at the top shelf of the cupboard. A cardboard box, open at the side, sat on the very edge of the shelf. The picture of a fluffy kitten looked at them from the cover. The box was filled with dry cat foot.

"Oh." Carlina's heart sank. *Why did he have to find that? I don't want to tell him.*

"Can you explain why he keeps cat food?"

"It's a snack." She closed her mouth with a snap.

"For which cat, if he doesn't own one?"

"Um." Carlina could feel her ears turning hot. "It's not for a cat."

"*Signorina* Ashley." He sounded patient now, too patient. "Will you tell me who ate that cat food or do you want me to keep guessing for another hour? Did he feed a rat?"

"No." Carlina swallowed. "He . . . he ate them himself. As a snack between meals."

His eyes bulged.

"You see, they are very healthy." She pointed at the box. "They contain loads of calcium, and vitamin B, and --"

"And they create silky fur."

"Em. Yes."

"Did your grandfather have silky hair?" A muscle twitched in a corner of his mouth.

She bit her lip. "I don't think I need to answer that."

He put his head to one side. "Did you ever try them?"

"Yes, when I was a kid. He fed us all with them." She bit back a smile. "We loved them."

"Did you, now?" He sounded thoughtful, as if he was already wondering which institute with extra secure bars would have room for the whole family.

"They're crunchy, salty outside, and soft in the middle."

"You make them sound delicious."

She grinned. "You can try one."

He lifted one eyebrow. "My hair is silky enough."

"Do you want to take them with you?"

"No. We know the morphine was given to your grandfather in liquid form."

"Oh." She swallowed.

He picked up the wine box. "I'd like to continue with your Aunt Maria's bathroom now."

They went to the hall, but before they could knock on the bright red door, Aunt Maria came out, dressed in a white coat made of a thin and shiny material. She looked like a giant snow ball. Her gaze fell onto the box. "What's in there?"

"Grandpa's carafe. The *commissario* wants to check it for fingerprints and stuff."

Aunt Maria's eyebrows soared. "I see."

"I need to inspect your bathroom, *signora* Mantoni," Garini said.

Aunt Maria's small eyes blinked. "Why do you need to do that?"

"Your brother-in-law was killed with an overdose of morphine, and I need to find out if you have morphine in your medicine cabinet."

Aunt Maria shook her head. "Do you really think an intelligent murderer would keep the morphine in his medicine cabinet after the deed?"

A glimmer of a smile appeared in those light eyes. "No. But it would be careless not to check."

"Oh, all right." Aunt Maria pulled her voluminous overcoat around her and stepped to the side. "But I won't wait for you, or I won't be back in time for dinner."

"No problem." The *commissario* nodded at Carlina. "Your niece will come with me."

Aunt Maria gave Carlina a surprised look, then she sailed off without another word, the overcoat billowing around her like a cloud.

Carlina led the way to the bathroom. "Don't you feel stupid?" she said.

He frowned. "Why?"

"Aunt Maria is right." Carlina went into the bathroom and perched on the edge of the tub. "If you want to do a thorough job, you have to search the whole house, not a few medicine cabinets here and there."

His light eyes assessed her. "I can't search everything at once, that's why I have to focus on the most obvious points first."

"But if it's obvious to you, it will be obvious to the murderer too."

"You'd be surprised how many murderers don't think of the obvious." He smiled. "Besides, I often learn other things I didn't know before. Facts that lead me to a better understanding of the situation. Like cat food snacks."

"Why has this led to a better understanding of the situation?" she asked.

He grinned. "It gave me a better feel for your family."

She narrowed her eyes.

The *commissario* opened the cabinet above the sink and started to dictate the things he saw.

Uncle Teo's habits were very different from his twin's. He used an expensive shaving lotion, different types of aftershaves, an automatic toothbrush, and even had a hook where he kept four different golden necklaces - thick chains in several styles.

Carlina smiled. "I wasn't aware that Uncle Teo is so vain," she said.

"You should have known," Garini said.

"Should I?" Carlina looked at him in surprise. "Why?"

"One glance at his clothes, and you can tell that he dresses with care and a certain finesse. It's natural that he extends his habits to his personal care."

You have sharp eyes, commissario. "What about Aunt Maria?"

He closed one cabinet door and opened the next. "Aunt Maria is more like her brother-in-law. Spartan." He lifted the wooden lid of a white porcelain container and recoiled. "Still, she left her mark." He held the container out to her.

Carlina looked into it. "Garlic?" Her voice rose high with disbelief. "Aunt Maria keeps garlic in the bathroom?"

"As an emergency snack, I imagine." His voice was dry.

Carlina shook her head.

He finished dictating the list, then looked at her. "Now your apartment."

Carlina led the way upstairs with a nervous churning in her stomach. *Is the bathroom clean? Did I throw away that old jar with rejuvenating face lotion from my mother? I don't want him to search every corner. It's my life, and it's private.*

She waited until he had come in, then closed the front door and went straight to the bathroom. From the window in the roof, the late sunlight illuminated the bath and played on the terracotta tiles. It smelled of lemon soap, as it always did. Home. Her home. If only he wasn't here to poke his nose into every detail.

As her bathroom was so small, she stepped to the side before entering it and made a move with her hand.

He followed her invitation in silence.

A whiff of his scent came to her, attractive, clean. She ignored the reaction inside her and leaned against the door frame. "Go ahead."

"Thanks."

So he does remember his manners sometimes.

He held the recording machine relaxed in one hand. "Toothbrush, toothpaste, rejuvenating face cream."

Damn. I should have thrown that thing away weeks ago.

He continued to list what he found.

I need to get rid of half that stuff. Carlina shook her head. How things accumulated when you didn't look.

"Almost done." Garini opened a drawer stuffed full with odds and ends. "Matches, rubber bands, bath salts, small hammer."

Carlina grinned in triumph. *That's where I put it!*

Garini pushed the hammer to the side and bent forward to look into the dark corners of the drawer. "Nail scissors, tissues." He stopped.

Carlina looked up.

He held a ring in his hand. The light sparkled on the large sapphire in the middle and the ring of diamonds all around. "An engagement ring?"

Carlina caught her breath. *Of course. That's where I put it.* The sudden discovery felt like a punch in her stomach. She nodded.

His hand with the recording machine sank. "From the prince?"

"He wasn't a prince."

"Tell me who he was."

Carlina jumped up. "Want a coffee?" She knew her voice sounded unfriendly, but she needed a bit of time to compose herself.

"Yes, thanks."

"Chamomile-peppermint not your favorite brew?" Carlina threw him a glance.

"Cat." He actually grinned.

Carlina turned away. When he smiled, he was a different man. She led the way to her small kitchen with the slanted roof.

He followed her, but she noticed he kept his distance. Did he now trust her enough not to attack him with a kitchen knife?

She spooned the fragrant coffee powder into the small round receptacle of her old aluminum espresso maker and pressed it down with her thumb, then she filled the base with water and screwed the parts together.

He watched her without interrupting her routine.

She lit the gas flame and placed the Espresso maker on top of the fire.

"About the prince," he said.

"He wasn't a prince." Carlina took out two saucers and tiny cups. "Sugar?"

"No. I drink it black."

Of course. Sugar doesn't fit this guy. Nothing sweet about him.

She had to tell him now. *Better make it short.* With feigned nonchalance, she leaned against her kitchen counter and faced him. If only his eyes conveyed more feelings. It was like talking to a wall. A wall made of concrete. "Five years ago, I was engaged to Giulio Ludovico Eduardo Montassori, heir to the Montassori vineyards and estates. We split up, and the family has been convinced ever since that I'll never get married."

"Why did you split up?" His light eyes never wavered from her face.

Carlina shrugged. "We didn't match."

"Who broke it off?" His voice sounded like a computer voice again, cool, without feelings.

She clenched her teeth and gave him a black look. "Do I have to answer all your questions?"

"No." He shrugged. "But it would help if you did."

Their eyes met.

He didn't have to say it, but it hung between them, unspoken. Her family would regale him with plenty of versions about her engagement, without the slightest encouragement from his side.

"You will hear different versions in answer to that question," she said with difficulty.

"Which one is yours?"

The Espresso maker started to gurgle. Grateful, Carlina turned her back to Garini, but he moved to the side, so he could see her profile.

"I broke it off," she said.

"Why?"

She had tried to explain it so often. Nobody had understood. "Do you know the Montassori vineyards?"

"Who doesn't?"

"Yes. Well." Carlina switched off the gas, picked up the Espresso maker, and filled both cups. The steaming coffee plumes twirled up, thin and white, and the fragrance of fresh coffee filled the small kitchen. *At least my hand isn't trembling.* "He asked me to give up my store."

"But --" he broke off.

"But what?" She narrowed her eyes and passed him his cup and saucer.

"Grazie." He met her angry gaze. "The Montassori vineyards are at least a two hour drive to the south, if I'm not mistaken."

"They are."

"So he agreed not to live on the estate?"

"No, he didn't." Carlina picked up her cup, then led the way to her living room. "You can sit over there." She pointed at a low armchair with a fake leopard skin as cover.

He sat down with care so as not to tilt his cup of coffee. His legs seemed too long for her apartment.

She crossed the room and perched on the windowsill which she had made especially broad. She loved her special seat, loved to sit here, looking over the tiled roofs of Florence, enjoying the soft evening air. Maybe it wasn't so hard to talk to him after all. At least he didn't interrupt her all the time. "I was willing to give up Temptation, though it made me unhappy." She paused, trying to find the right words. "I underestimated my attachment to my store. It wouldn't have been so difficult if Giulio had understood, but he expected me to give up everything." She blew onto her coffee. "I should have told him earlier, but it was so clear to me that I would continue with my profession somehow, I never even discussed it. Then, six weeks before the wedding, we happened to talk about it. I told him I wanted to start an Internet trade for underwear." She bit her lips. "He almost fainted."

Garini looked at her without twitching a muscle.

"When I realized this was a no-no, I suggested working as a freelance designer for underwear. I have a degree in fashion design, you know." Carlina picked up her cup and took a sip, then looked out of the window. "He thought that was even worse. The more I suggested, the more horrified he became." She bit her lips. "In the end, I asked him what he thought I would do all day long." She took another sip of her coffee. The September evening light lingered over the red roofs of Florence and smudged the edges a rusty red. A cloud of doves flew up, white flashes against the rosy sky.

"What did he say?" Garini took a sip from his cup, but his eyes never left her face.

Carlina gave a start. "Oh, he said I would oversee the estate. I would represent the Montassori vineyards. I would become a happy mother." She swallowed. "I loved him, but the future he painted for me . . . that wasn't me. Nothing of me would be left after that marriage. It took me one week, then I broke off our engagement. Thank God I hadn't yet found a buyer for Temptation."

"How did he take it?"

"Very well." A bitter smile curled up her mouth. "Within two months, he had organized a suitable replacement. He is married with three kids now."

"So your grandfather hit a sore point with his story about your bad past." It wasn't a question.

Carlina shrugged. "I'm quite used to all kinds of oblique and open references to my bad past, as you call it. Enough not to react with murder, I can assure you."

He placed his empty cup on the floor next to him. "What about the other family members? What did they say?"

"Oh, they thought it was a great joke."

"I meant their own stories. What did your grandfather tell them?"

Carlina shrugged. "I don't recall every single one. I know we all laughed about the one he flung at Uncle Teo."

"What did he say to him?"

"He said Uncle Teo had had a love affair with *signorina* Electra in his twenties." She chuckled. "Uncle Teo laughed the hardest. He can't stand her, you know."

"Did your Aunt Maria laugh as well?"

Carlina sat up with a start. *He's a policeman. This is a murder investigation. Stop treating him like a friend.* "Yes." Her voice sounded chilly. "But maybe you had better ask her herself."

"I will."

The front door banged open.

Carlina and Garini both jumped.

"Carlina!" Annalisa ran into the room, her silky red hair flying, and slithered to a full stop in front of them. Her gaze darted from the coffee cups to their faces. "What is this? Are you having a date?"

Carlina sighed and got up. "No. This is an interview, and every word is being recorded."

"Oh, that's all right, then." Annalisa smiled. "Carlina, could you lend me your silver scarf? I'm going out with Tonio, and it would be just perfect for my outfit."

"Sure." Carlina went to her bedroom and pulled the scarf from the basket where she kept her accessories. "Have fun. But don't forget to bring it back."

"Of course not! Thank you so much." Annalisa blew her a kiss and waved at the *commissario*. "Ciao!"

The *commissario* took his cup and got up too. "Your family is very . . . refreshing."

Their eyes met. "My thoughts exactly."

The door opened and Fabbiola rushed into the apartment. "Carlina!"

"Ciao, *mamma*."

Fabbiola's gaze darted from the *commissario* to her daughter. "What have you discussed?" She put her hands on her hips and faced the *commissario*. "How did you get into my daughter's apartment?"

His face remained impassive. "Your daughter opened the door."

Fabbiola turned to Carlina. "You should have told me, then I would have come with you! I don't think it's clever to talk to the police all on your own." She threw a glance at Garini. "You'll forgive my plain speaking, *commissario*."

He inclined his head. "Certainly, *signora* Mantoni-Ashley."

Carlina suppressed a giggle.

"This is not funny, Carlina!"

Garini went to the kitchen and placed his cup next to the sink. "I'm afraid I have to insist on talking to every one individually." His cool gaze assessed Fabbiola.

She swelled with indignation. "Certainly not."

"It's all right, *mamma*." Carlina placed her hand on Fabbiola's arm. "He needs to find the murderer of Grandpa. We want that too, don't we?"

"Of course!" Fabbiola crossed her arms in front of her chest. "But he won't find the murderer by talking to the family." She rounded on her daughter. "Why do you grin like that?"

Carlina bit back her smile. "I'm not grinning."

"I forbid you to talk to the police without me!"

Too late. I already told him everything.

"Maybe I can talk to you right now, *signora* Mantoni-Ashley."

"What do you want to know?" Fabbiola pressed her lips together.

"Which event from the past did your father throw at you?"

Fabbiola's mouth fell open. "What?"

"First, you have to agree that this conversation will be recorded," Carlina said.

Garini's mouth twitched. "Correct. Do you agree, *signora* Mantoni-Ashley?"

Fabbiola waved her hands. "Yes, yes, whatever. Now explain what you meant."

"Do you wish to take a seat?"

"No!" The strand of hair that kept coming loose from her bun fell forward. "Tell me!"

"You told me your father had a so-called bad past phase just before his death." Garini leaned his shoulder against the door frame of the kitchen.

Carlina slid onto her seat at the window without a sound. *Maybe he'll let me stay if I don't say anything.*

Fabbiola lifted her eyebrows. "Yes?"

"I understand that during this phase, he told several family members about their bad deeds of the past."

"Oh, that." Fabbiola made a dismissive gesture with her hand. "What about it?"

"What event from your past did he use?"

Fabbiola's glance darted to her daughter. She licked her lips and swallowed.

Carlina blinked. Her mother embarrassed? *What on earth is going on?*

Garini's light eyes never left Fabbiola's face. "Do you wish to continue this conversation without your daughter?"

Carlina held her breath.

"No." Fabbiola pulled back her shoulders and stood up straighter. "It was all nonsense anyway."

A dove landed on the roof with a scratching noise. It started to coo next to the window, the sound too loud for the silence in the room. Carlina frowned and waved her hand at it. The dove veered away and tripped around the window in a wider curve.

"Father said Carlina wasn't her father's daughter."

Carlina's hand fell into her lap as if she had been shot. Her mouth dropped open.

Garini didn't blink. "Isn't she?"

Carlina glared at him. Ruthless questions seemed to be his specialty.

"Of course she is." Fabbiola went to her daughter and put an arm around Carlina's shoulders. "Just because she has blue-green eyes doesn't mean she's from another man."

"What color were your husband's eyes?" Garini looked straight into Fabbiola's brown eyes.

"Blue."

Something hard and cold formed inside Carlina's stomach. Dad's eyes had been light-brown, amber. She would have to take his picture off the wall the minute the *commissario* left her apartment. *Oh, my God. What is going on here?*

"I see." Garini's voice sounded mild. "When did the conversation about your daughter's father take place?"

Fabbiola shrugged. "At lunch, in Benedetta's kitchen, a few days before Emma's wedding."

Nobody told me about it. Carlina felt as if a black pit opened in front of her feet. *I thought I knew everything about us.*

"I don't remember the exact date," Fabbiola spread her hands in an apologetic gesture, but she remained close to Carlina.

Garini nodded. "Do you remember what he said to the other family members?"

Carlina could feel her mother's rigid body softening. *Don't relax, mamma. This guy is dangerous.*

Fabbiola frowned in thought. "He said something about Angela."

"Angela?"

"My niece Angela, who married the young doctor Marco."

Garini nodded. "Yes, I remember. What did he say?"

"He said Angela had blackmailed Marco into the marriage."

Carlina remembered the blank look Marco had given his wife. *Blackmailed into marriage?* She shouldn't have stayed. She didn't want to hear all these terrible things about her family.

The *commissario* frowned. "Did he say how she blackmailed him?"

"No." Fabbiola shrugged. "It was all nonsense anyway."

"Anything else you remember?"

Fabbiola shook her head.

"Thank you." The *commissario* looked at her for a moment, his gaze cool. "I now wish to talk to the other family members."

"You have to come downstairs to do that." Fabbiola pushed back her strand of hair. "Benedetta is preparing Ravioli and can't spare the time."

Annalisa opened the door to Benedetta's apartment the instant they arrived on the landing. "There you are! I was just going to call you. Dinner is ready. Do you wish to join us, *commissario*?"

Carlina closed her eyes. *Oh, no.*

Fabbiola hissed in her breath.

"Thank you, that would be nice." The *commissario* smiled.

Carlina rolled her eyes. Of course he could smile at her lovely cousin. But wait until he started to grill her. Annalisa would wonder if he was the same man the minute he concentrated on her every secret with those hawk-like eyes.

Carlina waited until Garini and her mother had gone down to the kitchen, then she sidled up to Annalisa and said under her breath, "Why did you invite him? You said he's scary!"

Annalisa threw her a surprised glance. "I thought you liked him."

"Me?" It came out as a yelp.

"Yes. Besides, we always invite everybody who's in the house when dinner is ready."

"Not the police." Carlina threw his back a dark look.

"I'm sorry." Annalisa pulled at her lower lip with her pearly teeth. "But I can't un-invite him now. What should we do?"

Carlina shrugged. "Eat Ravioli, I guess."

Chapter 7

Carlina chose a chair as far away from the *commissario* as possible. Unfortunately, she could still see him very well. The kitchen smelled of garlic, hot butter and fried sage. It smelled of home. Carlina took a deep breath, but the feeling of wellness she usually got at home didn't filter through her fears.

"Carlina, pass me the Parmesan, will you?" Fabbiola nudged her daughter.

"Sure." Carlina felt like a puppet, stiff and awkward. *This is the Muppet Show*, she thought. *Mantoni-style. Watch us all play the piece to perfection. If only we remembered our roles.*

"So." Benedetta ladled molten butter and crisp sage leaves onto her Raviolis. "Do you have a sweetheart, *signor* Garini?"

Carlina choked.

"No." The *commissario* met Benedetta's searching gaze with one of his unemotional stares.

"Ha." Uncle Teo waved his fork. "That's not very clever of you. A man needs a woman."

Exactly. Carlina suppressed a grin and picked up another piece of pasta. She loved the taste of spinach with Ricotta. And she loved to see the *commissario* in dire straits.

"How about your family?" Benedetta's red mouth disappeared behind a fork-load full of Ravioli.

Ah, the big interrogation. Carlina started to enjoy herself. *How's that for turning tables, commissario?*

Benedetta swallowed her Ravioli and returned to battle, ignoring the *commissario's* silence. "Do your parents live in Florence, *commissario*?"

"My father lives in Fiesole." Garini continued to eat with unmitigated appetite.

"That's not too far away. Do you see him often?" Benedetta was like a dog with a bone; she chewed with relentless intensity.

The *commissario* speared his food with his fork. "These Raviolis are very good, Mrs. Mantoni-Santorini."

"Please call me Benedetta."

Carlina's food got stuck in her throat. *Hello?* Had Benedetta forgotten who he was? He wasn't Annalisa's latest boyfriend or Ernesto's current buddy. He was the *commissario* who was trying to find a murderer within the family!

"My name is Stefano." The *commissario* smiled.

Damn. When he smiled, he looked almost human. From the corner of her eyes, Carlina saw Annalisa's eyebrows going up. Oh, no. What if Annalisa started to picture herself in love with the *commissario*? How long had she been going out with Tonio? Four weeks? Five? Damn. That was about the time it took to make her bored with a guy.

"And your mother?" Annalisa flashed a hundred-watt smile across the table.

Great. Now her cousin had joined the big interrogation. Carlina almost felt sorry for the *commissario*.

The *commissario* regarded Annalisa for a moment, then he said without once drawing breath, "My mother died when I was twenty-one. She had cancer, but thank God she didn't suffer for long. I have one sister who lives in Switzerland. She works as an event manager at a luxury hotel. My hobbies are playing the saxophone and reading science magazines. My shoe size is forty-three, and I have lived in Florence for ten years."

Carlina burst out laughing.

The family stared at her in consternation. "What's so funny?" Fabbiola frowned at her daughter.

"Nothing." Carlina met the *commissario*'s gaze. The glimmer of a smile in his light eyes filled her with a hum of happiness. She averted her gaze.

II

Stefano Garini opened the window of Nico's living room and took a deep breath. He had suggested this room as neutral territory, but he had not counted on the stuffy smell. Carlina's apartment had been a lot more cheerful. He had felt at ease with her, something he didn't want and couldn't use. She was his main suspect, and it wouldn't do to look for the ready smile to emerge in those cat-like eyes, or for the crinkle of amusement in the corner of her mouth.

He closed the window and leaned with his back against the

sill, waiting for Benedetta to join him. If he was lucky, she would stick to his instructions and come without another family member in tow.

He shook his head. The Mantonis made him feel as if he was walking on eggs. You never knew when the next would crack. The whole case had started on a bad footing, and that's how it continued. First, his mistake not to take the death seriously. Second, Carlina with her cat-like eyes who didn't fit into any category he knew. Third, her family, a collection of crazy bats if he ever saw one. Cat food as a snack! What else would they tell him?

He had to handle them all on his own. He frowned. Where was Piedro anyway? He shouldn't be doing the interviews by himself. Stefano whipped out his cell phone and called his subordinate. "Piedro. Where are you?" This time, he didn't try to veil the threat in his voice.

"I missed the train in Pisa and had to wait for over an hour because the next train was delayed, but I'm only ten minutes away from the office now." Piedro puffed into the phone as if he was running.

"Don't go to the office. Come to Via delle Pinzochere 10 directly."

"Where?"

"To the house where the old man died."

"Oh, all right."

Stefano heard the suppressed sigh in Piedro's voice. "Get something to eat on the way. It'll be a long evening."

"Okay." Piedro sounded sullen now.

Garini hung up and shook his head. *How a man as wily as signor Cervi ended up with a son like Piedro will always remain a mystery to me.*

The door opened and Benedetta came in. "You wanted to talk to me?"

"Yes." Stefano made a move with his hand. "Please take a seat." He took out his recorder. "Do you agree to my recording this conversation?"

"Of course." Benedetta had applied new lipstick and smiled at him. "We all wish to find father's murderer."

Stefano explained what he wanted to know and watched her reaction.

Benedetta cocked her head to one side and pursed her lips. "Let's see. Uncle Nico said so many things I didn't pay attention anymore." She cocked her head to the other side.

Stefano started to feel as if he was in a theater show.

"No, I can't recall anything." Benedetta shrugged. "It was such nonsense; I never bothered to remember."

"How about the other family members? He suggested quite a few different things from the past, didn't he?"

"Well." Benedetta shrugged. "I think he once said that Aunt Maria had a drinking problem and compensated for it by eating garlic."

Jesus. "Did you believe him?"

Benedetta made a wary move with her hands. "Of course not. Even if he was my father, he was an old man and delighted in mischief. You couldn't take anything seriously, no matter what he said."

"I see." Stefano looked at her. *I don't believe a word.* "Where were you on your daughter's wedding day between eleven and two?"

Benedetta looked affronted. "Well, I was at Emma's wedding, of course."

"The ceremony only started at one."

"Yes." Benedetta drew herself up. "But, unlike Emma, I arrived early." Her red mouth twisted. "Very early. Emma was quite nervous and had asked us all to leave her alone."

He frowned. "All but her cousin Carlina, that is." *Maybe they killed him together.*

"Of course." Benedetta shrugged. "Carlina and Emma . . . " She shook her head. "They're inseparable, in spite of the age difference." She pressed her mouth together as if she did not approve of that friendship.

"How many years separate them?"

"Nine years." Benedetta shook her head again. "Carlina always helped Emma."

"Is that a bad thing?"

The red lips pursed. "She helped her to get into mischief more than once."

Stefano didn't take his gaze off Benedetta. She seemed like an overprotective mother. Still, he made a mental note to find out more about this mischief. "Thank you. Please ask Teodoro to come to me now."

Benedetta got up. "It wasn't anybody from the family, Stefano, believe me. You're wasting your time here. Better start looking further away."

He inclined his head. *No way.*

Benedetta collided with Piedro in the door.

"Ah, my long lost assistant." Stefano nodded. "Please take out your notebook and note everything that is being said, Piedro."

Piedro nodded and chose his old seat on the footstool.

Teodoro Mantoni skipped into the room as if he had been through a rejuvenating bath. "Carlina already told me what you need to know. I am to give you an account of the bad past stories."

Garini nodded. "That's right." *I wonder if you will.*

Uncle Teo sat down and lifted his thumb. "Number one: Nico told Fabbiola that Carlina wasn't her father's child." He looked up and stared at the *commissario* out of rheumy eyes. "Utter nonsense, of course. The child is a true Mantoni."

She will always be a true Mantoni because of her mother, no matter who her father was. Stefano made sure his face didn't show his thoughts.

Uncle Teo lifted his index finger. "Number two: He told Carlina she had rejected a prince and would end up marrying a garbage man."

Stefano bent forward. "A what?"

"A garbage man."

"Not a butcher?"

"A butcher?" Uncle Teo blinked. "I said nothing whatsoever about a butcher. Do you have problems with your ears, young man?"

"No." Stefano said with a small smile. "Not at all." *The little witch.*

Uncle Teo lifted his middle finger. "Number three: He told Benedetta she had killed her husband by nagging him into his grave."

And she doesn't recall that? Fat chance. Stefano narrowed his eyes. "How did he die?"

"He died of a gastric ulcer seven years ago." Uncle Teo shook his head. "The young men today aren't what they used to be. No stamina, if you understand what I mean."

Stamina to live with the Mantoni women? Stefano suppressed a desire to laugh and nodded with a grave expression.

Uncle Teo came to his ring finger. "Number four: He said Annalisa had cheated on her final exams in school."

Stefano looked at the old man in front of him. "Had she?"

Uncle Teo waggled his head. "She was very good friends with the young teacher. That's all I know."

Whoa. Stefano swallowed.

Uncle Teo's small finger came up. "Number five: He said Ernesto always comes home in the middle of the night by way of the balcony." He contemplated his small finger as if he had never seen it before. "I'm glad Nico didn't say that in front of Benedetta."

"Is it true?"

"Of course." Uncle Teo nodded so hard, his wisps of white hair started to shake. "I did it myself when I was his age. It's not a sin, young man."

"Of course not." Stefano glanced at Piedro. *I hope you manage to note all this without mistakes.*

Uncle Teo dropped his right hand into his lap and started on his left. "Number six: Nico said I had an affair with *signorina* Electra." He chuckled and seemed to sink into reminiscences.

Stefano waited. The nearly bald crown of the head in front of him sunk deeper, the dark age spots visible on the pink scalp shining through the tufts of white hair. "*Signor* Mantoni?"

The old man roused himself. "Where was I? Oh, yes. Electra. Well, I had a--" he stopped and stared at Garini from underneath his bushy eyebrows. "Are you related to her?"

"No. I got to know her years ago because of another case."

"Ah." Uncle Teo nodded. "Well, I had a crush on her, when I was a very young man." He winked at Stefano. "That was before Maria, you understand."

I wonder. "How old were you approximately?"

"Oh," Uncle Teo waved a pale hand through the air, "sixteen or seventeen." He nodded again. "A long time ago, as I said."

"Quite."

The index finger came up. "Number seven: He said Maria had a drinking problem which she kept in check by eating garlic cloves."

Stefano waited for Uncle Teo to continue.

"Utter nonsense, of course." Uncle Teo shook his head with a frown. "She has an eating problem which she manages to control with the garlic cloves."

Stefano bent forward. "I don't quite get this."

"Well," Uncle Teo shrugged, "she always carries around a garlic snack, and when the need to eat something becomes too big, she takes one."

"Why garlic?"

Uncle Teo looked at him as if the answer was evident. "Garlic has less calories than chocolate."

"I see." *I'm glad Piedro is here, or I'd start to believe I'm dreaming this case.*

"I would appreciate if you wouldn't mention this to Maria," Uncle Teo said. "She's a bit touchy about this subject."

Oh, my God. "How about stories concerning other family members?"

"Which ones?" Uncle Teo looked at him as if he could continue to list a million other family secrets.

"Angela?"

Uncle Teo shrugged. "Nico said she had blackmailed Marco into their marriage. No chance."

"No?"

"No." Uncle Teo hissed air through his teeth. "Not enough spunk." It was clear Angela wasn't a favorite niece.

Madre mia. I wonder if he would approve of blackmail if he saw it as a proof for spunk. Stefano nodded. "Anybody else?"

"Let me see . . . " Uncle Teo stared into the distance. His mouth started to twitch, then he wheezed like an asthmatic horse.

Stefano was about to start forward to support his shaking shoulders when he realized Uncle Teo was laughing.

"Number eight." Uncle Teo crowed with laughter as he held up his middle finger. "He said to Alberta she had educated her son to be a criminal."

"Who's Alberta?"

"Alberta is Fabbiola's eldest sister."

"And her son is in prison?"

"No," Uncle Teo slapped his knees. "He's an investor in Dubai and making a fortune."

"Right." Stefano's head started to ache. "Anything else?"

Uncle Teo waved his paper-thin hand again. "Oh, plenty of things, but I can't recall them all. I'll tell you later, when I remember them."

"When did your twin say those things?"

"Always with an audience." Uncle Teo twinkled. "Where would the fun have been otherwise?"

Where indeed? Stefano started to wonder if the demise of Nico hadn't been a blessing. "So all of these bad past stories were general knowledge?"

Uncle Teo shrugged. "I guess. On the other hand, we didn't

talk that much about them."

No wonder. Stefano stared at the aged man in front of him. "You realize you've just handed me several murder motives on a silver platter, don't you *signor* Mantoni?"

Uncle Teo's rheumy eyes suddenly looked sharp. "I do, *commissario* Garini."

"Why did you do that?"

Uncle Teo held his gaze. "Murder is wrong. My brother wasn't ready to die." He narrowed his eyes. "I trust your intelligence, *signor*. I'm too old to find the truth. I have told you all I know so you can find the murderer."

Stefano swallowed. "Right."

Uncle Teo pulled himself into a standing position. "You will find him." He turned to the door. "If you need help, ask Carlina. She's a sensible girl."

Stefano closed the door behind Uncle Teo and turned to his assistant who was still writing so hectically he was getting red cheeks. He crossed the room in two big strides and stopped next to him. "Did you catch everything?"

"I hope." Piedro looked up, his eyes filled with awe. "Do you think he's sane?"

Garini sighed. "I don't think anybody in this family is normal, let alone sane."

He looked over Piedro's shoulders and read the notes. "Think we can cross anyone off our list already?"

Piedro went through the list again, his finger following each line he had written. For once, Stefano didn't become impatient. He needed a minute himself to organize his thoughts.

Piedro's finger came to a stop. "We can cross off number five. Ernesto. Isn't that the youngest here, seventeen or so, red hair?"

"Yes. Why do you think he's innocent?"

"Well," Piedro blushed. "If he's only going out to party at night, that's no sin, as the old man said."

"That's no sin." Stefano nodded. "But are we sure that he goes out to party? What if he's out because he's dealing with drugs?"

Piedro's mouth dropped open. "You think he's doing that?"

Stefano shrugged. "I have no clue. But until I have evidence that he's only partying, he will stay on that list."

Piedro's finger moved up. "I didn't get that thing about the butcher."

"That's all right; don't worry about it. I will deal with that detail." Stefano smothered a smile. "So what would you do now?"

"Em." Piedro stared at his notes as if inspiration would come from them. "I would talk to the others."

"Good. What do you expect they will say?"

His subordinate hesitated. "I think they won't be quite as open. After all, these things are all rather embarrassing, aren't they?"

"Yes. And then?"

Piedro swallowed. "Then . . . I . . . em. I don't know."

"Then you'll confront them with the things we've just learned, hoping they will spill something else."

"Right."

"What then?" Stefano wanted to tap his foot with impatience, but at the last moment, he curbed himself.

"I don't know."

"Then you'll check out these stories."

Piedro's eyes grew round. "All of them?"

"All of them."

"How?"

"Let's see." Stefano reached for the notes and turned back some pages. "Check the birth certificate of Carlina, find a picture of her father, and talk to someone who was around when she was born. Next, find the almost-prince she was engaged to . . ."

"Huh?" Piedro's mouth gaped open.

"Sorry, I forgot you don't know this part yet. You can listen to the tape later on, then you'll understand." Stefano suppressed a feeling that the story wasn't for Piedro. He could not start to treat Carlina any different than the rest. He concentrated with an effort. "Once we have the prince, we have to get his version of the story, then get the death certificate of Benedetta's husband and talk to the doctor who treated him, talk to Annalisa's class mates and her teacher and check her exams, check the balcony at night and catch Ernesto climbing up, talk to Maria about her eating habits, talk to Electra about the past and discover when Teo started dating Maria, find out what Angela could have used to blackmail Marco, and check out that famous investor in Dubai. Then, we need to contact the family doctor and learn if he was really ill the day after the wedding. And last but not least, we need to find out when cousin Emma will return from her honeymoon and interrogate her immediately."

Piedro blanched. "You're kidding me."

"No. In the meantime, something new might crop up that will lead us into a totally different direction. This might mean that some things we considered important don't have to be checked anymore while new things will surface."

"And when do we have to be done?"

"We have about four weeks for the intensive part of the job."

Piedro gulped. "Only four weeks? Why?"

"Because, unless it's a political case, we get four weeks to work on something and then we have to concentrate on the next case. That doesn't mean that we stop there, indeed, many cases get cleared up years and years later, but from experience, we know that the first four weeks are crucial. So, where do you think we should start?"

Piedro clutched the notebook as if he was drowning. "I don't know."

"Start with the most likely suspect." Garini felt boredom creeping in. *Why do I have to work with Piedro Cervi?*

"The most likely suspect?" Piedro's gaze raked the pages. "Who's that?"

"Who lied to us about the time of death?" Garini pressed his lips together.

Piedro had a bright moment. "Carlina."

"*Signorina* Ashley, correct. Besides, she would do anything for her mother, or for any other member of her family. She's absolutely devoted to them." *And I could shake her for it.*

"But *signor* Mantoni said she's a sensible girl."

"That's what he said, yes." Garini's eyes were hard. "But since when do we trust every word a witness says?"

Piedro swallowed. "Do you think she isn't her father's child?"

Stefano decided to overlook the convoluted sentence. "I have no clue."

"She doesn't look like the others," Piedro said. "Her hair is different."

"True."

"And her eyes are so . . . so clear."

And cat-like. "Yes."

"She's also taller than the others."

"Yes."

"And not as pretty."

Isn't she? Stefano's patience came to an end. "Just what are you trying to say, Piedro?"

Piedro opened his eyes wide. "I think it's very possible that her father is not her real father."

Stefano closed his eyes for a moment. "You've never seen her father. You've just compared her to her cousins, without ever having seen her brothers and sisters."

"I saw her sister, and she doesn't look at all like her."

"Do you look like your sister?" Garini snapped.

"I don't have a sister."

Thank the Lord for small blessings. Garini closed his mouth with a snap. "When you get home tonight, go into the Internet and check out the basic rules of genetics."

"Tonight?"

"Tonight." Garini glared at him. "And in the future, try to think before you speak. Now please ask Maria Mantoni to join us."

Chapter 8

Maria Mantoni looked at Garini, her black eyes intelligent and without fear. "Of course Teo had an affair with Electra."

Piedro gasped.

"He never told me, but I knew." She moved in her chair as if it was too hot. "I'm not blind."

"You never confronted him?" Stefano had trouble with his breathing. Maria exuded garlic fumes out of every pore.

Maria shrugged. "No. It was an aberration, and now, he's ashamed of it. That's why he can't stand her."

"When did it happen?" Stefano took one step back. Maybe the garlic stench wouldn't reach that far.

"In the first year of our marriage." Her answer came without hesitation. It was clear she didn't have to think about it. "But it didn't last long."

"I see." *I wish I knew if she's as unemotional as she pretends to be.*

"He's just a man, *commissario*." Aunt Maria looked at him as if men were a sorry species to be treated with lenience. "And he went to confession."

Garini decided to switch the topic. "How about the things your brother-in-law said about you?"

Maria looked at the floor, so her three chins spread out over the collar of her dress. "I like garlic snacks," she said.

I know. Stefano tried not to breathe.

"But I'm not dependent on alcohol." Maria looked up. "I never was."

"Anything else?" He tried to make his voice neutral. He had to get her to tell him the truth, even if it hurt.

She pressed her lips together. "Gluttony is a Cardinal Sin."

Her words transported Stefano back to his mother's bedroom. How often had he come in as a child, only to find her on her knees in front of her bed. She always went to confession, burdened down by feelings of guilt for every tiny mistake. She chastised herself for every wrong thought and believed her cancer had been the final and just retribution.

Without thinking about it, he bent forward. "Don't forget that Humility is one of the Holy Virtues." He smiled, willing her to understand. "If you've never been tempted, you have no compassion."

She stared at him. "What are you telling me?"

"I'm telling you that your weakness makes you a better human." He glanced at Piedro. *I hope he won't write that down. Don't want anybody to think I've mistaken my calling.* He cleared his throat. "Have you heard any other bad past stories from your brother-in-law?"

Maria blinked. "Yes. He said Ugo had stolen the camera. I think Benedetta told you already."

"I didn't quite catch the name?"

"Ugo," Maria repeated. "He's my eldest son. He always takes the pictures at our family parties, and he got a new camera in January. A very good camera."

"I see." *I don't want to hear any more stories. I'll never be able to go through that list of suspects.* "What do you think about it?"

Maria clicked her tongue, and a cloud of garlic breath enveloped Garini. "Ugo wouldn't steal anything." She placed her head to one side. "It was an extraordinary good deal, though."

"According to Ugo."

She nodded.

"Fine. Anything else?"

Maria shook her head. "I can't recall."

You don't want to. Garini inclined his head. "Thank you. Would you please ask Annalisa to come now?"

Maria heaved herself to her feet with a low groan. She slid one hand into the pocket of her dress and pulled out a garlic clove. "Would you like one?"

Garini suppressed a shudder. "No, thank you." He closed the door behind her, jumped to the window and flung it wide open.

Piedro ran next to him, hung his upper body out of the window until his nose touched the iron bars, and groaned. "How can anybody stand that stink?"

Stefano took a deep breath. How sweet the air smelled.

"I can't believe she added another story." Piedro sighed. "We'll never get to the end of it."

"She only did so because she suspected Benedetta of having

shared that story before. Interesting, isn't it?"

"Em. Yes." It sounded vague.

Stefano winced. *How am I ever going to make a good investigating officer out of you?*

"Are you all right?" Annalisa's voice came from behind them.

They both whipped around. "Yes, thank you." Stefano leaned his back against the sill but left the window open. "Please take a seat."

Annalisa dropped into the old armchair and crossed her legs. Her short skirt rode up her long leg. She wore high-heeled sandals in silver and kept moving her foot in the air.

Piedro stood frozen. He looked like a monk fish, his eyes bulging, his face devoid of expression.

"Piedro!" Stefano made sure his voice sounded like a whip. "Sit down and take notes."

His assistant started and hurried to his seat.

Annalisa focused her wide brown eyes on Stefano. "What do you need to know, *commissario*? I will tell you anything to help you." She lowered her lashes and smiled. Her red hair looked smooth like silk.

Gag. This one needs a more brutal approach. "Your grandfather told everybody you had cheated on your final exams at school." He made a suggestive pause.

Annalisa stiffened. The change from angelic girl to fury happened in seconds. "That's not true!"

Stefano pushed her further. "He also insinuated that you were friends with your young teacher." He drew out the pause to enhance the impact. "Very good friends."

Her eyes shot flashes. "Grandpa had such a dirty mind!" She balled her fists and bent forward with a hiss. "Yes, my teacher and I, we are good friends, but that doesn't mean he helped me to cheat!"

"I see." He drew out the word and made sure she could read the disbelief in his face. "Did you finish with good marks?"

For an instant, he thought she would jump up and slap him in the face. He could see the effort she made to control herself, then she decided to chill him with offended dignity.

"Yes, I had very good marks." She shook her hair like an impatient thoroughbred. "Is that a crime, *commissario*?"

"Not at all, *signorina*. Please give me the name and address of your teacher."

Her bosom swelled in indignation and her cheeks flushed red.

She looked lovelier than ever. "I don't want you to harass my teacher!"

"This is a murder investigation." Stefano made sure his voice sounded like ice. "You don't have a choice."

She pressed her lips together and gave him a look of undiluted hatred. "His name is Giuseppe Auguri."

"Thank you." He tried not to sound ironic. He let the silence hang between them and sized her up, wondering how he could get her to say more.

Annalisa lifted her eyebrows and inspected her fingernails, then she said, as if she was making an unimportant remark at a social occasion, "I'm not sure you're a good policeman."

"No?" He bit back a smile. Here came the attack he had expected. "How come?"

"If you had more sense, you would look deeper." She smoothed a crease on her skirt in a suggestive gesture.

"Are you thinking of anything in particular?" He didn't take his eyes off her face for one second, intent on catching every nuance.

"You should check on Uncle Teo." Annalisa crossed her arms in front of her chest and pulled up her breasts until they strained against the blouse. "Teo and Nico were in eternal competition. They always wanted to outdo each other. Maybe Uncle Teo was afraid that Nico would win, so he decided to help fate along."

"Why would he suddenly think so, after seventy-nine years?" Stefano's voice was hard.

Annalisa shrugged her round shoulders. "I don't know. It's your job to find that out. I'm just saying it's possible. You should check it."

"I will." Stefano inclined his head. "Anything else?" *I don't want to hear more and yet, I need to.*

"I'm not sure about Carlina." Annalisa looked at him through her lashes.

Stefano clenched his teeth. "Yes?"

"She keeps telling everybody she broke off that engagement, but I don't believe it. She threw away the Montassori estate and vineyard. I mean, hello?" She bent forward. "If you ask me, he gave her the kick. After all, he got married a few months later, and she's still single."

"And why should that provide a motive for killing her grandfather?"

Annalisa shook her head. "He probably taunted her once too

often. She just flipped, you know. Besides, she tried real hard to make Marco sign the death certificate, though it was plain to see he had doubts."

"I see." Stefano forced himself to ask his next question. It didn't happen often that a load of filth got to him, but this one did. "Any other stories to share?"

Annalisa laid back against the cushion of the armchair. "I'm not one to tell tales."

"Of course not." *Stop sounding so ironic, Stefano.*

As soon as the door had closed behind her, Piedro led out a deep breath. He sounded like a collapsing balloon. "You were very hard on her."

Stefano turned around. "Do you know why?"

"No!" Piedro shook his head. "I think the police should always treat everybody in a polite way."

"Particularly young and good-looking women?" Garini's voice was hard.

"Well . . . I didn't say that . . . but . . . " his voice petered out.

"We're trying to find a killer, Piedro. I like that you've spoken up for her, but I would have liked it even more if you had done so for a less attractive suspect. Someone felt threatened enough to kill Nico, and we won't get him or her by being polite and friendly. We need to get to the core of these people. We need to find out what makes them tick, and we can only do so by understanding what they value most. If we don't, we'll never catch the killer." Garini scrutinized his assistant. "Do you understand what I'm trying to say?"

Piedro looked puzzled, but he nodded.

"Good. Then try to remember it."

II

Ernesto perched on the edge of the armchair, his hands clasped together on his knees. "The others said you want to hear about the bad past stories."

"That's right."

Ernesto lifted his pale face. "My Grandpa knew I often went out late at night by way of the balcony, but I never did any harm."

Stefano regarded him. "What did you do?"

Ernesto swallowed so hard, his Adam's apple moved in a jerk.

"I go to an Internet Café."

"An Internet-Café?" Stefano had expected a lot of answers, but not this one.

"Yes. You see, I have a computer at home, but I play with friends at the Internet Café."

"Just what do you play?"

Ernesto flushed. "We play Monster IV." He bent forward until he threatened to fall off his chair. "We're organized in Guilds, and we fight against each other. It's so cool, because you have several lives, and you can create several characters. I'm a barbarian and a druid and an archer, and each can do different things. When you fight the Master Spider, you enter another level, and then --"

Stefano held up his hand. "Do I take it your mother doesn't approve?"

Ernesto's enthusiasm wilted like a spring flower in frost. "She hates it."

"Why?"

Ernesto shrugged. "Just because of a bit of blood and the noise." He looked at Stefano through his tumbled red hair. "I mean the fighting noise and the cries when we die." He grinned. "That's half the fun, though."

"Would you give me the address of your Internet Café?"

Ernesto's eyes lit up. "It's on Via Taddeo Alderotti. Do you want to come?"

Stefano bit back a smile. "I might have a look." *But I won't join in the game, and I do hope for your sake this Internet Café doesn't sell anything else.* "Do you remember any other bad past stories from your grandfather?"

Ernesto shook his head. "No. I don't think he meant them seriously anyway. I never pay much attention to what they say."

"They?"

Ernesto shrugged. "My mother, my aunt, my sister, my grandfather. It's better if you don't react."

I bet.

III

When Carlina finally crawled into bed that night, she was so tired, her bones felt too heavy to carry around anymore. She snuggled deep underneath the fake leopard fur bed cover and closed her eyes with a sigh. They burned as if someone had rubbed sand into them. *I can't believe this is happening. Oh, Grandpa. If I had known . . . if only I had only known. For Emma, I'm glad we concealed your death. She had the perfect wedding she wanted, and now she has the perfect honeymoon. But for everything else . . . oh, Madonna.*

Carlina turned to the other side. *Who could have done it? Who had hated grandpa enough to kill him? Was it really because of some bad past story or other? Nothing he had said had been new. He had only pulled up old scandals and dished them out again. Okay, so it wasn't nice, and nobody had enjoyed hearing their own scandal fresh and embellished. But murder? I can't believe it.*

Maybe it wasn't a bad past story. Maybe it was something quite different, something nobody knew anything about. Something outside the family. Her mood lightened. She tried to think up something outside the family, but nothing came to mind. She sighed.

The commissario seems to be very efficient. Efficient, ruthless, and bent on finding the truth. Very exhausting type of guy and difficult to dodge.

Carlina turned again and freed her leg from the twisted sheet. Now she felt hot. *Do I want to dodge him? Don't I want him to find the killer?* She bit her lips. *What if it's mamma?* Cold fear grabbed her gut. *Never.* A thought seared through her, and she jumped out of bed. The photo. She had to hide her father's photos. She went to the wall where his picture hung and lifted it from its nail. "Sorry, Dad." She looked into his light-brown eyes. "I don't want the *commissario* to see your eye-color and dig up loads of misleading information about recessive genes." Something inside her crumbled. *He was my father. I believe it, and so did he. That's enough.*

She placed the frame upside down inside the drawer of her bathroom. Garini had already searched this drawer. It wasn't likely that he would go through it again.

Her feet felt cold as she crawled back into bed. *Did mamma cheat on dad before I was born?* The thought chilled her. *Even if it was true, would it have been reason enough for mamma to kill her own father?* Carlina shook her head. Impossible. *After all, dad died years ago. It can't hurt him anymore.* She rubbed her cold foot against her calf. *But it hurts me, and she would know that.* The thought came out of nowhere. *Had mamma killed granddad to protect me? If yes, she would never have talked about it in front of me, instead she would have insisted on a private interview. Or would she?* Carlina started to nibble on her index finger. *Maybe it was a sort of double bluff. Oh, God, this is too difficult to fathom.* Carlina turned around and pulled the cover higher. *It wasn't mamma. I know her, and that counts more than a million proofs.*

She tossed around again. *But if it wasn't mamma, who could have poisoned grandpa? Uncle Teo? Had he killed his twin in cold-blooded murder? They had been in eternal competition; I said so myself. But life will be without zest now for Uncle Teo, with nobody to compare himself to. He knows that. No, I can't imagine that Uncle Teo poisoned his twin.*

How about Benedetta? She is a devoted mother. Of course, she has to have things exactly her way, and she nags a lot, but on the other hand, she is so generous and always works hard. No way would she have poisoned her father. After all, he presented no threat to her.

Carlina gave up. *I can't imagine anybody in my family killing grandpa.* She sighed. *Unfortunately, the commissario can, and he seems to be doing it with growing enthusiasm. I have to talk to them. I have to find out more. Somebody did it, and I know my family best.*

Carlina pulled the sheet higher around her shoulders. *Tomorrow.* She would talk to them tomorrow.

Chapter 9

"Mamma?" Carlina pushed open the door to her mother's apartment and stood for an instant, blinded by the morning sun.

"Is that you, Carlina?" Fabbiola's voice came from the kitchen. She sounded cheery and upbeat.

With a sinking heart, Carlina went through the kitchen door. Unlike her sister Benedetta, her mother was the world's worst cook, but she made up for it by buying every electrical kitchen appliance available on the market.

Fabbiola stood hunched over a steaming coffee machine that looked like a miniature space ship. "Is everything all right?" Fabbiola turned to her daughter, then checked the huge digital clock above the door. It had been designed for a cooking contest and measured not only the humidity of the room but could also be set into four different alarm modes by remote control. "You're late for Temptation." Fabbiola poured a cup of coffee and held it out to Carlina.

"Elena is standing in for me." Carlina accepted the cup. "Thank you."

"Why do you look so gloomy, then?"

Carlina sat on a modern chair made of purple plastic. It had been the winner in a restaurant contest for most unusual furniture. "I need to ask you something."

Fabbiola's eyes darted to her trusted cushion, reposing on the purple chair next to Carlina, as if seeking guidance. She picked it up, fluffed it against the back of the chair, and sat down, her eyes apprehensive. "What is it?"

"The *commissario* . . . " Carlina had difficulty forming the words.

Fabbiola sat up straight. "What? What did he do to you? Did you talk to him on your own? I told you it's dangerous."

Carlina took a deep breath, but the heavy weight on her chest didn't budge. "Why did you say dad had blue eyes?"

Fabbiola jumped. She averted her eyes from her daughter and

pulled the cushion from behind her back with a hectic move. "Did I say so?"

Carlina closed her eyes. "You know you did."

"But he had blue eyes." Fabbiola stared at her daughter with an unwavering gaze.

It reminded Carlina of her niece Lilly whenever she was asked if she had brushed her teeth. "Dad had light-brown eyes, and you know it." The words sounded brutal.

Fabbiola flinched. "Oh, really? I must have forgotten." She waved her hand. "It's such a long time ago, you know . . . "

"*Mamma*." Carlina bent forward. "The *commissario* isn't stupid. We have pictures of dad all over the house, and they show his brown eyes." She swallowed. "Why did you lie to Garini?"

Now Fabbiola fluttered both her hands. "I didn't lie to him. I just misremembered."

Carlina winced. She could imagine Garini's face when Fabiola dished out that she had "misremembered" her husband's eye color. She wouldn't last a second.

Carlina tried another track. "Why did grandpa say dad wasn't my father?"

Fabbiola shook her head. "I don't know, darling. Honestly, I have no clue." She jumped up. "And I don't think it's nice of you to grill me. I'm your mother, and I think you should show some respect."

Carlina clenched her teeth. "*Mamma*, I--"

Fabbiola interrupted her with a hiss. "Did that *commissario* put you up to it?" She bent forward and stared at her daughter, a nervous hand plucking at the cushion. "Is that why?"

"No!" Carlina wanted to shake her. "But you shouldn't underestimate him, *mamma*. If you have something to hide, he will ferret it out."

Her mother sniffed with disdain. "There's nothing to find out."

"Nothing but who killed grandpa." Carlina's voice sounded flat.

"He's wasting his time." Fabbiola shook her head. "Nobody in our family would kill."

Carlina looked at her mother. "Nobody? Would you guarantee that you would never, ever kill someone, no matter the provocation?"

Her mother lifted her eyebrows. "Of course I wouldn't kill

anybody. I wasn't raised in a jungle." Her eyes narrowed. "And neither were you."

If only it was so easy. Carlina bit her lips. If she looked at herself, she knew the rules ingrained into her were strong. They felt insurmountable. But what if she felt her life was threatened or if she needed to protect someone? *I'm not so sure of myself.* Carlina sighed and looked at her mother who concentrated on picking invisible bits of dust from her cushion. *You would kill, mamma. You would kill for us.* The thought chilled her. She took a deep breath to fight the feeling of being sick. "Did you have a boyfriend before you went out with dad?" The minute the words were out of her mouth, she knew she shouldn't have said them.

Her mother flashed her a look full of anger and jumped up, still clutching her cushion. "You are impertinent, Caroline Arabella."

Carlina got up. "I'm sorry."

Fabbiola lifted her hand in a regal gesture. "I wish you would think before you speak. It's easy to say you're sorry, but you can't take back the words."

Carlina sighed. "I have to go."

She hurried from her mother's apartment and went upstairs. It wasn't until she felt the smooth wood of the railing underneath her fingers that she realized her mother had done it again. By making her feel inadequate, Fabbiola had skilfully turned the limelight away from her. *Damn.*

The bells of Santa Croce chimed the half hour. From downstairs, Carlina heard Aunt Maria's voice. She was saying good-bye to Uncle Teo.

Uncle Teo. Carlina stopped in her tracks. *I could talk to him.* She waited until Aunt Maria had left the house, then she clattered down the stairs.

Uncle Teo still stood in the door. "Good morning, Carlina." He smiled at her, his face a maze of wrinkles. "You're late today for your store."

"My assistant is minding Temptation this morning," Carlina said. "Can I come in and talk to you for a moment, Uncle Teo?"

His eyes assessed her in one sharp glance. "Of course. Come right in."

Carlina followed him to the sitting room with a hideous brown sofa. The window to the street stood wide open, and a reflected beam of sunshine shone through the iron bars. Carlina crossed the room and closed the window.

Uncle Teo raised his bushy eyebrows. "Sit down, dear." He lifted his pleated trousers at the knees with his thumb and index finger before seating himself. "What's troubling you?"

"Grandpa said my dad wasn't my father." She didn't care how confused it sounded.

"Hmm." Uncle Teo's eyes narrowed. "And you're asking me if it's true?"

"Yes." To her dismay, Carlina felt tears pressing against her eyes.

"You should ask your mother."

Carlina snorted. "She won't say anything. She's all offended dignity, and I can't get a single sensible word out of her."

Her great-uncle nodded. "I see."

Carlina bent forward. "Will you tell me the truth?"

Uncle Teo regarded her for an instant. "You're a true Mantoni, girl. You have nothing to worry about."

Carlina frowned. "Of course I am. After all, nobody questions my mother. It's dad I'm wondering about."

He frowned. "Why do you have doubts? After all, Nico invented plenty of things." He chuckled. "He even said I had an affair with Electra."

Carlina pressed her lips together. "His stories all held a grain of truth."

Uncle Teo sat up straight. "Nonsense."

"Oh, yes." Carlina nodded. "I don't mean the story about Electra, but everything else I've heard . . . he always mashed up some facts and embellished them with loads of rubbish all around, until nobody believed a word anymore."

Uncle Teo's eyebrows descended.

"And that's why I want to know more." Carlina gave him a belligerent stare. "Tell me. You know more. I know it. Don't tell me you don't."

Uncle Teo shook his head. "Carlina, I--"

"Please. It makes me crazy, not knowing what to believe. *Mamma* even told the *commissario* dad's eyes were blue, while all around him the walls were plastered with pictures that showed dad's brown eyes." A hysterical giggle escaped her. "I hid all pictures last night. It made me feel so awful."

Uncle Teo's nose flared, and he pressed his lips together. "So that's why," he murmured.

"What?" Carlina bent forward. "What do you mean?"

Uncle Teo shook his head. "The *commissario* was here early

this morning, just as Benedetta was leaving for work. He asked her if she could give him some pictures of Nico, and he also took some of the wedding, and one of your father."

Carlina could feel the blood draining from her face. "Oh, no. What will he think now?"

Uncle Teo shrugged. "It doesn't matter what he thinks. He's here to catch the murderer. All other scandals are of no interest to him."

Carlina dropped her head into her hands. "But it's of interest to me!" Her voice broke. "I want to know if dad was my father!" She didn't say it, but the thought that her dad might not have been her natural father made her feel as if the floor underneath her shifted. "What made grandpa tell that story? I can't believe he came up with it out of the blue."

Uncle Teo sighed and passed a hand over his eyes. "You were born seven months after the marriage of your parents."

Carlina lifted her head and stared at him. "I know. I was a premature infant."

Uncle Teo shrugged.

Carlina narrowed her eyes. "You mean I . . . I wasn't? You know more, don't you?"

Her great-uncle blinked, his face devoid of feelings. For an instant, he looked like a turtle - inscrutable and wise.

Carlina bent forward until she almost slid from her seat. "You're hiding something from me. What is it?"

Uncle Teo sighed. "It's nothing."

Carlina wanted to shake him. "So tell me about this nothing."

He sighed. "You should talk to your mother."

"She doesn't tell me anything!"

Uncle Teo shrugged. "It's her story to tell." He lifted his head and smiled at her, a warm smile, a smile that would have touched her if she hadn't been so angry. "Carlina, it doesn't matter if he wasn't your real father. True family isn't always about flesh and blood."

She jumped up. "You want me to believe that? You, of all people?"

His bushy eyebrows pulled together. "What do you mean?"

Carlina bent forward until her face almost touched his. "You are the most committed patriarch I've ever known. If things went your way, you would have every Mantoni living on this very street."

"That's not quite true." A smile appeared on his wrinkled

face. "I'm quite glad your aunt Alberta lives in Fiesole, for example. I disliked her way of dropping nasty remarks even when she was a child."

Carlina's jaw dropped.

Uncle Teo winked, leaned back in the chair, and folded his hands in front of his stomach.

Carlina's anger evaporated like spilled wine under the Tuscany sun. She burst out laughing, bent forward and kissed his cheek. "You're incredible. I'm going now. I have to recover from my family."

II

Stefano frowned at the report from the lab. It confirmed that the carafe had contained the morphine. A tiny trace had been found on one side, even though someone had taken pains to wash it. Not a single fingerprint showed on the smooth glass. *Of course not.*

Stefano bit his lip. *This case has too many dead ends, and time is running out.* Talking about which, Piedro seemed to have done another vanishing act. *I'd better track him down.*

He picked up the receiver and called his subordinate. When Piedro finally replied, he didn't waste time with preliminaries. "Where are you, Piedro?" Stefano leaned back in his chair and looked out of the window. The sunlight streamed through the dusty window panes.

"I'm on my way back from the solicitor." Piedro said.

"Good. What did he say?"

Piedro hesitated. "He used many complicated words."

Garini suppressed a sigh. *I shouldn't have sent him.* "If you don't understand something, you have to ask."

"That's what I did." Piedro sounded hurt. "And he explained it again. It was very simple. I don't know why he first made it so difficult, when it wasn't."

Stefano grinned. "That's because they use their own language."

"What?" Piedro sounded confused. "He spoke Italian. At least, I think it was Italian most of the time."

Garini forced himself to keep the impatience from his voice. "Just tell me the result, Piedro."

"Wait. I've written it down, so I wouldn't mix it up." A

rustling of paper came through the receiver, then Piedro started to read. "Nicolò Alfredo Mantoni had a savings account. First, the costs for the funeral and a donation of five thousand Euros to the Uffizi Museum Trust has to be deducted from that account. The rest will be divided into seven equal parts and will be given to each offspring." Piedro took a deep breath.

"Did they tell you how much money was in the savings account?"

"No." Piedro sneezed. "But they said each beneficiary," he stumbled on the word, "will receive roughly one thousand and three hundred Euros. It depends on the costs of the funeral, you see."

"Did he have any property?"

"I asked about that." Piedro sounded pleased. "He doesn't. The house on Via delle Pinzochere belongs only to Teodoro Mantoni."

Damn. No motive there. Garini sighed. *You don't kill for one thousand Euros unless you're desperate. Another dead end.*

"Shall I come to the office now?" Piedro sounded eager to return.

"No. We discussed it this morning. Please go to the Civil State Office now, to get the death certificate for Benedetta's husband."

"Oh, right. I forgot."

"When you've done that, go to the hospital where he died and try to find out if the doctor who signed the certificate still works there. Don't question him, just find out if he's still there. Also, find out if he's the doctor who treated him and knew his case. Got that?"

Piedro sighed. "Yes."

"And talking about doctors, call the Mantoni family doctor and ask him if he was too ill to work the weekend of the murder."

"All right."

"Did you note everything?"

"I won't forget." Piedro sounded defensive now.

I wonder.

III

The *commissario* rolled his motorbike to a stop. He glanced at the Mantoni house, grateful no one was out front to notice his visit to their neighbor. It would save a lot of explaining later.

"*Buongiorno*, Stefano!" Electra opened her door wide. Today, she was shrouded from head to toe in a turquoise garment covered with sequins. They glittered in the light.

"*Buongiorno*, Electra." Stefano smiled. "Do you have a minute for me?"

"But of course!" Electra waved him in and shut the door.

Stefano advanced into the dim room and almost fell over a black cat. "Gosh, sorry."

"Never mind." Electra went down the hall. "She's like lightning, always between my feet. I keep tripping over her all the time."

"Hmm." Stefano looked at the cat. "Did you ever try her food?"

Electra turned around and stared at him. "What?"

"I've heard dry cat food tastes nice. Sort of crunchy."

Electra shook her head. "Tsk, tsk. The people you have to associate with when you're a police man . . . I pity you. It's hard to imagine what strange things people eat. Disgusting." She gave him a brilliant smile. "Would you like some chamomile-peppermint tea?"

"No, thanks." Stefano hastened to decline the offer. "I've just had some coffee."

"Then take a seat in the living room. I'll get myself a cup and will join you in a minute."

"I'd rather be with you in the kitchen." The kitchen didn't have a window that could be seen from the Mantoni house.

"Oh, all right." Electra turned and led the way to the kitchen. Her dress billowed out like a turquoise cloud. She filled a kettle with water and put it onto the stove. "Now tell me. You didn't come to talk to me about cat food, did you?"

"No." Stefano leaned against the kitchen table. "I've come to ask you about your love life some thirty years ago."

Electra exploded with laughter. "Ha, this is right. My love life, thirty years ago! Who tells you my memory goes back that long?"

He smiled. "I hope it does. It's about Teodoro Mantoni."

She stopped mid-laugh and shot him a sharp glance. "Oh." She swallowed. "I see."

"Will you tell me about it?"

Electra turned her back to him and busied herself with her tea pot. "What do you want to know?"

"Did you have an affair with him in the first year of his marriage?"

She didn't reply.

"Electra?"

"Who says so?" Her voice sounded flat.

"Maria."

She whipped around, her eyes huge. "She knows?"

He didn't take his gaze off her for one moment. "She says she always knew."

"So that's why . . ." Her voice petered out. She stared into space.

He bent forward. "What?"

Electra pressed her lips together. "Maria is a devoted Catholic."

"I know that."

"She . . . she had some funny notions about the sex life of a good Catholic."

"Like you should only have sex if you want to create a child?"

Electra gave him a sharp glance. "You know that, don't you?"

"I do, even if I'm not a good Catholic."

Electra smiled. "Well, it was hard for Teodoro." She took a deep breath. "I'm still ashamed about it. At the time, I wasn't strong enough to resist."

"Why did it end?"

She lifted both hands. "One day, Teodoro came and told me it had to stop. He said Maria had changed, things were better. Then they had all those kids, so I figured they were fine."

"Did you remain friends?"

"Oh, no." Electra shook her head. "He avoids me whenever he can. At first, I wanted to move away, but then . . . you have to live with your mistakes, you see."

Stefano took a deep breath. *One thing cleared up. But is a thirty-year-old love affair enough motive for murder? I don't think so.* He shook his head and got up. "Thank you very much."

Electra gave him a sharp glance. "You won't talk about it, will you?"

"Not unless I have to due to the investigation."

Electra rolled her eyes. "Of course."

IV

When Carlina arrived at Temptation, Elena was deep in discussion with a female customer dressed in designer clothes from top to toe. Carlina waved at her assistant and took a seat at the computer. Contrary to most shop owners, she had placed her tiny office right at the cash register which was next to the door. That not only forced her to be well organized but it allowed her to get on with her work even if she was alone in the store. She could also see the street from her high bar stool in front of the computer and wave at acquaintances. The day was warm, so she had opened the glass door wide to catch the fresh air. *I love autumn. Not too hot, not too cold, and everything so warm, so intense, so rich.* Usually, it made her feel happy just to sit here, in the center of her universe, knowing she had things under control.

However, today was different. She tried to concentrate on her work and put together the order for the next season, but her mind kept drifting. How could she think of lace and pearls if her very being was questioned? She had always been a father's girl. The link to him was strong, and the thought that he might not have been her natural father left her feeling loose, as if her mooring had snapped off, and now she was floating, not knowing where she came from or where she belonged. She lifted her shoulders in a rolling motion to ease the tension. "It's all nonsense," she said under her breath and pushed the catalog away. Without making a conscious decision, she turned to her computer. Her fingers clicked onto Google and entered the words 'genetic eye color'. Seconds later, she was deep inside an article.

She didn't even hear the customer say good-bye as she left the store, but Elena got her attention by poking her in the ribs. "Is it true what people say?"

Carlina tore herself away from the article. "What?"

"Your grandfather was killed?" Elena's eyes, outlined with black eyeliner, widened.

Carlina hurried to close the article, so the screen wouldn't give her away. "Yes."

"They say he was stabbed, and the blood-stained knife was found in your apartment." Elena lifted both hands, heavy with massive silver rings.

"What?" Carlina blinked. "Who said that?"

"*Signora* Barberini."

"*Signora* Barberini?" Carlina shook her head. She knew that her formidable landlady liked to gossip, but she couldn't imagine her spreading such wild tales.

"Yep." Elena nodded. "She came this morning in full-battleship mode and--"

All at once, Carlina didn't want to hear another word. "*Signora* Barberini had better stop thinking up crazy stories." Carlina jumped up. "It's all nonsense. As far as we know, my grandfather was poisoned."

"Oh," Elena's shook her blond-dyed head. "No knife?"

"No." Carlina went to the window. "I really don't want to talk about the murder anymore. Let's talk about something else. How was your weekend?" She knew it wasn't an elegant change of topic, but she couldn't think of anything better to say. Besides, Elena loved to talk about her private life. Carlina lifted the mannequin and moved it to the side. It was time to finally put on those brown nylons.

Her assistant regarded her for an instant, then she shrugged and went to the storage room. "My weekend was great," she said. "We went to the Rio Grande. Have you ever been there?"

"No." Carlina opened the package that contained the nylons and pulled the hosiery out of their plastic bag with care. *How silky they feel.*

"It's the biggest disco I've ever been to. They have four dancing floors."

Carlina could tell by the sound of the cutter sliding through cardboard that Elena had started to open the box from the last delivery which was standing in the small storage room. "Wow," Carlina said. "Where is the Rio Grande?"

"It's right next to the Ippodromo, on--" Elena stopped with a shriek.

Carlina dropped the nylons and ran to the back of the store. "What's up?"

Elena bent over the box. Her trousers were cut so low that Carlina could see her thong on her hips. Above the thong, two curlicued tattoos decorated Elena's midriff.

"What. Is. This?" Elena lifted a skin-colored bra, padded like a saddle, large enough to wrap three times around her slim body. "Don't tell me you ordered this. There must be some mistake."

Carlina wiped her sweaty hands on her jeans. "God, you gave me a fright. First the murder, and now your scream . . ."

Elena turned around in slow motion. "You ordered this . . .

this atrocity?" The ring in her nose quivered.

Carlina nodded. "It's for *signora* Barberini."

"*Signora* Barberini? So that's why she came this morning! But since when is she our customer?"

Carlina grinned. "Since she came through this door and told me that her old retail store had been replaced by a supermarket chain and that she has no clue where to buy her bras in the future."

"Her bras . . ." Elena lifted the garment and wrinkled her nose. "Her suit of armor, you mean."

It sure looked like one in front of Elena's skinny frame and pink t-shirt. Carlina grinned. "*Signora* Barberini likes them, that's what counts."

Elena dropped the bra and poked around the box. Then she twisted her head so she could look at Carlina's face. "But you bought a whole box!"

"I know." Carlina picked up the discarded bra, folded it, and placed it onto the shelf to her right. "It's a new supplier, and they wanted a minimum order quantity."

Elena's mouth dropped open. "What on earth are you going to do with them? There must be at least ten!"

"Twelve." Carlina bent over the box to count them. "Believe it or not, they're already sold. Every single one."

"No way."

"Yes. Ten, eleven, twelve. All there." Carlina straightened, crossed her arms in front of her chest, and leaned against the door frame of the storage room. "I told Mrs. Barberini we have to reach the minimum, and so she asked all her friends to place orders too." She grinned at her assistant.

Elena blinked. "I can't imagine her doing that."

"Oh, she gets a commission."

"What? *Signora* Barberini works as a sales rep?" Elena shook her head. "You must have bewitched her."

Carlina nodded and spread her arms. "That's me. The lingerie witch from Via Tornabuoni."

They both laughed.

Elena looked at the huge bra once again. "You know, I'm just wondering . . ." She frowned. "My mother might like one of those, too."

Carlina frowned. "But wouldn't she want something more comfortable in bed?"

Elena shook her head. "She keeps wearing those, insists on

them, even if she doesn't get up all day."

"Does she still feel so bad? When I saw her last week, I thought she was getting better."

Elena sighed. "No. I even have the feeling she's secretly raising her morphine doses."

Carlina's mouth went dry. "Morphine?"

"Yes. I know for sure I bought enough to last all week, but she told me yesterday it was gone."

All at once, Carlina's legs felt too soft to bear her weight. "Elena."

"I think it's best if we place those bras on the shelf for commissioned goods, don't you agree?" Elena started to gather the boxes in her arms.

Carlina cleared her throat. "When did you buy the morphine for your mother?"

"What?" Elena looked up. "Tuesday. We went to the Andromeda Club, and I remember I went to the pharmacy before, so I--" she broke off. "Why do you look like death warmed over?"

Carlina felt sick. "I saw your mother on Thursday."

"Yeah, I know. Your mother came the same day, did you know that?"

"What?" The floor seemed to tilt beneath Carlina's feet.

"You must have missed each other by a few minutes."

"Elena, would you--" Carlina swallowed. "Do you think you could keep this to yourself until . . ."

"I've heard every word." The *commissario*'s voice came from right behind her.

Carlina screamed and spun around.

Elena dropped all the boxes.

"How dare you scare me like this?" Carlina wanted to slap his mocking face. "How dare you creep up and eavesdrop on us?" He seemed taller today, and more menacing than ever. His black leather jacket was open and revealed a white t-shirt that molded itself across his chest.

"I didn't creep up." Garini's face remained impassive as always. "I stood just in front of the door when your assistant screamed. Neither of you heard me coming in. Why don't you have a bell?"

"I don't need one. Usually. Don't tell me you tried to get our attention!" Carlina narrowed her eyes. "I wouldn't believe it."

His cool eyes assessed her. "I didn't."

"Who are you?" Elena stared at Garini.

"*Commissario* Stefano Garini from the Homicide Department."

Elena's gaze darted between Stefano and Carlina. "Are you . . . have you known each other for long?"

"Too long." Carlina replied before she could stop herself.

"May I know your name?" Garini looked at Elena.

"Elena Certini."

"Would you be willing to repeat the statements you've just made in front of a jury?"

Elena's eyes widened. "Why? What have I said?"

"You mentioned that a quantity of morphine has disappeared from your house, and that several people who are closely linked to the murder we're investigating had access to it."

Elena looked at Carlina and lifted both hands palm up. Her face was a question.

"Of course she would." Carlina felt as if someone was pressing the air out of her throat.

"I haven't asked you." Garini said without inflection.

"Yes." Elena shrugged.

"Would you give me your mother's name and address?"

Elena stiffened. "My mother has nothing to do with this. She's ill, and you shouldn't bother her."

"*Signorina* Certini, I'm looking for a murderer. If the morphine was taken from your mother's house, we might get valuable clues from her."

Carlina sighed. "Give him the address, Elena. He'll find out anyway."

Elena swallowed. "But--"

Garini said, "I promise I won't bother her more than necessary."

"Oh, all right. I'll write it down for you." Elena went to the desk at the entrance of the store and got out a piece of paper.

Garini's gaze turned to Carlina and hardened. "I wish to take you to the police station."

Carlina's heart stopped beating for two painful moments. "Am I . . . are you arresting me?"

"No." Garini looked as if he would have preferred to say yes.

Her stomach clenched. "Do I have to come?"

His cool eyes assessed her. "No. Not until the prosecuting attorney gives me orders to bring you in."

His words had such a sinister ring that Carlina grabbed the

shelf next to her.

"Here's my mother's address," Elena came back from the desk and gave Garini a piece of paper.

"Thank you." He turned back to Carlina. "Well, *signorina* Ashley? Are you willing to cooperate with the police?"

Carlina clenched her teeth. "How long will I be gone?"

"I can't tell you. It depends."

She didn't dare to ask what it depended on and took a deep breath. "Elena, do you think you can manage on your own for some time?"

"Sure." Elena gave her a smile that was a curious mix of bravery and curiosity.

Wrong answer, girl. Carlina forced a smile and followed Garini out of the store. She felt as if she was being led straight to execution. *Better me than mamma. I have to talk to her.*

"Put on your helmet," he said. "I will take you up on my motorbike."

Carlina went to her Vespa and unlocked her helmet, then locked the Vespa again.

He lifted his eyebrows when he saw the helmet. "Does everything in your life have to be with a leopard print?"

"That's none of your business."

He didn't reply, instead, he led her to his black motorbike on the sidewalk.

"This is a no-parking-zone." Carlina said.

He mounted his bike and started the motor. "Get up behind me and hold on tight." It sounded as if he spoke through clenched teeth.

After her slim Vespa, his motorbike felt like a sofa. Carlina ducked behind his back and resisted the temptation to lean her head against him. He drove fast, and she was obliged to hold on tighter than she wanted. It felt too close, too intimate. *I should have insisted on a taxi.*

Five minutes later, a narrow alley with several-storied houses on both sides multiplied the noise of the motor. Garini slowed down, took a sharp corner to the left, and stopped in a parking area filled with four black motorbikes and one police car. Carlina saw the black bars in the back of the car and averted her eyes. *I hope he didn't lie to me. What if he wants to arrest me? What will become of Temptation?*

He dismounted and waited until she stood next to him, then he held out his hand. "Your helmet."

Without a word, she handed him her helmet, and he placed it in the storage container on his bike. When he had locked it, he led the way to the back entrance of the police station.

They arrived in a cheerless room that smelled of dust and fear. Garini closed the metallic door behind them and locked it with a key.

The sound made her stomach lurch. Did he think she was going to run away? She pulled back her shoulders and looked around her. Three old metal chairs and one wooden table constituted all the furniture. The windows had bars in front of them. A sick shade of light-green paint covered the dingy walls.

"Sit down."

Carlina sat. A shudder of fear went through her stomach.

He chose a seat at the other side of the table and looked at her with his light eyes as if he wanted to x-ray her soul.

Carlina set her teeth and met his gaze without flinching. She could feel cold sweat trickling down between her shoulder blades.

He pulled a piece of paper from his pocket and unfolded it. "This letter informs you about your rights. Please read and sign it." He pushed it across the table.

Carlina took it and tried to make sense of the words. She had trouble focusing her fear-frozen thoughts on the things she read, but after having read it three times, the bare facts registered. It said that anything she said could be used against her in court and that she had the right to get an attorney before she was questioned. "I don't know any attorney."

"We can arrange one for you, but you can also decide to talk without one present."

She looked at him. He had never seemed so fierce. *I need to get out of here.* "Start with your questions." She flung her words on the table like a challenge. "If I find them too difficult, I'll stop answering them."

"You have to sign first."

She held out her hand. "Give me a pen." *No need to be polite with this guy.*

He fished a black ballpoint pen from the pocket of his jacket and pushed it toward her.

The pen felt warm from his body. *I wish he liked me.* Carlina's mouth went dry. *Where has this crazy thought come from?* Without a word, she signed the document. Then she lifted her head. "Now start."

He took out the recording machine. "Do you agree to my recording this conversation?"

One day, I'm going to stuff the stupid recorder down his throat. "Yes." Carlina glared at him. "Are we done with the preliminaries or do we have to agree on a million other things?"

"We're done."

"Then start." She pressed the words through clenched teeth.

His face remained set like a mask. "Please tell me about the assistant who works at your store."

"Her name is Elena Certini." Carlina placed a hand onto the table. It felt gritty with dirt. She grimaced and dropped both hands into her lap.

"How long has she been working for you?"

"Six months."

"Did you know each other before she started at your store?"

It felt like a tennis match where she had to run to catch each ball. "I had seen her a few times before. Our mothers are friends."

"Of course."

He said it so low, she wasn't sure if she had imagined the ironic answer.

"But we get along very well." Carlina felt she had to defend her choice of assistant.

"Since when have you known the mother?"

Carlina shrugged. "I've known her for years, but not very well. As I said, she's a friend of my mother's."

"Are you in the habit of visiting her?"

Damn. Here it came. "I . . . no." Carlina's hands started to shake and she pressed them together in her lap.

"Why did you visit her last week?"

"Because she's ill with cancer." *His mother died of cancer. Does he think of her now?* "Elena told me her mother was bored," she added.

"And so you decided to visit her?" He made it sound as if it was a vicious act.

"I decided to visit her because Elena asked me to do so." *Even if you don't believe it, Mister Policeman.* "Elena had told her mother about Temptation and--"

"About what?"

"About my store."

"Go on."

Carlina took a deep breath. "She also told her mother a lot

about her work and me, and so she had the idea that her mother would be diverted from her illness if I came one evening for an aperitif."

"And so you went."

"Yes, I did." Carlina lifted her chin. *Anything wrong with that, Garini?*

"Where does *signora* Certini keep her medicine?"

Carlina clenched her teeth. *If only I could say I have no idea.* "I think she keeps it on the side table next to her bed."

"You think so?"

"Yes."

"Why?" The word shot out like a bullet.

It hurt. *Yesterday, when I told him my story, he was so different. Maybe it's part of the interrogation tactics. Put the suspect on an emotional roller coaster.* Carlina bit her lips.

"*Signorina* Ashley? Have you heard my question?"

"Yes." Carlina gave him a dark look. "I saw Elena take a tablet from that side table. She gave it to her mother."

"Did you see what it was?"

"No."

"No?" His voice sounded ironic.

"No!" *Damn you.*

He contemplated her for a moment, as if she was a snail on a piece of lettuce. "You are aware that you are the prime suspect for the murder of your grandfather, aren't you?"

"What?" Carlina jumped up. "I haven't killed my grandfather!"

"Sit down, *signorina* Ashley." He sounded bored.

Carlina clenched her trembling hands and sat down. *I should have called an attorney.* "Why?" She bent forward. "Why do you think I killed him?"

The *commissario* lifted his right hand and started to count on his fingers. "Means. You had access to morphine a short time before the murder. You also had free access to your grandfather's apartment at any time you chose." His light eyes never wavered from her face. "Motive. Your grandfather harassed you with stories about your past and insinuated that you were not a legitimate child of your father, whom you adored."

"How do you know I adored him?" Carlina felt sick.

"I have eyes in my head, *signorina* Ashley." His voice was hard as granite. "Place. You were the first at the scene of the crime and managed to disturb it."

"But--"

He interrupted her. "General behavior. You lied to us about the time of death. You did everything you could to make an inexperienced doctor sign the death certificate and stop the investigation."

Carlina tried to swallow, but her throat was too tight. "I told you why."

"I have noted your reasons." The *commissario* inclined his head.

He doesn't believe a word I said.

The *commissario* lifted his hand again and counted another point. "Corruption of witnesses. You tried to convince your assistant to keep your access to morphine a secret."

"Only until I could have talked to you!" *and mamma.*

His eyebrow twitched in that ironic manner she had come to hate. "Indeed?"

Carlina felt tears springing into her eyes. *I won't cry in front of this monster.* She averted her face and concentrated on her clenched hands. "Are you going to arrest me now?"

"No."

"Why not?"

He was silent.

She lifted her head. "Are you going to play cat and mouse with me?"

His face was inscrutable. "No."

Hot rage filled her. "Just what are you trying to tell me, *commissario*?"

He bent forward. "Has it occurred to you that quite a few of the points I mentioned are also valid for the rest of your family?"

Carlina caught her breath. "My mother didn't do it!"

He narrowed his eyes. "Why did you think of your mother?"

She could feel hot blood mounting to her face. *Oh, God.* "I won't say another word!"

He cocked his head to the side. "What about your cousin Emma? She maneuvered you into a pretty tight spot, didn't she?"

"It wasn't Emma!"

"No? Did she love your grandfather so much?" His voice sounded too soft.

Damn him, damn him, damn him. Carlina clenched her teeth. *Don't reply, Carlina.*

He leaned back and tapped his fingers on the table. "Tell me one more thing, *signorina* Ashley."

She gave him her darkest look and waited.

"Why did you like your grandfather?"

"What?" Her mouth dropped open.

"Why did you like him?" He bent forward. "From what I've heard, he delighted in making everybody's life difficult."

"Then you got the wrong information." Carlina crossed her arms in front of her chest. "He wasn't like that."

"No?" The *commissario* lifted his eyebrows. "Is it a charming habit to drag everybody's black memories from the past into discussion when the whole family is around?"

Carlina shook her head. "That was just the last phase."

"How about the other phases?"

She smiled a bit. "It wasn't always easy to live with him, but at least it was never boring."

"Hmm." His light eyes assessed her. "Did you admire him?"

Carlina lifted her chin. "Yes, I did. He was a man with passion. Whatever he did, he did one hundred percent."

He narrowed his eyes. "It's called a fanatic."

Carlina shrugged. "So what? He dared to stand out from the crowd. He didn't do what people expected him to do. He did whatever he thought was right."

"A rebel?"

Again she shrugged. "Maybe. A man with courage for sure. A man who was able to laugh about his mistakes. A man who told you what he thought even if you didn't like it." *A man like you.* The thought came out of nowhere. Carlina jumped and shut her mouth with a snap.

The *commissario* looked at her, thoughtful. Then he said. "I wonder why nobody threw Nicolò's own past into his face."

Carlina sighed. "I did, once. When he told me I would never marry, I said at least nobody could ever say of me that I had flattened the family dog into a pancake."

Garini blinked. "Had he done that?"

Carlina smiled. "He claimed it was a mistake. You see, we were at a garden party in Fiesole, in the villa where Angela and Marco now live, and Grandpa started to rock on the old swing they had for the kids. He was never very sportive, but that day, he wanted to impress us, so he jumped from the swing." She giggled. "Unfortunately, Alberta's old dachshund chose just that moment to waddle past the swing, and Grandpa landed on top of the dog."

"No."

Carlina grinned. "Yes. Alberta threatened to kill him and--" She froze. "She didn't mean it, of course."

"Of course." His voice didn't betray the slightest feeling.

"The dog survived and lived a healthy, happy life for ages." Carlina snapped. "It happened eight years ago, maybe more. It's an old, old story, and completely unimportant."

He looked at her in a way that made her feel he saw every dark corner of her mind. "Who was the closest to your grandfather?"

Carlina put her head to one side as she considered. "Next to Uncle Teo? Me, I guess. I often dropped in when I came home from Temptation, and we had a cup of tea together."

"And a bit of cat food."

"No, a peppermint drop." Then she caught herself. "Is being close to him another proof that I killed him?"

He didn't twitch a muscle. "Ninety-eight percent of all murders are done within the closest family circles."

"That's what I thought you would say." Her voice sounded bitter.

He smiled.

Carlina blinked. "How can you smile now?"

"Shouldn't I?" The smile still sat in one corner of his mouth.

"No."

He lifted his eyebrows. "Why not?"

"It's not in character."

The smile fled. "I see."

In front of the locked door, somebody passed with heavy steps.

Then silence, so thick, it made breathing difficult.

"Who killed your grandfather?" His blank face was back in place.

Carlina shook her head. "I have no idea."

"Come on," he said. "Think. You know your family best. You know it's not right to kill a man. You say you loved your grandfather. He did not deserve to be silenced like that. Think." He bent forward. "Who could have done it? Don't tell me everybody loved him to bits."

Carlina swallowed. "Of course not. I'm not saying they're all angels." A fleeting smile. "They aren't." She looked up. "But murder? I can't picture any of them doing it." Her mouth twisted. "At night, when I can't sleep, I think about it. All the time. But it's impossible. I keep hoping that maybe it was a mistake altogether."

"Your grandfather wasn't on medication. He can't have taken it by mistake."

"I know."

"Once again, *signorina* Ashley, think. Who could have done it? You must be able to come up with something."

Carlina swallowed. Images swirled through her head. Emma's face, contorted with fury. Her mother, refusing to go into details about her past. Uncle Teo, inscrutable. She pushed them all away. "I can't!" Her voice was flat. "I have no idea who killed him."

He nodded with a slow movement, as if he was thinking about her answer. Then he got up. "Thank you."

"It was a pleasure." Her voice dripped with irony.

He smiled again, a knowing smile, a smile that told her he had caught the irony and found it amusing.

What a strange man.

He pulled a card from the pocket of his jacket and held it out to her. "If you ever think of something else, something that might help us, call me, no matter what time."

She took it and stuffed it into her handbag. "Right. You don't need to take me back. I'll walk."

He nodded and held the door open for her. "All right."

His quick agreement irked her. Carlina gave him a nod and walked past him. *I hope he saw it was a regal nod.* Her knees felt like jelly. *What on earth will happen next?*

Chapter 10

Stefano watched her walk down the corridor and suppressed a sigh.

Her curls were ruffled, her back straight and unforgiving. She left the building without a backward glance.

She's angry at me. No wonder.

"*Signor* Garini?" The voice of his boss startled him.

Stefano looked over his shoulder. "Yes?"

Signor Cervi poked his head out of the office at the end of the corridor. "Would you come to my office for a minute?"

Now what does he want? "Sure."

His boss held the door open for him and closed it as soon as he was inside. He indicated one of the leather chairs around the mahogany meeting table. "Sit down."

"Thank you." The office smelled of flowers. A vase with yellow roses sat in the center of the table.

"Wasn't that one of the Mantoni girls?"

"Yes."

His boss lifted his eyebrows. "You're about to arrest someone?"

Stefano shook his head. "No. I just wanted to scare her."

Cervi leaned back and linked his hands in front of his stomach. "Did it work?"

"Not at all."

Cervi nodded in thought. "How is the case proceeding?"

Stefano's mouth twisted. "Do you want the long or the short version?"

His boss glanced at his watch. "The short."

Stefano thought a moment, then he said, "I have a thousand leads, and one is stronger than all the others."

"But that's good."

Stefano shook his head. "I have a feeling it's all wrong. The facts speak against her, but--" He broke off.

"But?"

"My instinct tells me she hasn't done it."

Cervi looked at him from underneath his eyebrows. "Instinct is not to be underestimated. Tell me about the things that speak for her."

Her eyes. Stefano swallowed. "The whole family has an agenda."

Cervi shrugged. "Suspects usually do."

Stefano shook his head. "She doesn't. Oh, she lied to me and all, but she's the only one who was really fond of the victim. She's also fond of all the other family members, so much so that she refuses to throw a bad light on them."

Cervi moved in his chair so the black leather made a squeaking sound. "Have you tried to make her speak?"

"That's why I asked her to come here." Stefano sighed. "I scared her so much, she expected to be arrested immediately." *It made me feel like shit.* He remembered the way she had swallowed her tears. For one crazy instant, he had wanted to pull her into his arms. *Get a grip on yourself, Stefano!*

"I hope you didn't exaggerate."

"No." *I had to force myself to say every sentence.* "When I had her where I wanted her, I invited her to tell me who else could be a suspect."

Cervi bent forward with another squeak of the leather chair. "And?"

"Nothing." Stefano's voice sounded bitter. "The rest of the family was so creative when it came to pointing out motives for murder that I hardly know where to start. But she didn't say a word."

"Is she too naive?"

Stefano almost laughed. "No way. She knows all their faults." His voice turned even bitterer. "She finds them amusing."

"A woman with integrity, then."

"Yes."

Cervi looked at his hands. "I got a call from the mayor of Florence today."

Oh, no.

"It seems Nicolò Alfredo Mantoni had a few connections in certain circles. The mayor wishes to be informed regularly about the case."

Stefano clenched his teeth. "I'll send you an update every two days, if you wish. Your son is busy right now writing up our notes."

"That's good." Cervi nodded. "We need to make sure that the mayor is happy with our work." His eyes narrowed. "I think you understand."

You mean we depend on his support if we want to stay in our jobs. Stefano suppressed a sigh. "Yes."

"Fine." *Signor* Cervi stood up. "Thank you for your report." He picked up a gold fountain pen from his desk and placed it into his jacket. "Oh, by the way, is everything all right with Piedro?"

Stefano bent down to redo his shoelace. "His motor bike broke down."

"Yes, he told me."

A knock came on the door, then the receptionist Gloria poked in her head. "Your visitor has arrived, *signor* Cervi." She winked at Stefano. "Ciao, Stefano."

"Ciao, Gloria." *You came just in time.* Stefano straightened and nodded at his boss. "I'll give you the report later this afternoon." At the door, he stopped. "Oh, *signor* Cervi?"

"Yes?"

"How come you know Caroline Ashley?"

"Who?"

"The Mantoni I just interviewed."

Cervi grinned. "My wife likes gifts from her store."

II

Carlina walked straight through a flock of doves without seeing them. She held her back so stiffly it hurt, clenched her fists and marched on with grim determination, but her eyes still smarted with tears. *What an idiot I am. What an absolute idiot. He played me. He pushes me around as if I'm a stupid field mouse.* She crossed the antique market ignoring the gilt mirror frames and elaborate porcelain bowls and plunged into a narrow street beyond. *I can't avoid running into his traps, even if I see them coming.* She swerved from the sidewalk to make room for a black poodle sniffing at a house entrance. *I should never have mentioned the story about the dog. I should never have mentioned mamma.* She bit her lip. A metallic taste of blood spread in her mouth. *Great. How stupid are you, Carlina? And worst of all, why do you melt the instant he smiles? He uses his smiles as part of the interrogating technique.* She shook her head and marched on, her feet hammering the cobbled street. *What if he arrests me tomorrow? I need to do something to save Temptation. Elena can't cope on her own.* A three-wheeled pasta delivery van came toward her. Carlina pressed herself into a house entrance until it had passed with two centimeters to spare on both sides. In her mind, she went through the possible stand-ins. Benedetta? She had to work. Annalisa? She was busy at university. Carlina swallowed. *I have to ask mamma. She will fall asleep in the middle of the day, resting her head happily on her cushion right on top of the cash counter, and the tourists will rob Temptation empty without the slightest hitch.* She shuddered. *Oh, God.*

III

Angela's heels clicked on the marble floor as she led the *commissario* to the sitting room. "I'm afraid Marco is not at home right now, *commissario*. You'd think that as a doctor new in town, it would take some time to establish a reputation, but he is always booked out."

"That's no problem. I can first talk to you." Garini followed her into the room. The sunlight poured through the high windows and played on the deep red Persian carpet which covered the largest part of the floor. Thick curtains in a matching red framed the windows. Garini lifted his eyebrows. *What a beautiful and expensive room.*

"Please have a seat." Angela gestured at the antique sofa with a red-gold brocade seat and matching cushions.

Garini sat down and looked at the elegant woman in front of him. "I have come to talk to you about your grandfather."

Angela took out a white lace handkerchief and touched it to her large eyes. "Poor grandpa."

"Before we start, I would like to ask for your permission to record our conversation." Garini switched on the recorder and placed it on the marble table in front of him.

"Of course you can record my statement." Angela pressed the lace to her lips. "I want to do everything I can to catch this ruthless murderer."

She thinks she's in a movie. "Quite." Garini focused on her. "Your grandfather had fallen into a habit of telling the so-called bad past stories."

Angela gave a pretty smile. "He always had these unusual ideas, the dear."

The dear, my foot. "Please tell me what he said about your past."

Angela sighed. "I have to explain a bit more about our family to make you understand. My mother is his eldest daughter, and she always was the apple of his eye."

"Your mother's name is Alberta, is that correct?"

"Yes." Another pretty smile. "I don't think you've met her."

"No." *She's the one whose dachshund was flattened like a pancake.*

"Why do you smile?"

"Oh, it's nothing." Stefano concentrated on straightening his face. "Please continue."

"My mother married a very rich man, but he died early. It was so tragic." Angela sighed and leaned against the brocade cushion, playing with the string of pearls around her neck. "She mourned him for many years, but ten years later, she found another man worthy of her love."

I'm going to be sick in a minute.

"My father Clement is a professor at the Università degli Studi di Firenze. He's a wonderful man." She sighed.

"Please continue, *signora* Mantoni-Canderini." *As you've now made it clear how important you are.*

"Well, I am just like my mother and waited for many years for the right man."

He couldn't resist. "Just like your cousin Carlina." The nickname slipped out before he could stop it.

Angela sat up straight. "Who? I don't think you can compare me to Caroline."

No, indeed.

"When I met my Marco during the Christmas party at the golf course, I knew I had met the man of my life."

Congratulations.

"Do you know the Poggio dei Medici Golf and Country Club, *commissario*?"

"No."

Angela straightened her cashmere sweater. "It's a most exclusive place, and oh, the memories." She sighed. "It was a whirlwind romance. Six months later, we were married."

"You wanted to tell me about the bad past story, *signora* Mantoni-Canderini."

"I am coming to that, *commissario*." Angela looked at him through her lashes. "My grandfather mistrusted my choice, just because Marco is from Rome and not from Tuscany." She smiled. "I'm afraid the old dear wasn't much of a cosmopolitan. He would have preferred it if I had married the local cook."

"Not the garbage man?"

She blinked. "I beg your pardon?"

She brings out the worst in me. "Nothing. I'm sorry I interrupted you. Please go on."

Her look showed she found him odd. "My Marco is not only good-looking. He's also from a rich family and started less than a year ago to work as a general practitioner here in Florence." A self-satisfied smile played around her lips. "No wonder everybody thought it was too good to be true." She patted her long hair. "I myself often can't believe it."

"And the bad past story, *signora* Mantoni-Canderini?"

"But I am telling you, *commissario*." Her dark eyes narrowed. "My grandfather thought it couldn't be true. He was disgruntled because I had rejected the cook, so he made up a tale that I had blackmailed Marco into our marriage." She trilled a laugh. "It was a great joke among the family."

"Did he mention what you used to blackmail him?"

She opened her eyes wide. "But *commissario*! I've just explained everything to you; how can you ask such a stupid question? He made it all up, so of course he gave no details."

"I see. How about the other stories? Do you believe any of them were true?"

Angela patted her hair again. "I seriously don't recall them. You know, my grandfather was becoming a bit . . . shall we say odd? I didn't pay that much attention."

Garini nodded and got up. "Thank you for your time."

"You will want to talk to Marco too." Angela followed him to the door. "But I don't know when he'll be back. He works so hard, the poor darling."

"That's fine. I can always go and see him at his work."

Angela stretched out her hand in a gesture that came straight from a Verdi opera. "Oh, but please don't mention our conversation to him. He has no idea what Grandfather said, and he told me just yesterday that he even liked him." For an instant, she looked as if she couldn't understand this aberration of her husband. "I wouldn't want to disillusion him for the world."

IV

"And what's this?" Fabbiola stood in front of the cash register of Temptation and squinted at the golden display next to her. It was formed like a twisted horn that reached up to her hips, and it had an elegant engraving at the side that said 'special offers'. A puzzled expression crossed Fabbiola's face as she lifted one light-blue piece of lace up for closer inspection.

The sun glimpsed through the open door of Temptation and lured them outside with its golden light. Carlina longed to follow its siren call. Instead, she suppressed a sigh and continued training her mother. "It's a thong, *mamma*."

Fabbiola lifted one eyebrow. "You can't even use it as a handkerchief. Too many holes." She peered at the price Carlina had written with a gold pen onto the tag. "What's that? You want nine Euros for a bit of lace?" She turned to her daughter. "I have to say, Carlina, I had no idea what ridiculous prices you charge. Don't you think that's robbery?"

Carlina set her teeth. "You can ask *signora* Barberini if her rent is robbery, then talk to me about my prices."

"Ah." Fabbiola nodded. "I can imagine how ridiculous her rents are. She has never been a generous woman."

Carlina shrugged. "We're on Via Tournabuoni, *mamma*. *Signora* Barberini charges a normal rent for one of the top locations in Florence. She may not be generous, but she's fair. I like her."

Fabbiola sniffed and glanced at a man standing in front of the window. His nervous gaze darted over the bras on display, and he bit his lips as if working up the courage to come inside. "Do you ever have men as customers?"

Carlina nodded. "I do. Not as many as women, but yes."

Fabbiola shook her head from left to right. "Your father would have died of mortification if he had ever set a foot inside a lingerie store."

A twinge went through Carlina. *Don't answer.* She turned away and fluffed up the thongs in the golden horn display, then went to the right where a rose bra with matching slips was displayed. "You can see I have drawers for all bra sizes underneath each model shown. It always starts with the smallest size on the left hand side in the top drawer and ends with the biggest size." She knelt and pulled out a drawer on smooth hinges. The rose colored model above appeared, each bra folded together. The symmetry of the display never failed to please Carlina. "Look here, *mamma*. When you follow that order, it's easy to find everything, and we don't have to clutter up the small storage room in the back. The slips are no problem because there are just three sizes, but the bras would otherwise fill rooms." She couldn't disguise the pride in her voice. It had taken ages to get the drawer system working properly because the first carpenter had not worked with precision and it had been a tug-of-war to make the mechanism function, but now, it was a gem and Carlina enjoyed the soft feeling of the drawers gliding in and out without a hitch.

Fabbiola looked around. "The store really is tiny, isn't it?"

Carlina felt like a mother with a child too small for its age. She wanted to fling her arms around Temptation and tell everybody to go to hell.

"Yes." Carlina clenched her teeth. "Do you want to comment on anything else? So far," she ticked each argument off her fingers, "you said I charge too much, you said Temptation is too small, and you said dad would have been mortified if he had seen my store." Her voice rose. "I don't believe that for one moment! I'm an independent woman. I earn my own money, and it gives me a comfortable living. Underwear is nothing reprehensible; it's necessary." She glowered at her mother. "I think it was a bad idea to ask you to tend my store. You have no idea how to run my business."

Fabbiola stared at her daughter with wide open eyes. Her mouth slack, she went to the cash counter, where she had placed her cushion. "You really are touchy, Caroline Arabella. I've offered to help, but if you think I'm not good enough, that's no problem at all." She picked up the cushion and went to the door. "No problem at all," she repeated. Her voice floated through the door, then she was gone.

Carlina covered her face with her hands and burst into tears.

When she finally suppressed a hiccup and wiped her eyes, she saw Garini standing in front of her.

"*Madonna*." She closed her eyes. "I'm having apparitions." She averted her gaze and hunted through the pockets of her jeans for a handkerchief.

"It's not an apparition," he said.

"And it speaks." Carlina suppressed another hiccup and darted a glance from the corner of her eyes. He was still there. *Oh, God.*

He held out a paper tissue. "This what you're looking for?"

She took it. "Thanks." She wiped her eyes with rigorous care in the hope that she wouldn't smear mascara up to her eyebrows, then blew her nose.

Garini watched her like a man who had all the time in the world, his stance relaxed, his hands in the pockets of his jeans.

Carlina swallowed. "Is this store tiny?"

"Yes." He spoke without hesitation.

Of course it is. "Is it expensive?"

"Yes." Again, he didn't hesitate.

His answer was right, and it enraged her. She flashed an angry glance at him. "Do you never make compromises?"

"Rarely."

She knew she should stop right now, but her emotions took a firm hold of her saner instincts and roller-coasted ahead. "Are you never perturbed by anything?" She flung it out like a challenge.

A small smile appeared in the corner of his mouth. "I am. All the time."

She threw him a dark glance. "It doesn't show."

"It's not supposed to."

There. Now he put me into my place. Carlina swallowed. "Anything else you want? I've already told you all the family secrets."

He was silent.

Their eyes locked.

"Why did you cry?" His voice sounded soft.

She pressed her lips together. "Do you think my father would have been mortified that I own a lingerie store?"

He lifted his eyebrows. "Not unless he was bigoted."

She turned away and adjusted a hanger that was already hanging straight. "He wasn't."

"Then he would have been proud of you."

Carlina swiveled back to him. "What? Why?"

"You're loyal, hardworking, successful." He said it without any apparent emotion. "What parent wouldn't be proud?"

She narrowed her eyes. "I don't need your irony."

His face closed.

Carlina felt it like a kick in the stomach. What if he had been serious? *Don't forget he's still the commissario, trying to find a killer.* "What do you want?" Carlina folded her arms in front of her chest. "You came here for a reason, didn't you?"

He shrugged. "I was on my way home, and I--"

She narrowed her eyes. "Where is home?"

"I live next to the Hotel Porta Rossa." He answered her question with a smile, as if he understood why she sounded belligerent and found it funny.

"I see." *It's close enough to make sense.*

"You forgot something at the police station today, and I thought you would need it." He moved to the side so she could see the cash register. Her helmet with the leopard print sat on top as if it belonged there. "You didn't hear me when I came in," he added.

How embarrassing. It wasn't like her not to notice people walking into her store. "It seems you have a knack of moving without making a sound."

He smiled. "I have that reputation, yes."

"Thanks for bringing the helmet." She nodded in what she hoped was a dismissive way. "Good-bye, then."

He inclined his head. "We'll see each other again."

No doubt. Carlina wondered if it had been a promise or a threat.

Chapter 11

"Carlina!" Lilly ran into Temptation and hugged her aunt.

Carlina lifted her niece and buried her face in Lilly's fragrant hair. "It's good to see you, cara."

Lilly squirmed. "You're squashing me!"

"Oops, sorry." Carlina put Lilly back onto her feet. "Where is your *mamma*?"

"She's still next door, but she said I could already go ahead to Temptation." Lilly's gaze fixed on a red bra with little flowers in white. "Oh, Carlina, this is so pretty!" She stood on tiptoe and took it off the hanger, then placed it across her chest and paraded around the store. "Does it look nice?"

Carlina grinned. "Very."

"Can I have one?" Lilly smiled at her aunt in an ingratiating way that had gotten her almost everything she wanted in the past.

Her aunt shook her head. "You're not big enough yet, Lilly."

Lilly pouted. "Yesterday, I looked at the mirror, and I think--" She gave her aunt a mischievous look, "I really think my breasts are growing."

Carlina suppressed a smile. "Your mother would say I'm crazy if I start to give bras to seven-year-olds." She took the bra and placed it back onto the hanger. "You don't need a bra yet."

"What's this?" Gabriella came into the store, loaded with glossy shopping bags. "Is she trying to convince you she needs a bra?" Her brown curls looked as if she had been through a storm.

"Yes." Carlina smiled at her niece. "But I said it's too early."

Gabriella shook her head and dropped the bags onto the low wooden seat in front of the cash register.

Carlina smiled. The wooden seat had been an addition last week, for exhausted husbands and women carrying too much to shop in comfort. She was glad it found instinctive acceptance.

Gabriella sighed. "I've told Lilly a million times it's too early, but she keeps talking about bras." She eyed her sister. "Do you really own one with leopard fur?"

Carlina laughed. "I do." She turned to Lilly. "That was supposed to be our secret!"

Lilly had the grace to look ashamed. "I didn't mean to say it."

Gabriella grinned. "It slipped out while we were at the zoo. Lilly said the leopard looked just like your bra. At first, I thought she had mixed up something."

Carlina leaned against the cash register. "Why are you here, in the middle of the week?"

Gabriella lifted her eyebrows. "Don't tell me you forgot the birthday."

"Whose . . . ?" Carlina slapped her head with her flat hand. "Oh, no. Benedetta! I had such a dreadful day, it totally slipped my mind." *I don't feel like another birthday party tonight. I want to crawl into my bed and hide.*

Her niece looked at her. "Why did you have a dreadful day, Carlina?"

Carlina waved a hand. "Oh, many things." She checked her wristwatch. "You know what, I think I can close up and come with you."

Lilly clapped her hands. "Can I ride with you on the Vespa?"

"You don't have your helmet, love."

Lilly's face fell.

Carlina bent forward. "The next time you come to stay with me, you'll bring your helmet, and then I'll take you, okay?"

"That's a good idea," Gabriella said. "I wanted to ask you anyway."

"Ask me what?" Carlina took out the cash and started to count it. It had been a meager day. Well, no wonder, distracted as she had been most of the time.

"I have to attend a conference next weekend and wanted to ask if you can take Lilly for two nights."

Carlina stopped counting. "I don't think that's a good idea, Gabriella."

Lilly's face twisted. "Why not? Don't you like me anymore?"

"Of course I do!" Carlina smoothed Lilly's curls. "But I'm really very busy at the store and--"

"It's only Sunday to Tuesday," Gabriella said. "The store isn't open on Sundays, and Monday, Lilly will be at school."

"Where is Bernando?" Carlina grabbed at straws.

"Bernando promised his mother to drive her to a friend's house in Pisa on Sunday night. She will go on vacation for one week on Monday morning." Gabriella said.

"Yes, and her plane leaves soooo early." Lilly started to hop around the store on one leg.

Carlina turned her back to Lilly and mouthed a desperate "No" at her sister.

Gabriella frowned. "What's up?"

"I can't do it." Carlina said under her voice.

"Why not?"

Carlina glanced at Lilly who had hopped to the end of the store but was still well within hearing. She whispered, "I'm afraid Garini will arrest me."

"The *commissario* will arrest you?" Gabriella clapped her hand in front of her mouth.

Lilly pivoted around, her eyes too big for her small face. "You'll be arrested, Carlina?"

Damn. "I don't know." Carlina sighed. "He took me to the police station today and put me through an awful interview."

"Did he say he would arrest you?" Gabriella stared at her.

"No." Carlina shook her head. "But he said I shouldn't leave town without telling him."

"Oh, *Madonna.*"

Lilly's anxious gaze swiveled from her mother to her aunt. "Why does he want to arrest you, Carlina? Did you do something wrong?"

"No."

"Then why?" Gabriella frowned.

"He . . . " Carlina forced herself to say the words, but she said them in English so Lilly wouldn't understand. "He thinks I killed grandpa."

"But that's ridiculous!" Gabriella wiped the words away. "I'm sure you got him wrong."

Fat chance. Carlina could still feel his cool gaze, dissecting her.

Lilly tugged at Carlina's blouse. "What did you say, Carlina?"

"It doesn't matter." Gabriella picked up Lilly's rucksack. "If you can't do it, then *mamma* will have to stand in."

"But it's more fun with Carlina than with grandma!" Lilly pouted.

Gabriella gave her a soothing smile. "Well, if Carlina isn't arrested, she can still have you."

"You're mighty cool about it," Carlina said.

"I think it's utter nonsense." Gabriella shook her head so hard, her brown curls bounced. She added in English. "Nobody who knows you would ever think you killed grandpa."

"Then who did?" Carlina lowered her voice even though she answered in the same language. "Garini believes it's someone from the family."

Gabriella shook her head. "No way. He's totally wrong."

Carlina regarded her sister. *If only I could share your conviction.*

II

"And then she jumped onto the sofa, and all the fish landed on top of her." As Carlina finished her story, everybody laughed. Carlina looked at the smiling faces around her. Maybe it was the familiar routine of celebrating together, maybe it was the rich glass of Gallo Nero Chianti wine, but she felt much better tonight. It was good she had decided to come after all.

Benedetta's kitchen was crammed full with guests for the birthday party, sitting all around the big table. Everybody from the house was there, plus Gabriella, Bernando, and Lilly, Angela and Marco, Uncle Ugo and Alberta, and even their neighbor Electra.

Benedetta placed a new cake onto the table and took her seat. "What fell on top of her? Fish?"

"Yes, you know the mobile I bought on vacation in Venezuela years ago, the one with the wooden fish, painted red and white? They're all fixed onto a black branch with nylon strings."

Benedetta frowned. "I don't know it."

"Yes, you do." Carlina smiled. "It hangs on a rafter above the sofa in the living room."

"Oh, that one." Benedetta nodded. "But why did it fall off?"

"Because, whenever Lilly comes to stay with me, she jumps into bed, which happens to be my sofa."

"She always jumps into bed," Gabriella emphasized the second word, "not only when she stays with you."

Lilly giggled.

"Anyway, when she jumped onto the sofa the first time she stayed with me," Carlina said, "the sofa moved against the wall with a bang, and the rafter shook so hard that the nail dropped out, and the whole thing fell onto Lilly's back." Carlina grinned. "We couldn't stop laughing."

Uncle Teo frowned. "I can't believe this little girl shakes the walls so hard that nails fall out." He gently pulled Lilly's curls.

"Oh, it doesn't take much to make that nail come down," Carlina said. "For some reason, it never really holds, but I've always been too lazy to get a larger one, so I simply push it back in whenever it has fallen out."

Ernesto bent forward and took a piece of cake. "Does it fall very often?"

Carlina grinned. "Only whenever Lilly jumps into bed. It's a little ritual by now." She winked at Lilly. "Lilly says she can't sleep anymore when the fish haven't kissed her good-night on the back."

"You can be glad it's only a small mobile." Fabbiola lifted her glass of wine. "Otherwise, it could have hurt her."

"Oh, *mamma*, stop seeing dangers for your grandchild everywhere." Gabriella clinked her glass against Fabbiola's. "She's leading a charmed life. Nothing can hurt her."

Carlina felt a cold shiver run along her spine. *I hope the gods don't listen.* But the moment of fear passed, and as the evening wore on, she felt the dark worries slip from her shoulders. *I'm happy. I'm exactly where I want to be.* She spread a creamy bit of goat's cheese with sweet fig filling onto a toasted crust of white bread and popped it into her mouth. *Delicious.* The babble of voices from her family surrounded her, smiling faces everywhere. Her mother stood with Marco in a corner, their heads together. Carlina suppressed a grin. Fabbiola always had a soft spot for a good-looking man. Marco looked a bit pale. Probably he worked too much. Lilly ran to her grandmother and jumped into Fabbiola's arms with so much momentum, Fabbiola almost lost her balance. They all laughed. Carlina lifted her glass and took another sip of wine. The combination of cheese and wine was a match made in heaven. *Savor the moment. This is the essence of life, little sparks of happiness that make life worthwhile.*

Angela took the empty chair next to Carlina and crossed her elegant legs. "What's this I hear about you and the *commissario*?"

Carlina frowned. *Of course. Just as I have forgotten the commissario and everything connected with him, Angela has to haul me right back to reality.* She didn't reply, instead, she picked up the next piece of bread and eyed it. *Maybe I should not eat it until she's gone. She'll destroy the taste.*

"Are you playing deaf, Caroline?"

"No." Carlina shrugged. "I just don't have to say anything."

"So it's not true that the *commissario* is going all dove-eyed over you?"

Carlina glanced at her beautiful cousin. "Dove-eyed? The *commissario*? You mixed up birds. You mean a hawk."

Angela laughed. "Oh, come on. I know what a man looks like when he's interested. It showed right from the first time he met you."

"And I know when my cousin is trying to make me admit feelings I don't have."

Angela opened her beautiful eyes wide. "You don't like him?"

Carlina sighed. "If the way he looks at me is an indication that he likes me, then I never want to meet his gaze when he doesn't."

III

"Hi, Carlina. It's me, Rosanna."

"Rosanna!" Carlina put her phone on loudspeaker and dropped into her armchair. Rosanna owned the flower shop at the bottom of Piazza di San Firenze. They had been friends ever since school, and the friendship had intensified when they both started up their own retail stores. She placed the phone on her lap and stretched. "I've just come in."

"I know. I've been trying to reach you for hours, and you've switched off your cell phone."

"It ran out of power." Carlina wriggled her feet. They ached from standing too much. "Why do you need me so urgently? Is anything the matter?"

"Well, you remember your order for one basket of rose petals, to decorate Emma's apartment upon her return from the honeymoon?"

Carlina shot up. "Oh, no. Don't tell me it's the fifteenth today?"

"It is." Rosanna chuckled. "It's not like you to be forgetful. What rattled you?"

"Oh, it's a long story." Carlina ran to the kitchen to find the shoes she had dropped somewhere when she had come in. "What's the time?"

"Half past seven."

"Damn." Carlina found her first sneaker and slipped into it. "Emma landed at the airport at seven. Thank you so much for calling! Where are you? Are you still at your store? Do you have the rose petals with you?"

"Too many questions at once," Rosanna said. "I'm at home, but I took the basket with me, so you can come and collect it."

"You're fantastic!" Carlina found her second sneaker and put it on. "I'll be with you in two seconds."

She raced her Vespa across the Arno via Ponte Vecchio to Rosanna's apartment on Piazza Santo Spirito, conscious of an uneasy feeling that it wouldn't help her case if Garini saw her now, rushing through town way above the speed limit, the motor of her Vespa roaring like an angry lion, the sound magnified by being thrown back from the ancient walls.

A quarter of an hour later, she arrived out of breath on the landing to Emma's door and opened it with her key. The white tiles in the entrance area were too clinical for her taste, but at least they wouldn't stain if she left a trail of rose petals that led straight to the bedroom. Carlina hummed to herself as she sprinkled the fragrant rose petals on the floor. She knew Emma would be delighted. Hopefully Lucio would feel the same.

She stopped the trail of rose petals at the door to the bedroom and eyed the white carpet with a frown. Maybe she shouldn't risk it. Suppose someone stepped on a rose petal by mistake. Emma would throw a fit if her carpet ended up with red rose stains. No, she had a better idea. She dropped the basket, ran upstairs to her apartment and retrieved a pile of white saucers from the cupboard. Back in Emma's bedroom, she placed the saucers in a long row and put four rose petals on each. Carlina smiled at the uninterrupted trail of roses from the door to the bed. Perfect.

Then she checked the basket. Rosanna had given her more than enough. Maybe she could also cover the bed. Now that would look nice. But the pristine white bed cover didn't look as if it would be happy about crushed rose petals either. Carlina frowned. Then she remembered the plastic sheets Emma had put on the floor when her bathroom had been redone. She went to the kitchen and rummaged underneath the sink. Yes. Trust Emma to keep that roll of plastic. With her treasure under her arm, she went back to the bedroom and checked the alarm clock next to the bed. *I'd better hurry. They could arrive any minute now.* Carlina placed several sheets of plastic next to each other and sprinkled the rose petals on top. It looked great. She was just emptying the last rose petals from the basket when she heard a key in the lock of the apartment door.

Carlina jumped. *Damn.* She didn't want Emma to see her; it was supposed to be an anonymous surprise. Her eyes darted through the room. Maybe she could hide somewhere and slip out later, when they went downstairs again to collect their suitcases. Emma never traveled with less than four suitcases and hated to leave them on the curb as one had been stolen years ago.

Carlina's gaze fell on the built-in wardrobe with the large mirror. *That's it.* She threw the basket underneath the bed, dived into the wardrobe, and pulled the door shut behind her the very instant Emma said, "Oh, look at this! How sweet . . ."

Garini said, "Would you please step with me into the living room, *signora* Mantoni-Casanuova?"

Carlina stiffened. Garini? What was he doing here? Where was Lucio? Her slight movement made the door crack open and a thin sliver of light fell into the wardrobe. *Darn. It's too tight in here. If Garini finds me now, he'll cart me straight off to the next loony bin.* Carlina curled into a ball below Emma's clothes and pulled the door shut from the inside with her fingernails. *Better.*

"In a minute, *commissario*. I first want to check out the trail of roses. You have to admit it's irresistible." Emma's voice came closer.

Carlina suppressed a smile. Trust Emma not to let herself be intimidated by Garini. Their voices became louder now. She heard the door open, then they stood right next to her.

Emma clapped her hands together. "How pretty!"

"Quite." Garini sounded impatient. "However, I would appreciate if you could answer my questions now without any further delay."

"Let me just go upstairs and say hello to Carlina." Emma sounded a bit nervous.

"I'm afraid you can't do that." Garini said.

Carlina pictured him leaning against the wall, his hands in his pockets. No doubt he had already asked her if he could record the conversation.

"When did you last see your grandfather alive?" Garini asked.

"Alive? What do you mean?"

Carlina had to hand it to Emma. The astonishment in her voice sounded genuine.

"Your grandfather Nicolò Mantoni died on your wedding day, Mrs. Mantoni-Casanuova." Garini's voice seemed gentle.

Carlina winced. She knew the voice was misleading. He was coiled up like a panther, ready to pounce.

"No! I had no idea!"

Maybe Emma overdid it a bit. Was she going to pretend to cry? Carlina tried to shift her weight without making a sound. Her left leg was falling asleep.

"Could you please answer my question?" Garini said.

"I'd like to wait until Lucio comes." Emma stood right in front of the wardrobe now. "His plane must have landed by now." She sighed. "I really had no idea that he would take that article about the royal family so much to heart. Though it's quite flattering that he doesn't want me to die if his plane crashes, but it's also a bit complicated."

Carlina didn't trust her ears. Lucio had decided he couldn't share the same flight with his wife because it was too risky? She suppressed a giggle. The *commissario* wouldn't find it comforting to discover another member of the Mantoni family with a strange habit. She shook her head. It wasn't clever of Emma to talk about her husband's flying policies right now. She should have pretended to be a bit more astonished about Nico's death, should have asked some questions. *Damn.* The *commissario* would have noticed her mistake too. He was playing her.

"We can't wait for your husband, I'm afraid." The *commissario*'s voice didn't sound as if he regretted it. "I need to talk to you alone."

Emma sighed. "What do you want to know, *commissario*?"

From Emma's voice, Carlina knew her cousin now pulled a pretty mouth and fluttered her eyelashes at him. *Don't overdo it, Emma. This guy is made of granite.*

"When did you last see your grandfather alive?" The *commissario* repeated his question as if he was speaking to a child.

"When Carlina and I asked him to join us for the wedding."

"What did he say?"

Carlina cringed. How he led her on.

"He said he didn't feel like going because he could feel bad vibes. My grandfather sometimes felt vibes that prevented him from doing things, you see, and he--"

"I know about that," Garini interrupted. "Did he say anything else? Did he mention any pain?"

"No. He . . . he felt fine." Emma's voice faltered.

"Absolutely fine?" Garini insisted.

"Well, he . . . he said he felt a bit stiff."

Emma! Carlina clasped her hand over her mouth to stifle a giggle.

"Stiff? How do you mean, stiff?" No trace of laughter crept into Garini's voice.

"Well, sort of like a wooden board." Emma was in full fairytale mode now. "He said he had a bit of a problem with his muscles."

Carlina gasped for breath without making a sound. Her left leg was numb from top to toe. She clutched at a long dress on a hanger to stop herself from toppling forward.

"Did you touch your grandfather when you saw him the last time?"

"Oh, no!" Emma sounded revolted.

"Then how did you know he felt like a wooden board?"

"Because he said so!" Emma's voice moved away. "I really don't understand these nonsensical questions."

"One moment, please." The *commissario*'s voice was hard. "Didn't you worry about his illness? Why didn't you drive him to a doctor?"

Carlina held her breath. What would Emma say now?

"We didn't think it was serious." Emma seemed upset.

"Not serious? When he had claimed he felt stiff like a wooden board? It sounds pretty serious to me."

"We knew it wasn't serious." Emma gained confidence.

"How could you know?"

Emma took a deep breath. "Because grandpa was dabbling with self-hypnosis."

"What?" The *commissario* almost shouted the word.

Carlina hugged her knees and hid her face, but she couldn't suppress her muffled laughter. Her whole body started to shake. The door of the wardrobe trembled with every suppressed giggle, but she couldn't stop herself.

"Everybody in the family knew grandpa was trying new methods of self-hypnosis. He was becoming quite professional at it." Emma's brand-new explanation was delivered in a nonchalant tone. "We assumed he went a bit over the top this time."

That did it. Carlina lost her balance, toppled forward and fell out of the wardrobe, right in front of Garini's feet. She laughed so hard, her breath came in shallow gasps. Her eyes streamed, and she tried to gain control, but she couldn't stop.

"Carlina!" Emma, tanned and well-groomed as always, started forward. "What are you doing in my wardrobe?"

"Who is that man?" Lucio's voice came from the door. "Emma! What are you doing with this man in our bedroom?"

Carlina lifted her head, but she couldn't see Lucio as she was still sitting on the floor, hidden behind the bed.

Garini took a step forward. "I can explain--"

"I don't want you to explain!" Lucio interrupted him, his voice fierce, and turned on his wife. "What is going on here? How dare you cheat on me the very day our honeymoon is over? How--"

"Lucio!" Emma darted to his side and shook his arm. "This man is a *commissario*!"

"I don't care what he is! I want to know what he's doing in my bedroom, all alone with you, all covered with roses!"

Emma threw up her hands. "Oh!" She hissed in her breath. "How can you even start to think I would cheat on you!" She bent forward and stabbed at his chest with her forefinger. "I would never have thought that you have so little trust in me."

"Trust in you?" Lucio shouted so loud, the door of the wardrobe rattled. "How can you talk about trust when I find you with another man in the bedroom, all alone?"

"They're not all alone," Carlina raised herself on her knees and looked over the bed. "I'm here, too."

Lucio's jaw dropped. "Carlina! What are you doing here?"

Carlina got up and brushed off her trousers. "Not what you think," she said. "I suggest you apologize to Emma. This guy," she pointed with her chin at Garini, "is *commissario* Stefano Garini of the homicide department, and he is trying to find out who poisoned grandpa."

Lucio paled. "Poisoned Uncle Nico?"

"What?" Emma's hands flew to her throat. "Grandpa was murdered?"

"Yes."

Emma's eyes were huge. "But . . ."

Carlina put an arm around her cousin's shoulders. "You didn't take off grandpa's socks, and that's why Uncle Teo called the police."

"What?" Emma blinked.

Carlina nodded. "When they came, they not only found that grandpa had been dead too long to have chatted with you about stiff muscles or anything else, but that he had been poisoned with morphine."

"I don't believe this." Lucio shook his head.

"You'd better start," Garini cut in. "That's why I needed to talk to your wife right after her return. I had to hear her story before anybody else could tell her what to say." His eyes narrowed as he glanced at Carlina. "So I asked an officer to bring her to the police station after the plane landed, but she insisted on going home because she didn't want you to worry when you arrived home and found her not here. Stupid enough of me, I agreed to meet her at the apartment, and that's when that trail of roses led us to the bedroom." He gestured at the saucers on the floor.

Lucio held out his arms. "My darling! I've wronged you!"

Emma flung herself at his chest.

The *commissario*'s eyes met Carlina's.

She shook with laughter. "Romantic, eh?"

"Unbelievable," he murmured.

They watched the happy couple for a minute, then Garini said, "Do you wish to alter your statement, Mrs. Mantoni-Casanuova?"

Emma lifted her head. "What?"

"Tell him the truth." Carlina pushed some roses to the side and sat on the bed. The plastic sheet rustled underneath her. "He won't leave you a minute of peace otherwise."

Emma turned to the *commissario*, her husband's arms around her shoulders, and gave him a pretty smile. "My grandfather was dead when we came downstairs to pick him up."

Lucio turned his head and stared at his wife. "What? He was dead? You said he had felt a bad vibe."

Emma shrugged. "Maybe he felt one before his death, but when we came downstairs, he was certainly dead."

"Was he stiff?" Garini asked.

Lucio drew himself up. "I would appreciate if you could pose your questions with more delicacy, *commissario*."

Carlina chuckled, and Garini threw her an exasperated glance.

"It's all right, Lucio," Emma smiled at her husband, then turned back to the *commissario*. "No, he wasn't stiff. We put him to bed, and then I undressed him."

Lucio's mouth dropped open. "Why did you do that?"

Emma caressed his cheek. "I didn't want to leave you waiting at the altar, honey. Imagine what would have happened if I had told the world at large that grandpa had died."

"The flowers would have wilted," Garini said without a trace of emotion.

"What?" Emma frowned.

Carlina smothered a grin. "He means the wedding ceremony would have been canceled."

Lucio blanched at the thought.

"So you see, honey, I had to do it."

"But why did you put him to bed?" Lucio shook his head.

"Because everybody could see him from the kitchen window." Emma's gaze fell on the rose petals. "Oh, Carlina, did you think of the roses? I love them!"

"I did." Carlina shrugged. "Though I was too late. You caught me red-handed." She stopped and blushed. "I mean, I didn't have the time to leave the apartment, but I didn't want to spoil the surprise either, that's why I hid in the wardrobe."

Lucio stared at Carlina. "You hid in our wardrobe?"

"Amazing family, isn't it?" Garini said to no one in particular.

"Absolutely." Emma gave Garini a dazzling smile and turned back to her husband. "But when Garini interviewed me, Carlina started to laugh so hard she fell out of the wardrobe, and then you came."

Lucio opened his mouth and closed it again.

Garini took Carlina's arm and pulled her with him. "Thank you for your statement. I'll have it typed for you to sign tomorrow." He nodded at Lucio. "Have fun with the roses."

Carlina was still laughing when the door closed behind them.

Garini shook his head. "How can you laugh at a time like this?"

"Don't you think it was funny?" Carlina tried to calm down, but another uncontrollable gurgle broke out of her. "Lucio's face . . . gosh, did you see his face?"

He smiled.

"And when Emma said grandpa had dabbled with self-hypnosis until he accidentally killed himself . . . " Carlina held onto the wooden railing so she wouldn't collapse. "I could have shrieked with laughter."

"You did."

"Oh, well." Carlina wiped her eyes. "You have to admit it was ingenious."

"Very." The *commissario* regarded Carlina with an odd expression on his face. "Does he really think his wife needs to be protected?"

Carlina laughed again. She couldn't help it, anything set her off. "Oh, yes. He has no idea she's made of steel, our Emma." She grinned. "He was deceived by the sugarcoated outside. Just like a man." She felt high and giddy after her laughing bout, a bit as if she had drunk too much champagne, though she was stone cold sober. "It's the same with Marco. I don't think he had a clue what his wife was really like when he married Angela."

Garini leaned against the railing. "She's a handful, that one."

"Oh, yes." Carlina took a deep breath. "But beautiful."

He looked at her. "There are many good-looking women in the Mantoni family."

Carlina grinned. "And even more that are crazy. My mother thinks every man who marries into our family should be given a medal for courage or something."

"Does she, though?" The *commissario* smiled.

"Yes." Carlina chuckled. "But don't tell her so. She'll never admit it out loud."

IV

"Is he gone?" Emma poked her head around the door to Carlina's apartment.

Carlina giggled. "Yes. Come in." She hugged her cousin. "You look great! Did you enjoy Africa?"

Emma returned the hug, then dropped onto Carlina's sofa and stretched out her long legs. She picked an invisible speck of dust from her cream colored chinos while she answered. "Africa was wonderful. It felt like a whole different world."

"I can imagine." Carlina went to the kitchen with a wistful sigh. "What on earth made you say this thing about grandpa's self-hypnosis? I thought I would die."

Emma shrugged. "It was a good story. I could tell he wanted to hear something, so I made it up."

Carlina shook her head. "You're amazing."

"Do you think you can make us a cup of espresso?" Emma leaned her back against the cushions and drew both her hands through her long mane. "I'm dying for a cup. And while you do it, tell me what happened here. Is it true grandpa was killed?" Her eyes shone.

"Yes."

"Wow."

I wish she didn't look so pleased. But hadn't they all perked up at the idea of a family murder, that day in grandpa's kitchen? Carlina placed the full espresso machine on the fire. "We destroyed evidence when we moved grandpa, and the *commissario* thinks we're both suspects."

Emma shook her head. "He's really fierce, that one, isn't he?"

"Yes." Carlina leaned against the door frame and crossed her arms in front of her chest.

"Are you afraid of him?"

"Hmm."

Emma laughed. "No, really? Since when have you been afraid of anybody?"

Carlina sighed. "He's ruthless and immune to charm."

"Ha." Emma stretched her arms above her head and yawned. "I don't believe in men who are immune to charm. They are a myth, like Santa Claus."

"Don't underestimate him, Emma." The espresso machine started to gurgle. Carlina turned around and switched off the fire, then poured the black liquid into tiny cups. "When we moved grandpa that day, Emma, did you see anything suspicious? Anything at all?"

"Nothing." Emma replied without hesitation. "Everything was exactly like always. Too boring for words."

Carlina brought the cups to the sofa and placed them on the low side table, then she sat in the armchair with the leopard print rug. "I keep thinking and thinking, telling myself I should have noticed some clue."

"That's stupid," Emma picked up her cup. "You don't have second sight or something."

"It must have a connection to the bad past stories. I'm sure of that."

Emma shook her head. "We all know the bad past stories were utter nonsense."

"I'm not so sure." Carlina took her cup and sipped the espresso. It ran down her throat, hot and strong. "In fact, I have the impression grandpa always took a real event from the past and added something else, something he made up."

Emma started to laugh. "No, he didn't."

Carlina narrowed her eyes. "What's so funny?"

"I just remembered what he said to me."

"Well?"

"He said I had too many men at once, and that I only married Lucio because he was the most insistent." She drank from her cup, her eyes glittering with amusement.

"Did you?"

Emma sat up straight. "Of course I didn't! I married Lucio because he would jump off a bridge for me. He worships the ground on which I tread."

Carlina frowned. "He also has a tiny jealousy problem. Weren't you afraid what would happen if grandpa told him about the too many men in your life?"

"Not at all." Emma finished her espresso. "I know how to handle Lucio."

"But . . ."

Emma bent forward and laid a hand on Carlina's knee. "You worry too much, like always. Just relax. It'll blow over."

Carlina's mouth dropped open. "It'll blow over? Emma, we're talking about a murder here. It will not blow over!"

Emma shrugged. "Oh, well. But that doesn't mean we have to talk about it all the time, does it? Tell me about Temptation. Did you get that delivery with the yellow feathers on the bra?"

Chapter 12

"What can I do for you, *commissario*?" Marco got up and shook Garini's hand. "My wife said you would stop by. It's a terrible business, and I will do anything I can to help." His gaze fell on the recorder. "It's no problem if you record everything."

"Thank you." Garini took the seat Marco had indicated in front of his table. The walls of the office were painted white, but the famous picture of Monet's water lilies covered the free space at one side, softening the effect. From a sink in the corner of the room came a whiff of disinfectant and soap.

"I understand you've only recently married into the family." Unbidden, Carlina's words jumped into Garini's mind. *Every man who marries into our family deserves a medal for courage.* He suppressed a smile and tried to concentrate.

"That's right. I married Angela in June." The young doctor smiled. "We met at the golf club Christmas party."

"Yes, she told me." Garini didn't want to hear it again. "I would be grateful if you could once again tell me about the morning when you were called to certify Nicolò Mantoni's death."

Marco nodded. "We were still sleeping when the phone rang."

"What time was that?"

The doctor shrugged. "I'm not quite sure. Ten thirty? Eleven? It was Sunday, and we were still in bed because of the wedding the night before." He smiled. "My wife likes to dance."

Garini stretched out his legs. "I see. Please go on."

"Fabbiola was on the phone. She was in tears and asked me to come because her father had died. At first, I couldn't believe it. He had seemed like a healthy man."

"Was he your patient?"

Marco shook his head. "No. He was a patient of Enrico Catalini. I only started my practice here about a year ago. Fabbiola told me that Enrico had the flu and begged me to come instead."

I forgot about the family doctor. Stefano frowned. Did Piedro check if the doctor had really been ill? Maybe this illness had been an invention of Fabbiola to get the inexperienced young doctor to sign the death certificate instead?

Marco looked at his hands, folded on the table in front of him. "At first, I didn't want to go, but it's my wife's family, and Angela said I had to."

What hold does Angela have over Marco? "Are you in the habit of doing everything your wife says?" Garini didn't take his eyes off Marco's face.

The young doctor flushed. "Not always. But in this case, I thought it made sense, even if I didn't enjoy it."

"Go on."

Marco sighed. "When we arrived, everybody was there. I don't know where they all sprung from. Maybe they stayed over at the house; I have no idea. I checked the body." He swallowed. "I have to admit I didn't find anything unusual." He lifted his dark head and stared at the *commissario* with defiant eyes. "Maybe I should have looked closer. But his twin rattled me, hopping around in the background, and then, Nico was an old man, and I had no idea about his condition. Maybe he had a weak heart." He shrugged. "I decided to sign the death certificate and to talk with Enrico Catalini as soon as he was back at work."

"What happened next?"

Marco pushed a hand through his dark hair. "I didn't have a pen, so I had to go to the kitchen. They were all there, waiting. Carlina gave me a pen." He smiled. "She's a nice girl."

He's the second one who says that, but most killers seem nice. Garini shook off his thoughts. "And then?"

"Just as I was going to sign the death certificate, Uncle Teo charged into the room and told us that something was wrong because his twin was still wearing socks."

"Didn't that strike you as unusual?"

"God, no." Marco lifted both hands palm up. "How should I know what he put on when he went to bed? Many old people suffer from cold feet and sleep with socks."

"Hmm." *True enough. But shouldn't a doctor, even one without experience, have recognized the signs that showed the victim had died somewhere else?*

"Did you have a look at his feet while you examined the body?"

"No." Marco shook his head. "I only uncovered the torso. That's why Uncle Teo didn't see his feet until I had left the room. I assume he straightened the cover, saw the socks, and ran to the kitchen without missing a beat."

"Go on, please."

Marco shrugged. "They all went crazy. I admit I felt overwhelmed. Carlina was the only one who was comparatively sane. She said I should sign the certificate without listening to Uncle Teo."

Garini shifted in his seat.

"All the others seemed to delight in the situation. I thought they would calm down when I said it would create a scandal if we called the police, but it only energized them."

I bet. The *commissario* nodded.

"Finally, my wife said we should call in another doctor."

Once again your wife. I do wonder about your wife, doctor.

Marco said, "Angela was afraid it would throw a bad light on me if I signed the death certificate with a suspicion of murder. She didn't want me to have anything to do with it, even if the signature meant nothing but pronouncing him dead." Marco fell silent, lost in thought. "To be honest, I wasn't keen on being involved either. I'm new in town, and rumors have a way of getting out of hand." He shrugged. "Then Uncle Teo insisted on calling the police, and the rest you know."

The *commissario* nodded. "You have heard about the bad past stories, haven't you?"

Marco lifted his head with a sharp jerk. "Bad past stories? What do you mean?"

Garini narrowed his eyes. "Nicolò Mantoni had a habit of interjecting embarrassing episodes of the past into each family conversation. Haven't you heard about them?"

"Oh, that." Marco gave a forced laugh. "Yes, I know. He said Uncle Ugo had stolen a camera and Carlina would marry a garbage man because she had rejected a prince."

"Do you believe those stories?"

Marco shook his head. "Of course not. Old people often delight in mischief. They have nothing left to lose, and they love to rattle others." He smiled. "Sheer boredom, I believe."

"Have you heard the story about you?"

The doctor blanched. "What do you mean?"

"They say your wife forced you into marriage with a secret she threatened to spill."

Marco threw back his head and laughed. It sounded convincing. "*Commissario*, any man with eyes in his head would be happy to marry my wife. There was no need to force me into it. On the contrary. I can't believe that you considered that story even for one second."

Beauty isn't everything. "So far, I reserve my judgment." Garini got up. "Thank you for your time, doctor."

II

Carlina lifted her head and smiled at the man dithering on the door step of Temptation. She had opened the doors wide to let in some fresh air. "*Buongiorno*," she said without getting up from her bar stool behind the counter. He looked like one of those guys who needed a bit of encouragement but would be scared if she took a direct approach. She was proud of her instinct, honed by many years of retail experience. Some people turned tail the minute you talked to them, some did if you left them alone too long. He looked like an American, and Americans loved small talk. "It's a lovely autumn day, isn't it?" she added in English.

The man relaxed and returned her smile. "It sure is."

She had been right. His accent was American.

"Your English is very good," he said.

She grinned. Trust Americans to start with a compliment. "That's because I was raised in the US."

"Really?" He came closer. "Whereabouts?"

"Seattle."

"My best friend is from Seattle."

Someone usually is. Carlina nodded. "It's a great city. Wonderful landscape, with both the mountains and the sea so close."

"It sure is." His vague answer told her he had never been to Seattle. But it had done the trick. Now that the preliminaries were over, he felt confident enough to broach his delicate subject. "I was wondering if I should buy some underwear for my wife." His gaze darted over the golden horn display like a deer in panic.

Carlina still didn't get up, but she bent forward to show him he had her full attention. "That's a great idea," she said. "Do you have anything particular in mind?"

He looked at the floor. "I . . . um. I've never done this before."

"I will help you." Carlina smiled at him. "Let's start with her favorite color. What does she wear most?"

"Oh." Her customer looked nonplussed. "Green. She likes green."

How unusual. Better not trust this statement too far. "Does she wear more white or black underwear?"

He seemed more confident now. "White."

"Very good." Carlina gave him an encouraging smile. "Last question. Does she prefer flowery patterns or plain ones?"

"Oh, she likes flowers very much."

"Then I have just the thing for you." She led him to the display to her left and pointed at a white bra with a slim fringe of lacy flowers. "This is a very popular model because it can be worn beneath a t-shirt or white blouse, but it still has a special something. We also have a matching slip." She touched the fringe.

His face lit up. "I like it."

"Do you happen to know her size?" Carlina turned her back to him so she wouldn't make him feel embarrassed when he realized he had no idea. His silence told her enough. "Is she taller or smaller than I am?" She smiled over her shoulder and bent down to open the drawer.

His gaze darted over her figure. "Em. Taller. As in wider." He made a wide move with his hand.

Carlina suppressed an amused smile and fished out a bra two sizes larger than hers and a matching slip in size L. "Is your wife with you in Florence?"

"Yes, she is. We're celebrating our twentieth anniversary tomorrow, and I want to give it to her as a surprise gift."

"What a lovely idea." Carlina took the bra and slip to the cash register. "Shall I wrap the set as a gift, then?"

He gave a sigh of relief. "That would be great."

"That'll be ninety-five Euros." Carlina ignored his shocked silence and wrapped both items in the creamy tissue paper she used for gifts. "If the size should not fit, she can come back and exchange it as long as you don't take off the labels. There's no price on them." She dropped the parcel into a shiny little bag with 'Temptation' written on the outside.

He placed his credit card on the counter with a stunned expression.

Carlina processed the credit card and smiled at him. "Your wife will be delighted. I would be, if I were in her place."

He found his smile again. "I hope so. Thank you for your help."

"My pleasure." She followed him out of the store and lifted her hand in a farewell gesture. "Better hide the bag inside your jacket."

"Oh." He nodded. "I will."

She waved him off and turned around only to find herself nose-to-nose with Garini. Her smile faded, but her heart seemed to get something wrong, for it started to beat quicker. "Oh, it's you again. What do you want?"

"That was a very skillful manipulation."

Carlina narrowed her eyes. "It's called sales advisory service. I helped that man find a perfect gift for his wedding anniversary. Some even call it an art, an art that combines psychology with instinct and product knowledge."

He gave her a mocking smile. "Is it?"

She decided to change the subject. "How come you've been listening in again, Garini? Nothing better to do?"

"I was just standing in front of your window, admiring these, ah, brown nylons." He made a move with his hand toward her mannequin. It had hidden him from her view.

"Aha." Carlina lifted an eyebrow to show her disbelief. "Do you want to purchase the nylons?"

"No, I don't."

"Pity. I could do with some turnover."

He frowned. "I thought you're doing quite well."

"I was." Carlina relished each word. "Until I had to rush off to the police station all the time." She put her head to the side. "Have you come to take me somewhere again?"

He smiled.

Carlina's heart skipped a beat.

"No. This time, I've come to ask your assistant a favor."

"Oh." She averted her face so he wouldn't see how disappointed she was. "You're out of luck. She's not here this afternoon." And how come he never asked her a favor but ordered her about as if she held the lowest possible rank in his army?

"Do you know where she is?"

Carlina shook her head. "No. But I can call her on her cell phone, if you want."

He nodded. "Thanks."

Carlina talked to Elena with her back to him, so he wouldn't see the fake leopard skin cover on her cell phone. She didn't want to hear another snarky remark. When she had Elena on the line, she said over her shoulder. "She's with her mother."

"Good. That's what I had hoped. Can she stay with her for a while? I wish to come and talk to her mother."

Elena said she would wait and Carlina slipped her phone back into her handbag.

"Thanks." Garini looked at her, a curious light in his eyes.

"What's the matter?"

"Nothing." He turned around and left without a backward glance.

Carlina stared at his back, her feelings in turmoil.

III

Signora Certini laid propped up in bed, a cushion twice as large as herself behind her. Her brown hair had been combed back into a ponytail, and bony shoulders defined a fragile frame beneath the flannel night dress in pale rose.

"I'm sorry to disturb you, *signora* Certini." The *commissario* sat in an upholstered armchair next to the bed while Elena stood at the open door and watched them. The room smelled of menthol and lilies, and it was much too warm. "But I need to ask you a few questions. I'll try to make it as short as possible."

A faint smile creased *signora* Certini's mouth. Her tight skin looked papery and blotched, like brittle paper.

Stefano's heart constricted. His mother's skin had looked like that.

"It's no problem, *commissario*." Her voice was low but clear. "I quite enjoy visitors."

"Thank you." Garini smiled at her. "Your daughter mentioned that you take morphine. Is this true?"

"Yes." *Signora* Certini looked at her daughter. "Show him the prescription, love."

Elena handed Garini a piece of paper with the signature of Enrico Catalini.

"Enrico Catalini is your usual doctor?"

"Yes." *Signora* Certini moved her hands on the bed cover as if she wanted to feel its texture. "He's a nice man."

"How often do you get a new prescription?"

"Once a week." Elena answered. "The doctor comes every

Tuesday, and I take it to the pharmacy."

"Please tell me about the week when the morphine disappeared."

"It was the week when you felt so bad on Thursday and the doctor had to come again," Elena said.

Signora Certini nodded. "Yes, I know. On Tuesday evening, Elena bought the morphine as usual before she went out. That week, quite a few visitors came to see me." She straightened her shoulders with a smile that showed how proud she was of her visitors. "On Wednesday, Carlina from Temptation came because Elena told her I would like to meet her. She's a sweet woman. Right afterward my old friend Fabbiola brought some flowers." She looked at her daughter. "We laughed because they missed each other by a few minutes, and they live in the same house."

Elena nodded.

"Then Maria and Alberta came. You might know them. Maria is Teodoro Mantoni's wife, and Alberta is Fabbiola's eldest sister."

The *commissario* frowned. "They were both here that day?"

"On Wednesday, yes." *Signora* Certini inclined her head. "We used to play cards together, before I got ill. Now they often come to visit me, but I can't play cards anymore." She sighed. "It tires me too much."

"It seems incredible that so many members of the Mantoni family came to your house the very week the morphine disappeared." Garini wanted to hit his head against a wall in frustration. What a case. Every step forward was followed by two steps back.

"That's not unusual," *signora* Certini said. "Fabbiola and I have been friends since Kindergarten and we used to live next to each other, so I played with all of the Mantoni kids. When Fabbiola moved to America, I started to see the other Mantoni girls more often."

Garini bent forward with a sudden idea. Maybe the trail to the morphine turned out to be cold, but he saw an opportunity to learn more about Carlina's father. He had to take it easy, though, otherwise *signora* Certini would clam up. "I imagine many people missed Fabbiola when she left Italy."

"Oh, yes." *Signora* Certini looked into the distance, her mind more than thirty years in the past. "Her father was furious that she married a foreigner, and even worse, a foreigner she knew only four weeks." She smiled a little. "But he was good-looking and sexy, and we all envied her. Against him, poor Angelo didn't have a chance. Angelo was her boy-friend before, you see." She frowned. "He had a funny name, the American. Paul." Her mouth formed the word with care. "Like Paolo."

"She married him after four weeks?" Garini tried to sound amused and not like a terrier sniffing out a trail. He took off his jacket and wished he could take off his shirt too. It was way too hot in this room.

"Yes." *Signora* Certini sighed. "It was love at first sight." She shook her head. "Poor Angelo, he was so angry, he wanted to force her to stay, but I told Fabbi to follow her heart." She nodded to herself. "She made the right decision, though she was unhappy first in America. Who could have known that Paul would die so young?" She made it sound as if she had expected better from a nation as sturdy as the Americans. With another sigh, she folded her thin hands on the bed cover. "You never know the will of our good God."

"Did Angelo ever marry?" Garini made sure his voice sounded as if he enjoyed the gentle reminiscence and leaned back in his chair, pretending he wasn't interested in *signora* Certini's answer.

"Not he." *Signora* Certini shook her head. "He never looked at another woman. He's single to this day. We all thought they would get married when Fabbiola came back . . ." She fell quiet and stared into the distance, her face drawn in.

Elena leaned forward. "Here, *mamma*, drink a bit. That'll make you feel better." She handed her mother a glass of water from the table next to the bed.

Signora Certini took the glass and sipped from it like an obedient little girl, then handed it back to her daughter.

Elena bent forward to place it on the side table.

Signora Certini continued as if the interruption hadn't occurred. "She was such a pretty widow. But with three kids not his own . . ." She lifted her thin shoulders and dropped them again. "It would have been difficult."

"So he didn't even try to get her back?" Garini asked. *God, I sound as if I'm hooked on trashy romances.*

"He did." *Signora* Certini slid a bit deeper into the cushion. "But Fabbi sent him away. She said it wasn't the same." She shook her head. "I told her to marry him, but she refused. Not very wise, if you ask me. Carlina would have coped."

"Carlina knew of it?" Damn. His question had sounded too

sharp. He smiled at *signora* Certini to take off the edge.

Signora Certini didn't notice. "She was a teenager, and a true daddy's girl. She took it hardest. The other two, they were younger and soon settled in, but not Carlina. Fabbi was afraid Carlina wouldn't accept Angelo."

"But she never tried?"

"No," *Signora* Certini's face looked drawn now. She had paled in the last minutes until she looked as white as her pillow. "She never tried."

Stefano bent forward. "I won't bother you much longer, *signora* Certini. Just one last question: Do you know where I can get in touch with Angelo?"

She nodded. "He's an architect. They both were architects, Paul and Angelo. That's how they met." Her voice was so low now, he had to lean forward to catch it. "His last name is Soccio."

IV

"Roberto, it's me, Stefano." Garini dodged a Vespa and hopped across a puddle. It had started to rain while he was at *signora* Certini's. The street smelled of wet dust.

"Stefano! I thought you'd gone on vacation." Roberto's chuckle came through the phone. "Haven't seen you for ages."

Stefano sighed and crossed the Piazza della Repubblica with long steps. "We met some days ago at the pizzeria. Remember?"

"But that's what I mean," the pathologist said. "Normally, you call me every five minutes after a murder. What's happening this time?"

"I'm calling you now." Stefano hurried past the red-and-white merry-go-round. "Listen, is it possible that a certified doctor could have missed the signs of morphine poisoning on the body of Nicolò Mantoni?"

Roberto's answer came like a bullet out of a gun. "Not if he's a pathologist."

"He's a general practitioner, and a young one."

"Which university does he come from?"

Stefano frowned. "Does it matter?" He passed a little restaurant now, and a scent of roasted panini with molten cheese floated out. Stefano's stomach grumbled.

"Not really." Roberto's voice still sounded cheerful. "It's just nice to know that someone who's making an ass of himself isn't from my university."

"So are you saying it's possible or not?"

"Of course it's possible." Roberto's voice was light and happy. "'After all, the victim just falls asleep and you don't see why until you open him up. Still, the body was moved after the death. Even you noticed that."

"The young doctor said he only uncovered the torso."

Roberto clicked his tongue. "That's general practitioners for you. They're all the same. Superficial. Only used to the living, unable to read a body." He sounded disapproving, as if he was being forced to watch an apprentice mishandling a piece of art. "Never trust a general practitioner, I say. It's amazing, the things they miss. They wouldn't even notice if--"

"If a body rose up and bit them in the nose," Stefano supplied.

Roberto shouted with laughter. "Well said, Stefano! I didn't know you could be funny! Where did that come from?"

Stefano smiled. "Oh, go back to your bodies, Roberto. You've been no help at all."

"Thanks for the compliment!" Roberto hung up with a chuckle.

When Stefano reached his office, he looked up Angelo Soccio and arranged a meeting with him two hours later at the cafeteria of the Biblioteca delle Oblate. Then he found out the name of Annalisa's teacher and asked him for a meeting in three hours, sent an e-mail to Piedro with detailed instructions how to inquire into the background of Marco's university, and wrote a confidential letter to the bank where Alberta's son, the Dubai investor, was employed. He checked his watch. Forty minutes to go. Time enough to file a request to check the financial situation of Uncle Ugo who had such surprisingly good cameras. Then he had to commit every detail into his report. Just before leaving the office, he placed a copy of the report onto *signor* Cervi's desk. It made him feel he had covered all the ground he could, but a nagging feeling that it was all useless persisted.

V

The cafeteria of the Biblioteca delle Oblate was situated on the top floor of the library and included a large terrace. When

Garini went through the glass door that led outside, he stopped in surprise. He knew that the library was situated in a former convent, but nobody had told him that its terrace offered a magnificent view. Below, he could see into the atrium of the building, surrounded by two stories of graceful arcades that immediately made him picture nuns going to prayer. He turned his head. Beyond the red-tiled roofs of the neighboring houses the dome arose like a mirage. The sky had cleared up and now the sun was setting in soft pastel colors, tinting the red marble of the dome and the terracotta tiles in such intensive hues that it took his breath away. He smiled. The beauty of Florence made up for many ugly things he saw in his work.

Only a handful of people were scattered across the terrace, but from the corner of his eye, Garini noted a massive man who was looking as if he was expecting someone. Garini went up to him.

"Are you Angelo Soccio?" Stefano had trouble keeping the disbelief from his voice.

"I am." The man in front of him inclined his head. He was broad enough to hide three men, standing side-by-side, behind him. It was a wonder that the modern plastic chair in light green managed to support his weight.

"I'm Stefano Garini. Thank you for meeting me on such short notice." Stefano pulled out a chair and sat opposite the massive man. He had trouble imagining Angelo Soccio as a young man, as the boyfriend of Fabbiola Mantoni.

A group of boisterous students burst through the door and filled the cafeteria. It suited Stefano, as he knew it would be hard for anybody to overhear his conversation with Mr. Soccio.

Signor Soccio leaned forward. "You wish to talk to me about Fabbiola, you said?"

Garini nodded. "I'm investigating the murder of her father."

Again, *signor* Soccio inclined his head. "I've heard about it."

Stefano hesitated. He didn't know how to put his question in a way that would make him get at the truth without deviations.

Signor Soccio winked. "Ask me anything you like, *commissario*. I don't get bent out of shape easily."

I can believe that. Garini smiled. "Thank you. My question is quite easy, even if a bit delicate."

"A delicate question, you say?" Soccio regarded Garini with a hint of amusement in his blue eyes.

"Yes." Garini took a deep breath. *I have to jump right in.* "Is it possible that Carlina, Fabbiola's eldest, is in reality your daughter instead of Paul Ashley's?"

Soccio's mouth fell open. His massive hand clenched into a fist, then relaxed again. He cleared his throat. "I have to congratulate you, *signor* Garini. This is the first time in many years that someone has rendered me speechless."

Stefano laughed. "That wasn't my goal. Quite the contrary." He didn't take his eyes off the man in front of him. "The idea never crossed your mind?"

Soccio took a deep breath. "Never." He pulled out a white handkerchief and mopped his brow. "How on earth did you get that idea?"

"Her grandfather hinted at it before he died."

Soccia frowned. "He did? How strange. He never said a word to me."

"But it would be possible?"

Soccio frowned. "I was going out with Fabbiola for over a year, when the American came to work in Florence for the summer. He was the son of a friend of my boss, that's why he was invited to work with us as a trainee."

"You both worked as architects, didn't you?"

"Yes." Angelo looked into the distance.

Garini doubted that he saw the the beauty of the dome against the backdrop of rose-tinted sky. Soccio's mind was firmly rooted in the past.

"I took him with us one night, when we went dancing." He grimaced. "They took one glance at each other, and from then on--" He interrupted himself with a sigh. "It was as if I didn't exist anymore."

Garini didn't say anything.

"The American came later, to apologize. He said it was fate." A harsh laugh came from him. "Ha. Fate. What do they know about fate?" He shrugged. "Four weeks later, she followed him to America. Oh, I was angry. Very angry. I talked to her father; we all tried to talk her out of it. But she wouldn't listen."

"When was that?"

"September 14," Soccio said without hesitating.

Stefano swallowed. "Carlina was born in March."

"March, eh?" Soccio shook his head in disbelief. "You know, I can't believe she's mine. She never liked me."

"You got to know her after they came back?"

"Yes." Soccio leaned his head to one side. "Maybe Fabbiola

would have married me if Carlina hadn't made it clear she hated the idea. Fabbiola is a devoted mother. She always adored her kids."

"From what I gather, the feeling is mutual." *More's the pity.*

Soccio made a wide move with his hands. "Oh, that's the Mantonis for you. The whole clan is like one giant ball of chewing gum. You have one, you have them all. You can't detach them from each other." He squinted at the *commissario*. "It takes courage to marry into that clan. I had it once. Don't know about today."

"I see." Stefano regarded him for a moment. "But theoretically, Carlina could be your daughter, is that right?"

Soccio started to shake with silent laughter. "Theoretically, yes. But she would hate to know that." He looked at Stefano with misgiving. "We never told her that I was . . . an old friend. You won't share that, will you? I treasure my comfort, and that girl, she's quite a handful."

"I won't tell her," Stefano said, "unless I have no other choice."

VI

Annalisa's teacher was so tall, his hair brushed the door frame above him. He looked around the Café Duomo like a skinny rabbit expecting a wolf to jump out of the bushes.

Stefano got up and went to him. "Are you Giuseppe Auguri?"

The young man nodded. His short hair was bleached blond and his nose covered with pimples.

Stefano offered his hand. "I'm *commissario* Garini of the homicide department."

Again, *signor* Auguri cast an anxious glance around the café, but he took Stefano's hand and shook it without enthusiasm.

"Let's sit over there." Stefano indicated a small table to the left. He waited until the young man had taken a seat before he continued. "You taught Annalisa Santorini algebra and mathematics at school, is that correct?"

"Yes." His voice was low, almost a whisper.

Garini bent forward to hear him better.

A whiff of whiskey came from the young teacher.

"Was she a good pupil?"

"She was all right."

"What do you mean by all right? Could you be a little bit more specific?"

The young man cast a haunted look around the room. "I mean she was . . . all right. Not too bad."

Obviously, he had not done his masters in linguistics. *I wonder how he survives in class.* "But she finished her final exam with a top grade, didn't she?"

Auguri nodded.

"Weren't you surprised?"

The young man shook his head. It seemed he had given up on speaking altogether.

A waitress managed to fight her way through the overcrowded tables and stopped next to them. "*Signori*? What can I do for you?"

Couldn't she have come some minutes later? "I'll have a *panino* with *prosciutto*, please." Garini said. "And a coffee."

"And you, *signor*?"

Auguri pursed his lips. *"Un Grappa, per favore."*

She nodded and whisked away.

Garini bent forward. "Why not?"

"Huh?" Pale-blue eyes stared at him.

"Why weren't you surprised?" Stefano found he was speaking more slowly than normal. "'Wasn't it unusual for Annalisa to be brilliant in mathematics?"

"Uh."

Stefano clenched his teeth. If Auguri made another nonsensical sound, he was going to strangle him. An owl was more eloquent than this species. He tried a different approach. "Did you ever suspect foul play when Annalisa finished with a top mark?"

Auguri shook his head.

"Why not?" Stefano shot out the question. *I want to shake him.*

The teacher made a vague move with his hands. "Nerves."

"Nerves?" Garini blinked. "Can you explain this to me? In a whole sentence, please?"

The young man pushed a hand through his bleached hair. He opened his mouth and closed it again, then opened it again like a fish desperate for air. "Sometimes nerves can bring you to unexpected heights."

I am reaching unexpected heights right now. Garini pressed his lips together. *Unexpected heights of rage.* "That was how you explained it? Nerves?"

"Uh."

The waitress appeared out of nowhere and dropped their dishes on the table. "Here you are." She disappeared again before they could reply.

Auguri lifted his glass, opened his mouth wide, and downed the Grappa with one experienced twist of his wrist. He didn't meet Garini's gaze.

Garini wolfed down his sandwich without taking his gaze off the young teacher. *I can't believe Annalisa would ever start an affair with him. How on earth did Nico come up with that story?* He took a deep breath. Nothing for it, he had to try the brutal approach. "Did you have an affair with Annalisa Santorini?"

The young man's face exploded into an intense lilac hue. He opened his mouth, but no sound came out.

That's it. I've done it. He's blown a fuse; he'll never speak another word for the rest of his life. Garini curbed his impatience. "I'm sorry I have to ask you, but I need to know. If it has nothing to do with the case, I'll never mention it anywhere."

Auguri sat like a rabbit frozen with fear, his eyes fixed on Garini as if pleading not to bite him too hard.

"Did you?"

Auguri shook his head. "Uh-u."

Aha. Uh-u seemed to mean no. They were getting somewhere with their owl-talk. "No?"

"Uh."

Garini clenched his teeth. "I need a clear answer, *signor* Auguri. Can you please tell me the truth in one sentence? If you don't answer me, we might sit here until midnight."

That got him. Auguri opened his mouth in panic. "I didn't have an affair with Annalisa!"

"All right." Garini got up and slapped some money on the table to cover the bill. "Thank you for your time, *signor* Auguri."

He left the café with rage boiling inside him. Another evening wasted. Another dead end. *Damn.*

VII

"Looking for anything special, *commissario*?"

Her voice made him jump. He turned on the balls of his feet, his hands deep inside the pockets of his trousers. It was Carlina.

Of course. Who else? "No." *Attack is the best form of defense.* "Where are you coming from this late at night?"

She came closer. In the weak light coming from the unshuttered window above, she looked smaller than usual. For once, she wasn't wearing jeans but a short skirt and a jacket. "Is that question part of the murder investigation?" she asked.

"Yes." An unknown feeling of protectiveness rose inside him. He suppressed it. *This woman does not want to be protected.*

She leaned against the wall of the house and crossed her arms in front of her chest. "I'm not sure if I should believe that, but I'll answer it anyway. I'm coming from a meeting at the town hall, where the wife of the mayor presented a new project to support the businesswomen of Florence." She cocked her head to the side. "And you, my dear *commissario*, are trying to see how to get access to our house by way of the balcony, if I'm not very much mistaken."

He mirrored her posture. "How acute, *signorina* Ashley."

"You won't find it," she said.

He lifted an eyebrow. "No? Why not?"

"Because," she laughed, "it's a Mantoni thing."

Her laugh was low and soft, and did something to him he didn't want to analyze.

She walked up to him.

A hint of her alluring scent made him wish she would come even closer. He stood rooted to the spot.

Carlina smiled. "I'll show you."

"Why?"

She froze. "Why?" She sounded stunned.

"Yes, why? Why should you help the police?"

She shrugged. "Why shouldn't I?" She gave him a challenging glance. "I've got nothing to hide." She came closer. "Could you step to the side, please? You're right in front of the stone."

"What stone?" He wanted to wait until she was close enough to touch him, but he forced himself to step to the side.

"This one." She looked up and down the street, checked the windows, then bent with one fluid move and pulled out a loose stone just above the ground. It was the size of a brick, flat and rectangular. "Don't tell anybody." An impish smile, a hop, and she stood on the window sill of her grandfather's kitchen, the toes of her high-heeled shoes between two iron bars. Carlina stretched and inserted the stone into a hole at the side of the window, then used it as a stepping stone.

Garini narrowed his eyes. It looked as if she accessed the house every night via the balcony. With one more step, she reached a decorative ledge high above him. Now she already had one hand on the balcony railing. Instead of climbing across the balcony railing, however, she turned around and returned the way she had come, more slowly now.

As she stepped on the brick, she lost her balance. Arms flailing, she slithered the last meter and fell in front of his feet.

He steadied her. Her arms felt warm and soft. She was so close, he could smell the fragrance of her hair, the delicate scent of her skin. What would happen if he bent down and kissed her? He felt himself going hot. *Steady, Stefano. She's a suspect.* He clenched his teeth and forced himself to drop his hands. Not trusting himself, he took a step back.

"Sorry," Carlina said out of breath. "I've never gone down, only up."

It took all his concentration to ask a question that made sense. "Why didn't you go inside and come back through the front door?"

She grinned. "Because I won't climb over that railing in a skirt if someone's watching. Besides, the door of the balcony needs to be open."

He shook his head. "Risky. What if Benedetta closes it when you're gone?"

"No problem. Then I call someone inside the house and ask them to open the door. Anybody but my mother or aunt, that is."

He regarded her. "I see. Did you do it often?"

"Hmm. Not as often as Ernesto and Annalisa. Benedetta is an anxious mother."

"And your mother isn't?"

Carlina hopped onto the window sill again and retrieved the stone. "She is, but officially, I always stayed the night with my friend Rosanna. She has very lax parents." She returned the stone to its hiding place.

"Who created this . . . side entrance?"

"I have no idea." Carlina shrugged. "The knowledge has been passed on within the Mantoni family for ages, but only among the males. A cousin showed it to me when I turned fourteen."

"And you taught your cousins."

"Sure."

"Weren't you afraid of waking someone?"

Carlina giggled. "Oh, no. Benedetta wouldn't even wake up if you started a tap dance next to her bed."

"Then why didn't you use the front door?"

She laughed.

It was more a giggle, coming from deep inside her, sounding carefree and fun. He couldn't get enough of it.

"Because grandpa always closed the front door by midnight and left the key stuck on the inside. He was convinced that you can't force open a lock if the key is stuck. He also believed that ninety percent of all break-ins are done after midnight."

"He was wrong." Garini shook his head. "What happened if an adult returned after midnight?"

"Oh, they had to ring the bell. I always used the balcony and called Annalisa or Ernesto. Grandpa turned grumpy when you woke him."

He looked at her. "That reminds me of something. Did you teach Emma too?"

Carlina nodded.

"What other mischief did you do with her?"

Her eyes widened. "Mischief? Nothing out of the ordinary. Who told you that?"

"Benedetta."

She grinned. "Oh."

Madonna, this was difficult. When she grinned like that, her cat-like eyes shining, he wanted to--

He interrupted his train of thought and narrowed his eyes. "Come on, share the secret with me."

Her grin broadened. "I hadn't thought of that story for ages. One summer, Emma decided to go swimming in the middle of the night. She had a boyfriend with a very fast car at the time, and they drove all the way to the coast to go swimming." She bit her lips to suppress her laughter. "Unfortunately, while they were in the water, her clothes were stolen. She came back, dressed in nothing but her bikini, at four in the morning. That night, Benedetta had some sort of stomach problem which kept her awake. She closed the balcony door during the night, but she never checked Emma's room, thank God. So when Emma came and found the door closed, she rang me. I went to Benedetta's kitchen to let her in, and just as Emma had stepped inside, her mother tottered in with a hot water bottle."

"Sounds like fun."

Carlina shook with laughter. "Benedetta asked what on earth

we were doing, and Emma came up with a wild story about a bet going on between us, a bet that involved getting dressed in a bikini and dancing in the kitchen in the middle of the night."

"She's good at inventing wild stories, that one."

Carlina stopped mid-laugh and gave him a sharp look.

He pointed at the wall. "Aren't you afraid that one day, someone will use that knowledge to break into the house? I assume half the population of Florence knows by now how to use that stone."

She shrugged. "We remove it when we go on vacation."

He shook his head. "Has it ever occurred to you that your family is a bit . . . out of the ordinary?"

"Or, they're as crazy as drunken hens." Carlina smiled. "That's why I love them."

Chapter 13

"Good morning, Piedro." Garini frowned. Piedro looked like an old t-shirt, crumpled, white with a dirty rim, and out of form. "Did everything work out last night?"

"Ugh." Piedro sank into the chair in front of Garini's desk.

I hope he won't start owl talk with me. "Any trouble at the Internet café?"

"No." Piedro shook his head, then winced.

"Did you drink?" Garini's heart sank. *If he drinks on the job, I'll have to tell his father.*

"No. Stiff neck."

"Good."

"What?" Piedro's eyelashes fluttered, but in spite of his effort, his eyes remained half-closed.

"Nothing." Garini bent forward. "Did you see Ernesto?"

"Yeah. He stayed all night at the café." Piedro sat up straighter and swayed.

"Were you offered anything suspicious? Any mention of drugs?"

"Monster slasher. Black spider."

Garini frowned. He'd never heard of these drugs before. "Piedro." He made sure his voice sounded like a whip. "Get up."

Piedro sat motionless. A faint snore came from his mouth.

Stefano went around the desk and hauled Piedro to his feet. "Now tell me again. What drugs?"

Piedro's eyes rolled back. "No drugs. Game. Game all night."

"Nothing but a game?"

"Yeah."

Garini shook him. "Sure?"

"Yeah."

"All right." Garini dropped him and took out his wallet.

Piedro sank into his chair like a balloon without air.

"Here." Garini handed him ten Euros. "You take a taxi home and sleep. Don't return until you know your name."

Blood-shot eyes tried to focus on him. "My name?"
"Yes. You'll remember. Eventually."

II

"*Buongiorno*, Carlina." The voice came from Temptation's entrance.

Carlina looked over her shoulder. "Aunt Maria! You're up and about early. Let me just finish this, then I'll be with you." She took an old towel and rubbed the floor of the dressing room dry, then fished a bottle from a hidden corner and sprayed the uneven stone tiles that had seen more than a few centuries of business.

Aunt Maria watched her with a frown. She wore a light-green rain jacket and a matching green hat. "Why are you doing that?"

Carlina sighed. "Because you have to take off your shoes when you try on underwear, and in summer, many customers have smelly feet. I need to scrub the floor of the dressing room at least twice a week, and I always add disinfectant too." She straightened. "There, that's it. Clean and fresh for my next customer." *At least, it would be if you didn't reek of garlic*. She pushed the thought aside and went to the door of Temptation. "Let's air the place a bit." She slid the glass door open and fixed it while looking at the gray sky. A drizzle of rain was keeping the tourists away. Carlina sighed. It was the right weather for a museum, not for shopping.

Aunt Maria followed her and leaned against the cash register. Her small eyes were bloodshot.

Carlina frowned. "Are you all right?"

Aunt Maria nodded. "Yes. I had a bad night, that's all." She wiped her hand across her brow. "My thoughts kept me awake."

Her great-niece pointed at the bar stool. "Take a seat, Aunt Maria. I'll get you a glass of water. It'll make you feel better." She went to the tiny bathroom behind the storage room.

When she came back, her aunt had managed to climb onto the bar stool. With her green garments, she looked like a round nymph on her throne next to the golden horn filled with thongs. "You have a great overview from this chair." Aunt Maria's smile was triumphant. "Even if it's a bit difficult to climb."

Carlina handed her the glass of water. It was translucent red. In a small square on the front, the word 'Temptation' was written with golden curlicues.

"That's a great glass." Aunt Maria took a sip. "I didn't know you had these."

Carlina leaned against the counter. "I bought them in summer. So many customers asked me for a glass of water that I started to feel like a bar and became quite resentful, but of course, I couldn't refuse to give them something. After all, it was very hot."

"Yes, it was a hot summer." Aunt Maria took off her green hat and wiped her brow again though cool air was coming by now through the open door.

"So I talked to Francesca. She's a glass-blower with her own studio on Via Burchiello, and she made those for me."

Aunt Maria smiled. "So now you sell glasses too?"

Carlina nodded. "I also have another version in translucent black." She grinned. "If they buy the glass, I don't even have to wash it."

"And how much is one?" Aunt Maria held it against the light and squinted at the reflection on its red glass.

"Twelve Euros." Carlina said.

Aunt Maria's hand sank. "What?" She eyed the glass with respect. "How come it's so expensive?"

"It's handmade." Carlina pointed at the rim of the glass. "See the little swirls here? Every piece is unique."

"But do you make a profit too?"

"Of course." Carlina grinned. "I didn't want to risk selling more glasses than underwear and becoming bankrupt." She shivered but didn't close the door. The garlic smell that permeated the air around Aunt Maria was as dense as a fog. "In fact, it's a great bargain for a handmade glass."

"I'll take your word for it." Aunt Maria bent forward and placed her glass with care on the cash counter. Then straightened and folded her hands on her lap, crushing the green hat. "I didn't come to talk about glasses, Carlina."

Carlina looked at her.

"I've been thinking all night long." Aunt Maria stared into space. "I've been thinking about the murderer of Nico, and I think I know who it was."

"What?" Carlina's mouth dropped open. "You know who it was? How come?"

Aunt Maria looked past Carlina's shoulder. "I think we should close that door."

"Sure." Carlina moved with alacrity. Suddenly, she didn't care if the whole store smelled of garlic. *What does Aunt Maria know?* She rushed back to her great aunt and leaned against the counter. "Tell me."

Aunt Maria's small eyes regarded her. "Do you like the *commissario*?"

Carlina was taken aback. "I . . . no."

"Why not?"

Carlina swallowed. "He's rude. He pushes me forward, makes me try to lose control." *And he has a smile that makes my knees weaken.* Carlina shook her head. Where did that thought come from? She pushed it away.

"Hmm." The ample nymph on the bar stool nodded her head from side to side. "Funny, Annalisa says the same."

"Does she? I thought she was interested. I saw that gleam in her eye."

Aunt Maria shook her head. "No. She says he's impossible."

"Ah." For some reason, that statement made Carlina feel better. "She has more sense than I thought. But let's not talk about Annalisa. You said you knew who killed grandpa? Do you really know or do you just have a good guess?"

Aunt Maria took the glass of water and drank a thirsty draft from it. "I like Garini," she said, as if she hadn't heard Carlina's question.

"You do?" Now it was Carlina's turn to stare. "Why?"

"He understands weaknesses."

Carlina's mouth dropped open. "We're not talking about the same man."

Aunt Maria started to laugh. "Oh, yes, we are. I think he's leading you on, Carlina."

Nettled, Carlina said. "I can well believe that, but he has never given me the slightest reason to believe that he understands any human emotion. He reminds me of a police computer, that one. I keep wondering if he has a switch he turns off when he goes to bed at night."

Aunt Maria held onto the counter. Her whole body shook with laughter. "Oh, Carlina," she said, "you have to look closer."

"No, thanks." Carlina crossed her arms in front of her chest. She had difficulty with her breathing. If any unsuspecting customer came into Temptation right now, he would be blown out again by the garlic stench. "Now please tell me, Aunt Maria. Don't keep me hanging."

The laughter fled from Aunt Maria's face. "It's difficult," she said. "You see, if my theory is right, then a lot more people should be dead by now."

Carlina felt the blood draining from her face. "What?"

Aunt Maria nodded. "Because several people know the secret. That's what bothers me." She turned her hat in her hands. "But we aren't dead. So does this mean my theory is wrong?"

Carlina swallowed. "What is your theory?" She stressed the second word.

Aunt Maria didn't answer. "Should I tell Garini?" She lifted her head. "What if it's all wrong?"

"Tell me." Carlina felt like jumping onto the counter and shaking her great aunt. "Then we can decide together."

"That's why I came to Temptation," Aunt Maria said. "I wanted to speak to you without anybody overhearing."

An icy current ran up and down Carlina's back. *It's someone from the family. Oh, Madonna.*

Aunt Maria's mouth twisted. "Now I wonder. I would put you in danger." Suddenly, she looked old.

"You can tell me," Carlina held her breath and bent forward. "You can tell Garini too. He will know what to do."

Aunt Maria frowned. "I thought you didn't like him."

Carlina reared back. She bent down and pretended to fix something on her shoe so she could take a deep breath of pure air before she came up again. "I don't. But that doesn't mean he's a bad *commissario*. Actually, I believe he's quite good at his job."

Aunt Maria shook her head as if she wondered about her great-niece. She started to search for something in her large pockets and unearthed a fresh garlic clove which she held out to Carlina. "Do you want one?"

Carlina shook her head. "No, thanks."

Aunt Maria popped the garlic clove into her mouth and started to chew. "I think--" She broke off and choked. Her face turned red, then blue; her eyes looked as if they wanted to pop out of her head; her hands came up and grabbed frantic fists of air, then she toppled forward, straight into the golden horn.

"Aunt Maria!" Carlina jumped to her side to steady her, but she couldn't hold her weight. She went down with her great-aunt; the golden horn fell over with a crash, and thongs scattered right and left like lacy snowballs. "Aunt Maria!" Carlina shook her, forced her great-aunt's mouth open and took out the remaining pieces of garlic, then she jumped up, grabbed the glass of water, and flung the contents into Aunt Maria's mouth. It flowed out again. "Oh, *Madonna*."

Panic stricken, she looked around. Nobody was in front of the store. She grabbed her phone and called an ambulance, then she dropped to her knees again. "Please, answer me. Come on. Aunt Maria!" She rubbed her aunt's hands, touched her face, and wondered how to do heart massage, but she had no idea where to apply pressure and if it would help or make it worse. Tears ran down her face. "Aunt Maria!"

A siren sounded on the street. The next instant, a hand grabbed her shoulder and pushed her to the side. Carlina lost her balance, but when she saw it was the emergency physician, she only said, "It's poison. Don't touch her mouth."

She retreated to the back of the store and pressed her fists against her mouth, praying without knowing it.

The next minutes passed like a blur. Suddenly, Stefano Garini's lean figure emerged behind the doctor. He pushed himself through the crowd that had gathered in front of Temptation, took two big steps over Aunt Maria and the doctor, then stopped next to her. "What happened?"

Carlina's teeth chattered. She trembled so hard, her feet shifted on the floor though she tried to keep them still. She couldn't turn her eyes away from Aunt Maria, prostrate on the cold stone floor, her green coat covering her like a blanket. She had looked so cheerful on that bar stool.

Garini narrowed his eyes, then disappeared into the storage room. He returned with one of Carlina's small folding chairs, placed it onto the floor, took Carlina by the shoulders and made her sit on it, with her back leaning against the shelves. Next, he took an empty water glass from the display and went to the tiny bathroom in the back.

Detached, as if she wasn't really here, Carlina heard the water run from the tap.

The next minute, he returned and thrust the glass of water into her hands. "Drink this." His voice sounded commanding.

Carlina took the glass, but her hand shook so hard, she couldn't keep it straight.

He covered her hand with his and guided the glass to her mouth.

His hands felt warm and comforting, but her teeth chattered against the rim of the glass when she tried to drink. Finally, she managed to swallow a bit.

He took the glass away and placed it on a shelf. "Carlina."

His voice was compelling. "Look at me."

Carlina turned her gaze from her great-aunt and looked at Garini without seeing him.

He studied her with narrowed eyes. "What happened? Tell me. I can help."

Carlina gulped air. "It was poison." Her voice sounded flat, as if she was a machine on autopilot. "A clove of garlic. She put it in her mouth, and then . . ." Her face twisted. "She fell from the bar stool. I took the piece of garlic from her mouth, but she didn't wake up."

He nodded. "Stay here." One step brought him back to the doctor. He bent down and exchanged a few low words with him, then he searched the floor. He picked up something, placed it into a handkerchief, and put it into his pocket. Then he straightened and took in every detail of the store, the fallen bar stool, the abandoned glass of water on the floor with a small puddle next to it, the closed door.

Carlina watched him as if he was behind glass, as if this whole show didn't concern her. She had a feeling of floating above them, of not belonging.

Garini returned to her. "Why did you think it was poison?"

"Why?" She blinked. "It happened as soon as Aunt Maria started to chew. She . . . she didn't cough. She just changed color and collapsed."

"Did you give her something to drink?"

Carlina stared at him. She heard the words, but the sense eluded her.

He bent forward, his light eyes forcing her to listen. "It's important that you tell me. Did you give her something to drink?"

She nodded. Her tongue felt stiff when she said, "Water from the tap. I tried to rinse her mouth, to take out the poison. But it didn't work."

His hand dropped onto her shoulder for an instant, warm and safe, like an anchor to a world she had lost, then he turned around again, pulled out his phone and started to speak into it in a low voice.

Carlina didn't listen. She wanted to feel his hand on her shoulder again, wanted to lean against someone who would tell her that nothing bad had happened, that it had been a nightmare, that all would be well again.

The doctor sat back on his haunches, his face gray. He looked up and met her eyes, then he slowly shook his head.

Chapter 14

"Carlina!" Her mother's voice woke her.

Why didn't she come in? Carlina didn't move.

"Carlina!" A pounding on the door.

Oh. She remembered now. Carlina rolled out of bed and schlepped herself to the entrance of her apartment. She still felt groggy from the sleeping tablet she had taken, the very first in her life. The emergency doctor had given her one, and when Garini had said that they would need hours to finish documenting everything, she had handed him the key to Temptation, had jumped on her Vespa and had bolted home.

However, for the first time in her life, it hadn't felt safe. In the end, she locked her door with the key and placed a chair beneath the handle. Feeling ridiculous and small, she curled up in bed, crying like a small child before the sleeping tablet kicked in.

Carlina pushed the chair to the side and turned the key, then pulled open the door. "Oh, no."

Garini stood next to her mother. Around his mouth, he had deep lines she had never noticed before.

"Carlina!" Her mother placed her hands on her hips. "Why did you lock yourself in? I was so worried about you!"

Carlina rubbed her hands over her eyes. "I'm sorry. I didn't want to be disturbed." She looked at Garini. "Does Uncle Teo know?"

He nodded. "I told him."

She bit her lips. "What did he say?"

"Nothing much." His face was impassive as always.

A strand of Fabbiola's hair hung across her face. "I don't know what's going on here." She hunched her shoulders. "It scares me."

"Me too." Carlina took a step back. "Come in."

Her mother and Garini followed her into the kitchen. "Espresso?" Carlina started to make coffee without waiting for their answers. She was aware of Garini's gaze on her, sharp and intelligent, taking in every detail. She pressed the Espresso maker into his hand. "Can you continue? I'll just go to the bathroom for a moment."

She looked at her face in the mirror. Due to the smudged Mascara, she had dark circles beneath her eyes, her nose still looked red and swollen from crying, and her hair hung in tangles around her face. She brushed her teeth, repaired the worst of the damage and returned to the kitchen, feeling a bit more like a human being on the outside, but with a bleak and hopeless feeling inside.

The espresso was done. It was strong and hot, just what she needed. She finished it with a grateful sigh.

"I need to talk to you," Garini said.

"Now why doesn't that surprise me?" Carlina felt weak, as if she was recovering from an illness, but she tried to sound like always.

"Is that really necessary?" Fabbiola put her cup onto the saucer with a clatter. "You're not giving us much time to grieve, are you?"

His face hardened. "I wished I could leave you alone, but I don't think we have much time."

Carlina remembered Aunt Maria's words. *A lot more people should be dead by now.* She shuddered.

"You should start somewhere else." Fabbiola crossed her arms in front of her chest. "Carlina is still in shock."

His light eyes scanned Carlina's face, but he answered Fabbiola. "She was the last who talked to her. It happened in her store."

I'm a suspect. The air went out of Carlina as if someone had punched her in the stomach. Her hand trembled. She turned her back to the *commissario* and placed the cup in the sink. Maybe he hadn't seen her reaction.

Fabbiola put an arm around Carlina's shoulders. "There. I hope you're glad now. Do you enjoy tormenting us?"

Carlina glanced at him from the side.

For the very first time, a temper flared up in his eyes.

Carlina swallowed. She had been right the first time. He wasn't a man you wanted to make angry.

Garini narrowed his eyes. "I can stop tormenting you, as you call it, and leave the murderer to go on with his or her business." He pressed his lips together. "You'll have many funerals in the next months."

Fabbiola hissed out her breath. "How dare you?"

He opened the door of the kitchen. "Please leave me alone with your daughter. I need to talk to her."

"No way!" Fabbiola's face became stubborn. "I won't--"

"*Mamma.*" Carlina pulled her mother by the arm to the living room. Out of earshot, she said in a low voice. "Aunt Maria said many more people should be dead. She had a theory, but she didn't have the time to tell me."

"What?" Fabbiola's eyes widened until the whites showed all around. "She said that?"

"Yes. I think the *commissario* is right, and I need to tell him everything she said. Maybe he can make sense of it." She sighed. "I sure can't."

"But I should stay with you! I'm your mother!"

Carlina suppressed a sigh. How could she tell her mother that instead of helping, her presence made things more cumbersome? She gave her a quick hug. "Thank you. But I think it'll be better to obey the *commissario*. I don't want him to take me to the police station again."

"Again?" Now Fabbiola's eyes threatened to fall out of her head.

Damn. How could I forget? She had spared her mother the details of that awful interview. Carlina went to the door of the apartment and opened it. "Please."

"Oh, all right." Fabbiola took a deep breath. "You've always done as you liked anyway." With a regal toss of her head, she swept out of the room.

When the door had closed behind her, Carlina leaned against it and braced herself.

"Congratulations." Garini's voice was dry. He came into the living room and handed her another cup of coffee. "Sit down, please."

Without a word, Carlina accepted the cup and sat on the sofa. "I won't be much help to you, Garini." His last name slipped out before she could stop herself. "My head is a big muddle."

"I'll take you through everything step by step." He took out the recorder and pointed at it. "All right?"

Carlina sighed and nodded. "What happened to your assistant?"

"The flu." He looked as if he made the assistant personally responsible for such an untimely illness. "Tell me everything your great-aunt said." He placed the recorder on the low table and sat on the armchair across from her.

Carlina looked at her cup. "She came to Temptation this morning and wanted to talk to me. I made her sit on the bar stool because it's the sturdiest chair I have." She smiled. "With her green coat, she looked like a triumphant little nymph when she had managed to climb onto it." A tear ran down Carlina's cheek. She wiped it away.

"Did she often come to Temptation?"

"From time to time. She never bought anything, but she came to chat."

"Was she different this morning?"

"Yes. She was troubled. She said she knew who the murderer was."

He sat up straight. "She said that?"

"Yes." Carlina nodded. "But before she could tell me who it was, she took out one of her infernal garlic cloves and--" She broke off. "She first offered one to me."

"She offered her cloves to everybody, but there was no danger anybody would ever have accepted one," Garini said.

Carlina smiled, a sad smile. "I know."

"Did she give you any clue about the murderer? Male or female?"

Carlina frowned and tried to recall every word. "I don't think so . . . no. She only said if her theory was right, then many more should be dead. That's why she wasn't sure. She said she would endanger me by telling me."

"Endanger you?" His eyebrows lifted. "How?"

"She didn't say. Just by knowing about it, I guess."

The *commissario* frowned. "If she said many more should be dead, and she was wondering about it, then a possible reason could be that the murderer was away in the last weeks."

Carlina caught her breath. "You mean Emma! She didn't do it." Her cousin's face, twisted with fury at finding Uncle Nico dead, appeared in front of her inner eyes. "No," she repeated. "I don't believe it for one minute."

"Poison is a typical weapon for a woman," he said.

She balled her fists. "She didn't do it."

He put his head to one side and regarded her, his eyes like steel. "No matter who I suggest, you always say it's impossible."

She wanted to stamp her foot. "It is. It's your job to provide irrefutable proof. Maybe I'll believe you then."

"Knowing you, I doubt it."

Was there a glimmer of a smile in his eyes? Carlina looked away.

"Tell me about your conversation with your great-aunt. Tell me everything, even if you think it doesn't matter and doesn't belong."

Carlina sighed. "I'm not sure if I remember everything, and if I remember it right. I might have misinterpreted something." She shrugged.

"I know," Garini said. "I'll count that in." He leaned back and placed one arm across the back of the sofa. "Shoot."

"She smelled of garlic as always, and she looked worn out. I offered her a glass of water." She clenched her teeth. "With fresh water from the tap. Next, we talked about my water glasses. They're handmade, and I sell them if someone is interested. Suddenly, she said she knew who had killed grandpa. She asked me to close the door."

He bent forward, his elbows on his knees. "What then?"

Carlina suppressed a smile. "Then she asked me if I liked you."

Garini blinked.

She started to enjoy herself. "I said no. She asked why. I said you were rude, pushed me around, and tried to make me lose control."

His face didn't betray what he thought.

"She told me Annalisa felt the same, but that she, Aunt Maria, liked you because you understood weaknesses. She also said you were leading me on, and that I had to look closer."

Their eyes met. The room was silent. Carlina tried to read his feelings, but his face was shuttered. She felt ridiculous. "Next, she mentioned that bit about more people dying. It chilled me." She fell silent. "She wasn't sure about her theory, because several people knew the secret, and if her theory was right, then they should be dead."

"Did she tell you who else knew the secret?"

"No." Carlina swallowed. Now came the hard part. "But she came to Temptation to talk to me out of earshot, to ask my advice." She hurried on, hoping against hope he wouldn't catch the implication. "She wondered if she should share her knowledge with you. I said yes."

He lifted his eyebrows. "Are you sure of that last bit?"

She glared at him. "Yes. Aunt Maria was surprised too. Even

if I don't like you, I can still think you're good at your job." She crossed her arms in front of her chest. "That's what I said, believe it or not."

"And then?"

Her face twisted. "Then she pulled out that garlic clove, offered it to me, and put it into her mouth. She turned red and fell off the chair. I took the garlic from her mouth, but I didn't dare to try mouth-to-mouth treatment."

His gaze never left her face. "Why didn't you think she'd had a heart attack or something like that?"

Carlina swallowed. "I guess because it happened the very second she started to chew, and because we were just talking about grandpa's murder. Did . . . did she have a heart attack?" Her eyes widened. "Could I have saved her if I had tried?"

He shook his head. "No. She was poisoned with cyanide."

"Cyanide?" Carlina stared at him. "Why cyanide?"

Garini lifted his eyebrows. "It's quick. Why not?"

"Don't . . don't killers usually stick to one method?" When she saw his gaze sharpen, she hastened to add, "I've read that somewhere."

"This killer sticks to poison. So far." His words had an ominous ring. "There are exceptions to every rule."

Carlina felt cold and rubbed her arms. "Is it easy to get cyanide?"

He watched her, impassive. "It can be extracted from apricot and peach pits. Not easy, but not impossible either."

Ernesto is the only one in the family who's interested in chemistry. I wonder if Garini knows that? Carlina pressed her lips together. "I see."

"What happened after your great-aunt fell down?"

"I called the ambulance. The rest you know."

"Why didn't you call me?"

"I thought you'd be informed quickly enough. As you were."

"Do you still have my number?"

"Yes." Carlina waved her hand. "It's somewhere around."

"I want you to program my number into your phone right now."

Carlina lifted her eyebrows. "Why?"

"Because I want you to be able to reach me."

Carlina shrugged. "Fine." She got up and retrieved her handbag from the chair where she had dropped it the night before, pulled out her phone and started to punch in his name.

"Put me on speed dial," he said. "So I'll be right on top."

She looked up. "Aren't you exaggerating a bit?"

He held her gaze. "No."

"My phone isn't that modern, and your name doesn't start with A."

"So make something up."

Carlina threw him a glance and programmed "Aaawful *commissario*". Then she held it up for him to see. "Like that?"

He grinned. "Fine."

Carlina suppressed a smile. "So tell me your number."

He dictated it to her.

She saved it and lifted her head. "Anything else?"

"Yes." He got up and took something shiny from his jacket. "I've bought you a latch. From what I've seen, you're able to attach it yourself, aren't you?"

Her chin dropped. "You bought me a bar? To block my door?"

"Yes. And I want you to fix it right now."

"But Garini . . . " his last name slipped out before she could stop herself. "That's not necessary. I mean--"

"You blocked your door today," he said. "Don't tell me you did it because you wanted to sleep in peace."

She swallowed. "No. I didn't feel safe."

"Exactly." He nodded. "Now get a drill, will you? The bar will only serve its purpose if it's well fixed into the wall. I also brought the screws and screw anchors."

When she didn't move, he got up. "Shall I get it? Is it in the bathroom?" An ironic smile played around his mouth.

She jumped up. "No, it's not. I'll get the drill." She went to the kitchen and retrieved it from a drawer, looked at the screws he held out to her and chose a matching drill bit.

In silence, she got a pencil, marked the right spots on the wall and drilled the holes. Then she punched in the anchors, placed the latch in the right position, and tightened the screws. Garini's presence made her nervous, but she liked that he didn't offer to fix the bolt. Instead, he passed her whatever she needed without comment. It made her feel that he respected her independence, and because he did, she said, "Try to tighten the screws some more, please."

He nodded, took the automatic screwdriver from her hand, and tightened them.

Carlina swallowed. The fleeting touch of his fingers set

something alight inside her. She took one step back and lifted her chin. "Tell me something, Garini."

He turned and looked at her. "What?"

"Why do you think this bolt is going to keep me safe if the preferred method of murder is poison?"

Garini didn't reply.

"Well?"

"It won't keep you safe," he said. "But it'll make me feel better."

II

The next morning, Carlina got up with a gloomy feeling, trying in vain to chase away the memory of her troubled dream. She had seen Ernesto and Uncle Teo in an unknown kitchen, bent over a hot stove with satisfied smirks on their faces. A copper saucepan filled with a green liquid had spewed hot bubbles. Carlina shook herself. Evil. How could such nasty suspicions fill her mind and filter into her dreams?

The sky was overcast, and a chilling wind came through the open window. She closed it with a shudder. What a day for a funeral. No wonder she had slept with nightmares.

When she had dressed all in black, she opened her fridge. A bit of yogurt looked at her in challenge. She had not finished it yesterday morning. What if--? Anybody could have had access to her apartment while she was away. Oh, *Madonna*. She picked up the yogurt with two fingers and smelled it. It smelled as always, a bit sour, milky. Her stomach grumbled in anticipation. She was hungry and could already taste the creamy yogurt combined with grains of sugar, melting on her tongue. But did she dare to? She remembered Garini's eyes, the way he had looked at her just before he had left. So maybe he had feelings after all.

A rattle at her door made her jump. Something pounded against the wood. "Carlina! Open up!" Her mother's voice.

Carlina pushed the yogurt back, shut the door of the fridge and ran to the door. "I'm coming!" She slid back the bolt and opened the door.

Her mother was dressed all in black, her hair pushed back from her face in a tight bun. "Are you ready for the funeral?"

Carlina nodded. "Almost. I still have to eat something."

"How can you eat at a time like this, just before we bury your grandfather?" Fabbiola pressed a handkerchief against her lips.

Great. Now she felt like an oaf. A frightened oaf. "Wait a minute." Carlina decided to take some biscotti which were still wrapped in their original packaging. She returned to the kitchen and got them from the cupboard, then she went to join her mother. "Are we leaving already?"

"Yes." Fabbiola pulled her jacket closer around her. "Marco offered to drive us. He's downstairs, drinking coffee with Benedetta."

On their way to the funeral, they were subdued. Angela and Marco sometimes exchanged a few comments, but Fabbiola and Carlina in the back didn't join in the conversation. Carlina tried to steel herself for the ordeal ahead. If only she didn't know that another funeral would follow soon. "You will have many funerals." Garini's words echoed through her. She closed her eyes.

When she got out of the car, the first person she saw was her ex-fiancé. She caught her breath. Giulio. Giulio Ludovico Eduardo Montassori. She hadn't seen him for years.

He came up to them and took Fabbiola's hand. "My deepest sympathy, Fabbiola."

Fabbiola blinked away a tear. "How kind of you to come, Giulio."

Carlina could tell she still regretted not having him as her son-in-law. Giulio turned to her and took hold of her hand. "I'm so sorry, Carlina."

"What are you doing here?" She didn't manage to make it sound friendly. "Where's your wife?"

Giulio frowned. He had aged. His hair had thinned, and a paunch showed above his belt, but his brown eyes hadn't lost their kindness. "Your grandfather was a friend of mine, surely you remember that? As he's dead, I only thought it natural to pay my respects."

Carlina suppressed a sigh. That was Giulio all over, accepting conventions and following them.

Fabbiola shot her daughter a look like a dagger. "That's very thoughtful, Giulio."

He offered her his arm, and together they went up the hill to the church.

Angela followed with Marco. She hung on his arm like a heavy shopping bag, tottering on her high heels.

Carlina crossed her arms in front of her chest. At least Giulio hadn't brought his wife. She probed her feelings. It had been a shock to meet him again, but it felt good to see how much he had aged. *What an uncharitable thought.* Maybe he had thought the same when he had seen her? She bit her lips. What else did she feel? Regret?

She frowned and slowly shook her head. No. No regret. None at all.

She smiled. Feeling much lighter, she went up to church with a determined step. As she came inside, the smell of incense combined with gloomy twilight covered her like a suffocating blanket. *I don't like churches.* The thought came out of nowhere. She felt shut in, cut off from fresh air. *If I ever get married, it'll be in the American way, in a garden, with sunlight and flowers all around.* Carlina followed her mother to the front, but when she saw Giulio sitting next to Fabbiola, she stopped dead. How dare he? He had nothing to do with the family! Without stopping to think, she slipped into the next pew to her left. She was not going to sit next to Giulio. No way. So busy was she with her angry thoughts that she missed the sermon and only caught the tail-end.

"Nicolò Alfredo Mantoni was a much beloved man, strong and wise. He was a true family patriarch, and everybody adored him."

Gag. Who had instructed the priest? Alberta? It sounded just like the kind of drivel she would tell. Carlina crossed her arms in front of her chest and leaned back. *I'm not going to have a funeral service when I die. It's so fake. And it's torture.* Her throat tightened, her breathing became harsh, and she felt dizzy. *I have to get out of here. I can't stand it anymore.* She slid out of the pew and went to the door with bowed head, her steps as quick as she could make them without actually running. Thank God all heads were now bowed in prayer. She tried not to make a sound as she pulled open the heavy doors with her last ounce of strength and burst outside.

Thank God!

Light!

Fresh air! She bent forward, her hands on her knees, and took deep breaths. In-Out. In-Out. In-Out.

A hand fell on her shoulder. "Are you all right?" Garini's voice sounded free of emotion, as always.

Carlina straightened. "Yes." Maybe straightening as if an elastic had snapped wasn't a good idea. For an instant, everything went black, and she swayed.

She smelled his leather jacket, the faint trace of aftershave, and opened her eyes. He held her arms in a vise-like grip, so she had to stand close to his chest.

Her eyes focused on the faint scar next to his mouth. "Where did you get that scar?" she asked.

"What did you eat this morning?" he answered.

"You know, you always appear out of thin air," she smiled. "Like an apparition. Funny habit, that."

"Yes, you said so before." He shook her, but gently. "What did you eat this morning?"

"Nothing." Carlina smiled. She had the impression of floating above the ground.

"Drink?"

"Coffee."

"On your own?"

"No." Carlina couldn't move, he held her so tight. "I shared a pot with the others before I left."

"Who were the others?" His light eyes scanned her face.

"Everybody. We all met in Benedetta's kitchen."

"Did anybody have a chance to place something into your cup?"

"You hurt me." She started to feel more down to earth and wondered if it was a good thing. The floating sensation of the last minutes had felt quite nice. Had he answered her question about the scar?

His grip loosened. "Carlina. Answer me."

She raised her eyes to his. "Nothing. I paid attention. Nothing in my cup."

He expelled a breath. "Good."

She smiled at him. *I think you could kiss me now.* The thought came out of nowhere. It shocked her out of her dream-like state, and she straightened her back.

His eyes narrowed. "Why did you feel faint?"

"I don't like churches," she said. "So dark and fake. Do you like churches?"

He didn't miss a beat. "No."

"The priest talked utter rubbish. I couldn't stand it anymore." She frowned. "I'm not a good Catholic."

He removed his hands. "It could be worse." His face softened. "You need to eat something."

She nodded and opened her handbag. "I've got some biscotti

in my handbag."

"How providential." He took the package from her and examined it, then handed it back to her.

She opened it, and they shared a few biscotti.

The organ boomed out.

"The service is over," she said.

"Let's move to the side." He took her arm. "We can join the others from the side, then nobody will notice you left early."

They watched the coffin being carried outside. The bells overhead started to peal. They sounded too loud in the crisp air. Dark clouds scuttled over the top of the hill and obscured the sun. Today, Florence looked like a shivering chick down in the valley, waiting for the next downpour of rain.

Uncle Teo followed. He seemed to have shrunk. Carlina's heart filled with pity. She took a step forward to join him, but before she could do so, his eldest son and one daughter, having come from out of town for the funeral, appeared from behind and supported him, one on each arm.

"Who are they?" Garini asked.

"Cousins," Carlina answered.

"I guessed as much." Garini said.

Carlina chuckled. It felt strange to chuckle at such a moment, but it made her feel better. "They're Uncle Teo's children. Rinaldo and Gina. They both work in Milano."

Others followed, in groups, silent, mournful. Emma, looking sexier than ever in a tight black dress, leaning on Lucio's arm. Annalisa and Ernesto, their hair like flames above the black clothes. The bells continued to peal. They made Carlina think of war, of chances lost, of grim reality.

Next came Fabbiola, still leaning on the arm of Giulio. "I don't believe this," Carlina said under her breath.

Garini's sharp gaze was on her. "What?"

"The guy next to my mother is my ex-fiancé. He came here as if he was invited and now pretends to be a chief mourner."

"Did he know your grandfather?"

"Yes, but not well. He claims he was a friend of grandpa, that's why he came to pay his respects." She imitated Giulio's voice with scorn.

"Do you see him often?"

"Never."

"Does it--"

A voice from behind interrupted them. "Here you are,

Carlina."

They both turned around.

"Hi, Enzo." She nodded at the *commissario*. "Meet my brother, Enzo Ashley. He lives in Pisa."

Enzo stretched out his hand.

"Enzo, this is Chief *commissario* Stefano Garini from the homicide department."

"Oh, you're the Chief *commissario*," Enzo shook Garini's hand with delight. "I thought you were a friend."

"Enzo has a reputation for always finding the right word for every occasion." Carlina glared at her brother.

"So I notice," Garini said.

She was glad to hear amusement in Garini's voice.

Enzo looked from one to the other. "What have I said?"

"Nothing." Carlina took his arm. "Let's follow the others."

III

Garini waited until Carlina and her brother were lost in the crowd, then he went to the man Carlina had almost married. The thought turned him cold. "*Signor* Montassori?"

"Yes?" Giulio turned around.

"I'm *commissario* Stefano Garini from the Homicide Department. Would you step aside with me for a moment?"

Montassori lifted both hands. "I've no connection with the family; I've just come to pay my respects to the dead. *Signor* Mantoni was a friend of my grandfather."

What a louse. "I understand." Garini made sure no trace of emotion crept into his voice. "Still, I would like a few words with you."

"Is that really necessary, *commissario*? I'm a busy man, and I--"

"If you prefer, you can accompany me to the police station." Stefano met his gaze without blinking.

Montassori clenched his jaw so hard, the muscles bulged. "What do you want to know?"

"You used to be engaged to Caroline Ashley."

"Is that a problem?"

"Not at all," Garini said. "Is it correct that you ended the engagement?"

Montassori hesitated. "We didn't suit."

"And who decided to end the relationship?"

Both hands came up. "Listen, *commissario*, I see no reason to reply to these very private questions. It was all more than five years ago, besides, they can in no way be related to the murder of Nicolò Mantoni."

"They are." Garini made sure his voice sounded hard. "But I can note that you refuse to help the police, if you prefer that."

Montassori's chest swelled with indignation. "Really, I see no reason to become so aggressive, *commissario* . . . What was your name again?"

Stefano lifted his eyebrows. "Garini. Can you tell me how you didn't suit?"

Montassori laughed. "I didn't offer her enough. She wanted more. You can see what her behavior got her. She's still waiting for someone to top what I had to give."

Stefano wanted to hit him. "She refused a prince."

Montassori looked a bit confused. "Well, I might not be a prince, but I'm not a nobody either." He laughed so loud, the people behind him turned their heads. "Nice comparison, though." He splayed out his legs and rocked on his heels.

"When did you meet your wife, Mr. Montassori?"

"My wife?" Montassori shook his head. "Now what does that have to do with the price of fish?"

"Please answer my question."

"I've known her since school. Our mothers are friends. My family was delighted when we tied the knot. They had never liked Carlina." He shook his head. "She's too independent. Too headstrong. You know, I didn't think so at the time, but I may have had a lucky escape."

Stefano smiled at him. "I think she did."

Chapter 15

"Hi, Gloria." Stefano walked past his colleague with a nod.

"Stefano!" Gloria waved to stop him. "How come you're all dressed in black? You look sexy."

"I was at a funeral." *If only she didn't make those outrageous compliments all the time.*

"Which one?"

"The old man close to Santa Croce."

"I remember." Gloria nodded. "The crazy family."

"Exactly." Stefano said. "Have you heard from Piedro?"

"He's ill for another two days."

I don't believe this. Stefano shook his head. "Thanks." He went up the stairs to his office and hung up his jacket. *If this so-called illness continues much longer, I'll have to talk to Cervi about it.* He didn't relish the idea.

At least Piedro had managed to hand in his report about genetics before he fell ill. Stefano took it from the pile of paper on his desk and started to read. A minute later, his hands sank, and he stared unseeing across the room. *Piedro didn't write this.* He returned to the file. It was written in a complicated way, full of medical expressions. Two paragraphs long, it continued in this style, then a transition that didn't make sense followed before it went into another rambling report.

He shook his head. Piedro had remembered to add the sources of his information, so Stefano pulled up his keyboard and typed in the website. He found the same paragraphs, but this time, set in their context, he managed to follow them. Because more than one gene makes up eye color, a child could have blue eyes even if both parents' eyes were brown. His mood lifted. Finally something good to tell Carlina.

He stopped dead and re-examined his feelings. *I'm becoming too involved. It shouldn't matter to me.* He couldn't deny it; he enjoyed being in her presence. He enjoyed her sense of the ridiculous, admired her readiness to fight for her convictions, for her family. Not for one second did he believe she had killed her grandfather and her great-aunt, not any more, but he couldn't afford to overlook any details. Too many clues pointed her way, but not all of them. A sense of urgency gripped him. He knew the killer was dangerous, even more so now, after having had a taste of killing without being found out. He had to find the truth, and soon.

Hours later, he stifled a yawn. He had listened to the taped conversations, had paid attention to every inflection of voice, had recalled how they sat and looked while they spoke, and had written his report. It helped him to organize his thoughts and to find the things he had overlooked.

First Benedetta's husband. Piedro had returned from his trip to the hospital with the name of a doctor, but the doctor had died in the meantime. Upon looking up gastric ulcers in the Internet, Garini found they were often attributed to stress, but not always. *Great.* Stefano sighed and made a note in his report.

Next, the Mantoni family doctor. He confirmed a severe case of the flu which laid him low for a whole week. No lies there.

Stefano continued checking the report for holes. He was fishing in the dark, every lead a dead end. Aunt Maria's death had not brought him a single step forward. She mentioned a secret many people knew. He had suspected as much. But if so many people knew about it, why hadn't the killer acted earlier? It must be obvious, so obvious that nobody talked about it. His head ached.

With a sigh, he opened a drawer and took out a picture. Carlina's father looked at him with amber eyes. He thought he could see Carlina in the shape of his eyes, in the twist of his mouth. Disgusted with himself, he pushed the photo back and picked up another. Carlina with her cousin at the wedding, both smiling into the camera. Maybe he shouldn't trust her too much. Seeing them like this, nobody would ever have believed they had carried around a body two hours previously. He remembered the way she had smiled up at him at the funeral, her cat-like eyes luminous, her mouth so inviting. He shook his head. She had told him in no uncertain way she didn't like him, and it was better to believe her. Besides, he couldn't become involved with a suspect.

Too late, Stefano, a voice inside him whispered.

His office door opened with a squeak of protesting hinges.

Stefano jumped.

"Ah, I see you're still working." *Signor* Cervi came in and dropped onto the chair in front of Stefano's desk.

"Yes." Stefano suppressed a sigh. If Cervi stayed long in the office, it meant his wife was not at home and so Cervi had time to chat for ages. Unfortunately, he never remembered that others might have different plans for that night.

"I've read there's another murder."

"Yes."

"Any clues?"

"A few. Not enough." Stefano glanced at the window. Soft drops of rain ran down the pane. Too bad. Cervi hated to get wet and would stay even longer than usual.

Cervi placed the tips of his fingers together so his hands built a tent. "I just got a call from the manager of the Banca di Italia here in Florence. He was upset about a letter you sent."

Garini frowned. "A letter?"

"Yes. Something to do with an inquiry about one of his employees in Dubai."

"Ah, now I know." Stefano nodded. "Alberta raised her son to be a criminal."

Cervi looked blank. "Am I supposed to understand that?"

"No. It's part of my investigation."

"Well, in the future, consider that your investigation might ruffle some important feathers. If you can avoid it, do so."

Stefano pressed his lips together. "I don't see how I will ever get anywhere if I treat people like fragile flowers. They don't offer their secrets voluntarily."

Cervi shook his head. "You're treating them all in the same way. That's not clever. Look at the flower and think about the political consequences before you act. That's all I want."

How about justice? How about treating everybody equally? The questions burned on Stefano's tongue, but he held them back.

"Anyway, the bank manager said his employee is working exactly as he should, hasn't been to Florence in the last six months, and he, the director, would appreciate if you would in the future arrange a personal interview instead of sending a letter anybody could read."

"It was a confidential letter, addressed to him personally. The hint about the bank employee in Dubai was one of the weakest leads in the Mantoni case, and I just didn't have the time to see him eye-to-eye."

With one impatient hand, Cervi wiped the time problem away. "As I said, look at the flower before you act. You need to consider that when you set your priorities."

Yeah, sure. Trample on the weak and bow before the strong. Stefano clenched his teeth.

"One other point." Cervi narrowed his eyes. "The mayor called."

Oh, no.

"He's asking us why we still haven't arrested anybody. He's asking us if any citizen of Florence is still safe or if we're all going to be killed in our beds." His tone of voice made it clear he was quoting.

"The latter." Stefano made sure his voice sounded dry.

Cervi's mouth tightened. "I know you like to be ironic, but this is not the right moment to be funny. You don't want me to tell him that, do you?"

Stefano didn't reply.

"So?" Cervi bent forward. "What about this owner of Temptation? Didn't you say all clues point in her direction? The second victim even died in her store."

"I said she didn't do it." Stefano made sure his feelings didn't show.

"Do you have proof?"

"No." Stefano closed his mouth with a snap.

Cervi looked at him critically. "I believe you have to re-think your strategy, Garini. If you want to advance in this job, you have to keep other factors in mind."

Stefano clenched his teeth. "You mean a quick arrest would make the mayor happy."

"No need to put it as crudely as that."

"The mayor would only be pleased for a short time." Stefano bit off the words. "If a third victim crops up the minute *signorina* Ashley is in prison, we would be ridiculed."

Cervi shrugged. "If the killer is clever, he wouldn't continue but let well enough alone."

Their eyes met, hard and challenging.

Then Stefano slowly said, "I must have misunderstood what you mean."

His boss got up. "I think you understood very well."

Stefano jumped from his chair. "You want me to arrest an innocent to satisfy the killer and the mayor?"

"I never said so." Cervi picked a bit of dust from his navy-blue jacket. "The interpretation is up to you." He went to the door. "You still have a lot to learn, Garini."

If learning means arresting innocents, I don't want to learn. It cost Stefano a conscious effort of will to keep his mouth shut.

"We need results." Cervi's eyes were hard like polished marble. "Soon. I think you get my meaning."

He opened the door and left the office without another word, leaving only a trace of aftershave and a sense of fear coupled with desperation.

Stefano hit his balled fist on the table. He had no other choice. He had to scare Carlina into action.

II

Carlina draped the last thong over the back of a kitchen chair and sighed with relief. What a job, to wash thirty thongs, all smelling of garlic. It had taken her longer than expected. Now she only had a few minutes left before she had to leave home and rush to Temptation. Her hands were white and bloated from the long contact with soapy water, but they were nothing compared to her mood. She missed her grandfather. She missed Aunt Maria. She missed the sense of security she had taken for granted before someone had suggested she wasn't her father's daughter. A hush had fallen over the house; a sense of fear and death permeated every corner.

The door bell rang. Carlina jumped. Who would call her so early in the morning? She went to the intercom. "Sì?"

"Garini here."

Her heart did a somersault.

"I need to talk to you." He sounded ruder than ever.

What had put him into such a bad mood? She pressed the button that would open the door downstairs and looked around the apartment. Garini would have to manage.

A knock came on the door. Carlina opened it and stepped to the side. "Ciao."

"Ciao." His leather jacket was black with rain. With him, a wave of aggression and cold air came into the room.

Carlina watched for his reaction and chuckled when she saw his eyes widening.

Without a word, he took in the lacy thongs spread out in the apartment, from the window sill to the sofa, from the armchair to the low table.

Carlina had used every imaginable surface, knowing it wouldn't take long for them to dry.

He pushed a hand through his hair. It remained slicked back, making him look more than ever like a hawk, lean and dangerous. "New decoration?"

She shook her head. "I had to wash them all by hand. They stank of garlic."

"Can we sit somewhere?"

"Em. Not really." She looked at him.

He was watching her out of narrowed eyes as if she might start to pull out a gun any minute.

"I have to go to Temptation in a few minutes," she said. "You can join me. I have a very comfy footstool there. You might remember it."

He didn't smile; not even a hint of warmth entered his glacial eyes. "All right."

She turned to get her handbag and raincoat. "Why are you in such a black mood?"

He didn't reply.

He's back to being a panther. Great. Just great. She led the way downstairs without a word, her fingers caressing the smooth wooden railing for comfort. His black motorbike stood right in front of the door. *Signora* Electra hung out of her window and watched the street. Sometimes, she pretended to clean the window pane, but in the pouring rain, she had omitted the camouflage. "Hello, Stefano!" She waved at him.

Garini acknowledged her with a short nod.

"You're here mighty often." Electra laughed. "One could believe you're hunting more than a murderer."

Carlina glanced at Stefano.

His mouth was pressed into one thin line. If she was Electra, she would stop teasing him right now.

"Have a nice day, you two." The tone suggested much more.

Garini swung himself on top of his bike and started the motor with a roar that filled the narrow street.

Carlina grinned, started her Vespa and followed him at slow speed.

When they arrived at Temptation, he waited until she had opened the door wide and gone to the cash register. Then he said, "I'm supposed to arrest you."

Her keys dropped to the floor. She stared at him, her mouth

half open. "You . . .you're supposed to? What do you mean?"

His hard eyes bore into hers. "It means I need to close this investigation. Soon." He bent and picked up the keys, held them out to her.

Carlina took them without a word. She tried to get some order into her hectic thoughts. He hadn't arrested her. Yet. If he had wanted to do so, he could have done it at home. So what was going on? "Why don't you?"

He frowned. "Did you know your grandfather was a friend of the mayor?"

"What?" Carlina blinked at the abrupt change of topic. "Yes, I did. They sometimes played cards."

"Nico was a lousy card player," a voice behind them said.

They both swiveled around.

"Uncle Teo!" Carlina gave her great-uncle a hug. "What are you doing here, so early in the morning?"

"It's not early." The skin around Uncle Teo's eyes looked crinkled and saggy. "I've been up since six. I walked here. I'm still fit for my age." His stance was a far cry from his old swagger.

Her heart went out to him. With both his wife and his brother dead, what was life like for him now? "Would you like some water? I'm afraid I don't have coffee."

"No." Uncle Teo shook his head. "I came to make you an offer."

Carlina gulped. "An offer?"

"Yes." Uncle Teo looked at her with a determined expression. "I wish to work at Temptation."

Garini turned to the shelf behind him with a sudden twist and studied the label on a golden bra as if he couldn't find anything more fascinating on the whole earth.

Carlina's mouth went slack. "What? But . . . you don't have to work, Uncle Teo."

Her great-uncle frowned and made an impatient move with his hand. "I know that. But I think I could help you. A free worker is always welcome."

"I'm honored that you'd consider working for me."

"I don't consider it. I'm offering it. You just have to snap it up." He rocked back on his heels and beamed at her.

Carlina swallowed. "Yeah. I mean, thanks. It's only--" She threw a helpless look at Garini's back. Was he shaking with silent laughter? "Actually, I need especially trained people. Selling underwear may sound easy, but you have to know a lot and be very tactful."

His eyebrows pulled together until they looked like a scraggly ridge. "Are you telling me I'm not tactful?"

You're the least tactful man on earth. With the exception of the guy standing behind you. "Em."

Garini turned around. "It sounds like a great idea."

Carlina glared at him. "This is none of your business."

Uncle Teo shook his head. "That wasn't a tactful thing to say, Carlina."

She clenched her teeth. "I don't think it would work, Uncle Teo."

"Why not?" Her great-uncle adopted a belligerent stance.

Damn. Carlina threw a fleeting glance at Garini. He seemed to be having the time of this life. At least he'd snapped out of his bad mood. *I don't have time for this.* "You have to know a lot about women's underwear to work here."

Uncle Teo winked. "But I do know a lot. More than you'd think."

Carlina suppressed a shudder. If he winked like that at any of her female customers, they'd turn on their high heels and vanish quicker than the last piece of tiramisu at a family party.

Garini chuckled.

That did it. Carlina clenched her teeth. "All right," she said. "Sell him something." She leaned her shoulders against the shelf and pointed with her chin at Garini.

Garini's eyebrows went up. "Me? I don't need underwear."

"Never mind. Pretend you're buying something for--"

His eyebrows climbed even higher.

"For your sister. It's a gift. For . . . for her birthday."

"She'd faint if she ever got underwear for her birthday from me," Garini said.

Carlina nudged her great-uncle. "Go ahead. He's only shy. Many men are. Get him out of his reserve."

Garini looked revolted.

Carlina smiled. Maybe this was fun after all.

Uncle Teo cleared his throat. "*Buongiorno*, young man."

"Do you mean that young bit ironically?" Carlina cut in.

Her great-uncle frowned. "But no. From my point-of-view, everybody is young."

"I'm thirty-four." Garini sounded put out. "In my book, that's not old."

Uncle Teo beamed at him. "But that's what I'm saying, young man."

Carlina grinned. "Go on, Uncle Teo."

He waved at the display. "Anything take your fancy?"

Garini rolled his eyes. "No."

"Come on," Carlina said. "Be a bit more spontaneous. You have to buy a birthday gift for your sister. You only have two days left, and this is the last chance."

"Her birthday is in six months."

"Spoilsport."

Their eyes met.

A smile quivered in a corner of Carlina's mouth. "Waded in too deep, Garini?" She made sure her voice sounded sweet.

A tiny flame sprung up in his eyes. He turned to Uncle Teo. "She has the same size as your great-niece." A move with his chin left no doubt which niece he was talking about.

Damn. Carlina could feel her face going hot. She was not going to discuss her size with him or anybody else, for that matter.

Uncle Teo nodded, his face split into a delighted grin. "Now we're getting somewhere."

We're not. Carlina clenched her teeth.

"What's your size, dear?"

He had no shame. Carlina took a deep breath. "Few men know the sizes of their wives, lovers, or sisters." She looked at Garini. "In fact, many women don't even know their own size. The size of a bra is separated into two different units, the circumference of the chest, and the size of the cup. As we have a lot of tourists in Florence, you don't only have to know the Italian size, but also the American, the British, the French, and the Australian sizes. They all differ. Depending on the system, you have at least ten different circumferences, some in centimeters, some in inches. The size of the cup varies from A to H." She saw Uncle Teo's eyes glazing over. "Depending on the use, you have different styles. Some bras are especially made for sports, some have straps you can take off for evening wear, some are made to maximize the size, some to minimize. I offer stick-on bras for dresses without a back, and on request, I order bras for breast feeding as well as bras that help the healing process after operations."

Uncle Teo held up his hand. "All right, my dear. I can see it's a complicated business."

"I haven't finished." Carlina said.

"Please don't." Uncle Teo shook his head. His shoulders sagged forward. "I can see you don't have any use for an old stick like me."

Carlina bit her lips. "I'm sorry." She cast around for something to offer, anything to make him feel better, but nothing came to mind. She felt like a louse.

"Maybe you can work for the police," Garini said.

Carlina thought she'd misunderstood.

Uncle Teo's face brightened. "Really?"

Garini looked at the old man. "We sometimes need people to spy for us. You would blend in better, sitting somewhere in the sun, than many other people."

Uncle Teo nodded. "Yes, I could do that."

"However, we can't start until this case is solved," Garini added.

He got cold feet. Carlina frowned. *I hope he won't leave Uncle Teo hanging for ever.*

"When will you solve the case?" Uncle Teo asked.

Garini's eyes met Carlina's. "Soon. Very soon."

Chapter 16

"Ciao, Carlina!" Bright eyed, her pigtails crooked, Lilly bounced into Carlina's arms. "Hmm, it smells nice here!" She wriggled out of her aunt's arms and ran to the kitchen.

"I've made a cake for you." Carlina picked up the pink backpack Lilly had dropped. "Oh, my, this is heavy. Are you planning to stay a week?"

Lilly answered from her place in front of the oven. "I only packed what I need."

Carlina opened it and took out a box with colored pencils, a drawing book, one teddy bear and one tiger with a missing ear, a package with cards, and a Nintendo player. She placed everything on the low table in front of the sofa. "Hmm," she said. "One tiny thing is missing. Where are your clothes?"

"*Mamma* will bring them." Lilly hopped back into the living room. "When can we eat the cake?"

"Carlina!" Gabriella's voice came from below. "Come and help me!"

Carlina went to her door and looked down the staircase. "Don't tell me you can't carry Lilly's suitcase. She's only staying two nights."

"It's not the suitcase. It's Lollo."

"Lollo? Who's . . ." Her voice faded as she saw her sister coming up the stairs with a bird cage in her hand. It was covered by a pink shawl. Carlina blinked.

"It's my canary!" Lilly ran to her mother and stopped right in front of her. She lifted the pink shawl, looked underneath, and clicked her tongue. Then she crooned. "We're almost there, Lollo. Don't be afraid. I'm with you."

Her mother gave an exasperated sigh. "Lilly, if you'd step to the side for a minute, I could go upstairs and get rid of this heavy cage. Now move, will you?"

Lilly turned on her heels, bounced upstairs to her aunt, and took her hand. "You don't mind that I brought Lollo, do you? Mom said you would be angry, but I knew it would be fine."

Carlina's gaze met her sister's for a pregnant moment.

Gabriella looked defiant.

Lilly tugged at Carlina's hand. "Lollo would be sad all alone at the house."

Carlina glared at her sister. "You said two nights, didn't you?"

Lilly gave her an anxious glance. "Are you angry, Carlina?"

Carlina took a deep breath. Exasperation and amusement fought within her, but finally, the latter won, and she started to laugh. "No, I'm not. Let's get Lollo inside, shall we?"

As they settled the cage in the kitchen, Gabriella gave many contradictory instructions about how to deal with any possible crisis and how to take Lilly to school the next morning. Then she helped to make a bed out of Carlina's sofa and took her leave.

Carlina looked at her niece who was munching cake with a happy grin. "Well, Lilly? What do you want to do today?"

Lilly didn't hesitate. "I want to ride with you on your Vespa. You said you would take me to the hills."

Carlina smiled. "Did I?"

"Yes." Lilly shoved another piece of cake into her mouth. "I brought my helmet."

"But we can't take Lollo."

"Oh." Lilly put her head to one side and gave her canary a considering look. "I think Lollo is tired from moving. He will enjoy a rest now."

Carlina suppressed a smile. How easy to interpret everything the way you wanted. "That's settled, then."

Lilly's helmet was bright pink. It had been Carlina's birthday gift for her niece two months previously. Feeling her arms circling her waist, holding on tight, hearing her squeal with glee

when going round corners, and stopping whenever they saw
something they liked, filled Carlina with happiness. They had
agreed that two tugs meant "please stop", and so they ambled
through the hills of Florence, alongside vineyards filled with
heavy bunches of grapes, dusty, purple, and sweet. Their way led
them alongside low stone walls, giving off heat after a morning
full of sun and sheltering them from the autumn wind. They
found a donkey with ears that looked as if somebody had chewed
on them, an olive tree that reminded them of an old mountain
troll Lilly had in one of her picture books, and a quiet church
built of beaten sandstone where every whisper returned with an
echo. At a small inn, they had Lilly's favorite pasta, spaghetti
with pesto sauce. Their last stop was at the historical Gelateria
Vivoli where they both devoured a huge portion of homemade
ice-cream. When the sun set, they trundled home, happy,
exhausted, and full of good food. Carlina decided to warm Lily
up with a hot bath before putting her to bed. While her niece
soaked in the hot water, singing a song for Lollo to compensate
for the long day all alone, she went to the living room to get
Lilly's pajamas from the sofa they had already turned into a bed.

As she bent down to retrieve them, she stumbled and caught
her balance with one hand on the bed. The bed moved against
the wall, a swoosh rushed past her ear, and just as she started to
laugh, remembering the fish mobile, the laughter froze in her
throat. A long, thin knife was stuck in the middle of the bed. On
top lay the mobile with the wooden fish. They had come down
together, but the knife, sharp and thin, had penetrated the
mattress at the exact point where Lily's back would have been
had she jumped into bed as usual.

The room around Carlina receded, then started to turn in
circles. She sank to her knees. Her hand curled into the fake
leopard skin on the armchair next to her.

"Carlina!"

With an effort that felt as if it came from outside her body,
Carlina pulled herself together. She opened her mouth. Nothing
came out. She swallowed and tried again. "Yes?"

"Why aren't you coming back?"

Carlina stared at the knife, mesmerized. *Garini. I have to call
Garini.* She forced herself to get up and looked around the room,
blinded by panic.

"Carlina!" A splash followed the words. "Come and have a
look! I have great soap bubbles."

"I need to call someone. Stay in the bath." There. Carlina pounced on her phone, lying on her favorite window seat. Thank God he had made her program his number. Aaawful *commissario*. She pressed the button with shaking fingers. *Please. Answer the phone. Please.* It rang once, then it clicked, and an unknown female voice said. "This is the police operator. How can I help you?"

Carlina swallowed. "I need to talk to Stefano Garini."

"I'm afraid he's not in the office right now. Try to call him on his cell phone."

"I did." Her voice sounded as if it came from a long way off.

"Oh. I'm afraid I can't help you in that case. Can it wait?" The operator sounded stressed.

Carlina looked at the knife stuck in the sofa, at the closed door to the bathroom where Lilly sang, happy and without a clue of how close she had been to death, at the useless bar on the entrance that had failed to protect them.

"Hello? Are you still there?" The female voice snapped.

Carlina felt unable to explain anything to the impatient woman on the phone. "Yes. Thanks." She cut off the connection.

"Carlina!"

"One moment, Lilly!" Her next move was instinctive. Without thinking, without asking herself why she acted as she did, she put on her coat, slid the phone into its pocket, pulled out Lilly's suitcase, threw in Lilly's clothes for the next day, the tiger with one ear, and the picture book, placed a big cushion in front of the knife so it wouldn't be seen, then took Lilly's pajamas and went to the bathroom. "I have a surprise, Lilly." She forced herself to sound cheerful, but it sounded stilted, even to her own ears.

Lilly looked up. "A surprise?"

"Yes. We're going to sleep somewhere else tonight." Carlina took a large towel and held it out to her niece. "Get out. I'll rub you dry." Thank God Lilly hadn't put her head underneath the water or she would have caught a cold when going out again.

Lilly obeyed and stood dripping in front of the tub. "Where are we going?"

Carlina gathered her into her arms with the towel and hugged her tight. *I don't know.* "It's an adventure." Carlina forced a smile. "I won't tell. Get ready. Quick."

Lilly jumped into her pajamas. Then they added a sweater and a pair of jeans. She giggled. "It's not right to dress like this."

"It's an adventure dress." *Please don't ask why.*

Two minutes later, they stood at the door, ready to leave. "Let's make it a secret adventure." Carlina said. "We're leaving the house on tiptoes. Nobody should hear or see us. All right?"

Lilly nodded.

Bless you. Carlina opened the door a crack and looked out.

"But what about Lollo?" Lilly's voice rang out, clear and loud enough to be heard all over the staircase.

Carlina shut the door again with a hasty move. "Lollo? He'll stay here. He's still so tired from the last move."

Lilly's mouth turned down at the corners. "He wants to stay with me. I know he does. I have learned at school that canaries are unhappy if they're on their own." Her voice rose. "They pull out their feathers, and then they die!"

Carlina bit her lips. She had to get Lilly out of here, now, without being seen, without being heard. If Lilly was upset about the canary, she had no chance, unless she gagged and bound her niece. She clenched her teeth. "All right." She pushed the suitcase at her niece. "You take this. I take the cage." In two steps, she was in the kitchen, grabbed the cage, flung the pink shawl over it, and returned to the door. "Now quiet. No sound. Okay?"

Lilly nodded. Her eyes shone.

Carlina wanted to hug her, keep her close to her chest, covered by her arms. The responsibility for her niece choked her. How close to death Lilly had been. She had to make sure nothing happened to the child.

The door closed with a soft click behind them. They tiptoed downstairs. Just as they reached the landing to Fabbiola's apartment, they heard a door opening further down.

"*Buona notte*, Benedetta," they heard Fabbiola say.

Carlina turned on her heels, grabbed Lilly's shoulder, and raced upstairs again.

"Good night," Benedetta's voice floated up. "Do you know if Carlina and Lilly have returned from their spree?"

"They have." The stairs creaked under Fabbiola's weight. "Lilly's just taking a bath. I heard the water gurgle."

"Well, if you see them, say good night to them too."

"I will." Fabbiola had reached the landing which led to her apartment.

Carlina, one floor higher, opened the door to her apartment with a shaking hand and darted inside, pulling Lilly with her. She flung the suitcase behind the door and dropped the cage on the low table in front of the sofa so it hid the cushion before the knife.

"Now don't say a word, Lilly, all right?"

Fabbiola appeared at the open door. "Have you finished your bath, love?"

"Yes, she has." Carlina blocked the entrance to her apartment and pulled Lilly close to her.

"How nice." Fabbiola bent down and gave her granddaughter a kiss. "Hmm, you smell good." She looked up and frowned. "But why are you dressed again? Isn't it time to go to bed?"

Desperate, Carlina cast around for an explanation. "It's an experiment." She made an airy move with her hand.

"An experiment? What kind of experiment?"

"Em." Carlina swallowed. "A . . . a clothes experiment. We were talking about the life of adventurers, and we have read how often they sleep in their clothes, so we decided we would try that too."

Lilly nodded with vigor.

Bless her.

Fabbiola crossed her arms in front of her chest. "But that's ridiculous. It's much too hot and uncomfortable."

Carlina took a step forward, crowding her mother's space. "Never mind. It's my evening with Lilly, and tonight, our own rules apply." She tried a carefree smile. "Grandmothers not allowed."

Fabbiola frowned and shook her head. "How unkind."

"Pirates are never kind." Carlina made her voice gruff to make it sound like a game while underneath, she felt sick with fear. *Who can I trust? How can I protect Lilly?*

Lilly giggled.

"Oh, well." Fabbiola shrugged. "Sleep well, then."

"Good night." Carlina closed the door as soon as her mother had moved away from the doorstep and sank against it. Through the door, she heard Fabbiola muttering something and let out a sigh of relief. "Gosh. That was close."

"Carlina." Lilly looked at her aunt with troubled eyes. "I think it's a bit scary, our game."

Very scary. And no game at all. "But no!" Carlina hugged her niece and continued in a conspiratorial whisper. "We'll only wait until grandma has closed her door, then we'll try to escape again. We're pirates!"

Lilly didn't look convinced.

"Okay, I'm a pirate," Carlina improvised. "You're a princess and my prisoner. I'm taking you away."

Lilly nodded. "Okay. But we'll take Lollo."

"Of course." Carlina clenched her teeth.

They descended the stairs a second time. The second they hurried down the last steps, the door to Uncle Teo's apartment opened a crack.

"Good night, then," Angela's voice came through the opening.

Carlina jumped a foot. She grabbed the front door of the house, pulled it open and rushed through side by side with Lilly, then turned to the right and ran along the street toward her Vespa. "We have to hide here." She pulled Lilly into a crouching position behind the Vespa's seat.

"Carlina?" Lilly shivered. "Is this really a game?"

"Shh." Carlina put her finger on her lips and looked around the back of the Vespa.

At this instant, the bells of Santa Croce started to peal. Carlina shivered. They used to sound so comforting, so familiar. Tonight, they seemed to herald danger, spoke of death and fear. She narrowed her eyes to see better though the dark.

In the light shining from above the entrance to their house, Angela appeared, followed by her husband Marco, Uncle Ugo, and Ernesto. Ernesto's red hair shone in the light. They turned to the left and walked down the street, their loud voices ringing with echoes, their steps hollow sounds between the ancient walls.

Carlina felt limp with relief. She waited until the voices had disappeared in the distance, then straightened. "All right. Let's go." She put on her helmet, fixed Lilly's, mounted the Vespa, placed the suitcase where she usually put her feet, placed Lollo's cage on top, and helped Lilly sit behind her. "Hold on tight." With care, she accelerated, her feet held high because she had no space to put them. One last glance over her shoulder assured her nobody was following them from the house.

Her hands trembled. The panic inside her, held at bay by the need to act, now threatened to surge over her like an all-engulfing wave. Driven by the urge to flee, she flicked her right wrist to push the Vespa to maximum speed.

They roared away from her home, from the place that used to be her shelter. Sudden tears blurred her vision.

Two tugs at her midriff stopped her mid-thought. She slowed. "What's up?" she shouted loud enough to be heard by Lilly.

Two more tugs. "I'm afraid, Carlina. You're going too fast!"

"Sorry." Carlina forced herself to return to her normal speed and looked over her shoulder. Nobody pursued them, but the move of her head made the overloaded vehicle wobble. *Damn.* Her left leg hurt with a sudden cramp. She had to figure out where to go. Now. Lilly wouldn't last much longer, and if the police discovered the canary on her Vespa, they would become even nastier than Garini at his worst.

Garini.

Carlina frowned. He had told her where he lived. Next to the hotel Porta Rossa. It wasn't far. If he wasn't at work on a Sunday night, maybe he was at home. She could go and see him, ask his advice. Even if he wasn't at home, she could check into a room at the hotel next door. It would be as safe as any other hotel. She only had to hide the Vespa.

At the next street light, she did a U-turn and roared into the other direction. Five minutes later, they arrived at the end of Via Porta Rossa. Carlina knew it became a one-way street at the end, so she went part of the way, then stopped the Vespa at the intersection with Via de Sassetti. They had to walk a few minutes, but on the other hand, nobody would find them easily, even if they discovered the Vespa.

By now, Lilly was so tired, she stumbled over her feet, but Carlina dragged her on, carrying the suitcase under her arm and the canary with her free hand. When they came to the hotel, Carlina first checked the name plates to the left. No mention of a Garini. Maybe he hadn't told her the truth. Maybe it had been a fib so she wouldn't wonder why he came so often to Temptation. The thought hit her like a fist. Carlina swallowed. She hadn't realized how much she had counted on finding Garini. *I can always check-in at the hotel.* The thought gave her some stability.

"Let's check the other side." She persuaded Lilly to go the few steps to the right of the hotel and checked the name plates. Shiny brass bells in two rows blinked at her in the light from the street lamp. There! S. Garini. *If only he's at home. Maybe he has returned to the station. Maybe--*

The door opened and a young woman with a ponytail came out. She held the door open for Carlina who went inside without hesitating. At least nobody could find them now, hidden behind the doors.

"Carlina, I don't want to go on." Lilly's face was pale. "Can we go home now?"

"Not yet, love." Carlina hated to push her forward. "We first have to see if we can meet someone."

"Why? Who do you need to meet?"

"A . . . a friend." Carlina stopped dead on the words. She had run to Garini as if he was a friend, someone she trusted. *Nonsense. You've run to him because he's not connected with your family, because he's the investigating commissario, and you know he has to be informed. That's why.*

On the third floor, she found his name on the door. Exhausted from her flight and the ascent with the canary, child and suitcase, emotionally drained and shaking, she pressed the bell. Then she bit her lips so hard they hurt. *Please. Let him be at home. Please.*

Footsteps came closer. The door swished open, and Garini stood in front of them. He wore a white t-shirt, molded over his chest, and a pair of black jeans. His feet were bare. When he saw her, his mouth went slack. "Carlina?"

"Ciao." Her voice cracked. To her dismay, tears sprang out of her eyes and ran down her cheeks.

He took in Lilly's tired face, the canary, the suitcase, her tears, and opened the door wide. "Come in."

Lilly stared at him. "Are you Carlina's friend?"

He didn't miss a beat. "I am. My name is Stefano. And yours?"

"Lilly."

He took the canary cage from Carlina's hand and looked underneath the shawl. "And who's that?"

"His name is Lollo." Lilly came closer as if she was used to visiting men in the middle of the night. "He's tired."

"I see." The *commissario* led the way to a small living room and placed the cage on a low bookshelf that stood next to a leather sofa all in black. "I think he will be happy to sleep here."

Carlina followed them into the room, glad for the moment to recover her equilibrium. She unearthed a tissue from her jeans and blew her nose. Garini's living room smelled of coffee. Now that she was inside, she realized how cold the wind outside had been. The tension in her shoulders eased. She looked around. It seemed Garini didn't spend much time here. The sofa, the TV, and the low bookshelf represented all the furniture. A blue carpet covered most of the floor, but Stefano didn't have curtains at the windows, nothing on the window sills. To enhance the sterile atmosphere, the walls were painted stark white. One was dominated by a framed picture of modern art. Carlina couldn't make out what it showed, but it had huge blotches of yellow, red, and blue paint, as if the artist had thrown whole pots of paint at the canvas in a temper. She averted her eyes with a shudder.

Lilly had discovered a new reserve of energy and tested the sofa for its flexibility. "It's not a good sofa to hop." Her tone sounded disapproving.

"I'm sorry." Garini smiled at her. "I forgot to check that point when I bought it. It won't happen again."

Lilly gave him a forgiving smile. "It doesn't matter. Is that where we'll sleep? Carlina said we're staying the night."

Garini lifted his eyebrows and shot Carlina a look, but he replied without hesitation. "Yes. The sofa is very comfy. Let me get you a blanket."

He disappeared through a door to the left.

Carlina opened the suitcase and got out the tiger with one ear. "Here's tiger."

Lilly took the stuffed animal and buried her face in it. "Will you sleep on the sofa too, Carlina?"

Anything to reassure her. "Yes." Carlina didn't hesitate, even though the sofa was much too slim and short to allow the two of them to sleep on it together. "I'll help you undress."

Garini returned a minute later and covered Lilly with a thick blanket. "Are you warm enough?"

"Yes." Her eyes were drooping.

Carlina sat on the sofa next to her niece and took her hand. "Sleep well, my love." She kissed her smooth forehead. Lilly's hair smelled of the flowery shampoo Gabriella always bought for her. Tenderness pulled Carlina's throat tight. Lilly had been so close to death. Thank God they were here, safe.

Lilly grabbed her hand tight. "You won't go away?"

"No. I won't go anywhere without you."

"You're still wearing your coat."

"So I am." Carlina laughed a little. "But if you keep on holding my hand, I can't take it off."

Lilly released the hand and Carlina slipped out of her coat.

Garini had watched them without a sound. "I'll hang it up." He took the coat from her. They heard him go to the entrance of the apartment, then he went to another room – the kitchen? - and rummaged around.

"He's nice." Lilly said.

"Hmm."

"Can you sing me a song, Carlina?"

"Sure."

Carlina sang the familiar lullaby she always sang when Lilly came to visit her. *"Fa la ninna, fa la nanna, nella braccia della mamma."* When she came to the part where it said "Sleep well in the arm of your mamma", she sang the word *zia*, aunt, instead, because she knew it would make Lilly chuckle. The familiar song soothed Lilly into sleep.

When Garini came back several minutes later, Lilly's breath came deep and regular, and her tight hold on Carlina's hand had relaxed.

He placed a box with a red cross on its cover upon the table and turned to Carlina.

"Take off your blouse."

Carlina blinked. "What?" Wild thoughts tumbled through her brain. *I'm having a nightmare. He's the murderer himself, and now he's going to finish us off. Why the blouse?*

"You needn't look like that; I'm not going to attack you." His voice was dry. "You're bleeding." He pointed at her shoulder. "It has soaked through. I saw the blood on your coat. We need to stop the bleeding. Does it hurt?"

Carlina turned her head. The sleeve of her blouse hung limp, wet with blood. Her mouth fell open. "I don't feel a thing." *The knife must have slid along my shoulder before it hit the sofa.*

"You're in shock." He opened the box, picked up a bandage, and removed the plastic cover. "I suggest you start to take off that blouse now." He looked at her without emotion. "Alternatively, I could cut off the sleeve, but to do so, I would have to move your arm, and I'd rather not do it before I've seen the damage."

Carlina shot a look at Lilly. Her eyes were closed, her mouth half open. "I'll take it off." She dropped Lilly's hand and started to undo the buttons. Her fingers shook. She'd never felt so clumsy.

He watched her for an instant, then he caught her hands and pulled them to the sides. His hands felt warm and firm. "Let me do this." In no time at all, he had undone the buttons.

Carlina's mouth went dry. She was wearing her favorite bra, the one with the imitation leopard fur. *Great.*

He pushed the blouse from her shoulders without touching her skin. "Damn."

Carlina looked at him. That wasn't the reaction she had expected.

But Garini was looking at the cut on her arm, just off her shoulder. "It's a deep cut."

Carlina craned her neck. "Does it need suturing?"

He frowned. "I'm no physician."

She swallowed. "Just bind it up real tight. I'm not going anywhere tonight."

A smile appeared in one corner of his mouth. "Aren't you?"

Carlina bit her lips. "No. I . . . there's a reason."

His light eyes focused on her face for an instant. "I thought as much. Don't talk now. Let's first stop that bleeding." He lifted her arm and looked at the wound again, then took a spray from the box. "This might burn, but I prefer to disinfect the wound." He applied the spray.

Carlina clenched her teeth and suppressed the urge to flinch away from his hands. The spray first felt cool, then it burned like hot pepper on her open wound.

Garini frowned. "Was the knife clean?" He placed a pad on top of the wound and pressed it down.

"How do you know it was a knife?"

He looked at her. His face was so close, she could see the small scar next to his mouth, the flecks of dark color in his light eyes. "I'm a policeman, Carlina. I know a knife wound when I see one." With surprising speed, he started to bind up her arm. "Well? Was it clean?"

"I--" a funny feeling had taken possession of Carlina. She felt light and floaty. What would he do if she leaned against his chest now? Would he hold her tight? It was a tempting thought. "It looked clean to me. But I didn't go very close."

"Hmm." He finished the bandage and fixed it with a broad stretch of band-aid. "We need to watch this. If the bleeding doesn't stop, I might have to take you to hospital."

"I won't go." Carlina lifted her chin.

"You won't, eh?" For an instant, a smile softened his face. It looked tender, and amused, not like Garini at all. He had never smiled like that before. He got up. "I'll get you a shirt."

He returned with a checkered flannel shirt and helped her to put it on, then he started to do up the buttons, relaxed, easy, as if he did it every day.

Carlina held her breath. He was so close. She could smell his aftershave, could feel the heat coming from his body. It took all her willpower not to topple into his arms. She concentrated on his t-shirt, avoiding his eyes.

"There. Warm enough?"

She cleared her throat. "Yes." *Hot, rather*. She dared to lift her head and looked at him. "Thank you." She meant more than the first aid help, and she knew he would understand that.

Their eyes locked. Nothing moved. Lilly's quiet breathing was the only sound in the silent apartment. For an instant, she thought he would bend down and kiss her, but just as she leaned forward, he took a step backwards, moved a few books from the low shelf at the side, pushed Lollo's cage to the edge, and perched on the shelf. "Now tell me what happened."

It felt like theft not to have him close anymore. Did he think she was coming on to him? How embarrassing. Carlina could feel her face going red. She'd better concentrate on telling him her story. He needed to know everything, and fast. Who knew what was going on at home. Maybe some well-meaning person had come up to the apartment and found the knife. Carlina looked around. Lilly occupied the better part of the sofa, but the carpet was thick, so she slid to the floor, folded her legs, and leaned her back against the sofa. "Do you speak English?"

He lifted his eyebrows. "I do." He said it with a British accent.

"Good." Carlina continued in English. "Because I don't want Lilly to understand a single word."

He looked at the sleeping girl. "She's fast asleep."

"You never know with Lilly." Carlina shook her head. "You should get out your tape recorder before I start."

He shook his head. "You might not believe it, but in my spare time, I don't tend to walk around with a recorder."

"Of course." She felt silly. "First, I wanted to thank you for taking us in. I didn't know where to go. When I tried to call you, the operator told me you weren't in the office."

He frowned. "She has my private number. I routed my cell phone to her, so I could catch some much-needed sleep this afternoon, but I told her she should wake me if anything urgent came up."

Carlina shrugged, then winced.

"You shouldn't move that shoulder." Garini said. "It might start to bleed again."

"I forgot." Carlina took Lilly's hand. "Someone tried to kill her tonight."

His eyes narrowed. "Tell me."

"To make you understand, I have to go back to Benedetta's birthday party last week. We were having fun, and we were talking about Lilly's odd habit of jumping into my bed whenever she stays with me." She explained the connection to the wall and the falling fish mobile.

He nodded. "Got it. Who was at the party?"

Carlina stroked Lilly's soft hand. "Everybody who lives in the house. Then my sister Gabriella and her husband Bernando, Lilly herself, Angela and Marco, Uncle Ugo and his mother, Augusta. Even Electra from across the street came over to celebrate with us."

Garini shook his head. "Of course. Too much to hope that the field would narrow down at some point."

She looked at him. "They might have talked about it after the party. It was a funny story, one you might repeat somewhere else when in a good mood."

He grimaced. "Good point. Go on."

"Someone rigged up a knife together with the fish mobile." Carlina's mouth went dry. "It was sharp and thin and long. A butcher's knife." She swallowed. "If Lilly had jumped into bed as usual, it would have gone straight through her back."

He didn't take his eyes off her. "What happened instead?"

"She took a bath, and I wanted to get her pajama, but I stumbled against the sofa. I heard the sound of something falling through the air and started to laugh, thinking of the fish mobile, but then I saw the knife." She felt sick remembering it.

"Did you touch it?" He was back to interviewing mode; his questions came hard and fast.

"No."

"Hold on a second." He jumped up and left the room. A moment later, she heard him speak.

To whom is he speaking? Carlina slid lower against the sofa. Every bone hurt, and she felt a trembling deep inside her, telling her without mistake she was still far from her usual self.

Glasses clinked, then Garini returned with a phone fixed between his ear and his shoulder. He held two glasses in his hand, filled with a transparent liquid. "Yes," he said. "Via delle Pinzochere 10. You got that? I'll join you there. Wait for me. Ciao."

He gave one of the glasses to Carlina. "It's only water, but I think you should drink it."

She nodded and accepted the glass, then started to sip. The water ran down her throat, soothing, cool. It made her feel better.

He placed the phone on the shelf, emptied his glass in one thirsty draft, and put it down next to the phone. "Please continue."

"Are you going to my apartment?"

He nodded and glanced at Lilly. "I would like you to join me, so you can explain everything while we're there."

"No way." Her response was unequivocal. "I promised I'd stay with her."

Rather to her surprise, he didn't insist. "Can you give me your keys?"

"Yes." Carlina looked around. "They're in the pocket of my coat." She made a move as if to get up.

"Don't." He held out his hand to stop her. "I'll get them on my way out." With a twist of his wrist, he glanced at his heavy wristwatch.

She had never noticed it before, but then, he usually wore his leather jacket.

He said, "I have to get to the apartment before anybody from your family does. Above all, I need to get the knife." He clasped his hands around one knee. "Tell me as much as you can. We still have about ten minutes before I have to leave. What happened after you discovered the knife?"

"I was paralyzed at first. When I could think again, I called you, but you weren't there. Afterward, I acted by instinct." She looked at him in the hope that he would understand. "I was on autopilot. I just had one goal, to get Lilly out of there. I felt it was too dangerous to stay another minute. So I told Lilly we were pirates, and I hid the knife behind a cushion, but I didn't move it."

"Well done."

"I'm sorry I brought the canary. Lilly insisted, and I didn't want to upset her." The words rushed out of her like a gush of water. It was a relief to share the responsibility.

"Did anybody see you when you left the house?"

"No. We saw Angela, Marco, Ernesto, and Uncle Ugo leave from Uncle Teo's apartment, but they didn't see us."

She took a deep breath. Now came the embarrassing part. "When we hit the street, I realized all of a sudden I had no idea where to go. Then I thought of you, and that you lived next to a hotel. Lilly was tired, so I figured I would try to find you, and if that failed, I would book ourselves into the hotel next door." She shot him a glance. "I'm sorry I imposed on you."

"No problem." He seemed to grapple with another problem. "Do you know when the knife was rigged up?"

She shrugged. Pain shot through her, and she winced. *Damn that shoulder.* "Anytime during the day. Lilly I and were out for hours. We went around the hills on my Vespa. It was great." Tears darted into her eyes. "I'm responsible for her."

"Did you see anybody during your trip on the hills?"

Carlina brought herself up short. What did that question imply? Did he want to check if she was lying? Did he think she had set up this whole rigmarole to clear herself? That she had cut herself with the knife? Tried to seduce him on top of everything else? Her face burned. "We stopped at an inn and had lunch." Her voice was glacial. "I can't recall the name, but I can take you there."

His hard eyes met hers.

She knew he had sensed her change of mood, had followed her thoughts. *Damn.*

"We can do so tomorrow," he said. "I have to leave now."

She felt embarrassed to be here, in his apartment, and if it hadn't been for Lilly, she would have left that very minute. But the idea of moving Lilly again made her swallow her words. Lilly's needs came first. Besides, his apartment was safer than a hotel room where anybody had access.

Apparently, Garini's thoughts were going along the same lines. "Where did you leave your Vespa?"

"Down the road, at the next intersection."

"Good." He got up. "I think it's safest if you both stay the night." His immobile face didn't betray a single trace of emotion. "I'll place Lilly in my bed, then you can sleep next to her."

Carlina jumped up. "But I can't take your bed." She shook her head. "I'm sorry. I should never have come."

"I'm glad you did. I'd rather have you here than anywhere else."

Her heart stopped beating for an instant. Had he really said that?

"It's the safest place I can think of under the circumstances. I would hate to explain to my boss that I had not managed to prevent a third murder."

Carlina swallowed. So that was why.

He bent forward and gathered Lilly in his arms. Without a word, he carried her through the door and into the next room. With his elbow, he switched on the light and placed Lilly on his bed, then gathered the blanket around her.

Carlina blinked. His bedroom surprised her. *It's the complete opposite to the living room.* The wall behind his broad bed was covered with fitted shelves which went from floor to ceiling, leaving a free square around the head of the bed. In the middle of the free square, the latest Bang and Olufsen CD player hung like a futuristic piece of art, flat like a painting. The right half of the shelves was filled with CDs, the left with books. In the four corners of the room, just below the ceiling, expensive looking music boxes tilted at an angle, and next to the window, a glittering saxophone on a stand waited to be used again.

Garini played the saxophone? She had never thought about him outside his job, about his interests and life. How self-centered she had been.

The shelves right above the bed had four hidden spotlights, flooding the bed for easy reading. They were muted by the wall opposite the bed, painted in an unusual blue-green shade. It was a vivid room, a room to live in, a room with a personality. Carlina felt like an intruder.

Garini pointed at a flat light switch at the side of the bed. "If you touch the switch in one swift move, you turn it off or on. However, if you leave your fingers on the round centerpiece, you can dim the light."

"Listen, I can't accept this." Carlina crossed her arms in front of her chest. "I've no right to take your bed tonight."

He looked at her, an ironic smile in the corner of his mouth. "You don't have a choice. I can only offer this bed and the sofa. Unless you or Lilly wish to share the bed with me, you have to accept it."

Carlina opened her mouth and shut it again. He was right.

"It's no big deal." He grinned. "I often fall asleep on the sofa. I've slept in worse places."

Did he enjoy seeing her embarrassed? "Right." She pressed her lips together.

"When I'm gone, I want you to stay put. Don't answer your or my phone, and don't open the door, no matter what happens. I'll lock the door when I leave."

"You'll shut us in?" She didn't know if that made her feel safe or trapped. A bit of both, maybe.

He regarded her for a moment. "No. I'll leave you my key, so you can get out if there's a fire. But please, stay here unless you absolutely have to go."

It wasn't like him to ask her something. So maybe he was rattled too. It didn't show in his face, though. He seemed as unruffled as ever. She frowned. "How will you get in?"

"I've got a second key." He went to the entrance of the apartment and took a key from a hook by the door. "Here you are."

Carlina took it. "Thanks. Will you . . . will you be long?"

He nodded. "Don't wait."

Her mouth twisted. "I don't think I'll be able to sleep."

"No?" He looked as if he was considering something, then he said, "Go to the bathroom, take off that shirt and check in the mirror if the bandage is still clean. If not, I'll ask the police doctor to come here. The bathroom is over there." He pointed down the hall.

She obeyed like a puppet on strings. His bathroom, like the living area, had no personality. White tiles, white walls, a thin shelf above the simple sink, faded brown towels with an orange pattern that had been modern in the seventies. It seemed Garini spent his life in his bedroom.

She unbuttoned the shirt. Her shoulder hurt when she pushed it off to have a look, but she couldn't tell if that was because of the tight bandage or because of the cut. Thank God everything was still snowy white. She dressed again and found him in the kitchen. It was small and practical, no fancy kitchen gadgets anywhere. Apparently, Garini didn't like to cook.

"No blood." she said.

"Good." He leaned against the stove and watched a kettle coming to boil.

Carlina frowned. "I thought you wanted to leave."

He glanced at his wristwatch. "I'll leave in a second, but first, I want you to have this tea." He switched off the stove, picked up the steaming kettle, and poured the boiling water into a teapot. It smelled strange, of herbs and hay on a hot summer day.

Carlina wrinkled her nose. "What kind of tea is that?"

"Something to help you sleep." He placed the kettle back onto the stove and pushed a mug next to the teapot. "Now wait three minutes before you pour a cup."

She lifted her eyebrows. She'd have bet her last shirt that

Garini wasn't the kind of man to drink herbal tea.

He glanced at her and misunderstood the skeptic expression on her face. "It helps, believe me."

"Have you tried it?"

"Yes."

She had to ask. "Do you suffer from sleeplessness?" It was hard to keep the incredulity out of her voice.

"Not in general. But a few months ago, we had an ugly case." His mouth tightened. "It involved a kid."

Carlina blinked. She had learned more about him in the last few minutes than in all the time she'd known him. "I see."

"Three minutes, don't forget." He went to the door, took his leather jacket off a hook, found the key in her coat, then turned.

Carlina stood in the frame of the kitchen door, awkward, feeling like a wife watching her husband going to work.

"I'll see you tomorrow."

She felt a twinge of fear. "Garini, wait."

He lifted his eyebrows and scanned her face. "Yes?"

"Is she safe?"

He nodded. "Right now, she is." He stretched out his hand and touched her cheek for a fleeting moment. "Don't worry. You've done all you could. Now sleep. You need it." He opened the door, went through it and shut it behind him with a soft click.

Carlina heard the key in the lock, turning twice, then his steps, going downstairs. *I wish he had stayed.* She heaved a deep sigh. *Where is this going to end?* Weariness settled on her shoulders like a heavy blanket. *Who wants to kill Lilly?* She shivered. Aunt Maria's voice came back to her. *A lot more people should be dead.* Someone out there was prowling, ruthless, efficient. Someone from the family. Her family. She couldn't deny it any longer. Someone was desperate. Restless, she walked to the living room and back to the kitchen, going in circles, just like her thoughts. *It has something to do with grandpa's bad past stories, I'm sure of it. But those secrets are not secrets anymore. Everybody knows about them.* Carlina frowned. That fit to Aunt Maria's words. *A lot more people should be dead.* So maybe it was a secret nobody took seriously. Something they all knew and laughed about. But what could it be? *The family has changed ever since grandpa's death.* They didn't mention the secrets anymore, not even as a joke. Was that why the murderer took his time, killing them off one by one?

She went to the bedroom and checked on Lilly. Her niece had

turned around, arms flung out, the blanket halfway to the floor. Carlina covered her again with the blanket. How on earth was she going to spend the rest of the night? She stood and listened in the silence. No sound but Lilly's breathing. She felt cut off from the world, alone on a foreign planet. Not a sound from outside, no steps from the apartment above her. Maybe Garini had insulated the walls because of his saxophone.

Sleep was impossible. She gave a start. The tea. She had forgotten the tea. She went to the kitchen, poured herself a cup, and sipped the brew. Nasty stuff. She wrinkled her nose. It smelled of cat pee. Looked like it, too. It would make her sick, not tired. She held her breath and gulped down the contents of her mug. There. Hopefully Garini would be happy.

She returned to the bedroom, took off her shoes, covered herself with his blanket, and dimmed the light. The bed smelled of laundry soap. Maybe he had just changed the sheets. Carlina felt a twinge of disappointment. She would have preferred a trace of him, for comfort. Then she shook her head. "You have to stop these fantasies, my girl. Anyone can see he's not interested." Even his touch just before he left could be interpreted as a simple gesture of comfort.

Lilly moved in her sleep. Carlina gathered her in her arms, gave her a kiss on the cheek, and curled up around her. Nobody would hurt her niece while she was close. Nobody. At first, she thought she would remain wide awake the whole night, but the tea's effect was stronger than she had expected, and she soon dozed off.

She woke from a scream.

Lilly! What was happening to Lilly?

Carlina shot up. Lilly was next to her. They were both on Garini's bed, the muted light showing an empty room.

Lilly stretched both arms straight into the air, her face averted, convulsed with fear. "No," she screamed. "I didn't tell anybody!"

Carlina took her by the shoulders. "It's me, Lilly." She gave her a gentle shake. "Carlina. You're safe. Don't be afraid."

Her niece shuddered and fought against her arms.

Carlina released her. "You're safe, Lilly. Everything is all right." What was troubling the child? Was it a dream? Or something more sinister? Gabriella hadn't mentioned any nightmares. Her heart pounded against her chest.

Lilly opened her eyes and stared at her aunt, the whites

showing all round the iris. "Oh, Carlina!" Tears flooded her little face.

"Ssh." Carlina bent forward and hugged her. "It was a nightmare. It's over now."

Lilly hiccuped and held on tight. "I thought he would kill me."

Carlina suppressed a shudder. "Who?"

"Uncle--" Lilly gulped and clamped her mouth shut.

"Uncle?" Carlina held her breath.

Lilly jerked upright. "I can't tell. It's a secret. I have to keep the secret."

"Lilly, don't worry. You can tell me."

"No!" Lilly shook her head and retreated from her aunt's hug. "Don't make me tell it. I mustn't tell anybody. It's a secret." Her voice rose to a high pitch, broke. The terror in her eyes was tangible. "I can't tell."

"But--"

"No!" Lilly turned around and hid her face in the pillow. "I won't tell." The muffled words were ladled with anguish.

Carlina swallowed. She didn't know much about child psychology, but she knew it was dangerous to force her niece to tell the truth, terrified as she was.

She would ask Garini tomorrow. The police had more experience; they would know how to extract a secret without traumatizing the little girl.

"It's all right." Carlina caressed Lilly's hair. "You don't have to tell. It's fine."

Lilly's tight shoulders relaxed. "Carlina?"

"Yes?"

"Will you stay with me?"

"Yes."

Her niece gave a little sigh.

It brought tears to Carlina's eyes. She bit her lips. Lilly had the key to the secret, and the murderer knew it. Fear grabbed her by the throat and pressed down her lungs, so she had difficulty with her breathing. Lilly had said it was an Uncle. Not *mamma*, not Benedetta, not Emma. A wave of relief washed over her. Then she stopped short. Who could it be? Lilly called all male family members Uncle. Not Uncle Teo. *Please*. Ernesto? *Impossible*. Marco? *No way*. Uncle Ugo? Lucio? *Oh, God*, she'd never considered Emma's husband Lucio. Her mind balked. *No. No, no, no. This is making me crazy.*

Where was Garini anyway? What was the time? She waited until Lilly's breathing had returned to normal, then slid out of bed and padded to the living room. The sofa was empty. Maybe he had decided to stay somewhere else tonight. *Damn.* The need to talk to him felt like a physical ache.

She went to the kitchen, looked into the tea pot. The nasty tea had developed a thin film on top. Carlina averted her eyes and looked for a clock. There it was, next to the fridge. One o'clock in the morning. Where was Garini?

Chapter 16

"Carlina, wake up!"

Carlina opened her heavy eyes. For an instant, she had no clue where she was, then her gaze came to rest on the saxophone in the corner, and the memory flooded back.

Lilly stood next to Garini's bed, a piece of paper in her hand. "Stefano has gone," she said. "But he left a note." She looked offended. "I can't read it."

Carlina took the paper and focused her tired eyes to decipher his message. "Had to go." His scrawl was difficult to read. The message was written in English. It felt like a sudden gush of cold water. Wide awake, she sat up. "Bring L. to school, but warn the headmaster. Call me then. Stefano."

"What does it say?" Lilly's hair was tousled, but her eyes were bright like those of a cocky sparrow. She did not seem to remember her nightmare.

"It says he had to go, and that I should bring you to school."

"What about Lollo?"

Carlina blinked. "Lollo? What do you mean?"

"Will I take Lollo to school?"

"No." Carlina kept her voice firm. "Lollo hates to ride on the Vespa."

"How do you know?"

"He told me last night."

Lilly looked impressed. "Can you talk bird language?"

"Sort of." Carlina swung her legs out of bed and went to the living room, where she took the pink scarf from Lollo's cage. Thank God the bird looked all right. "You should give him some water and clear out his food tray while I prepare breakfast," she said. "Then we'll get dressed, and I'll take you to school."

"What about Lollo?"

"We will return after school and collect Lollo." *I have to keep the keys to Garini's apartment. Hope he won't mind.*

Apparently, Lilly heard the tone of finality in Carlina's voice because she didn't insist. Instead, she started to clear the cage as instructed. Carlina left her to it and went to the bathroom. Her shoulder still felt stiff, but the bandage had done its job. No sign of blood. *Who will bind it up later?* She pushed the thought away and washed her face, then brushed her teeth with her finger. What a featherbrain she was, packing a whole suitcase for Lilly and forgetting every essential for herself. She shook her head and went to the kitchen.

A bit of butter, a half-empty jar of Nutella chocolate spread, and a loaf of bread had appeared on the table overnight. Next to the bread, she found the key to her apartment. *Bless him.* Carlina hunted for a knife and some plates, made herself a cup of coffee and a glass of milk for Lilly, then called her niece.

As Carlina sipped her coffee and watched her niece eat, she analyzed her feelings. It felt strange to be in his apartment. Then again, everything felt strange right now. She still couldn't believe what had happened last night. It felt like a dream. A scary dream.

"Why are you shaking your head, Carlina?"

"No special reason." Carlina got up. "Are you done? I have to drive you to school."

When they arrived in front of the school, Carlina parked the Vespa. "I have to talk to your teacher, so I'll go in with you."

Lilly's eyes widened. "Why? Is anything wrong?"

Carlina glanced at her. How much should she tell her? She knelt and looked at her niece. "You have done everything right, Lilly. However, I believe you are in some danger right now." She swallowed. "Promise me not to leave the school today with anybody but me, no matter who comes to get you."

Lilly's eyes grew wide. "No matter who?"

"Yes. Don't go with anybody, not even grandma, no uncle, no aunt. Nobody at all, no matter what they say. Even if they say I'm in hospital and that I have sent them. All right?"

Lilly swallowed. "But . . . if you don't come?"

Carlina took a deep breath. "If I can't come, I will send Stefano."

"I can go with Stefano?"

"Yes."

Lilly nodded. "All right."

Carlina straightened. "Good. I'll tell your teacher the same." She led Lilly to the entrance of the ancient school building. Lilly walked by her side like a grown-up. No hopping, no singing today. Carlina bit her lips. *We will catch the murderer, and then life can be carefree again.*

She brought Lilly through the busy halls to her class. A boy ran past them, shouting. A group of girls giggled as they came into the building. It smelled of industrial detergent. A feeling of nostalgia gripped Carlina. It seemed so normal, so safe. How deceptive.

The teacher had not yet arrived, so Carlina left Lilly with her friends in the classroom and went to find the school secretary. A helpful boy pointed out the way. As Carlina pushed open the door, a wave of heat came out to her. Somebody had turned on the radiator to the max. The room smelled of cheap perfume. Carlina wrinkled her nose and advanced toward the desk at the side of the room, where a woman with a mop of brown curls was busy typing.

Carlina smiled at her. "Good morning. I'm Caroline Ashley, the aunt of Lilly Lombardi. I'd like to speak to the headmaster, please."

The secretary shook her head. "I'm afraid the headmaster isn't in today."

Damn. "Then I need to speak to Lilly's teacher. He's not yet in the classroom."

"Which class is she in?"

Carlina swallowed. "I don't know."

The secretary frowned. "I'll look it up." She continued clicking for what seemed an eternity.

Carlina checked her watch. She still had two hours before Temptation opened, but she expected a delivery early this morning. The carrier had already missed her last week and had left a message that he would return on Monday morning. Too bad.

Finally, the secretary lifted her head. "Lilly's teacher is *signor* Arredi, but he's ill today. His replacement is *signorina* Biffi." She looked at a big clock above the door frame. "She should be in the class room by now."

Carlina suppressed a sigh. She should have stayed with Lilly. "Thank you."

By now, the halls were empty, and her steps echoed with a hollow sound from the walls. Carlina knocked on the closed classroom door and peeked inside. Lilly waved at her from the third row. Carlina smiled back.

"*Buongiorno, signorina* Biffi." Carlina looked at the woman in front of the class. She was small and round and reminded her of a rubber ball.

Dressed in jeans and a pink sweater, the young teacher responded with a vague smile. "Yes?"

"Could you step out with me for a minute?"

The teacher lifted her plucked eyebrows, but she joined Carlina outside the classroom.

Carlina waited until she had closed the door. Only then did she realize that she had no idea how to bring across her message. "I'm Caroline Ashley, the aunt of Lilly Lombardi."

The teacher looked as if she had never heard Lilly's name.

"I understand you're not the usual teacher."

"That's right." *Signorina* Biffy looked offended.

"But you know the class, don't you? You know who Lilly is?" God, she was making total hash of this. No wonder the teacher was looking at her watch. Carlina hurried on. "Em . . . there's a bit of trouble at home."

"Trouble? What do you mean?"

Someone is trying to kill her. "We have reason to believe that someone is trying to harm Lilly."

Signorina Biffi's eyebrows rose until they almost reached the hairline.

"Please don't mention it to Lilly, but keep a close eye on her. Make sure she doesn't go with anybody, no one but me or *commissario* Garini."

"How about her parents?"

"Her parents are not in town right now."

"I'm afraid I can't accept the responsibility in such a case." *Signorina* Biffy shook her head with a little snorting sound that showed Carlina what she thought of her request. "You'd have to talk to the headmaster."

"He's out of town."

Signorina Biffi shrugged. "Then talk to his replacement."

Carlina clenched her teeth. "Who is responsible when the headmaster is away?"

"It's *signor* Arredi."

"But he's not in today, either!" Carlina wanted to shake the teacher. "Please. I've told you about it, and I rely on you."

Signorina Biffi pressed her lips together. "I'm not--"

Desperate, Carlina interrupted her. "It is a request from *commissario* Stefano Garini. He's a police *commissario*." *Better not mention the homicide department.* "If you wish, I can get him on the phone, so he can tell you personally about it."

Signorina Biffi opened the door. "I have no time to talk to anybody right now. I have a class to teach. And I certainly can't take over the responsibility for a child that's involved in domestic fights. *Arrivederci.*" She nodded at Carlina and disappeared inside the classroom.

II

His phone rang. Garini checked the display. It read Carlina. *Finally.* His heartbeat accelerated. "Ciao."

"This stupid teacher didn't believe me. She said she couldn't take the responsibility. She said--"

"Hold on." Garini leaned against his desk. "Where are you?"

"I've just left school. The headmaster is away today, and so is her normal teacher. She has a substitute, a stupid teacher who doesn't listen and doesn't want to take over any responsibility. I wonder if she has a clue who Lilly is! Maybe she mistakes her for some other girl, and--"

He frowned. "Carlina. Stop talking for a minute."

"What?" She sounded out of breath.

"Did you leave Lilly in class?"

"Yes." Carlina sighed. "But I wonder if that was a good decision. Should I go back and get her? Maybe she's safer with me. Maybe--"

"Where are you going?"

"First home to get a change of clothes, then to Temptation. I'm expecting a delivery this morning, but I could keep Lilly with me at the store. Only, she would be so bored, and she would like to go outside to play, but I couldn't allow that, and she would be so upset."

He blinked. It wasn't like Carlina to be so rattled, but he concentrated on the gist of what she was saying and revised the possibilities in his mind. "For the moment, I think she's safest at school."

"Do you think so?"

"Yes. The further she's away from the family, the better."

A silence told him she was digesting his words. Had he offended her? He couldn't help it.

She cleared her throat. "I need to tell you something else."

"Go ahead."

"Lilly had a nightmare last night. She kept saying 'I didn't tell the secret.' I tried to pry more information out of her, but she said she had promised him not to reveal anything. I asked her who 'he' was, and she said, Uncle--"

Stefano held his breath. "Uncle who?"

"She didn't say. At that point, she woke up, and she was so terrified that I didn't dare to question her further. I wasn't sure how far I could push her without hurting her."

"At least we know it's a man." *If I believe what you say.* The thought made him swallow. He had lost his detachment a long time ago.

"It could be any man of the family." Carlina said. "She calls them all Uncle."

"I need to talk to Lilly."

"Yes."

Her willingness surprised and touched him. "We have a psychologist on the force, a woman, who would be with me."

"Good. Do you want to talk to her right now?"

Garini checked his wristwatch. "No. My boss has asked for an urgent meeting. I need to talk to him first, see what he wants. Then I'll work out a plan."

"Right." Carlina swallowed so hard, he could hear it. "But let me be with her when you talk to her."

"If you promise you won't influence her."

"I promise." It sounded reckless.

Yes, she would promise anything to help her family. Anything. He felt cold.

"You still have Lollo," she said.

"Who?"

"The canary. We introduced you last night."

"Oh. I'd forgotten about him."

"I told Lilly he couldn't go to school with her, so we left him at your apartment. I took your keys, so I can collect him later. Was that all right?"

"Sure." He checked his feelings. It did feel all right. *Odd.* "How's the shoulder?"

"Okay."

He didn't want to hang up. "Managed to sleep?"

"Sort of. And you?"

"Too short. I came in at three and left at six."

"What did you do all night?" she asked.

"I went dancing."

She laughed. "Sure."

"Well, if you want to know, I searched every inch of your apartment, talked to an amazing number of Mantoni family members, bullied the lab people to give me the results double-quick, went over every bit of information again and again, and prepared a report."

"Sounds like fun."

"It was." His voice matched hers, dry, ironic. He waited for the inevitable question, but she didn't ask about his results. Probably she knew he couldn't tell her anything, even if he had found a definite trace of the murderer. Which he hadn't. Now he had to go and tell Cervi all about it. He wished the interview was already over.

"What did the innumerable members of my family say?"

"Your mother caught us when we left your apartment. Apparently, she had heard funny noises."

"Yes, the walls in our house are thin."

He had to ask it. "Does it never get on your nerves?"

"What?"

"Being so close to your family all the time. Having them meddle with everything."

"I . . . no, not really. I do my thing, and block them out if I don't want to listen. Besides, I always thought they were funny."

"I see." *Funny.* She thought they were funny. A bunch of lunatics, they were.

"What happened then?"

"Well, when she saw me, she screamed loud enough to wake half Florence. The rest of the family stormed out of their apartments."

Carlina chuckled. "Wow."

"You really think that's funny, don't you?"

"I do." Her voice was full of suppressed laughter.

In spite of himself, he had to smile. "They said I had spirited you away, put you into prison, killed you."

"Wow, how creative. In that order?" She still sounded as if she found it all amusing. "What did you say?"

"I said you were at a safe, but undisclosed, place, together with Lilly, and showed them the knife."

She gasped. "No."

"Yes. It belongs to Benedetta."

Silence. "Had she missed it for long?"

"No. She had used it the evening before."

"Damn."

He heard her swallow.

"What happened then?" she asked.

"I told them they were all under surveillance and that you would return the next day, so they could stop trying to lynch me."

"Oh. So they'll wait for me?"

"I should think so."

"Damn. I don't want to talk to them."

He grinned. "I seem to remember you said they were funny."

"Ha. I'm not going to discuss my family with you."

"Too late. We've never done anything else." He stopped himself short. Their tone had changed after last night. He'd lost his distance for good, but since last night, he had gone one step further. Now he had even lost the ability to hide it. It felt like a flirtation, something he could ill afford. All at once, he remembered his conversation with Roberto at the restaurant, eons ago. He had not understood how anybody could spend time with a mother-in-law they didn't like. How naive he'd been. *If I start anything with Carlina, I have to deal with the whole family. She only comes as a package deal.* The thought chilled him. He swallowed. "I have to go."

"Yes." She sounded reluctant to hang up.

"Be careful. Don't eat anything at home. Anything. You hear me?"

"Yes, *commissario*."

He bit back a smile. "Talk to you later."

III

"What's this I hear about an attempted murder? A child?" Cervi leaned across his desk and glowered at Garini. "I got several calls this morning. Just what is going on here?"

Stefano nodded. "The attempt was made last night. A knife rigged up, so it would pierce the victim. She was lucky."

Cervi pressed his lips together. "You know how the press loves a crime that involves a child. Anything to create crocodile tears. What do you have to say to them?"

Garini kept his face impassive. "We're working on it."

"Ha. Doesn't sound convincing enough. Can't you give details?"

Garini shrugged. "Sure I can. The child's aunt, Caroline

Ashley, dislodged the knife before it could do any damage."
Well, almost. I wonder if her shoulder is all right. "She decided
to run for it and managed to get her niece away from the house
without being seen."

His boss narrowed his eyes. "Where did she go?"

"She came to me." Garini faced Cervi without batting an
eyelid. "She first tried to call me, but the operator told her I was
at home." He clenched his teeth, waiting for the comment he
knew would come.

Cervi's mouth slackened. "She did what? How did she know
where you lived? Are you involved with the suspect?"

"I had mentioned my address to her before, when she
wondered why I was passing by her store so often. It's around the
corner. And no, we're not involved." He clenched his teeth. *I'd
better not say anything else. I'll only regret it.*

A sharp glance made him feel uneasy. "You'll remain
professional, won't you? Or should I put somebody else onto that
case?"

It was an empty threat, and Stefano knew it. Nobody had time
to enter into all the details at this point of the investigation, but
still, the idea chilled him. "I'll manage." He tried to make his
voice dry and unemotional, bored even.

"Did you consider that she might have rigged up the whole
show to make herself seem innocent?"

"Yes."

Cervi lifted both hands. "Yes, he says. Nothing else but yes.
Come on, man, tell me more. Our reputation is at stake."

And a child's life. Stefano suppressed a sigh. "Believe me, I'm
doing all I can. I typed a report last night, knowing that you and
the mayor would need to be informed." He pointed at the sheaf
of papers he had placed onto Cervi's desk.

"Tonight, Garini." Cervi narrowed his eyes. "I want a result
tonight. Have I made myself clear?"

"Crystal clear."

Chapter 17

Carlina opened the door and tiptoed into the hall. If she was lucky, nobody would see her. She lifted her foot onto the first step and decided to run up the steps as fast as she could when the door to Uncle Teo's apartment flew open.

"Carlina! There you are!" Uncle Teo came toward her with outstretched arms. He looked pale. "I was so worried about you."

Her heart melted, and she hugged him. How frail he felt. "I'm sorry, Uncle Teo. I had no other choice."

"Where's Lilly?"

"She's--" Carlina caught herself mid-sentence. She couldn't tell anybody. "She's safe."

His sharp eyes focused on her, then he nodded. "I see."

The sound of quick steps came from upstairs, then Fabbiola arrived on the landing with the speed of a cannonball. With her left arm, she pressed the ubiquitous cushion against her side. The henna-colored strand of hair fell into her face.

I've never seen her so upset. Carlina smiled at her mother to show she was fine.

Fabbiola pulled her daughter with her right arm against her chest. "Carlina! My darling! How are you?"

Carlina winced. Her shoulder hurt from the hug, and her face got pressed into the velvety cushion. It smelled of her mother's perfume, lily of the valley. She managed to break away from her mother's firm grip. "I'm all right, mamma. Really."

"What did he do to you?"

Carlina blinked "Who?"

"That policeman! The dark one. What did he do to you?"

He saved me. "Nothing."

"Where is he?" Fabbiola looked around her as if Garini had hidden in a corner beneath the staircase.

Has mamma gone crazy? "Garini? I don't know. I guess he's at the police station. Why?"

Fabbiola put her arms akimbo. "He said he would protect

you. Where is he, I ask? How can he protect you if he isn't here?"

Something warm shot through Carlina, but she hid her feelings. "Maybe he ordered an invisible angel."

Uncle Teo chuckled, but Fabbiola threw her daughter a dark glance. "I don't think that's funny, Carlina."

"No?" Carlina started to ascend the stairs. "I do."

"Where are you going?" Fabbiola demanded.

"I'm going to change my clothes." She checked her watch and sighed. "I had hoped to be in time to receive a delivery at Temptation, but I'm afraid I'll miss the guy once again. He'll return the goods." She sighed. "It'll mean a lot of hassle, doubled transport costs, and another delivery, but I can't help it."

"I could go and accept the parcel." Uncle Teo looked delighted at the prospect.

"No, you can't." Fabbiola said. "You've promised Benedetta you would go to the market and buy Gorgonzola."

His face fell. "So I did."

Fabbiola drew herself up. "I'll do it, Carlina."

Carlina hesitated only a second. Her mother would manage to accept a parcel without mishap, wouldn't she? It would avoid all the extra trouble. "Thank you, mamma." She took out her key ring and detached the key to Temptation. "Here you are. Let's hope the driver hasn't yet come. I'll join you as soon as I can."

She turned to go up, but was stopped by a male voice coming from the door. "Hi, Carlina. What's going on here? Family party in the hall?"

Carlina smiled at Marco's handsome face. "Not really. We're just figuring out who's going where. *Mamma* is about to leave for Temptation, I'll go up, and Uncle Teo will shop at the market."

Fabbiola nodded. "Otherwise, the house is empty. How about you?"

He lifted his eyebrows. "Benedetta isn't in?"

"No."

"How odd."

Carlina pricked her ears. "What do you mean?"

"Well, she called me this morning. She said she had a splitting headache and asked me to come and see her."

Uncle Teo shook his head. "That's strange. I saw her leaving for work this morning. Are you sure she called from home?"

"Yes." Marco frowned.

"How kind of you to come." Fabbiola laid a hand on Marco's arm and smiled at him.

She really dotes on Marco. Carlina suppressed a smile. *But then, she dotes on any man who dares to marry into the family.*

He returned her smile with his usual charm. "Well, if Benedetta doesn't need me, I'll leave again. Do you want me to drive you to Temptation?"

Fabbiola brightened. "That would be great."

Carlina waved goodbye and turned up the stairs for the third time, waiting for Uncle Teo to hold her back. However, he only nodded at her and returned to his apartment, no doubt to get his shopping bag for the market.

The thought of Benedetta's unexplained call made her uneasy all the time it took to freshen up and get dressed. In the end, she couldn't stand it anymore and called her aunt at work. As she listened to the dialing tone, her throat constricted. What if Benedetta hadn't arrived at work? What if someone had poisoned her too?

"Tell me!" Benedetta's bright voice came through the receiver.

A weight fell from Carlina's chest. "Ciao." It sounded like a croak.

"Is that you, Carlina?" Benedetta asked. "Is everything all right?"

"Yes. How about you?" Carlina leaned against the kitchen table, limp with relief.

"Everything's under control." Her aunt took a deep breath. "But what happened last night? I can't talk right now, but the *commissario* said--"

"I know." Carlina didn't want to discuss it. "Just tell me one thing: Did you call Marco this morning?"

"Marco? Angela's Marco?"

"Yes. Did you?"

"But no! I'm not ill."

"Funny." Carlina shook her head. "Something strange is going on, and I don't understand it."

"Well, I never called him. Maybe someone played a prank." Benedetta sounded decisive. "How about dinner? Will you be at home tonight? Emma and Lucio will be there. We'll have gnocci with Gorgonzola sauce, and a fresh--"

"I'm not sure." Carlina heard Garini's voice again. *Don't eat anything.* Until the murderer was caught, she wanted to stay away from home, but she couldn't very well invite herself and Lollo and Lilly to stay with the *commissario* indefinitely. "I have to go, Benedetta. I'll let you know if I'll be home tonight. Ciao."

Carlina hung up and hurried downstairs, her hand flying over the smooth wooden railing. If she didn't reach Temptation soon, her mother would sell the whole inventory at a huge discount.

II

"Ciao Stefano," Gloria, the receptionist, purred into his ear.

Stefano suppressed a sigh. "Is it urgent, Gloria? I'm busy."

"I don't know if it's urgent," Gloria drew out the words. "But Piedro called. You've given him some kind of research job, and he said he'd found something, or rather, he didn't find something that should have been there, and you should call him back. He didn't sound excited, so I've no clue how important it is."

How typical of Piedro to leave such a muddled message. "Thanks, Gloria. I'll call him later."

"I had a hard time reaching you, Stefano. Where have you been all this time? A woman tried to call you yesterday. She was rude, hung up before I could talk to her."

"Caroline Ashley?"

"Maybe. Sounded stuck-up."

She was scared to death. "Never mind. If she should try to call me again, put her through, no matter what."

Gloria tittered. "No matter what? Oh, my, this sounds so serious, Stefano."

"It is." He hung up before she could reply.

Two minutes later, the door opened on squeaking hinges, and Gloria peeked in.

Stefano clenched his teeth and glared at her. "What?"

She looked hurt. "There's an express delivery from the U.S. for you. I thought you might need it."

He felt bad about showing his impatience and held out his hand for the envelope. "Sorry I snapped at you. Things are difficult right now."

"I know." She gave him the envelope, but instead of returning to the door, she lingered. "Stefano?"

He curbed his impatience, even tried a smile. "Yes?"

"When this case is over, I'd like to invite you to dinner." She bent forward, revealing her attractive cleavage.

He didn't see it. Instead, he saw a bra with leopard fur, the gentle curve of a firm breast, a white shoulder, a spattering of freckles on a smooth cheek, cat's eyes. God, it had taken all his self-control to act as if he was blind. *I hope Carlina is safe.* An uneasy feeling lingered in the back of his mind. He had overlooked something. Somewhere, he had missed a clue and--

"Stefano?"

He blinked. "Sorry, Gloria."

She narrowed her eyes. "Are you all right?"

"Sure." He slid the envelope open with his fingernail.

Gloria muttered something and left the room.

He stared at the note in his hand. "Dear Mr. Garini," it read. "You were looking for information about the architect Paul Ashley. We have found a video tape with a speech he held at the Chamber of Commerce in 1978. Sorry it took so long, but we first had to transfer it to a modern medium. We hope it'll help with your investigation. Best regards, Morgan Waller, Seattle Homicide Department."

Stefano slid the CD into his computer and waited with bated breath for the speech to begin. At first, Carlina's father was only a shadow, half-hidden behind a speaker's lectern. The light came from behind him, and in the glare, nothing but his outline was visible. Stefano felt a pang of disappointment. What kind of loser had taken that film? Someone who had never mastered the basics of creating a video, that much was sure. What rotten luck. With mounting impatience, he watched the speech progress and was about to switch off the CD, when the camera man moved to the side. A pillar blocked out the glaring light and all of a sudden, Paul Ashley appeared as a man, not as a cardboard figure anymore.

Stefano sucked in his breath with one sharp gasp. It was Carlina, cast into a male mold. The shape of her eyes, her smile, the way her hairline curved over her brow . . . heck, even the way she moved her hands . . . it was all in front of him. He opened his drawer and took out the picture of her father. It held only a fraction of the truth. The likeness had never come across.

He felt a surge of relief, then realized with a sinking heart it didn't help him at all. If Fabbiola wasn't sure who the father of her eldest daughter was, she might well have been rattled enough to protect her daughter's happiness. She knew how important the father was to Carlina. *Damn, damn, damn.* Worst of all, he knew Fabbiola had indeed been insecure, otherwise, she would never have lied about her husband's eye-color. She must have been blind not to have seen the likeness between father and daughter. Or maybe it had only developed later, as Carlina had grown up. At thirteen, she might have looked different.

Besides, Lilly had said it was a man, not a woman. Or so Carlina had told him. What could he believe? He had to talk to Lilly. Stefano grabbed the receiver and asked the psychologist to join him at Lilly's school. Thank God she had time. As he got up, he remembered Piedro's call. It could wait. He wasn't in the mood for Piedro's slow intellect this morning. Then again, maybe he had found something. *Even a blind squirrel finds a nut once in a while.* He dialed Piedro's number.

"Piedro, it's me. Keep it short; I'm in a hurry. You said you've found something?"

"Yes." Piedro sounded insecure. "That is, I haven't found something, and I think it's odd. Or maybe it isn't. At least, I've been thinking about it for a while, and I think you should know about it, because I think that you'll think it might be important."

Garini rolled his eyes. "Just tell me."

"Well. You know you told me to research the diploma."

"The diploma?" *It was a mistake to call Piedro. I should have known better.*

"Yes. The one from the doctor."

"You mean Marco Canderini?"

"Yes." Piedro sounded triumphant now.

Is it because I have guessed the name or because of his news? "Go on."

"Well, the thing is, I looked everywhere, the way you told me."

Stefano clenched his teeth. *Be patient.*

"And I didn't find a diploma for Marco Canderini anywhere. I mean, I found one, but it was issued in 1953, and I think that's not him because he would be older now, wouldn't he?"

Garini frowned. "He would. And you looked everywhere, you said? All of Italy, not only in Tuscany? I believe he's from Rome."

"Everywhere," Piedro said. "It took ages."

Marco? Garini's mind raced. What if Nico had told Marco he had falsified his doctor's certificate, telling it as a joke, as one of his famous bad past stories? What if he had done so, for once, without an audience? It was a motive strong enough for murder. Marco's whole professional life depended on it, not to mention his private life. Angela wasn't the kind of wife who would stay married to a fraud.

Something clicked in Garini's mind. That would explain the willingness of the young doctor to sign the death certificate without comment even though he should have known better. He swallowed. What else had he missed?

The image of Elena Certini and her sick mother rose before his inner eye. What had she told him? The doctor had come on the very day the morphine went missing. But her doctor was Enrico Catalini, the same doctor who usually came to the Mantoni family. However, he had been ill the very next day. What if he had been ill the day before too? Hadn't he mentioned he had been ill a whole week?

Garini swallowed. *Oh, God, I have been blind.* Marco had stood in for his colleague, had taken the morphine from *signora* Certini, had given it to Nico. A quick and clean execution, with one flaw only: Nico had managed to share the secret before his death. He had informed Maria Mantoni, and Lilly must have overheard. Then a casual remark had alerted Marco. He had killed off Maria, had tried to kill Lilly. *I have to talk to Lilly. Now.* "I have to go," he said.

"Do you need me?" Piedro sounded hopeful.

Garini hesitated. He had to haul in Marco to the police station, but he couldn't send Piedro on his own, and he first had to talk to Lilly. She held the key and could provide the proof he needed. "No. I need to interview a child, and I don't want to intimidate her with too many people. You stay here and take all messages for me. Anything that sounds in the least bit connected with the case, you call me. Got that?"

"Yes." Now Piedro sounded sullen.

Garini cut off the connection and ran to his motorbike. He had to get Carlina from Temptation, then drive straight to Lilly's school. *I hope to God the child will talk.*

Chapter 18

The door to Temptation stood open, but Fabbiola was nowhere to be seen. Carlina entered the store with a critical look. The delivery man had come, she could tell by the parcel behind the desk. *Good.* She frowned. *But where is mamma?*

Then she heard voices behind the curtain that shut off the small storage room. She went closer . . . and froze.

"I don't want to do it," Marco's voice said. "But you haven't left me any choice, Fabbiola."

What? Carlina inched closer. *He doesn't want to do what?*

"Are you feeling quite well?" Fabbiola sounded concerned. "Why don't you sit down for a minute, Marco, and I'll--"

"I'm feeling perfectly well, thank you." Marco's voice sliced like a knife through the small storage room.

Carlina could tell he was standing to her right, just behind the curtain.

"I'm upset about doing this to you, but I don't have any choice."

What? Carlina's hand grabbed the mannequin at her side to steady herself.

"I'm sure you've confused something," Fabbiola's voice was soothing as if he was a five-year-old with a lost lollipop. "I can't believe you ever harmed anybody. It would be against your conviction! You're a doctor. You save lives."

His laugh sounded harsh. "You know I'm not."

Carlina's mouth dropped open. Marco wasn't a doctor? Was that the secret? *Madonna.* Her hand crept up to her cheek. It was a secret worth killing for. His reputation, his life, even his marriage would be gone if it became public. Her mother had never mentioned this. Had she known it all along?

"I don't agree," Fabbiola said. "To me, you are a doctor."

"I'm afraid few people would take such a liberal view of it, Fabbiola."

Fabbiola's voice became pleading. "Marco, don't do anything

you'll regret. Think of Angela. We are your family."

Carlina blinked. Had her mother realized that Marco had already killed two people of "his family"?

Suddenly, Fabbiola's voice became shrill. "What's this?"

Carlina's surged forward. With one quick move of her left hand, she drew the curtain to the side and tightened her grip on the mannequin with her right. For a split second, she saw Marco, a gun in his hand, then she lifted the mannequin and brought it with a crash down on his hand. Pain shot through her injured shoulder, the gun exploded, Fabbiola shrieked, and bits of polystyrene foam from the mannequin flew everywhere.

Carlina hit Marco again.

The head of the mannequin fell off, then an arm.

The gun crashed to the floor.

"Grab the gun, *mamma*!" Carlina lifted her arm in spite of the sharp pain in her shoulder and brought the rump of the mannequin down on Marco's head.

The mannequin cracked in two with a loud plop.

In slow motion, Marco dropped to his knees.

Fabbiola stood frozen, the cushion pressed against her chest. The gun had skidded across the room and was now behind her, out of Carlina's reach.

"Get the gun!" Carlina wanted to shake her mother into action, but she didn't dare to take her eyes off Marco.

He seemed stunned, his eyes glazed over, his expression vacant.

Carlina tore a box from the shelf to her left, ripped it open, and twisted the strips of a bra around Marco's hands. Before he could collect his wits, she pulled a pair of nylons from the next shelf and bound his feet with a tight knot. Out of breath, she stepped back.

"Can I hand you another bra?" Stefano said from the counter. "The one you used looks a bit fragile."

Carlina turned to him, her lips trembling. "But it's a sports bra. Very robust." Then she burst into tears, surprising herself. She was so glad to see him.

Garini took her by the shoulders and pushed her to the side, gentle, but firm. He pulled out a pair of manacles, clasped them on Marco's hands and said. "I arrest you, Marco Canderini, for the murder of Nicolò Alfredo Mantoni and Maria Mantoni, also for the attempted murder of Lilly Lombardi. You have the right to remain silent."

Marco stared at him as if the words didn't register.

"You've battered him into speechlessness, my dear," Garini said. "Unfortunately, I came too late to watch the show." He glanced at the broken arm of the mannequin in front of his feet and grinned. "But I gather from the debris that it was quite impressive. Accept my congratulations."

Carlina managed a watery smile. She hunted for a handkerchief in her jeans, pulled it out, and blew her nose. She looked at her mother. "Did he hurt you, *mamma*?"

Fabbiola shook her head, her mouth slack. "Did . . . did Marco kill my father?"

"I'm afraid he did," Garini said.

"And . . .and Maria?"

"Yes. He also rigged up the knife for Lilly."

Her face twisted. "I thought it was somebody from outside the family. He . . . he said he would never harm anybody. He said it was embarrassing and asked me to keep it to myself."

"Keep what to yourself?" Garini didn't take his eyes off the stunned Marco.

"That he didn't manage to pass the final exam at university. That's why he could never qualify as a real doctor."

"Did he tell you that?"

"Oh, no." Fabbiola hugged the cushion a bit tighter. "Father did, on the morning of the wedding."

Carlina closed her eyes. "Why didn't you ever tell us, *mamma*?"

Fabbiola's eyes widened. "I thought it didn't matter. I completely forgot."

For one pregnant moment, Carlina's eyes met Garini's.

She said, "So Marco had no idea you knew his secret? How did he find out?"

"I told him."

Carlina gasped. "You told him you knew he wasn't qualified as a doctor? That was like signing your own death certificate! When did you do that?"

Fabbiola plucked at the corner of her pillow. "At Benedetta's birthday party. He turned so pale that I felt very sorry. I promised I would never tell anybody."

Carlina caught her breath. *I saw them talking.*

Marco had closed his eyes now. He sat slumped with his back against the shelves, motionless.

Carlina swallowed. *I hope I didn't kill him.*

"Was Lilly around when you had that conversation with Marco?" Garini asked.

Fabbiola's mouth grew slack. "I don't know. Maybe. I . . . yes. Possibly."

Carlina threw Garini a warning glance. *Better not question her further.* Her mother would never overcome the feelings of guilt when she realized she had been the unwitting cause for the murder attempt on Lilly.

She knew he had understood her silent message, but the slight shake of his head showed her he was not going to stop asking questions.

"When did you tell Maria?" he asked.

Carlina frowned. "Maybe grandfather told her."

Fabbiola shook her head. "No. I let it slip, a day before she was killed. But I made her promise not to tell anybody, and I'm sure she didn't!"

Carlina swallowed. It hurt. *Damn.* Maybe, if Garini didn't question her further, Fabbiola wouldn't notice that her carelessness had caused Maria's death.

But no, she couldn't count on that. He wasn't quite the human computer she had thought at first, but he would not spare her mother. He had a job to do.

She put her arm around her mother's shoulders and met his gaze with defiance. No need to speak, he would know exactly what she was thinking. Yes, there it was. A tightening of his mouth, right next to that interesting little scar. She suppressed a sigh. Enemies once again.

"When you talked to Maria, was Marco anywhere near?" he asked.

"Oh, no." Fabbiola pushed the strand of hair back from her brow. "Marco came later, but he wasn't in the house when we talked."

"Where were you?" His question came hard and fast.

"We were in Maria's living room. I stood next to the window. Maria always smelled a bit . . . intense, so I opened it during our conversation."

Carlina glared at the *commissario*. Enough was enough. He didn't need to spell it out.

Garini met her gaze, then knelt to feel Marco's pulse.

Carlina bent forward. "He's not dead, is he?"

Garini straightened. "No." He lifted his hand, picked a bit of polystyrene foam from Carlina's hair, and dropped it to the floor.

"But your mannequin certainly is." His face softened. "How's the shoulder?"

"It hurts."

"Make sure you see a doctor."

She swallowed. Having him so near did things to her she couldn't control. "I will."

Stefano' gaze never left her face. "You look a lot like your father. Remind me to show you a video I got this morning."

Carlina's heart skipped a beat. "My father?"

He nodded.

"Of course she looks like Paul," Fabbiola said. "That's what I said all along."

Garini grinned.

Carlina couldn't avert her gaze. *I love it when he smiles.*

Their eyes locked.

"I'll call you," he said.

She had trouble with her breathing. "When?"

His smile deepened. "Yesterday."

THE END

If you've enjoyed reading Delayed Death, would you please consider writing a review? Reviews are the best way for readers to discover great new books.

But before you do so, enjoy this sneak peek
at the next book in the series:

Charmer's Death (Excerpt)

Temptation in Florence #2
Copyright 2013 Beate Boeker

Chapter 1

I

A shadow fell over her.

Carlina looked up from the cash register of her lingerie store Temptation, and a smile of pure welcome spread across her face. "Is it Christmas already?"

"What a nice greeting." Trevor took off his wet raincoat and dropped it onto the low bench in front of the register. "I feel like Santa Claus, coming early." He went into the area Carlina kept for herself and placed both hands on her shoulders. "Let me have a look at you, my girl." His blue eyes shone. "You're looking well."

She laughed and removed his hands from her shoulders. "Not good enough for your standards." One of her eyebrows lifted in a half-reluctant question. "Who is it this time?"

He gave he a mischievous smile. "A ravishing redhead. She's exquisite."

"Of course she's ravishing." Carlina shook her head. "I never expected anything else." She leaned against the cash register and pushed both hands into the pockets of her trousers. With a slight frown, she looked at him for a moment, the silence between them easy, as if they were friends, which maybe they were . . . though their friendship was unusual, to say the least. Then she surprised herself and him by asking. "Are you never going to settle down?"

He opened his eyes wide in mock surprise and pushed a tanned hand through his black hair. It was graying at the temples, but that didn't make him less attractive – on the contrary.

Carlina suppressed a grin. *He knows how attractive his arm looks when his muscles bulge like that. That's why he's wearing a tee-shirt.* She slanted a look at the rain outside, beating down on the ancient buildings of the historical center of Florence and rubbed her hands over the sleeves of her light-green cashmere sweater, glad to be warm.

"Of course I'm not settling down." Trevor's heavy signet ring blinked in the store's light. "Life would be without zest, wouldn't it?" He shook his head. "What kind of a question is that anyway? I'm your customer." He winked. "Have they taught you no manners?"

"I save them for those who appreciate them." Carlina grinned back. "I'm sorry to hear she's a redhead because I've just unpacked a delightful Christmas set in a gorgeous red color." She pointed to the shelf at her left. "It's over there. The slip ties at the side and is decorated with white feather balls. I thought of you when I ordered it."

He smiled. "Keep it for next year, Carlina. I'll find a raven-haired woman to match that set."

He called her with the nickname her family and half the town used – Carlina instead of Caroline. She didn't mind that at all, but at his words, she didn't know if she should laugh or be offended. "Do you have no shame?"

"Why should I?" He shrugged. "I'm not promising them everlasting love. They know what they let themselves in for. I'm always honest."

Carlina cocked her head to the side. "But what if they hope for more?"

"I can't help it if they choose to delude themselves." He made a move with his hand as if to wipe away the conversation. "Enough about that. How about you? Have you settled down, as you call it?" He grinned. "Or something better?"

The image of Stefano's face rose in front of her inner eyes, but she pushed it away. Even if her relationship with Stefano had developed into more than a romantic craving, which, alas, it had not, she would not discuss him with Trevor. Her feelings were too . . . private, too precious to share with this man who went out with a different woman every Christmas, as if they were Christmas trees, raised to shine for four weeks a year, discarded afterwards. "No."

"No? Just a simple no?" Trevor shook with laughter. "How can the owner of the most wonderful lingerie store in Florence, no, in the world, live like a nun?"

She grinned. "For the first part of that sentence, thank you. For the second, no comment."

He sighed. "Ah, you're hard."

Carlina shook her head. "Nowhere near as hard as you are."

"Me?" The blue eyes opened wide, mesmerizing her. "I'm not hard."

"I wonder if your many exes agree." She regarded him, thoughtful. "How do you do it?"

"What?" Trevor stroked his cheeks as if he had just finished shaving.

If only he didn't know what a determined jaw he has, and how good his chin looks when he pushes it forward like that. I would like him even better. "How do you get rid of them so easily?" she asked.

"It's all a matter of preparation," Trevor said. "I tell them from the start we're going to have some delightful weeks. Not more, not less. When my vacation comes to an end, the relationship ends, too. It's as easy as that. Every Christmas."

His words were callous, but his honesty disarmed her. *He's too charming for his own good.* "Was it always that easy?"

Trevor flinched. "Let's not talk about the mistakes of the past. It's way too nice to be back in Florence again. Now show me what you think would suit my stunning redhead."

Carlina didn't move. "What will happen if you ever fall in love?" she asked.

He turned to a black lace bra and grinned over his shoulder. "But I do, my dear. I do. Every single time."

II

Annalisa leaned against the cash counter of Temptation and glared at her cousin. "It's time to close this shop." She pronounced each word with care, as though Carlina was deaf. "Now."

Carlina tidied her desk with hurried moves. "Just a minute, Annalisa. I only need to file this invoice, and then . . . " She hated to leave stuff lying about when closing up for the night.

"You've been saying this for a quarter of an hour, and I'm bored." Annalisa rolled her eyes. "I'm also hungry, and you promised me dinner."

Carlina smiled at her. "You won't starve. Besides, do you know that you sound like a five-year-old kid and not like an almost-twenty-year-old woman?"

"Ha. Almost twenty." Annalisa turned a strand of her long

hair in her hand. "That's just the point. I'm spending my life waiting, and before I know it, whooosh, I'm twenty, past the age of all fun."

Carlina shook her head. "Dreadful. But there is a life beyond twenty, believe me. At thirty-two, I have sufficient experience to tell you."

Annalisa made a contemptuous move with her hand. "Your universe is this store."

"Quite right." Carlina looked around. Her gaze came to rest with pride on the clever storage drawers beneath each hanger that kept bras of all sizes in well-assorted rows, on the brand-new window mannequin, on the red Christmas bra and panties she had put on display today. "It's enough for me," she said. "You shouldn't underestimate how attractive a tiny universe can be if it's all in your own hands. You can manipulate it, and it's up to you to make it a success. Few things equal that feeling."

Her cousin perked up. "Yes, I see what you mean. I love the name of your store, always have." She sighed. "Temptation . . . it's perfect." Then she frowned. "But isn't it boring to deal with the same stuff year in and year out?"

"There is a lot of variety, believe me." Carlina smiled. "The lingerie industry may not advance in the same huge steps as mobile communication, but there are always changes. In a few days, for example, I'll exhibit at the Florence Christmas Fair for the first time."

"I've heard about that." Annalisa said. "Doesn't the wife of the major organize it?"

"Yes, Sabrina does. It's her dream to support the businesswomen of Florence, so she came up with the concept of the Christmas Fair. Do you remember my school friends Francesca, the glass blower, and Rosanna, who has that great flower shop?"

"Nah." Annalisa shrugged. "Unless you mean that tiny woman who looks like a cross between a troll and a fern?"

Carlina grinned. "That's Rosanna. Sabrina invited them both, and some others, to exhibit the crafts of Florence during the fair."

"Hmm." Annalisa looked at an embroidered bra. "But the underwear you sell isn't exactly Florentine art, is it? So how come you were invited?"

"They still had some room to fill, so Rosanna thought of me and suggested that I join, and I developed a concept for lacy underwear. The lace is from Bartosti."

Annalisa started to shake with silent laughter. "Bartosti? The big lace company? You're kidding me."

Carlina swallowed. "Stop laughing. My underwear has nothing to do with their usual lace coverings for toilet rolls. It's sexy, believe me."

"Lace coverings for butts." Annalisa shook her head. "Whatever will you do next?"

Carlina wanted to change the subject. It had taken her weeks of hard work to develop something she liked together with Bartosti, and she didn't like the idea of consumers laughing at her efforts. Hopefully other people wouldn't react like Annalisa. Maybe it had been a mistake to team up with such a traditional manufacturer.

"Can I see that super-lace-thing?" Annalisa asked.

"No." Carlina pressed her lips together. "Come to the fair on December 23rd, then you'll see it." *And don't you dare to laugh in front of strangers at my work.*

Annalisa frowned. "Aren't you a bit touchy?"

Carlina tried to get a grip. Yes, she was touchy, damn it. It was her work, her life, and this whole project was new, something she had never tried before. *Better change the subject.* "I've got something else to show you, something you'll like for sure."

She went to the tiny storage space in the back of her store. "Come here." To make more use of the limited space, she had installed two rows of shelves, one in front of the other. The front row was set on wheels that ran in guiding rails, so she could push it aside whenever she wanted to reach into something beyond or get access to the bathroom door. With a flick of her wrist, she moved the front shelf aside and reached into the cubicle behind.

Annalisa looked around. "It reminds me of a galley; no millimeter is wasted here."

Carlina laughed. "Spot on. I got in a yacht builder when I set this up. He had great ideas." She pulled out a flat cardboard box and opened it.

Her cousin chewed on her lower lip. "You know, I start to see why you find it so interesting."

Well, that's something at least. "You've seen nothing yet. Look here." Carlina held out her hand.

"A pair of nylons?" Annalisa raised her slim eyebrows.

"What's so special about them?"

"They've been woven with the latest technology. They guarantee you'll have no more runs."

Annalisa's eyes widened. Her fingertips touched the soft material. "No more runs?"

"Yes. Ricciarda and I tested it." Carlina beamed at her. "It's a special way of weaving that makes sure any small hole at the toe remains a hole and won't create a run up to your hips."

Annalisa blinked. "Are you telling me one pair of nylons will now last a lifetime?"

Carlina laughed. "No. It's still a fragile material. But at least you won't have to chuck them the minute a tiny hole appears somewhere."

"Wow. That's cool." Annalisa put her head to one side. "But isn't that bad for your business? I mean, people will buy fewer nylons if they don't tear them anymore."

"No." Carlina smiled. "I happen to have the exclusive rights for these nylons in Florence. It took two months of hard negotiation before they agreed to the deal." The memory still filled her with pride. "Even if eventually the nylons will be available elsewhere, people will start to buy more expensive nylons now that they last longer, so for me, that's fine." She held out the package. "Here, take a pair. I'll officially start to sell them tomorrow, but you'll get a few hours' head start."

Annalisa's face lit up. "Wow, that's great. Thank you." She slipped the nylons into her golden handbag and looked around the storage room. "You know, I think your business is quite fascinating after all."

Carlina looked at her cousin with affection, her irritation almost forgotten. "Says the jaded almost-twenty year old who thinks she's past the age of fun."

Annalisa's smile revealed a row of pearly teeth. ". . . and starving besides."

How gorgeous she looks. Carlina made a shooing motion with her hands. "Back up. I'm done now, and we'll walk to Gino's."

Annalisa obeyed with a shudder. "Walk? But the weather is dreadful."

"It isn't raining, and after all these hours inside, I need a bit of air." Carlina turned off the light at the back, leaving on the ones that illuminated the shop window. A sharp gust of wind tore at their jackets as they left Temptation.

"Brrr." Annalisa hunched her shoulders. "Are you sure you want to walk?"

"The Vespa isn't warmer." Carlina locked the door and set the alarm. Temptation's top location on Via de' Tornabuoni was an attractive target for thieves.

Annalisa opened her eyes wide. "I'm not talking about your Vespa. Ever heard of taxis?"

Carlina took her cousin by the arm and walked her along the ancient houses toward the Arno river. Festive decorations glittered from the shop windows in the luxury stores they were passing. "Oh, come on. You're not made of sugar." She took a deep breath. "This wind is invigorating, don't you think?"

Annalisa gave her a look that spoke volumes. A sudden gust whipped up her red hair so that for an instant, she looked like a wild witch flying on a broom.

Carlina tightened her scarf around her neck. "Funny, I'd have thought there would be more people about, just a week before Christmas."

"Not at nine o'clock in the evening." Annalisa held back her hair with one hand. "Every respectable shop owner closed the door hours ago; only you insisted on staying late."

"I still had to unpack the nylons. I hope for a great pre-Christmas rush tomorrow because I put ads in several papers." Carlina dug her hands deep into the pockets of her red coat. "I'm so glad they arrived in time. They got held up in customs. I was afraid people would storm Temptation tomorrow, and I would have nothing to sell." She grinned at her cousin. "And you talk about it being boring. It's more exciting than a thriller."

Annalisa laughed. "Yeah, sure."

They reached the Lungarno Corsini and turned left.

Annalisa slanted a look at the Arno. "The water looks awful. So gray and dirty."

Carlina leaned over the stone wall that separated the sidewalk from the steep embankment. Her gaze swept over the row of houses on the other side, taking in the mix of green wooden shutters, red tiled roofs, and the soft colors of the house fronts. Cream, faded terracotta, and soft yellow alternated, creating a mellow blend. Each house had a different height. Some were slim, crooked from age, some broad and feisty; some windows had arches, some grilles, some barren flower boxes. They looked weather-beaten, standing with clenched teeth in the icy wind, but they stood their ground, as they had done for centuries.

She smiled and turned her head to get her favorite view of the Ponte Vecchio bridge, loaded with shops. Additional rooms clung like fat beetles onto the back walls of the shops, hanging in precarious positions over the foaming water.

A feeling of tenderness swelled her heart, and she took a happy breath. "It's no wonder the tourists are in rapture whenever they see the Ponte Vecchio. It's so . . so Italian. This bridge could not stand anywhere else in the world."

Annalisa lifted an eyebrow. "Must be because you're half American. I see nothing special in it. It's decrepit, that's what it is."

Carlina shook her head. "You only think so because you were born here. Isn't it fascinating to think how unique it is because it grew with time and was constantly adapted to changing needs? Another bulging room added here, another layer of paint there, peeling off again, revealing the bridge's age, and so making it irresistible?"

Annalisa eyed her. "If a bulging something and a peeling layer of paint is making me irresistible, then by all means, let's buy a pot of paint." She linked her arm through Carlina's and dragged her away from the stone wall. "Come on, get over your romantic moment. It's freezing, and even if you're enjoying your fling with poetry, that doesn't mean I have to get pneumonia."

Carlina followed her cousin with a grin. "I wonder what it takes to make you feel romantic."

"Easy." Annalisa looked like a smug cat. "A bottle of golden champagne, a brand-new pair of flaming diamond earrings, and a whirlpool with rose leaves."

"A whirlpool with rose leaves would get clogged up immediately."

Annalisa gave her sharp glance. "Now who's unromantic? Really, Carlina, I wonder about you. You start to rhapsodize over an old bridge that's falling apart and give me a cleaning woman's remark when it comes to whirlpools." Her high heels clattered over the uneven stone slabs. "Besides, they don't. I tested it."

Carlina stopped dead. "You tested it? Who has a whirlpool? And who was stupid enough to throw rose leaves into it? Don't tell me Tonio treated you to a day in the spa. It's not his style at all."

Annalisa lifted her chin. "Tonio is history. Has been for ages."

Carlina blinked. "You mean five days."

"How do you know?"

"Six days ago, he had dinner at our house, and it didn't look then as if he was history."

"Oh, well." Annalisa conveyed Tonio to the past with a careless shrug. "I fell in love. It's different this time." She turned away and crossed the street to reach the restaurant.

I've heard this before. Carlina followed her without a word.

"You don't need to be so disapproving," Annalisa gave her cousin a defensive glance. "He's older . . . and . . . and different. He's not a boy."

"Hmm." Carlina held open the door to Gino's restaurant. "Come on in. You can tell me all about it while we're having dinner."

Twenty minutes later, Carlina inhaled the aroma of the rabbit ragout with gnocchi in front of her. "Just the right dish for a cold winter night." She savored the first bite in silence and smiled. "The first bite is always the best, don't you think?" Her cousin didn't reply, but Carlina didn't notice, filled with happiness. "I guess it's because your taste buds are not yet used to the treat they get."

Annalisa sighed and continued to nibble on her lettuce leaf. "Don't tempt me."

"Why didn't you take the ragout as well?" Carlina frowned. "You're not too fat."

Her cousin clenched her teeth. "It has to stay that way. I have to be perfect."

Oh, oh. Carlina blew onto her ragout to cool it and slanted an inquiring glance at her cousin. "The new lover is very demanding?"

"He isn't." Annalisa speared a piece of lettuce with her fork. "But I have a plan. A big plan. That's why I won't take any risks." She took a deep breath. "I want him to marry me."

Carlina dropped her fork. "What?"

Annalisa finished her confession in a rush. "He's rich, and handsome, and . . ." she gave a wistful sigh, " . . . so experienced. After him, I can't ever go back to those young guys." Her face twisted. "Besides, he needs to settle down."

Her cousin swallowed. "Does he know that?"

"Not yet." Annalisa's face clouded. "I tried to give him a little hint, and he reacted a bit . . . strangely." She shook herself. "However, there are ways to overcome that. I don't believe him at all when he says it'll be over after the holidays. After all, he never met a girl like me before." She pushed back a strand of her red hair.

Something sharp pierced Carlina. A man rich and handsome, here for the Christmas vacation, her beautiful cousin with red hair . . . She gasped and sat up straight. "Don't tell me your lover's name is Trevor?"

End of Excerpt
Charmer's Death by Beate Boeker
Temptation in Florence #2

About the author
- Mischief & Humor from Page 1 -

Beate Boeker is a USA Today bestselling author with a passion for books that brim over with mischief & humor. She writes sweet sophisticated romantic fiction and cozy mysteries, many of them set in beautiful Italy.

Beate's first novel was published in 2008 by Avalon Books. In the meantime, her work was shortlisted for the Golden Quill Contest, the National Readers' Choice Award, the "Best Indie Books" contest, and the RONE Award.

She's also a marketing manager with a degree in International Business Administration, and her daily experience in marketing continuously provides her with a wide range of fodder for her novels, be it hilarious or cynical. Widely traveled, she speaks German (her mother language), English, French and Italian and lives in Germany together with her husband and daughter. If people came with instructions, hers would say, "Make sure she'll always get enough chocolate and sleep, and she'll be a sunny companion."

While "Boeker" means "books" in a German dialect, her first name Beate can be translated as "Happy" . . . and with a name that reads "Happy Books," what else could she do but write novels with a happy ending?

Learn more about Beate at happybooks.de. Here, you can also contact her directly and sign up for her newsletter. Alternatively, you can also get in touch with her on Facebook (Beate Boeker Author) and Twitter (@BeateBoeker).

She loves to hear from her readers, and if you liked this book, please consider leaving a review.

Cozy mysteries
by Beate Boeker

Delayed Death – Temptation in Florence #1
Have you met the Mantonis? This eccentric Italian family has a fatal tendency to fall over dead bodies, and their unique reactions to murder will keep you giggling all through the night.

Charmer's Death – Temptation in Florence #2
A charming but older millionaire desires the most beautiful Mantoni, Annalisa, as his lover for the Christmas season and ends up being strangled by a pair of pantyhose.

Banker's Death – Temptation in Florence #3
Carlina's attractive cousin Valentino is the most unpopular member of the wide-spread Mantoni family. When he is murdered, only *commissario* Garini is sorry because he has to investigate the Mantoni family once again.

Expected Death – Temptation in Florence #4
The family patriarch, Uncle Teo, has fallen in love, and the whole family hates her with good reason. Nobody is surprised when she's killed, but this time, the Mantonis are in for it, and one of them ends up in prison.

Seaside Death – Temptation in Florence #5
The Mantoni family is going on vacation, but the holidays at the shores of the Ligurian Sea are anything but relaxing. When the hotel manager is shot, Carlina's young cousin, Ernesto, has to explain more than he wants to reveal.

Classic Death – Temptation in Florence #6
Commissario Garini has to investigate the death of an eccentric fountain pen collector while his engagement to Carlina turns out to be a lot more stressful than planned. In the end, only a race against time can prevent another death.

Contemporary romances
by Beate Boeker

Sweet Voice

Surely nobody falls in love with a voice, but Bridget is mag-netically drawn to the man who claims that her voice bewitched him. Should she stay engaged to Bobby or trust the charmer, Daniel?

Venetian Tangle

Lorena doesn't believe in ghosts, but this Christmas, she's forced to face her past and her feelings while traveling to the beautiful city of Venice.

Mischief in Italy

In this hilarious romantic summer comedy a father-son con-versation leads to unexpected results and manages to turn both their lives upside-down.

A New Life

How often have you wondered if A New Life wouldn't be fun? Circumstances force Anne to start from scratch in Flo-rence, Italy. Will she learn to love again in spite of another murder?

Rent a Thief

Tina can't believe she's falling in love with a thief when all she wanted was to get closer to her grown daughter. Her feelings and a mystery get thoroughly mixed up before she finds what she needs in Seattle.

Stormy Times

Joanna is lost in a blizzard on her way home from a difficult foaling. Just one man can save her – but he's strangely reluctant to come to her help. However, when they find a puppy, every-thing changes this Christmas.

A Little Bit of Passion

Karen loves her life as ski instructor and part-time book store owner, but when she meets John, she has to make a choice. How much independence does she have to give up in return for love?

Take My Place

Maren is busy setting up her own business and being a single Mom for her daughter. She doesn't have time to fall in love with a man who's way too charming to be true, but her heart doesn't seem to know the rules.

Wings to Fly

Cathy's trip to Seattle catapults her into a series of events that will change her life. Is Mick the right man for her or does she first have to learn to manage on her own?

It's Raining Men (co-written with Gwen Ellery)

Four cousins inherit one bedraggled umbrella, and each of them has to keep it for three months. Join them during this magic, amusing, touching and romantic year, and you'll finish this novel with a happy feeling deep inside.

Manufactured by Amazon.ca
Acheson, AB

12168268R00144